RANDOM HOUSE LARGE PRINT

Snowed In

Christina Bartolomeo

Snowed In

RANDOM HOUSE
LARGE PRINT

Published in the United States of America by
Random House Large Print in association with
St. Martin's Press, New York.
Distributed by Random House, Inc.,
New York.

**The Library of Congress has established a
Cataloging-in-Publication record for this title.**

0-375-43424-0

www.randomlargeprint.com

FIRST LARGE PRINT EDITION

10   9   8   7   6   5   4   3   2   1

This Large Print edition published in accord
with the standards of the N.A.V.H.

To Dan Murphy, with much love

Acknowledgments

Many, many thanks to my talented and tremendous editor, Jennifer Enderlin, who has turned this into a much better book than the one I first finished and has given it such incredible time, energy, and enthusiasm. Many thanks also to Jane Rosenman, who set me on the path of novel-writing, chose this book for St. Martin's, and shaped (and greatly improved) its first draft.

Thanks, as ever, to my wonderful agent, Henry Dunow, a tireless advocate for my work. Much gratitude to Jennifer Carlson and Rolph Blythe of the Dunow & Carlson Literary Agency for their unfailing kindness and expertise. Thanks also to Ethan Friedman of St. Martin's for his constant encouragement. For helping me to be a better nonfiction writer (and thus a better fiction writer), thanks to terrific editors Barbara McKenna and Roger Glass of the American Federation of Teachers.

For their invaluable friendship and support, my thanks to: Larry Doyle and Sylvia Mapes, Mary Quattlebaum and Christopher David, Karl Ackerman, Kate Bannan, Peter Clement,

Sam Wang, Laura Baker, Susan Lieberman, and Carol Goodman. Heartfelt love and thanks to Denis and Noreen Murphy and to Timothy Murphy and Clint Ramos. For the kindest of welcomes since I first came to New England, many thanks to the Foley, Rage, Ackerey, and Panto families. For making me feel at home in Boston, and for their warm friendship, thanks to Peter Leopold, Leslie Nystuen, and Ann Winslow. And to Matt Jacob and Jeff Campbell, thanks for a treasured friendship that included your braving the coldest of springs in Maine and Massachusetts.

Love and thanks to my mother and father, Dorothy and John Bartolomeo, and brother-in-law Eddie, whom we miss. Love and thanks always to my sisters and brothers, Mary Theresa, Anna, Angela, Nick, and John; and my brother-, sister-, and niece-in-law, Phil, Annie, and Kate. Getting you as my family is such amazing luck. Thanks and much love to my nephews, John, Brendan, Christian, Devin-the-writer, Sam, and Liam—you bring me great joy. Thanks and love, too, to our extended family: Mary and John Heneghan, John Schlecty, Gary Lattimore and Jennifer Ellis, and Leta Davis.

Finally, more love and gratitude than I can express to Dan Murphy, my partner and kindred spirit, who kept this book (and its author) going with his love and support—and who taught me how to merge. I love you always.

Late Autumn

One

Courage is not my leading virtue. I've always avoided change of any sort, operating on the principle of safety first. I married a "safe" man. I've made my living performing humdrum work, work that bored other people so much that they'd pay someone else to do it. All my life, I've watched those around me—my sister Delia, my friend Marta—dash forward to seize the day. I've admired them, cheered them on. But, if threatened by opportunity myself, I make sure to hide under the covers until the moment passes.

Evade life's twists and turns this assiduously, and the Fates will get their revenge by quietly ambushing you. When the alarm clock squawked 7:30 on that sullen October morning, I had no clue that by nightfall I'd finally be ready for what Marta refers to ominously as "taking steps."

Marta takes steps when an express mail package fails to arrive on time, or her morning toast is served up a shade too brown at the coffee shop. She plunges into eloquent, daunting reproaches, she storms out of rooms—only to return an hour later, cheerful and unaware of any ill-feeling she might have left behind. My sister, Delia, is equally assertive but calmer. If her husband Tom casts an admiring glance at a passing woman, the stray look of a faithful husband noting the scenery, she merely says briskly, "Snap out of it," and carries on. She doesn't pout or bluster, but neither does she let things slip by until she slips right down under them, as I do.

But for me, all acts of bravery are overthought, and anger is a feared eventuality, a thundering waterfall away from which I'm always frantically paddling upstream. But that October day, in a city that was still strange to me—Portland, Maine—I began, in spite of myself, to inch toward something different. Well, not even "toward" anything. Just away from what I had. Coward that I am, I took the smallest of steps. Life being contrary, and life being kind, that's when things finally started to happen—small things, with large consequences.

The Monday morning when everything got to be too much, my still-new husband Paul and I woke up cold, as usual. Our radiators had mysteriously shut themselves off during the night. This had become a habit with them, and one of us was going to have to talk to the landlord about it. The one of us who was going to talk to the landlord wasn't going to be Paul.

"You handle him better," said Paul, who always shied from minor confrontations. He'd never challenge a waiter about a miscalculated bill, or ask a hotel for their best room rate, or require that his office manager commandeer him a desk chair that didn't collapse when he leaned forward. Paul had been trained early in the stiff upper lip. He could have led troops over the top as an officer in World War I, or survived a winter at Valley Forge without a fuss, but he got weak in the knees when required to act "pushy."

That was why, since our August arrival in Portland, I'd been steadily getting to know our landlord Donald, who was also the resident plumber, electrician, roofer, and tile layer.

Summer had departed with a suddenness that surprised us. Over the course of my first few attempts to get the heat fixed, I'd heard the history of Donald's early career, the sad tale of his first marriage, the vicissitudes of his twenty years of motorcycle ownership, and his difficulty in getting his dog to breed with his friend's dog. Paul hadn't had to listen to any of this. He was intimidated by Donald's surly, obtuse air and liked to disguise it by saying I had "a way" with him. No one had a way with Donald, unless it was his second wife, who was rarely seen but often referred to with fear and respect.

It wasn't Paul's fault, really. Paul was already burdened with fighting the tiny battles of someone else's life—his mother Patricia's.

When I first got married, my new mother-in-law made me uncomfortable, but I'd believed our relationship would improve with time. "My friends all call me Pepper, and you should too," she'd said when we met. I'd thought then that we'd ultimately be friends. But Pepper didn't want any more friends. She wanted a certain kind of daughter-in-law, and I wasn't it.

Pepper **was** peppery, in a perky, blond, tight-mouthed way. At fifty-eight, she was entirely competent to take care of herself and her catering company, Comfort Foods. Unfortunately for Paul and his brother James, Pepper was a woman who expected things of men, old-fashioned, manly things: handling income taxes, cleaning out the gutters, and dropping a lady off in front of the restaurant before going to look for a parking space.

In the five years since Paul's lawyer father had died quietly from a heart attack, Pepper had formed the habit of calling on her sons to look after her in any number of petty and large matters, as if she were a consumptive young widow at the turn of the century. Thus, any spare time Paul had for disputing electric bills and writing letters to county property tax assessors was already claimed. When it came to the sticky administrative details in our married life, I was usually tapped.

This was good practice for a person like me, whose main goal in adulthood has been avoiding raising her voice in any consumer situation.

"So you'll get on the phone to Donald, right?" Paul said.

He was standing in the bathroom, jerking his tie into place under a row of flickering fluorescent "vanity" lights Donald had installed in a strip above the sink. We both looked green under those lights, but Paul didn't mind that. For men, getting ready to go out seems to be a question of establishing order in their appearance: shaving, knotting the tie, zipping the pants, and tying the shoes. Battening down the hatches to face the day.

"Should I call from the office and remind you, Sophie?"

"No, I can remember that it's cold."

He sighed and brushed a bit of lint from his pants cuff with a reproachful look in my direction. True, I hadn't dusted under the bed lately, but neither had he. Paul's quotient of these "why haven't you" looks had risen sharply since Natalie had been hired at his office, Natalie, the career gal who was also a domestic whiz, Natalie, the living embodiment of the idea that there's always one woman so perfect that she spoils it for the rest of us.

"I'm not trying to boss you, Sophie."

That had been my accusation to him in a recent fight.

"Yes, you are."

"It's just that I don't have time for this maintenance stuff."

"And I do?"

He paused, comb in midair. Even when fighting with him, I was sometimes struck by the handsomeness of my husband. It was a handsomeness that (under the theory that people wind up with their approximate physical counterparts) my own on-again, off-again attractiveness didn't merit. Paul had regular features, thick, light brown hair, and hazel eyes. His chin was nicely square, and his muscles were the well-defined muscles of someone who grew up playing tennis and swimming. His gaze met an on-looker's gaze head-on; even here, where we were so new, he was often stopped on the street for directions. He had a clean-cut, fearless, Protestant American face, a face that only generations of upper-middle-class sureness can create. When he smiled, you could see evidence of a saving sense of humor. He wasn't smiling now.

My own looks were unimpressive. Everything about me was almost-but-not-quite. Eyes: an unspectacular medium blue. Hair: darkened to ash from its childhood gold. Skin: pale and usually colorless. When all was right in my world, I was attractive in an offbeat, unphotogenic way. All had not seemed right with my world in a while. My face and hair seemed drab and dim—though it could just have been the lighting in that bathroom.

"You know what I mean," Paul said. "Your time is less . . . structured."

"I have a major layout to get out the door today."

"So how long does it take to call? You can work while he's here. You don't have to give him coffee and scones or whatever you do. He's the landlord, not your friend. Be firm."

He was pulling a V-necked sweater over his

shirt and tie, his new office attire for Portland. Natalie had advised him on this. She was full of opinions on matters of style. I myself preferred him in the light gray and navy blue suits he'd worn in D.C. He'd seemed so lovable to me in those suits, like a boy dressed up for a cousin's wedding. I'd met him at a wedding, in fact; he'd been sitting, well behaved, in one of his very nice suits, his hair slicked back with water and his elbows off the table as he'd been taught. He'd looked very young. He would in some way always look young in that he frequently had the appearance of following rules he didn't truly understand, rules made by grown-ups whom he didn't think to question but didn't sympathize with either.

"Most people manage to handle a job and these other things that come up in life," his voice came at me through the sweater.

I said nothing. I knew whom he meant by "most people." However, I didn't think even Natalie—or any other superwoman of the new century—could hurry Donald up.

"You have to show him you mean business, Sophie. You have to show him who's in charge."

"I think Donald and I both know who's in charge."

"That's because you're too soft on him."

He was rifling through the black canvas bag that had replaced his calfskin briefcase, the one I'd gotten him for his thirty-fifth birthday. No one in Portland carried a briefcase, apparently.

He smelled nice, of witch hazel and the hard-milled soap Pepper sent him from Caswell Massey. I've always been partial to men whose own particular smell makes me want to bury my nose in their necks. My first love, Rory, had sometimes smoked a cigar, a youthful affectation that meant Rory's sweaters had often smelled faintly of the best Cubans. Even today, that smell floating outside a restaurant or from the jacket pockets of an elderly man strolling by could turn me weak at the knees.

Paul was outlining what I would say to Donald, the magic words that would turn Donald's current benign tolerance of me to awed obedience.

"You just put it to him simply. You say, 'Donald, this is far below the housing code standard and I want it fixed immediately.' Don't say, 'Oh Donald, it would be so nice if you could see your way to getting us a teensy bit more heat.'"

It wasn't fair. Paul knew I wasn't a take-charge type when he married me. Confronted with dilemmas that demand a confident tone and a commanding gaze, my voice squeaks and my eyes dart around furtively. In this state I can appear a little wanting—in fact, downright moronic. "Speak up!" the nuns at St. Catherine's would say. I knew even then, though, that speaking up got you in trouble far more often than **not** speaking up did.

I'd also learned young that stupidity was my best defense. My mother was a determined social activist and good-deed doer. Early on, I figured out that when Mom needed me to man a ring-toss booth at the muscular dystrophy carnival or fill in as a Roman guard in the church Passion play, she'd soon grow discouraged if I seemed slow and scattered, if it promised to be more trouble than it was worth to enlist my services.

My sister Delia, older by three years, was louder in her refusals. Her first word had been "no" and she'd been saying it to Mom ever since. Someone had to. My father found his wife hugely entertaining in all her altruistic endeavors, and I'd always been too awed by the sheer force of my mother's personality for anything but the most passive resistance.

When you've spent your childhood hiding under a rock, hoping to avoid being dragged along to benefit folk concerts and dawn tree plantings, it's hard to mature into an incisive, self-possessed woman who can stare down a Motor Vehicle Department functionary and say, "I've been standing here for three hours. I am **not** going back to Table A for that form." My friend Marta was capable of such feats, but then she worked on Capitol Hill and was used to kicking up a ladylike dust until she got what she wanted.

"Like I said, I'd do it but it's gonna be a hell of day," Paul finished, dragging his coat on. It was a navy pea coat with a red-plaid flannel lining, bought at a rugged outdoor store in Freeport. I remembered with a sigh his Washington coat, tweed with a silk lining.

"Try not to be timid with Donald," were his last words before he left. Then he kissed me, quite tenderly.

How, I wondered as I watched him drive away, could you kiss someone like a lover while criticizing her like . . . like a husband. Criticism, I'd begun to conclude, was a side effect of marriage. Then again, I visibly bit my tongue a lot with him. Marriage meant biting your tongue.

Still, we hadn't grated on each other this way back home. They said the first year of marriage was the hardest, but this second year was more difficult by far. I'd liked our first year. I was thirty-three and I'd been, let's face it, so damn relieved to have someone. I'd positively rejoiced in our little domestic rituals. Grocery shopping together, painting the bathroom, buying mixing bowls. Other lovers had broken my heart and disappeared; Paul had stayed around to participate in the purchase of a hand-held vacuum cleaner.

Paul was charmed by my faults back then. He'd called me "charmingly soft-spoken," not "timid." But now, as we approached our second anniversary, his morning embraces were being steadily replaced by a list of important tasks I should consider completing before his arrival home. And "Did you have a productive day?" were his first words of greeting at night, accompanied by a tepid, G-rated hug.

This overseeing of my schedule was probably on the advice of Natalie, Paul's workmate. I brooded over Natalie as I made the first of many pots of coffee of my day. They said coffee gave you jitters, but it had little effect on me.

Natalie. I'd had a few years of practice hating Pepper, but in three short months, Natalie had almost caught up with my mother-in-law on my secret list of the top ten people I'd like to see shipped permanently to a research station on a polar ice cap.

Paul had taken to implying that, unlike me, Natalie managed her life. She was beginning to manage Paul too, in all sorts of small, slightly sinister ways. In her high, clear, confident voice, Natalie had probably reminded Paul that depressed stay-at-home types need action to lift their moods. I should be prodded for my own good.

The trouble was, I didn't want to be prodded. None of this was really my fault. No natural laziness or gloom had brought me to this low point. I was stuck at home, working in solitude and chill, and I'd never intended that when we moved to Portland. I'd had plans, lots of them.

First off, I'd hoped to give up freelancing for a "real job." But we soon discovered that any position available in Portland's tight employment market wouldn't pay half of what I made on my own, at inflated Washington rates. So: no new job. This was daunting, but what the heck. I'd explore in my free hours, discover Maine, make the most of the short year we'd have here. Paul was going to leave me the car sometimes.

Then it turned out that a car was essential for Paul's work. He had meetings all over the region, last-minute demands, unpredictable hours. No roving up and down the lovely coast but only as far as my legs could take me.

That left joining things. Getting involved, which is hell itself for a shy person. So far, I'd attended one meeting of the local community group, West End Forward. The discussions there centered on homeowners' grievances: zoning regulations, property taxes, dogs messing on lawns. I nodded and smiled, but they could tell I was a fake.

A child would have led us to places where parents make friends with other parents, but we'd decided to put children off. Paul thought we should be married for at least three years before attempting parenthood. It was too bad that renting a child occasionally wasn't an option. People can place you if you're holding a kid by the hand: you're a neighbor, a community member, a good citizen who'd produced another miniature good-citizen-to-be.

These obstacles had temporarily deflated me and made Paul touchy. It was his fault for dragging us here, he said. No, no, I replied. We'd miscalculated a little, that was all. We'd thought Portland would be a smaller Boston, a bustling metropolis with lots of ways in for the just-arrived. We were wrong. Portland was a town, not a city, an old-fashioned town with an understandably reluctant attitude to newcomers, especially spoilt urban professionals who talked about Maine's stunning natural beauty, then left after their first winter. The handshakes at the community meeting were courteous but brief, the faces polite but wary. Standing there with a falsely vivacious smile, holding a West End Forward mug full of tepid coffee, I'd felt as if I were trying to infiltrate a secret society.

Yet, despite these discouragements, I wasn't depressed. I was a little stymied, a little homesick, but not the hopeless moper Natalie clearly pegged me as. My listlessness wasn't related to the move. I had other woes, and they came down to one un-ignorable fact: Paul had changed. Since we'd arrived in Maine, the easygoing, affectionate husband I'd known was disappearing fast. "My man," as Billie Holiday sings in that old standard, "was not the angel I once knew." He was different, and the difference boded ill for me. For us.

"Different how?" said Marta. She likes specifics.

I'd called Marta's work number as soon as Paul left because I didn't want to sit and cry over my cereal. Marta is a great antidote to the urge to weep. Though it was early, I knew she'd be there. Marta's elegant slenderness is the outward sign of a highly strung nervous system sustained only by hard work and cigarettes. She relaxes at her office and wanders restlessly when at home.

"Different than he used to be," I said.

"Not just this business of trying to oversee your schedule? Because all men are bossy if you give them an opening. You've let him get away with too much, but it's not too late to slap him down a little." Marta is a great believer in keeping men in their place.

"Not just that."

"Then what?"

"I don't know."

"There must be a reason for all this free-floating anxiety, Sophie. No, wait. Sorry. I forgot who I was talking to. The woman who's sure she'll die of a septic ingrown toenail. The woman who worries that she'll accidentally commit tax fraud and be sent to a high-security women's prison where she'll be molested with a broomstick like Linda Blair in **Born Innocent**. The woman who thinks she'll catch TB when someone coughs on the Metro."

"Those are all very valid fears."

"Well," said Marta, who didn't believe in encouraging my morbid tendencies by arguing with them, "the subject at hand is Paul. I thought it was going along fine, the marriage experiment."

I tried to explain. Where once in Paul's eyes I'd been adorable, disorganized Sophie, I was now slipshod, inefficient Sophie. Where he once thought it was cute that I drove like a grandmother, now he made a throttled noise in the back of his throat when I hesitated at yellow lights. Paul had always seen my meals as interesting culinary excursions—who else would think to put prunes in chicken curry when the raisins ran out? Nowadays I was a failure as a woman because occasionally I overcooked a roast. Natalie, of course, practically sang over the stove, and **she** worked a real job.

"Did he really say that?" said Marta. "About the real job? The nerve of him. You bring in every bit as much as he does."

Marta knew almost to the dollar what I made a year. She'd referred several of my clients to me and still advised me on what to charge, which was always far more than I'd dreamed of. My work was so routine that I forgot sometimes it was worth money. Routine, and hardly sexy, hardly likely to rouse admiration in a bored husband. What three-to-a-pack men's T-shirts are to fashion design, my clients' jobs were to print design. They didn't need cutting-edge graphics or funky typefaces. They needed someone who could speed on the production of technical and legislative publications of the dullest variety: newsletters, manuals, white papers, low-end annual reports. For sleep-inducing documents produced on a budget, call Sophie Quinn.

I was also a fast, accurate proofreader, which brought me a nice sideline in research papers and the annual meeting proceedings of medical subspecialty groups. This work was even more tedious, full of dreary footnotes and charts. It paid well, but wasn't the best choice for a borderline neurotic like me, as it provided far too much up-to-the-minute information on brain-melting Caribbean fungi and obscure sight-destroying retinal diseases that struck with no warning symptoms.

"Sophie, does he know how hard it is, what you do? The concentration it takes?"

"He sees me sitting here in my sweatpants,

working when I want to, going out when I want to. To him it must seem like I have it easy."

"Does he also see you staying up till three A.M. because the client called you at five P.M. with some silly change to a table in an appendix that affects the study narrative on sixty other pages and wants it completed the next day?"

"He just falls asleep when I have night work. Then he complains that the house is a mess."

"Is that your fault? Did he break his leg?"

"He says he's concerned about me. He says I seem lethargic."

Natalie speedwalked to work, no matter what the weather. At the end of a long, productive day, she'd carry groceries home in an ingeniously designed backpack she'd picked up at the L.L. Bean factory store on Congress Street. Natalie's fiancé ate like a king, instead of being served ready-made roast chickens from the grocery store with microwaved vegetables on the side. And when the dishes were done, Natalie's idea of a fun evening was to single-handedly sponge-paint the dining room or mat their vacation photos to hang in the breakfast nook. I reeled off these accomplishments to Marta.

"What is this woman, some kind of sinister

throwback to the 1950s?" said Marta. "What does she do for a living that gives her all this time?"

"She's the PR person for the project."

"Huh," said Marta. "The stupid project." She had little respect for Paul's job, which had taken me from the cozy habits of our friendship to distant Maine, a place Marta had always assumed was part of Canada if she'd thought of it at all.

I huddled in my bathrobe and listened to her exhale cigarette smoke at the other end of the phone, a sound like ocean waves. **Shush-shush, shush-shush**. My bathrobe—English felt, a going-away present from Marta—covered three other layers of sleepwear piled on for warmth. This might account for the lackluster quality of my sex life lately.

"You think **your** work's boring. How do you even pretend to care about Paul's job?" Marta said. "The one time he explained it to me I was yawning in five seconds."

I knew this, since Paul had taken deep offense on that occasion.

Paul had been working for five years in fundraising and development for the National Science Learning Consortium when he got the chance to launch a new Consortium venture called The

Science Project. The Project aimed at "increasing the quality, effectiveness, and innovativeness of science instruction for all children at our nation's public schools," as Natalie's press release grandly put it. ("Innovativeness?" I'd said to Paul when I read Natalie's release. "I'm sure it's a word," he'd said. "Natalie looks everything up.")

In reality, the Project boiled down to new teacher training programs and large corporate donations of lab equipment. The whole enterprise was starting with a pilot year in Maine, where the school system was excellent and a few of the board members had summer homes.

It was a nice concept—who could be against science? against learning? against children? But while I found the Project admirable, Natalie behaved about the whole endeavor like some sort of John the Baptist proclaiming good news in the wilderness.

Marta said, "You're being quiet because you can hear me smoking."

"No. Well, yes, maybe."

I didn't tell her the sound soothed me. She was my friend, and I wanted her to live a long time. I wanted to be old ladies with her someday.

"I can't quit and stay human, Soph. And don't

tell me to try that patch because I may as well keep Scotch tape on my arm for all the good it does."

"You have to keep the patch on your arm, Marta. You can't just rip it off when it doesn't go with a sleeveless outfit."

"You know I'll quit one of these days. Back to this Natalie. It's no wonder she has all this time. Nowadays, PR is nothing but a refuge for light-weights," said Marta, who'd started out as an assistant in one of the big K Street agencies. She'd gotten me a job there too, right out of college, a good job in the graphics department where I'd learned all the latest computer layout programs. I did that job for eight years. Then they "out-sourced" me. In other words, they fired me, then hired me back as a freelancer with no benefits but a generous hourly rate that was passed on directly to the client.

The funny part was that once I was freelancing, people at the PR firm thought of me differently: as an expert, instead of that quiet girl down the hall. My first new client was accidental. Someone at the firm had a friend at a research institute. The friend hired me to lay out a report on the effects of mothers' education levels on children's success in school. Then it happened that the research institute client knew an editor at an association for cardiac specialists, and I whipped out their convention program. And so on. Washington isn't that big a city when it comes to its professional population, which is always generating piles of paper to show each other. Jobs came to me without much effort on my part, and the work began to fill my hours and keep my bankbook healthy. It was the best I could do, I told myself, and kept doing it.

Marta's career path had been far more strategically planned. She was a lobbyist for an association that represented the cosmetics industry. It was a highly paid career she'd chosen because, as she put it, "I knew that if I could be very talented at one thing, I could afford a cleaning service and take-out meals for the rest of my life."

She **was** good. Very, very good, a skilled diplomat and wily strategist who could never have been accused by carping competitors of using her sex appeal to get ahead. No one could have accused her of it, that is, because the whole effect was carried off with such adroitness. Marta, one senator's aide had remarked, was the only woman in town who gave the impression of changing into a bikini just by removing her reading glasses.

Marta didn't need reading glasses, of course; they simply accentuated her cool, snowy blonde loveliness. With her tortoise-shell spectacles propped at the tip of her impudent nose, Marta resembled a prim but secretly lusty librarian in a blue movie. Her given name—Martha—**was** prim. She'd changed it to Marta on the day she'd left Passaic, New Jersey, forever. She thought that "Marta Lindstrom" sounded intriguing. Even her own family called her Marta nowadays.

"To give Natalie her due, she does slave away," I said. "The guys at the office adore her."

"Of course they do. They think she's a great kid with a terrific attitude. She's not going to murmur in Paul's ear that if he'll sample her home-baked dinner rolls, she'll be his geisha girl every night. She'll just imply it by smothering him with attentions. Does she smother **you** with attentions?"

"She tried to be nice. In the beginning."

"Yeah. I bet Paul thinks you're the one who's standoffish for not wanting to be Natalie's best friend. After she's been so nice and everything."

Natalie had been pleasant and chatty the first few times I'd stopped by the office, giving me the inside scoop on where to buy Shetland wool sweaters, asking me about my freelance career. It was only recently that her advice had started to take on a faintly critical tinge. In fact, it was becoming eerily like my mother-in-law's advice.

I was a disappointment to Pepper. Not a wild, glamorous disappointment, as if Paul had married a showgirl or a Hindu or someone equally unacceptable in Pepper's Presbyterian, Daughters-of-the-American-Revolution eyes. Just a slightly spineless, uninteresting choice, a woman with no verve and few domestic skills. What good was a daughter-in-law if you couldn't shop or cook with her?

Pepper hadn't entirely given up hope, though. Her gift for my last birthday had been a glossy illustrated book entitled **Easy Gourmet Meals in Under An Hour**. It weighed eleven pounds and was full of confusing instructions such as "boil the stock until it is fully reduced" and "reserve the clarified butter for glazing."

"What does she look like?" said Marta. "This Natalie person."

Marta puts too much stock in how people look, but then for her it's been a determining factor. It is a factor when you're beyond just-pretty and into the category where men do things for you because you're **so** pretty.

I told her that Natalie was attractive, in what

they used to describe as a gamine way, with very dramatic coloring. Black hair held back by an Alice comb. Big, dark eyes.

"She's half French Canadian but doesn't like to admit it."

"Why?" Marta said.

"Somehow that's seen as not being classy up here. When we met I said, 'Oh, Pelletier, what a pretty name.' I said it the French way, trying to be correct. And she said, very sharply, 'It's pronounced Pell-a-tear.' I never meant to offend her."

"Of course you didn't. You can't be expected to spot every self-hating Canadian who comes down the pike. How does she dress?"

"Scaled down. You know, little angora sweaters. Short pleated skirts."

Natalie even had a blouse with a Peter Pan collar. I stood five-eight, with wide shoulders and long legs. My feet were a size nine. Natalie's doll-like shoes looked as if she bought them in the children's department.

"I don't like this," said Marta. "I don't like it at all. She's got homewrecker written all over her."

"She's more of a home**maker**."

"The two are not mutually exclusive," said Marta, who felt very bitter about recent trends encouraging women to return to the kitchen and the craft table. Marta saw no reason why she should kill herself to construct a lampshade out of waxed paper, pressed autumn leaves, and a hole punch when she could buy a perfectly good lampshade from a catalog for two dollars less, without the risk of contracting poison ivy. As for home cooking, any man who wanted Marta's favors had better learn to use a microwave or a Diners' Card, because she didn't express her love through casseroles.

But Marta wasn't married. I couldn't tell if, as husbands went, Paul was unusual, but he seemed to need lots more care and feeding than I'd bargained on. If only he'd come with an instruction booklet, like our new steam iron did, or even with a little plastic stick with tips about watering and sunlight, like a florist's azalea.

"Paul's a good guy," I said to Marta. "I know I'm lucky to have him."

"Sure, he's a good guy," said Marta. "But is he being good to you?"

"He was," I said, remembering that first year of marriage when our dinners were full of leisurely small talk, and our nights spent, if not curled in each other's arms, at least touching—a hand held in sleep, his leg flung over mine, keeping me warm. These days, Paul snored in a cocoon of blankets, and dinner often as not featured complaints about items I'd neglected around the house, like not returning that defective snow shovel, or doing the towels in the wrong kind of laundry detergent.

I never "got around" to things, he'd mutter. Many of these things involved getting Donald to fix problems with the apartment that Paul knew and I knew and Donald knew that Donald had no intention of fixing.

"Am I too sensitive, Marta? These criticisms of his . . . they're not harsh, exactly. More like pinpricks."

"You can be pinpricked to death," said Marta. "I think the Chinese have a torture along those lines."

"Maybe he's just adjusting," I said. "New job, new surroundings."

"You're running a business out of a place where you can't even get decent heat and Paul's the one who's complaining?"

I loved it when Marta called what I did a business.

"Maybe Paul is just feeling fragile and can't express it."

"If I were up there to kick his ass for him, he'd feel a hell of a lot more fragile than he does now."

In the background, I heard a door open, and the soothing voice that Marta's executive assistant uses when she has to interrupt. Marta was in the middle of mark-up on a bill limiting colorant additives in facial-care products, and I'd already kept her on the phone too long.

"Hold on," said Marta.

"No, no," I said. "You go."

"I can easily get rid of this call."

"And then stay until eight tonight? Go. You've helped already."

I could picture her stepping lightly around her office on the Georgetown waterfront, flinging the curtains open, flipping on the cappuccino machine, adjusting her favorite sapphire bar pin on the collar of an off-the-rack suit tailored to perfection by a neighborhood seamstress. Marta might look expensive, but her bankbook said otherwise.

At this moment it wasn't her wardrobe I envied, though. It was her confidence. There are lots of lovely blondes in Washington, but few made the impression that Marta did. Marta thought of herself as God's gift to men, and because she believed it, they agreed with her. I didn't even feel like God's gift to the one man who might reasonably have been expected to think I was.

The phone rang.

"Did you call Donald about the heat?"

"I left a message." A white lie, to keep the peace.

"Damn him. Okay, if he doesn't answer, go over there and knock."

"The German shepherds."

"Those dogs wouldn't hurt a fly. Have they ever even barked at you?"

"I'll knock if he's not here in an hour," I said.

"Half an hour. I hate thinking about you there, freezing to death."

"Sorry I snapped at you this morning."

"Me too," he said cryptically. "Now get that loser over there and tell him to bang that radiator until it works."

He cared if I froze. He was, in his own way, being protective. And for once I hadn't heard Natalie's piercingly sweet voice in the background, making helpful suggestions. So I took heart and called the only other man I knew in Portland: Donald, the landlord who gave landlords a bad name.

Two

Donald's pager answered. Across the back alley I could see him moving around the upper story of the garage ("carriage house," he called it) where he lived with his pinch-faced wife and three German shepherds. Donald never answered the phone, even when he was at home. He apparently believed that to pick up the telephone directly was an admission of hopeless amateurism.

I left a plaintive message about the heat, sounding even to myself like someone who was trying to get away with something she hadn't paid for. Then I took a shower, before the building's hot water supply for the day could run out. Donald arrived two hours later, his face startled and aggrieved, the universal expression of challenged landlords everywhere.

This was the third time in a week that our radiators had broken down, although you couldn't say that they'd ever worked. Normally, Donald ceded his tenants a brief morning blast of heat around six A.M., and an evening blast at six P.M., when people got home from work. Those unfortunates who hung around during the day were on their own. In actuality that meant only Donald and me, and Donald no more felt the cold than a vampire would. He was a real Mainer, skinny but unflaggingly tough.

Donald often reassured me that in a year or two, three at most, I'd be as impervious to the temperature as he was. He knew all about extreme temperatures, he said, since he'd spent his childhood in Caribou, far north near the frozen New Brunswick border. "I thought **this** was the frozen north," I'd answered, but he'd looked so hurt I'd never joked about the weather in Portland again.

"You think it's not comfortable in here?" he said. "It's seventy degrees."

I handed him a pumpkin muffin and said coffee would be ready in a minute. Donald always inspired an immediate urge to feed him. His pale brown hair was lank and dull, as if he lived on a moistureless diet of dried apricots and melba toast. You could see his ribs through his shrunken T-shirt, and his tool belt hung precariously from his narrow hips. No sweater. No socks between his bare white ankles and his grimy sneakers. My sympathy was a little dimmed by the fact that, out the window, I'd seen him don the tool belt just before ambling up the side stairs to our apartment, probably to demonstrate that I'd interrupted him in more important tasks.

I displayed how the mechanism of the wall thermometer he'd given us "to monitor the heating situation" had uncoiled and popped out at the back.

"Look at this," I said, trying to speak confidently.

"Seventy degrees, like I said," Donald observed.

"But we put this in the icebox yesterday at dinner time, and an hour ago when I took it out, it still said seventy degrees."

"How much could you need the radiators yet? It's not even November," said Donald, who always had a backup defense. "You can't be cold."

The first snow of the season had arrived early, on Columbus Day. It was a driving, icy snow announcing a winter that meant business. In fact, that winter of 2000 would be unusually bitter, even for Portland. There would be eight feet of snow over the course of it, and no January thaw. But all I knew on that late-October morning was that, despite Donald's contention that it was physically impossible, I was cold. Cold in my bones. Colder than I'd ever been before.

"We live in a mansion," Paul liked to tell people. It was a good joke, because we did live in a mansion. In the servants' quarters, in an apartment outfitted with so few modern conveniences that we'd both developed a keen appreciation for what Victorian parlor maids and skivvies had to put up with.

Donald's house was a dilapidated, misplaced relic of the Old South, built in 1906 by a homesick robber baron from New Orleans. It had a deep, shady front veranda held up by massive white columns, a circular sweep drive, and the famed carriage house, or garage, above which Donald lived.

On the August day when we first saw the place, the overgrown garden was crowded with roses in bloom, and tiger lilies leaned drunkenly against a wrought-iron fence. We were giddy with our own daring. Paul was thirty-six and I was thirty-four, and we'd both spent our childhoods in Maryland river suburbs and our young adulthoods in the quiet, leafy neighborhoods of northwest D.C. As we stood on the walking path that edges the Fore River Bluff, and gazed across at Donald's transplanted Tara in the cranberry light of sunset, we felt worlds away from the familiar.

"I know you find these rundown wrecks captivating, Sophie, but there's a limit," Marta had said, upon receiving my Polaroid. "If there was an outhouse in one corner of that photo, I wouldn't have been surprised."

Even then, Paul and I would have taken the lease. Housing stock in Portland was at a premium. Besides, we were on an adventure, and adventures required hardships. Driving up to Maine in a moving truck full of our winnowed-down possessions, Paul had said that he wanted this time to be special. The work would be hard, but the hours wouldn't be crazy. We'd swim in the ocean, and breakfast in small-town diners, and take overnight trips to the woods. This was going to be our year, he said.

Buoyed by this carefree spirit, we agreed that quaint was the word for our new digs. The living room was quaint, with its fireplace and transom. The bathroom was quaint, with the claw-foot tub and toilet pull chain. The kitchen was quaintest of all, featuring what Donald touted as "the original linoleum."

Even our new neighborhood, grandly known as the Western Promenade, was quaint, full of sea captain's stone mansions and Victorian clapboards. If you squinted, you could picture the river view that had once drawn the rich to this side of town, a view that now included the airport, a decrepit strip mall, and three steaming factory towers.

Of course, you can be too much of a sucker for quaint. The one time my fear-mongering might have done us some good, I switched it off in favor of a newlywed winsomeness worthy of Jane Fonda in **Barefoot in the Park**.

"We could never afford all this room in Washington," Paul had enthused. "And he'll give us half the garage to park in."

"Carriage house," said Donald.

Donald had stressed the covered parking, a valuable rarity here, where cleaning off your car after an overnight snow could add twenty minutes to a morning routine. There were also snow bans, nights when all cars had to be removed from the streets in order for the snow-ploughs to operate. "Were there many nights like this?" I asked Donald.

"Last year wasn't too bad. Not more than eight of them."

I'd thought he was kidding.

Donald said he'd recently taken over the property, left to him by his grandmother. He hinted at all sorts of schemes for improvements. Only later did we learn that he'd owned the mansion for years and that it would remain as it was, since Granny had left Donald no accompanying money for upkeep.

This always seems to be the way with these old family properties. At least it is in novels about impoverished English peers and their country estates. My own parents' house, a hideously utilitarian ranch, was never "kept up" at all. My mother was too occupied with saintly projects, and my father would scratch mosquito bites for months rather than take two minutes to patch the screen door.

Yet even my folks' house was cozier than our present drafty barracks. Nothing worked. The shower had the water pressure of an asthmatic spitting into the wind. The kitchen sink drained so slowly that we could only wash four dishes at a time. Because Donald's self-installed insulation left much to be desired, gales off the Promenade rattled the shaky windows. And, although "chrmg frpl." had figured prominently in the rental ad, Donald had blocked up the fireplace with inexpertly laid bricking before we moved in, so that it now appeared as if a murderer had hastily walled away a corpse in our living room. Too much trouble to keep the chimneys clean, he said.

Six months ago, we'd have laughed in the midst of our griping, made a good story out of it for our friends. Now Paul was overworked, tired, and not inclined to see old-fashioned inconveniences as anything but another headache.

It seemed it wasn't really our year. We never took those trips to the woods Paul had raved about; he was working too hard, with a smaller staff than he'd been promised. We ventured into the ocean only once, fleeing blue lipped to our towels after ten minutes' swimming. We never ate in a diner, either, because Paul was counting fat and calories. After a week in the same office with Natalie and her pedometer, he'd discovered a burning need to watch his cholesterol. These days, instead of a stroll down to the waterfront or a ride to Portland Headlight, he'd lace on his jogging shoes and race off on a six-mile run, returning gray faced and exhausted.

I poured coffee for Donald, who seemed less than swept off his feet by my fetching morning outfit: fleece-lined trousers, sheepskin slippers with boiled wool hiking socks, and a cableknit fisherman's sweater handed down by my sister Delia. Delia's chest is larger than mine, so the sweater bagged strangely.

"You can see that the radiator's ice cold," I pointed out to Donald.

"The temperature regulator doesn't go by the temperature in **here,**" he said. "It's taking the temperature from the front hall, where there's more of a direct morning light."

Since the front hall faced out upon the **Western** Promenade, even I knew that this could not be true.

"In these old houses," Donald added censoriously, as if the house belonged to someone else and he was just the visiting plumber, "the deposits on this cruddy copper piping really build up. There's only so much I can do. I flushed it clean at the start of the season, you know."

I knew. I'd watched him, to the accompaniment of much groaning by both Donald and the pipes. He'd left a pool of foul-smelling black water on the floor in the kitchen that soaked the edges of the living- room rug.

"Good coffee." He grabbed the sugar bowl and stirred in half its contents. "My wife's coffee isn't half this good, and I tell her you use the store brand just like her."

This, though not exactly sound marital policy on Donald's part, was a bigger compliment than Paul had paid me lately.

"Thank you," I said. Donald tossed off the rest of the cup as if it were whiskey. I refilled it, and he put it on the windowsill, near to hand, and stooped down, grunting. For a skinny little runt, he moved with the mannerisms of someone much heavier.

"Let's see what we got here," he said.

I huddled on a kitchen chair. There was a layout for the Pernicious Anemia Society newsletter to finish before five, when the last shipment departed from the Congress Street UPS office. But if Donald were left alone, he'd come up with some plausible story about operations he'd performed on the radiators, and leave without accomplishing anything. Then I'd be back to square one in this particular round of fruitless negotiating.

Besides, I was lonely. I must have been, for Donald's tuneless humming and ominous sighs to be a source of companionship.

"You got your snow tires on yet?" said Donald.

"He has all-weather," I said. I didn't think of Paul's car as ours.

"That's not enough. You need actual snow tires on that vehicle."

Donald had a poor opinion of the secondhand Volvo that Paul had purchased after considerable legwork involving the Blue Book, Consumer Reports, and three different used car buying guides. To Donald, a real man had two options: a truck, by which he did not mean a sport-utility vehicle, or a motorcycle. Donald obviously considered Paul a snot-nosed tenderfoot, and I couldn't blame him, since Paul treated Donald as if Donald were a member of the unwashed peasantry and Paul was the squire's oldest son.

Donald unscrewed the radiator cap and banged at its side with a ball peen hammer he clearly did not know the correct use for. I listened to his rhythmic clanging and thought about the advice in the marriage manual I'd bought two weeks before, skulking up to the checkout counter as if purchasing a copy of **Hustler**.

The manual was titled **Making Marriage Work: The One-Person Solution to Rescuing the Wedded Relationship**. In the first chapter, the book suggested lavishing your mate with simple acts of affection until he fell all over you in gratitude.

So I'd remarked to Paul, the morning before, that I liked his tie. He said, "I've had this tie for years." I'd made Cream of Wheat for breakfast, and he'd complained that it was lumpy. I'd given him a kiss good-bye and he'd turned his face away and said, "Brush your teeth yet, honey? Hah-hah."

Donald was now poking about under the radiator covers, which were original and decorated with beguiling curlicues that he'd painted over with six coats of institutional greenish-white. Donald rooted around the floor like this every time I complained about the heat, even though we both knew it accomplished nothing. My dealings with him—our mutual collusion in the pretense that I'd been forceful and he'd been responsive—reminded me of the old saw about life under the Soviet economy: "They pretend to pay us, and we pretend to work."

"Here," he said, handing out an envelope covered in grime. "Right up against the baseboard. Probably blocking the conduction flow valve."

I suspected that there was no such valve, but short of going down on my knees with a flashlight, how could I prove it?

The envelope had been a pale pink linen

stock, with deckle edges. It was soot-spotted and dingy, but the note inside was perfectly legible.

"Paul," it said in a large, unformed script, **"You did it! Save lunch Thursday. We have to celebrate."** The words "have" and "celebrate" were heavily underlined.

One of Natalie's "booster notes." She distributed such notes to everyone at work, Paul said. She'd sealed the letter with maroon sealing wax imprinted with her initials. Pretentious, but not really flirtatious. Judging from the date, the event that called for celebration was Paul's recent success in netting The Science Project a large grant from a big petroleum company for the Predators of the Briny Deep fifth-grade curriculum.

We had celebrated that past Friday night, with dinner at Walter's in the Old Port. I'd told Paul over and over again what a feat he'd pulled off. Now here was Natalie, with her sealing wax and her celebration lunches.

A mere collegial gesture. I was fretting about nothing, I told myself. Then why, holding Natalie's pink stationery in my hand, did I have this nasty, unmistakable feeling, like the opening sneeze of a bad head cold or the initial hasty search through your purse for a wallet that you suddenly know isn't there?

There was no difference, really, between this and a dozen notes and phone calls from Natalie to Paul since they'd been working together. Natalie rang up on weekends with "just quick questions." She phoned during dinner to tell Paul that **Field of Dreams** was playing on Channel Four. She located the best allergist in town when the unfamiliar Maine pollen gave him a runny nose. Just last Sunday, she'd called him from the office supply store at the mall to see what sort of desk blotter to order for him.

"Why is she bothering about your desk blotter? Don't you have a secretary?"

"She's just being nice, Sophie. We have one secretary for the whole office, and she barely remembers to order pens."

"Is Natalie getting anyone else a desk blotter?"

"How should I know? Should I go around checking everyone's desk Monday? She makes my life easier, hon. Since when were you the jealous type?"

I hadn't been, until recently. A strange phenomenon occurs when you take that vow. You start to trust the guy, to count on the fact that he's not going anywhere. He married you, didn't he, and of his own free will? But how could I not feel outshone by a predatory female who was up with the lark, buying office supplies in bulk and cooing into Paul's receiver about filing cabinets and laser printers?

"What we've got here is a very rickety system," said Donald from under the radiator. "You wouldn't believe what a chore it is, maintaining an old place like this," he added, shamelessly implying that he did maintain it.

Donald's family had money somewhere, but he seemed satisfied to eke out an income from renting apartments to suckers and occasionally rehabbing an old motorcycle and selling it at a small profit. He also chopped wood, for which he charged a fortune. The other tenants, whose fireplaces, unlike ours, did work, were mostly young doctors at the Maine Medical Center down the street, and they gladly paid for the extra warmth. The leftover cords Donald tied with blue plastic twine and stacked on the front porch.

Paul called him shiftless, one of those abominable words Pepper had taught him for referring to members of the blue-collar class. You might have argued that Pepper, as a caterer, was also in that class. But Pepper would have been horrified at that notion. To Pepper, one's social identity wasn't determined by how you toiled, but how **necessary** it was for you to toil. Work was a form of amusing self-expression to Pepper and her friends, several of whom had never earned a paycheck since their post-college year when they taught kindergarten or played secretary while waiting to meet Mr. Right.

Pepper would have disapproved if she'd known how many hours I spent with Donald, for whom I'd developed an entirely unromantic fondness.

"**. . . little fool, you never can win,**" sang Donald, holding out his coffee cup for a third refill.

Was this what I'd come to, hanging around the kitchen listening to Donald massacre Ol' Blue Eyes' greatest hits all morning?

"You should get out more," Paul had commented last night. "If you walk down Pine Street a half mile or so, there's a coffee shop and a Laundromat and all sorts of things."

"There's a coffee shop and a Laundromat."

"Aren't there a few other places?"

"There's a Cumberland Farms convenience store."

"You see? It's all about making yourself leave the house, Sophie."

What did Paul expect me to do, linger in the Cumberland Farms choosing lottery numbers and squeezing the Hostess Fruit Pies to see if they were fresh? Certainly, I needed to take action, but what sort of action? I was a shy, backward outlier in a generation raised on the mantra that people who need people are the luckiest people in the world.

"I'm done," Donald said, rising heavily. "I only hope those dogs haven't made a mess up there."

He washed his hands in the kitchen sink, spattering gray droplets all over the counter.

"When should this get hot?" I asked him.

"I'll do a test run this afternoon. If the boiler will cooperate."

The boiler, of course, would not cooperate. We'd be cold again tonight. Paul would fume, and I'd apologize, and tomorrow Donald would be back again. It was like some French existential play where none of the characters can leave the room or the park bench or the weekend house party. It would go on and on all winter, with no cuts, no intermissions, and no director to tell me, the most poorly defined character in the whole production, what my motivation was and how it all would end.

"Ames has space heaters on sale," Donald threw over his shoulder as he slouched down the porch stairs.

Natalie's large, looping script danced in front of my eyes. If Paul were to be tempted to stray at this moment, what would he see as the choice before him? On one side, the slovenly, depressed wife, shuffling around the apartment in moccasins, leaving saucepans of chicken noodle soup curdling in the sink. On the other hand, a petite, energetic young PR maven with a can-do attitude, a rigorous exercise program, and a cold-weather wardrobe that was both practical and seductive. Which would you pick?

I ripped up the note, childishly, and threw it into the trash can beneath the sink, the pink fragments pretty as confetti against the pile of grimy paper towels Donald had carelessly thrown in. I would not dwell on trifles, I resolved. I would not choke my healthy marriage with the weeds of jealousy. In years to come, on the day of our silver anniversary, I would turn to Paul and say, "Remember how jealous I was of that girl in Maine? What was her name?" And he'd say, "Nancy" or "Nadine," getting it wrong because she had been of so little significance, and we would both laugh, ha-ha-ha.

Ha. Ha. Ha.

Three

At high noon every day I put on my outdoor shoes and walked the hundred yards to fetch the mail, which was delivered to a row of tarnished brass postboxes in the foyer of the main house. Paul's name and mine were listed side by side on our box: Stoddard and Quinn, like a vaudeville act.

My mother-in-law had been upset that I was not taking Paul's name.

"It causes confusion when a woman keeps her name," she said.

"What sort of confusion?"

"How will people address invitations to the two of you?"

This was no small point to Pepper, who loved being listed on charity programs and alumni contributor lists as Mrs. Paul's Father.

"His name and my name. Or my name, then his name. Or both our names connected by an ampersand."

"I don't think you realize how complicated these issues can be, Sophie. What about your children?"

"Quinn-Stoddard would be a wonderful last name."

"Very British," Paul said helpfully, as hundreds of my wearing-of-the-green ancestors spun in their graves.

"I understand that women's rights and all that are important," said Pepper, "but now that we've come so far, isn't a name just a petty detail?"

There were so many possible replies to this assertion that I couldn't speak. What I wanted to do was grab one of Pepper's antique garlic presses from the hand-tooled rack on her Provence-yellow kitchen wall and beat her about the head and shoulders with it. When I was able to open my mouth again, Paul had changed the subject with a wink at me. Thereafter, every letter and package Pepper sent us was labeled "Paul and Sophie Stoddard." Paul suggested we return them marked "Not known at this address," but in the interests of family harmony I'd vetoed this idea.

Getting mail was a ridiculously important ritual to me just then. Today my "Hike Cape Breton" packet from the Nova Scotia Tourism Bureau (with free Cabot Trail map) had arrived. There was also a large manila envelope for Sophie

Quinn, which was reassuring in the face of Pepper's assumption that such a being no longer walked the earth. Paul had three thin notices informing him of stock transactions related to his pension plan. Finally, there was a printed form letter addressed in my mother's hand letting me know about a marvelous opportunity to give money to a rain forest cooperative. I opened that standing at the mailbox, to get it over with.

The circular contained a handwritten postscript, **"Sophie, you might consider this group for your Christmas giving. Hope all is well. Best to Paul."**

My mother always wrote, "Best to Paul," as if he were a mere acquaintance. It wasn't because he'd taken away her little girl; we weren't that sort of mother and daughter. Paul was simply irrelevant to Mom's attempts to press her family into the service of good. Paul had a civic heart, and gave a generous amount to various good causes, but he had no desire to mingle with the great unwashed at soup kitchens or attend sit-ins at the nuclear power plant up at Calvert Cliffs. Since he couldn't be conscripted for charity, Mom settled for sending him greetings by phone or letter from time to time.

My mother's handwriting created in me the

usual feeling of guilty obligation. I'd have to respond, even though she'd sent only a token communication, and it would be difficult, because I never had anything to say that would truly interest her. Mom was a good mother in that she'd always provided the basics—food, clothing, school supplies—but somehow, early in life, Delia and I perceived that motherhood didn't interest her very much. I think my mother had children because that was the thing to do back then. More telling was the fact that she'd gone against the dictates of the Church and had only two.

I couldn't say to my mother, "My husband is drawing away from me and I'm afraid." My anxieties only baffled and worried her, and so I didn't confide in her, sure though I was that in her undemonstrative, practical way she loved Delia and me. My mother would have done better with bouncing, energetic, can-do daughters. Delia, a math and computer whiz, was too intellectual for her, and I was too quiet.

The air was heavily damp and still, promising the snow Donald had predicted. Clutching Paul's corduroy weekend jacket to me, I ran back in and sprawled with my haul on the living-room sofa, an overstuffed white elephant covered in ivory cotton brocade. We'd bought it at a resale shop on Congress Street for only a hundred dollars.

The manila envelope contained new samples from Ann, my oddest client. I painted watercolors for her greeting card line, Life Markings.

Ann's samples always gave me a thrill—the thrill of the failed but still aspiring artist. I'd had promise once, according to my high school teachers, but my parents didn't see the use of art school when a fine liberal arts college in Pennsylvania had offered me a scholarship. At Wilkinson I majored in studio art, thinking to go on for my MFA. Somehow, once I was done paying off college loans, grad school became one of those "future plans," like going to Europe or getting more exercise.

Over the years, I'd always drawn and painted, taking adult ed classes with all the other dabblers. Then, a few months before I'd married Paul, Ann had signed me on.

My business involvement with Ann was one of those accidents produced by old acquaintanceship. She was a friend of sorts from my college newspaper days. I'd been layout manager (they paid me work study money for it), Ann had written a women's sports column, and Marta had been features editor, hated for her reviews by the college drama, fine arts, and music departments with a unity they brought to nothing else.

I'd remembered Ann as a wiry young woman with protruding, river green eyes and lank brown hair in a Dutch boy bob. When I'd seen her again a few years earlier, she hadn't changed a whit. She lived in Philadelphia, but was in D.C. for a one-day conference on entrepreneurship at the Sheraton in Woodley Park, and stopped by my apartment on her way to the train station afterward, since I was right around the corner. I had the distinct impression she wouldn't have gone farther to see me.

She was visibly unimpressed with my tiny studio and my store-bought "dessert" cookies. But, returning from the bathroom, she'd spotted a watercolor thumbtacked above the bookshelf. It was just a painting class exercise, a still life of a bowl of eggs, three black-eyed Susans, and an azure-blue pottery jug.

"I **must** have this for my new venture," she'd said, fixing me with her bulging eyes.

I was so impressed with anyone who had the confidence to throw the word "venture" around like that, before I knew it, I'd agreed to crank out three paintings for her every couple of months "for a small stipend." I guess "small stipend" sounds better than "measly pittance."

Ann hadn't revealed the subjects for this latest set of cards. Her last note had ordered simply, "Three florals, please. Purple iris, white roses, and pale peach gladioli."

I'd located a stalk of wilting gladioli in a grocery store, but peach is an uncertain color, and the result was mottled, like spilled tea. I'd had fun with the roses, using for background a length of amethyst velvet picked up in a remnant bin. The effect was pretty, but only the irises really worked.

Every April, in my parents' unweeded backyard, there bloomed a glorious stand of purple irises just suited to the swampy Maryland river soil there. I'd been painting them since I was nine. That was the year I had Sister Paulina, who'd let me draw freehand and taught me about perspective and shading while the rest of the class was making construction-paper Indian headdresses and Easter Bunny cutouts. She'd also encouraged me to paint from life. When I was outside, doing this, I felt reverent and transported, the way you were supposed to feel at mass during the consecration of the host. Bless Sister Paulina. She brought me as close to God as I'm ever likely to get.

For Ann's irises, I painted wet on wet, stroking cobalts and purples at full intensity onto an ochre wash. To create the gleaming highlights that shine through the underside of an iris petal, I used a thin sable brush to pick up streaks of the paint here and there. The result was a veritable riot of irises, dripping in the sun from a recent rain.

"That's one of your best ones yet," Paul had commented approvingly. He never stinted on praise unless I began talking about graduate school. Then he grew worried, as if I'd suggested joining an ashram. Paul was proud to have an "artistic" wife, but he'd been raised to think of contemporary artists as weird, unstable, and not very sanitary in their dress or living conditions. While he admired my paintings, he didn't rush out to grab catalogs from the Maine College of Art so that I could follow some idyll of youth.

But what was I going to do for the rest of my working life? A feeling of vertigo overcame me when I considered spending the next four decades in the effort to ensure that the Vegan Food Watchlist went to press on time, or copyediting articles titled "Three Cases of Atypical Myocar-

dial Infarction in Alabama Factory Populations"
for obscure medical journals.

The new cards slithered out of their plastic
liners. There were my irises, and they **did** work,
better than I'd hoped. And superimposed on the
painting, in Ann's clumsy amateur calligraphy,
were the words, "On the sudden passing of your
loved one."

The inside copy read:

When death comes unexpectedly
Grieving is so much harder.
Your loved one was taken away in a
moment,
But your memories will last forever.

The roses and gladioli were also condolence
cards: Death of Your Aunt, and Death of Your
Uncle. Ann's note said, "Soph, I think you'll be
pleased with these! Check to come."

This was what came of doing a favor for an
old friend.

Well, the art world would survive. I went to
my computer and caused the dull columns of
the **Pernicious Anemia Gazette** to take shape.
Of all the diseases my clients dealt in, the
chronic, drawn-out ones were the most discour-

aging to read about. Come to think of it, that was what my freelance career resembled: a chronic disease, never quite going away, never quite worsening enough to come to a crisis.

The **Gazette** was an easy job, a reliable gig that put four hundred a month in my pocket between layout, proofing, and pre-blueline changes.

"While patients may occasionally present with symptoms of chronic figure," I read (or something of the sort), **"the diagnosis of pernicious anemia can be verified with three simple testing protocols: the Marsh Lieberman count, a white cell–specific CBC, and the more rarely employed Hartz-Bozewell analysis."**

Interesting, I thought, checking myself mentally for signs of pernicious anemia. There were none. Physically, I was depressingly healthy.

I printed a hard copy for the client and packaged the file in a Zip disk for overnight mail. Then I began pulling on the bulky, cold-repelling garments I donned for trips down to the UPS office. The walk was merely a mile and a half, but the wind off the bluff made it feel more like three. Just as I was about to leave the house, sweating in my wraps, the phone rang again.

"Did you get it fixed?"

"He was over. He's doing a test run of the boiler this afternoon."

Paul's jaw clicked audibly. His dentist said that if Paul couldn't stop clenching his jaw he'd have to start wearing a bite guard at night.

"You can't let him get away with these tests and trials of his. Tell him that our living conditions are unacceptable. Use that word. Unacceptable."

"I think they're getting warmer. The radiators."

"They aren't, Sophie. You always think that. It's your whole life, wandering around, putting your hand on those radiators every ten minutes."

"Actually, I just finished the **Anemia Gazette** and I'm running it down to UPS. So if that's all we needed to talk about . . ."

He sighed again.

"I'm sorry. I just . . . the guy's a charlatan, that's all. He wastes too much of your time. Anyway, I didn't really call to check on the heat. I called to say my mother wants to come for Thanksgiving."

"Did you tell her yes already? You did, didn't you?"

"What could I do? Apparently Ellen is having her whole damn family over from Dublin or somewhere and Mom felt she'd be in the way."

Ellen was the wife of Paul's brother James, a soft-voiced daughter of Erin who was more than a match for Pepper. I'd often wanted to ask Ellen what her secret was, but figured her immunity came from the centuries of willpower bred in the Irish from resisting the English intruder. After Oliver Cromwell, even Pepper would seem easy.

"She wants to come Tuesday to Friday," said Paul. "It's only four days. I'm sorry. You know she does the poor widow act and I can't say no."

"I have three deadlines in those four days. And you'll be at work through Wednesday."

"I'll take the night shift with her and you can work then."

"Do you think she'll really understand when I toddle off to my light table after dinner? Last time she saw you with the laundry, she said, 'Can't Sophie do that during the day?'"

"I know, I know. But she's very excited about this visit. She wants to help you get the place all set up. Buy some sheets. Do the kitchen up. And Natalie knows her way around the outlets at Kittery blindfolded. She volunteered to go with you two on Friday. Then there's that cooking store down at the Old Port. I bet my mother would love that."

The store was called the Whip and Spoon. "The Whipped and Spoon," Paul had dubbed it last time we'd passed, watching women dragging their husbands in to buy expensive copper-bottomed frying pans.

Paul admitted that his mother was nagging, tactless, exhausting. But while he himself didn't get along with her wonderfully, he believed that my getting along with her was just one of those things women should know how to do. My sister Delia was bossy, he pointed out, and I managed to have a perfectly dandy relationship with her.

The difference was that Delia loved me, while Pepper had to work hard to flog herself into lukewarm liking. If I ever got run over by a train, the best I could hope for in the way of posthumous attentions from Pepper was that she'd dash over to Saks to pick out a suitably tasteful outfit for my corpse to wear at the wake—since in her eyes, none of my current clothes would qualify. "Sophie has such a delightfully gypsy wardrobe," she had commented once when I arrived at a barbecue in what I'd thought was a stylish and tasteful batik sundress.

"We've had three out of four holidays with her since we've been married."

"What do you want from me, Sophie? She has no one."

"Except your brother, his wife, three grand-children, and a host of friends all willing to crowd around at the slightest need. As well as ten sycophantic employees."

Pepper was a diva at her catering firm, Comfort Foods, where she compensated her staff extra well in order to ensure the kind of slavish employee loyalty that went out with circle skirts. It paid off. Pepper's whole enterprise was a fore-ordained success. The opening of Comfort Foods had coincided perfectly with upscale Americans' nostalgic yearning for the lower-middle-class foods of yesteryear: meatloaf, pot roast, mashed potatoes. Macaroni and cheese. Shoofly pie.

Pepper's versions of these specialties were, of course, more pricey and creative than the origi-nals. Her bread pudding came with a raspberry-brandy sauce, and her mashed potatoes were topped with a chive-and-cheddar crust.

"She's lonely," said Paul.

"How can she be lonely when she's never alone?" I asked, sounding like a Simon and Gar-funkel song.

"Maybe you wish you'd married an orphan," said Paul.

Yes, I thought to myself, picturing the orphan. He would be a man who often said, "Don't cook tonight, honey, we'll go out," a man who'd massage my shoulders and carry my easel, a man who'd take us on winter cruises instead of spending holidays perspiring over turkey and glazed ham at Pepper's gleaming, three-acre dining-room table.

"I know she's hard on you," said Paul. "She just can't believe anyone, even you, is good enough for me."

"Even me? I'm not remotely in the running. But sure, she can come for Thanksgiving. We'll have to figure out where she'll sleep."

"That's a problem. You know she's had that disc that's been acting up."

This was the first I'd heard of Pepper's disc.

"I thought if we borrowed an air mattress from one of the guys at the office we could use that and she could have our bed."

Perhaps Anita Loos had been right when she wrote that family life was only fit for those who could stand it. At the thought of my mother-in-law's impending visit, I wanted to check myself into a mental asylum.

"By the way," Paul said, "I'm going to be a little late tonight. I'm going to look at a Ford Explorer Natalie's brother is selling."

"An SUV? But you love your Volvo."

"It's not right for Maine, I'm realizing that. Everyone says you absolutely have to have an all-terrain vehicle up here."

"Aren't the snowploughs excellent? Donald said they were. It's not as if you need to drive up into the mountains or off-road or anything."

A mistake. Men considering sport-utility vehicles never like to be reminded that they don't, in fact, live the sort of lives that require one.

"It can't hurt to test drive. He'll even give me a trade-in on the Volvo. He's giving it away for peanuts. They don't know the market value of anything up here."

"But would you feel comfortable lending me such an expensive car?" We had an agreement: I bought gas from time to time in return for using the Volvo when I absolutely needed it. This wasn't very often, as Paul's agonized expression when handing over the keys was inhibiting.

"Sweetie, you don't actually need to drive all that much. Look how good all this walking is for you. Anyway, we'll talk about that after I've seen the thing."

"So when will you be home?" I said.

I had never thought I'd turn into one of those women who said, "So when will you be home?"

"I don't know."

"What about dinner?"

I'd also never thought I'd be one of those women who said, "What about dinner?"

"Ted mentioned something about catching a bite when we were done," said Paul. He added kindly, "Go ahead and eat whenever you want to."

I took a chance on making it to the UPS office by five, and first phoned my sister Delia to sputter about the Pepper visit.

"I can't believe Paul did that," Delia said. "Just said she could come."

"Pepper can be pretty imperious."

"He should at least have pretended to ask you."

I could picture her frowning, her lovely black eyebrows drawn together, her round chin stuck out. Delia takes after my mother's side of the family, the Welsh side, which is short and dark, while I take after my father's Irish and Scots side, which is tall and long limbed but not really willowy.

"It's kind of sad that I can't love Pepper even a little."

"You don't have to love her. You don't even have to like her. You just have to be polite to her when necessary."

"You're good to Tom's mother."

"She's good to me, that's why. She beat Mom to the hospital when Ben was born and waited there the whole time. Mom left halfway through for some committee meeting about Haitian refugees."

"The doctor did say you had hours to go, let's give her that."

"You stayed," said Delia. "Speaking of which, he'll be awake in ten minutes, so we should talk fast. I swear, that child's nap seems to get shorter every day."

Delia complained, but cheerfully. Even working part-time and raising the baby didn't faze her. She was a software and networking troubleshooter who made big bucks consulting, and justifiably so. My sister stilled the troubled waters just by walking in a client's door, and her brilliance was tempered by a winningly smart mouth. Tom had proposed to Delia, he always said, because she made him laugh.

"So let's get back to you," said Delia. "Because I have nothing to report except that, while we're on the subject of in-laws, Tom's sister Marie came over yesterday, and told me we had to buy a new couch. She implied that our current one is shabby."

The couch was worse than shabby. It had springs that mimicked a proctology exam. Delia, for all her easygoing ways, was very careful with money. Tom was a dermatologist, well established, and she was raking it in, yet they had furniture still hanging around from their college dorm rooms.

"I said, Marie, Ben may want to be a doctor too some day and we're going to have the tuition ready when the time comes. God knows what state school she'll have to send her kids to, the way she throws it around. Anyway, about Pepper. You'd better set some ground rules with Paul."

"Setting ground rules sounds easy in theory."

"Soph, these are the crucial years. Look, is Tom a great husband? He is, isn't he."

"Yes," I said sincerely.

"Because I **trained** him. You have to say, "Paul, honey, if you ever again tell your mother she can stay for four days without at least calling me first, I'm going on a long vacation to the Bahamas on **your** gold card."

"And if he doesn't listen?"

"He'll listen. Get angry if you have to."

"I don't like getting angry."

"I know that. What's more, Paul knows that. So he takes advantage."

"What if he gets angry back? What if he says, I know lots of women who'd be delighted to have me and my widowed mother in their lives?"

"Is this about that girl at work again? Forget her."

"I can't. She's wonderful. She's a domestic goddess."

Delia said, "You know, when we were first married Tom used to mention this ex-girlfriend of his, sort of plaintively, when I was rough on him, or what he thought was rough on him, like asking him to do the dishes once a week. He'd make little comments like '**Cheryl** thought it was cute when I showed up two hours late' or '**Cheryl** loved camping.' Well, I told him that every time he mentioned Cheryl, I was going to cast my mind back to sex with Stan DiMoglio, and think about it, right in front of him."

Stan DiMoglio was pre-Tom. He was a photographer for a convenience foods association, the kind of gorgeous Italian American guy who perfects the type. No good for the long run, but it was Stan whom Delia thought of when she missed the single life.

"Did it work?"

"He mentioned her one more time. I sat back and let my eyes get misty, and that was the last I heard about Cheryl."

I pondered this.

"Look," said Delia, "next time something like this comes up, say you're a bit upset and need a minute to think. Then go in another room. That alone will make him nervous. Men hate to be left alone in rooms."

"I had no idea there was this much strategy involved in marriage," I said.

"There isn't, not once you get a working routine going. I give in to Tom a lot too, you know. Him and his stock market flings."

"If we could get to where you and Tom are . . ."

"You'll get there."

A wail rent the air. Delia had a baby monitor, but she'd never needed one. Ben made it known when he was awake. He wasn't the sort of baby who gazes up sleepily at a mobile and chirps to himself when arising from a nap. Hearing him made me miss him more than ever: his inquiring blue eyes, so much like Tom's, his squiff of golden hair, his untranslatable babbling.

"Whatever else you do, don't worry," said Delia, and her voice saying those words gave me comfort as Delia's voice always had.

I raced down the long, gradual hill of Congress Street and arrived at the UPS office with five minutes to spare before closing time. Then I headed farther downhill to the Old Port and my favorite coffee shop, JavaNet. At JavaNet you could sit in a corner and log on to a computer, or read in one of the deep leather armchairs, or buy the latest **Vogue** and flip through pages of resort wear, pretending you might someday need an evening coverup for casual St. Tropez dining.

The place had high, pressed-tin ceilings and wooden floors that exuded a comforting cedar-polish scent. The staff left you alone and so did the customers. People in Maine seemed to need a context for you before making friendly advances. The problem with me was that I had no context.

The best seating at JavaNet was at the row of high stools facing the front window, from which one could overlook the cobblestone slope of Exchange Street. This was Portland's "tony" shopping neighborhood. In summer the block was crowded with tourists who meandered through the tiny bookstores and the dozen-or-so boutiques. Now, in the off-season, you'd be more likely to see what few customers there were wandering into the art house movie theater or hanging around the self-consciously hip record store that seemed as if it should always smell of reefer, but didn't.

A wet snow, almost rain, had begun, but it wasn't heavy. On my walk down I'd admired how it veiled the gray marble of city hall and softened the harsh red Victorian brick of the College of Art. The sky was silver, the harbor silvery blue. One of Portland's stunning beauties was that there was no ugly color for water here. At home the Potomac could turn brown and sluggish, a poisonous opaque brown that made one think of water moccasins sliding under the surface. Here there were only shades of blue and green and slate, shifting constantly with the weather and the changing, high-vaulted sky.

The pavement was slightly slippery, no more. This was baby weather, Donald had informed me repeatedly. The worst snowfalls came after Christmas, he said. But still, to a transplant from the temperate Mid-Atlantic, it felt cold. I felt virtuous walking, and promised myself that for a reward after my tea I'd go by Anthony's Restaurant and pick up a meatball sub. Anthony's produced the platonic ideal of the meatball.

I pulled a ballpoint and some folded notepaper out of my jacket pocket to start a list. Making a list allows one to sit around in a public place without feeling self-conscious. A busy, competent person making a list is not someone other people felt sorry for, as opposed to a pathetic lingerer drinking chai because she has nowhere else to go.

But this particular list was serious, a game plan. Paul had said this morning that I had no structure. That comment alone showed that it was time for a change. I wanted to become booked up. I didn't know yet how to make it happen, but since I'd never accomplished anything without writing it down first, that was clearly the place to begin. I'd make a list of actions to improve my life. I'd post the list on the kitchen wall and every day I'd cross off three items. Three, I swore it solemnly. I'd show Paul, and his horrible mother, and horrible interfering Natalie. I would show everyone, I thought, and took up my pen.

Four

I started with a comparatively easy category: Grooming and Personal Appearance. I wrote:

Haircut

It wasn't only the haircut, long and straight and boring. It was also the color, which in childhood was the soft buttery yellow of a Breck Girl's and had darkened over the years to its current uninteresting shade of ash. Delia never bothered to touch up the gray strands that were cropping up here and there in her chestnut curls, but then Delia was thirty-seven and still looked thirty, with her big brown eyes and peachy skin. Blondes aged faster. I wrote:

Haircolor

Then, squeamish, I crossed out "haircolor" and put:

Highlights

On to Exercise and Diet.

My food vices were childishly harmless: jelly beans, black licorice, butterscotch hard candy. And my height had kept me slim—but it wasn't enough for the modern woman just to be slender anymore. We were also supposed to be strong. How I envied my mother's generation, who'd had the Charlie Perfume Girl. All the Charlie Girl had to do was wear pantsuits and stride about the streets of New York with her shoulders back, exuding confidence and tallness. The Charlie Girl didn't have to win any marathons.

My own generation, unfortunately, preferred the Nike Girl, who ran through her day with sexy sweat beading on her forehead and arm muscles bulging. I detested the Nike Girl, but surely, with diligence and application, I could at least achieve a level of fitness such that I wouldn't get winded on the way from the grocery checkout to the car. My current practice of running errands on foot didn't seem to be doing the trick. I wrote:

Get stronger

And under that:

Join gym?

I'd need a car to get to a gym, and exercise clothes.

Go to swimming pool

I did own a drearily serviceable black maillot suit, and the elementary school a few blocks from our apartment had an Olympic-sized swimming pool that was open to the public a few afternoons a week. The first time I'd been there, a swim meet was taking place. The second time, construction crews were patching the roof directly above the pool. The last time, a large sign declared, "Pool temporarily closed for health violations."

Speedwalk

Natalie sped. That's how I thought of her, as always in motion, her piquant little face animated by some goal or other. But I doubted I'd have the energy to go at that pace. Weren't there walking clubs that gently challenged the sedate exerciser? Surely I'd seen advertisements in the **Casco Bay Weekly.**

A walking club. How English. How pastoral. How unintimidating. I wrote:

Join walking club

And put a star next to it.

The **Casco Bay Weekly** was kept in a stack near the door. It was free, and the personal ads could be intriguingly racy. Apparently somewhere in Portland there was quite a thriving community of swingers.

As I pushed my stool back, it met resistance. Turning, I was caught in the ribs by a plate of cinnamon scones. A deep voice said, "Goddamn leg."

The voice came from a burly, bearded man about thirty-five years old, wearing a beautiful suede and shearling jacket and tottering on crutches. A cast on his left leg went from his slippered foot to halfway up his thigh. He was carrying a cup of Earl Grey in one hand and a copy of **The Magic Mountain** under his elbow.

I apologized. He apologized. I settled him on the stool next to mine, eased the book out from under his arm, and took his Earl Grey to the counter to ask for fresh hot water, since the tea had slopped around quite a bit.

In the course of all the apologies, it became clear that the man was gay. At least, I thought so. Then I felt guilty for making such a snap judgment. "What **don't** you feel guilty for?" Marta would have asked.

"Sorry I popped up like that," I said to the man. "I was getting the paper."

"No, no," he said. "My fault. I can't get used to these crutches."

"Skiing accident?"

"If only. Work. I renovate houses. I was poking around some attic beams in this place my partner and I are rehabbing, up on the Eastern Prom, and the ladder broke."

"Ladders aren't supposed to break."

"Tell me about it. Now I'm hobbling around, not much help with anything, and my partner is going crazy trying to finish this frickin' job."

"And you're cheering yourself up reading Thomas Mann?"

"Sometimes I like to work **with** my depression."

Something about this man loosed me from my usual shyness. Perhaps it was his jovial appearance, with the reddish face and the hair and beard that gleamed a rich russet in the wavering light. Maybe it was his accent, northern but definitely not a Maine accent. Donald had told me that people who were not from Maine were referred to as being "from away." This guy was definitely from away, like me.

I said, "I agree with you. Sadness never hurt anyone. A **little** sadness, that is."

"Don't worry. I like eating way too much to ever consider suicide. I'm just planning on buttering these scones and gaining another chin."

"Scones demand butter," I said. "And besides, you don't want to be **too** thin."

This was no kind social lie. His reassuring, solid stoutness would look very odd if it were diminished.

"Tell my boyfriend that. My cholesterol is the tiniest bit high, and ever since I broke my leg he's been trotting arugula salads out for dinner and giving me hot water with lemon when I'm begging, pleading, for a latte."

"You didn't get a latte today."

"It was the latte or the scones. I told you, I'm not suicidal."

I laughed, probably too heartily. It had been a week since I'd had a conversation in person with anyone but Paul or Donald.

"Stephen Moore," he said. He enveloped my

hand, which is not small, in a bearlike clasp and began on his scones with the other hand.

"Sophie Quinn."

"Quinn. That's nice. Irish, is it?"

"I'm a quarter Irish."

"What's the rest?"

"A quarter Scots, and half Welsh. And you?"

"Classic New England mix, Irish and Italian."

"Where in New England?"

"Amesbury, Mass. The infamous Merrimack Valley."

I must have looked blank, for he went on, "Lawrence, Lowell, Methuen, Haverhill, Amesbury. The old industrial towns. The Valley hasn't changed since 1952, and doesn't want to."

"You miss it that much, huh?"

"Oh, I live in the South End of Boston now. My partner does too."

His accent wasn't a Boston accent, though. He pronounced his **a**'s very broadly, but on a higher register than the Boston **a.** Stephen's **a** was more like the sound you might produce if a dentist told you to go "ah."

I began to sip my chai again, relaxing.

"So," said Stephen. "What's a nice girl like you doing in a place like this?"

"My husband's job."

I added hastily, lest he imagine I was a lady who lunched, "I freelance."

"Freelancing's nice. But lonely."

He said it matter-of-factly, as if loneliness were a simple occupational hazard, not a shameful weakness.

"And what do you think of Portland?" he said.

I temporized.

"My husband's work friend told him it was the San Francisco of the East."

Stephen Moore snorted.

"That's a good one. Do they ever call San Francisco the Portland of the West? Do they write songs about Portland? Do people leave their hearts in Portland? I don't think so."

"People who live here seem to like it," I said.

"Homesick?"

Suddenly I was, more than ever. Delia had written me that Tom had framed the pastel I'd done of her rocking the baby and hung it in his "study," a renovated walk-in closet in their house in Cleveland Park. Ben had been crawling when I left. By the time I got home for Christmas, he'd be toddling.

I nodded mutely.

"I am too," said Stephen. "Although I'm not

as far from home as you are. I thought Amesbury was fucking Brigadoon, but this place wins,
hands down."

"I should try harder to blend in," I said. "People seem to know I'm not a Mainer."

"If you're trying to blend in, where's your
Bean cap? They'll think you're a housebreaker in
that dark one you've got there. And your
sweater's all wrong. Get yourself something with
snowflakes or a deer on it. Then you'll fit in."

He let out a laugh so loud the counter guy
turned around to check on us. Stephen nodded
at him, and the guy turned around again.

We talked of this and that as the light started
to go down outside. He related a few stories
about old houses, and the terrors to be met in
restoring them. I told him how Donald's mansion had cured me of window-shopping for Victorian splendor.

"Oh, for myself I'd want nothing older than
1925," said Stephen. "I do enough rewiring and
plastering on the job."

He was easy to talk with. Why are gay men so
often observant and witty? Maybe it's that any
condition of birth that sets one apart—being
gay, being brilliant, being an orphan—heightens
your sense of being a spy in this world. You keep

your cover by noticing details that other people don't have to notice. I could imagine Stephen growing up in the Merrimack Valley, being the class clown, watching himself for gestures and expressions that would be considered campy, "faggy," punishable.

His third cup of tea was gone long ago, and my second chai, and still I lingered. Partly for the treat of company, partly because I dreaded the walk home, especially the solitary stretch of Pine Street after the Cumberland Farms. There were shadowy alleyways and flickering street lights and big dogs that raced up to iron railings to bark at you. At dusk there were also strange types who liked to hang out on the bluff: cruisers, schizophrenics, vandals who enjoyed tossing bottles down the hill into the weeds below. It was another feature of the neighborhood Donald hadn't bothered to warn us about.

I began to assemble my things. Stephen was gazing longingly toward the pastry display case. Or perhaps at the counter guy. I couldn't tell.

"I should go. I'm not sick of your company but it's getting dark."

"Hey," Stephen said. "I hope you won't mind but I noticed that you wrote a note here about joining a walking club."

My writing isn't large like Natalie's but it's even more legible. Like most people who do layout, I print in small caps rather than using cursive.

He said, "Sorry I peeked but it was irresistible."

"Just New Year's resolutions a little early."

"But do you really want to join a walking club?"

"I do," I said, trying to mean it.

"Because I run one," he said.

"You run one? Wow. Then it's really lousy about the leg."

"Oh, I didn't start it for exercise. I started it because I'm stuck here for eight months working on this damn house, and I wanted to meet other people like me. You should join. Only . . . it depends on your attitude."

"I'm not a swinger," I said jokingly, remembering the personal ads.

"If there's a swinger in a five-mile radius of here, I'm Charlton Heston. No, it's just that it's a gay-themed walking club. It's called Happy Trails."

"Happy Trails?"

"You know. Gay . . . happy."

"Cute," I said. "Whose idea was the name?"

"My partner Ned's. He can be funny sometimes, although not as funny as he thinks he is.
Anyway, we welcome new people and we have
nothing against straights."

He pulled a battered orange card from the
pocket of his corduroys. The card listed meeting
times and places: one location on Mondays,
Wednesdays, and Fridays for walks that began
on the West End, and another on Tuesdays and
Thursdays for East End walks.

Stephen said, "Half our people live near the
Eastern Prom and half near the Western so we
split the difference and nobody's pleased. They
bitch and bitch. But it's a good group on the
whole."

"How fast do they go?"

"Let's put it this way. The day this cast comes
off I'll qualify to start walking with them again.
The people in front, the real fitness buffs, keep
up a good pace. But there's always a number
bringing up the rear. So to speak."

He grinned at me ferociously.

"You have lovely hair," I said. "The color I've
always wanted."

"Going thin up top, but what can you do? You
could really play around with yours, you know.
Color-wise."

"Cheater. You saw that on my list."

"Yes, but you're right. It's time. And not just highlights. Try new day."

"Excuse me?"

"It's a hairdresser's. New Day. Up by Longfellow Square."

"**How** long did you say you'd been here?"

"I get around. Or I did until this. Now I'm stuck mostly in one four-block radius, driving my partner crazy, being no use to anyone."

"You've been of use to me. And I'm sure your partner's a very lucky man."

For some reason he burst out laughing.

"Ned will like that. By the way, tell him who you are if you come walking so he can let me know. I like to think I'm a good recruiter."

"Seven-thirty's early for me," I said.

"It was the only hour of the day I could get them all to commit to. You wouldn't believe what time people go to bed and wake up around here."

"It's the cold," I said. "It makes you sleepy."

"Not me. God Almighty. And they say winter's not even started yet. The heating system was the first thing we fixed. I blast it, morning to night."

I subdued a stabbing pang of envy. I was now buttoned and zipped into all my outdoor clothes, bolstered to twice my size like Tweedle-dum in **Alice Through the Looking Glass.** And the sad part was, my outdoor clothes were also appropriate indoor wear for the temperature of our apartment. If only eating my way up to another layer of fat was an option. After all, it only made sense in this climate. You never saw Inuit women sticking their fingers down their throats or dieting frantically to reach a size six.

"How do I enroll? If I'm interested?" I asked Stephen.

"It's really simple. Just show up."

"Maybe I will. Good to meet you," I said.

"Good to meet **you,** Sophie Quinn. I hope you'll come walk."

He waved through the window as I headed up Exchange Street. When I was barely out of his sight, I slipped on the cobblestones and fell hard on my left knee. And I thought I'd be joining a walking group. That was a good one.

Just for fun, I stopped in at the Christmas shop a block up from JavaNet. There were candles burning that smelled like pumpkin pie, and two dozen sets of Christmas villages laid out along the walls: a Tyrolean village, a 1920s Main Street, a London scene after Dickens. Each village had its complement of villagers: barber, cook, matrons with packages. It would be nice, I thought, to shrink yourself down to three inches tall and take your place in one of these perfect worlds.

There was even a Wedding Christmas Village on a top shelf, a sweet little Jazz Age set piece that had a miniature snow-roofed stone church with a tiny white roadster parked in front, a little groom with painted hair parted in the middle, a flapper bride with a point-lace cap and a fur stole, and four diminutive bridesmaids in dark red capes with holly pinned on their muffs.

I'd have liked to go to this pint-sized wedding, as opposed to many I'd attended—and I'd gone to **lots** of weddings. There were a few very bad years in my late twenties when I developed a second career in bridesmaidhood, dragging myself, listless and oppressed, down any number of ribbon-swagged aisles.

"Your problem is, you're the perfect choice," said Marta. "You're blonde, so you look pretty in all those icky bridesmaid colors like aqua and lavender. Also, you'll wear anything. Brides sense that. They're evil that way."

There was a deeper reason why I was weary of weddings by my thirtieth birthday—what they used to call "a disappointment in love." Until I married Paul, the only nuptials that had played a decisive role in my life had been those of Rory McLaughlin, my dashing, unreliable first love. I didn't go to Rory's wedding. It's bad form when you've been having an affair with the groom up until three days before the ceremony.

Rory was the boy next door, in every goopy sense of that phrase. He was also the only person I'd ever known who was fearless. A fearful person like me has the choice of resenting the brave or helplessly admiring them. I'd been firmly settled in the helpless admiration camp since the day I saw Rory scamper from a maple tree branch onto the McLaughlins' roof to retrieve an errant softball. I was six, but I knew foolhardy charm when I saw it, even then. Besides, Rory was born to be admired. He moved in a glow of female worship and male emulation, a glow as powerful as the aura that surrounds some beautiful girls.

When I was twenty-nine years old, a wonderful thing happened. Rory, whom I'd loved my whole life, fell in love with me. He was in love with me, madly, for exactly seven weeks. Then he married Liz, the practical, spunky young woman he'd always intended to marry, and left to promote the cause of democracy in a distant country. Poland, to be exact, in a town whose name I couldn't even pronounce.

Rory worked for an international agency, the Foundation for Overseas Democracy. FOD was one of those Washington organizations that I'd heard of all my life, without being quite sure of what they did. Rory held a desk job in their downtown headquarters for several years before they promoted him to international outreach officer. His promotion precipitated his proposal to Liz Brody, and his engagement to Liz precipitated, you could say, his affair with me. That's what it is to live in Washington—the movements of the spheres of power wind up affecting your own puny, quotidian life.

And so he broke my heart.

In the months after the Rory debacle, I went a bit crazy with grief and took a risk that was greatly out of character: I invested my small savings in the stock market. Because my brother-in-law Tom has a God-given eye for spotting rising companies and knows when to take the profits and run, this heartbreak-inspired gamble resulted in a financial cushion—small, but bigger than I'd ever had before. It gave me a novel feeling of safety.

Three uneventful years passed. I was content with my life. I was even happy in my mild way—as happy as a woman can be who can't resist picking up any magazine with a cover teaser that reads, "Ten Tests Your Doctor Should Order for You." I dated a few guys who didn't mean much to me, and to whom I didn't mean much. Then I met Paul, while subbing as a bridesmaid in yet another wedding.

This particular wedding was a rather dreary September affair that had neither the golden romance of summer nor the hopeful atmosphere of nuptials held in crisp autumn. The bride and groom were college sweethearts, an uninteresting pair no one ever doubted would marry. Everyone there seemed to have been a guest too many times at too many weddings, going through the motions at the tail end of the bridal season.

One of the original bridesmaids had come down with chicken pox, and the bride took shameless advantage of our years together in grade school to call me in as a pinch hitter. Paul was a stony-faced usher. We were seated next to each other at the head table. All through the endive salad and the tournedos of beef, Paul made overpolite conversation on topics of the day, conversation that revealed, better than any rudeness could have, his lack of interest in me and my opinions. He seemed snobbish and withdrawn; I later learned that at the time, he'd just been dumped by his girlfriend of four years, Allison, a stockbroker who left for better opportunities in New York.

If Rory was the big love of my life, Allison was Paul's great romance. I saw her picture once, in our early dating days. She was slim as a greyhound, with narrow nostrils, smooth light hair, and an ungenerous mouth. In our early months together, Paul spoke of her with sadness. Later, he hardly spoke of her at all. Allison spent four years "making up her mind" about him in his presence, and her going had left Paul in the polite daze in which I first saw him at the wedding.

What broke the ice between Paul and me was that, after three bites of the wedding cake and a duty dance, Paul escorted me back to the table and collapsed on my lap. He'd drunk only a sip of the inferior champagne, and hadn't sneaked out to indulge in the fine Colombian pot that the bride's adolescent cousins were passing around. What could it be, I wondered in the split second after his head landed in an area usually not accessible on the first date.

It turned out that he was allergic to hazelnut. Normally he made sure that none passed his lips, but a goldenrod allergy had rendered his taste buds unable to pick up the thin layer of hazelnut paste cleverly concealed under the shiny chocolate ganache of the wedding cake. The dancing sent the dangerous substance quickly into his bloodstream. Before either of us knew what happened, he'd passed out into the frills of my salmon pink strapless tulle.

You can't very well shove a fainting man into the backseat of an usher's car and not accompany him to the emergency room. After Paul was revived with a shot of epinephrine and was able to sit up and sip some apple juice in the ER at Georgetown Hospital, we started chatting. We talked for an hour, while waiting for them to let him go home.

"I thought I dreamed that dress," was the first thing he said to me. "I didn't think it could be real."

"You should see the last four I wore. Enough fabric to clothe a developing nation."

"If the developing nation didn't mind looking very silly."

"At least," I said, "I managed to stay conscious through the entire event."

"If you have dinner with me, I promise I'll stay conscious," he said.

Our dates, in the beginning, were quite studious. We went to the National Gallery, where

I showed Paul my three favorite paintings: Turner's **Santa Maria della Salute,** Whistler's **The White Girl,** and Leonardo's **Ginevra.** No other straight man had ever volunteered to go to the gallery with me, but Paul stood in front of each painting, frowning in concentration, inquiring as to why I liked it. I told him that I liked the Turner for the luminous colors, and the Whistler because he had done so dazzlingly much with such a limited palette. And **Ginevra,** I said, because everyone liked the **Ginevra.**

"She's not much to look at," said Paul.

"She was considered a beauty."

"I like the landscape in back of her."

"That's called sfumato. That smoky light on the hills."

We strolled through the nineteenth-century galleries where he greatly admired a gruesome early-Victorian depiction of a sinking whaling ship surrounded by menacing sharks, and I tried not to hold it against him. Then I treated him to lunch at the fancy café in the East Gallery. We had roast chicken and salad niçoise, and Paul kissed my cheek when he left me at my apartment door.

After that we went to see an ACLU benefit showing of **The Shawshank Redemption,** then to a new Mongolian restaurant in Chinatown where Paul asked the chef many intelligent questions about the ingredients.

I was touched by his air of being always a tourist in his hometown.

"Why are you so interested in the inner workings of everything?" I asked him one afternoon in mid-October, after we'd gone out four weekends in a row. We'd had a slow, meditative Saturday at the Botanical Gardens, strolling through the yellow oaks and reading the fascinating history of the bonsai collection—Paul read it, anyway. We'd wound up at my place in Woodley Park, on my old broken-down chintz sofa, eating ham and cheese on crusty bread and drinking gin and tonics.

"The inner workings? I don't know what you mean," he said. He was a little tipsy. I was a little tipsy too.

"Those bonsai trees. Why do you care how they grow them?"

"How can you not care? They're right in front of you, so strange looking."

He was smiling, the sweet relaxed smile I was beginning to see more often.

"I'm right in front of you so strange looking," I said. "Do you want to know what makes **me** tick?"

"People are harder," he said. "You could give me a list of facts about Sophie, but it wouldn't tell me what I want to know."

"What do you want to know?" I said, lazily.

"I want to know if . . ."

"If what?"

"If you would do this." He stayed on his side of the sofa, but reached out and pulled me into the circle of his arm. Then he kissed me, a kiss that was practiced, as any thirty-three-year-old man's should be, but not presuming. One hand stayed on my arm, the other pushing my hair back lightly. I felt for the first time in the presence of a man who could be patient. And so I went to bed with him, in a spirit of goodwill and the sheer joyousness of that golden autumn day. When we awoke, early in the evening, he kissed me and went home, saying that he had work to do but really, I think, to allow me my solitude back. Before I fell asleep the phone rang.

He said, "I just wanted to make sure today was a good day for you."

"It was a very good day."

"You're sure?"

"An exceptional day," I said.

"That's all I wanted to know," he said. "Can we see each other soon?"

"I'd say we'd be foolish not to."

He laughed. His laugh was lower than his speaking voice, and it affected me strongly. After all, I wished he'd stayed the night. It was my first hint that I was getting into new territory, but I ignored it. I didn't want to think about what was happening with Paul; I'd done nothing **but** think with Rory and it had done me only harm. Sometimes it's better to let life sneak up on you.

I continued to sleep with Paul, to wander the city with him in the warm days of that mild November. Very slowly, I began to love him. Paul took nothing for granted. Allison had taught him that. And he had none of the Washington bachelor's preening self-confidence that he was doing me a favor with his attentions. Rory hadn't had that either, but Rory hadn't been my lover long enough to cherish me. I hadn't realized how hungry I was for a little cherishing until Paul came along.

When I grew angry with my husband, as I often did these days, I'd call to mind those early months, and his solemn, meticulous tenderness toward me. The Paul I'd fallen in love with was a man who, for my thirty-second birthday, gave me a silver-and-amber bracelet, cool as water on my wrist and so simple and lovely I wore it with everything. That Paul had taken us on weekend trips to small Chesapeake towns and old-fashioned country hotels in the Blue Ridge. For every trip he packed a bag of the Anjou pears I craved but was too cheap to buy. Paul expressed his affection in a thousand sweetnesses easy to forget now that we'd grown into a habit of mutual reproach.

I'd given away every other bridesmaid's outfit inflicted on me, but that salmon tulle reposed in a clear-plastic dress bag alongside other treasured possessions in a storage bin in Bethesda. At the time Paul fell into my lap, I'd been suffering from searing heartache for months and months. Paul opened a door to the world that was still going on outside, sunny and oblivious and full of quiet pleasures. He never knew about Rory, or what a bad way I'd been in when he found me. But on the first cold night of winter, he brought me a fleece blanket he'd picked up at Lord and Taylor's because "I noticed you get chilly easily" and I began to cry.

"You're so nice to me," I cried. He sat beside me on the sofa and stroked my head and finally said, "Is it that weird, for me to be nice to you?

Wouldn't anyone want to be? Or do you mean that I'm so nice to you that it's even harder to dump me?"

"Dump you?" I said nasally. "That's the last thing I'd want."

"Good, then," he'd said. "By the way, I guess you should know I love you."

I loved him too, I said. Six months later he proposed, and we were married in an uncomplicated ceremony in Delia and Tom's living room, surrounded only by immediate family, plus Marta. The service was performed by a former priest, an old friend of my mother's who had a sideline in marrying lapsed Catholics to Protestants. I wore a plain, blue silk dress with elbow-length sleeves and Paul wore one of his office suits, and afterward we took everyone to lunch at the Old Angler's Inn, up the river.

Pepper could not keep an expression of peeved disbelief entirely off her face during the proceedings. Her first mother-in-law's embrace was accompanied by the words, "I hope you'll make Paul very happy." I didn't care, not then. I'd found someone wonderful to keep me company, and I'd have suffered through far more than Pepper's persnicketiness to keep him.

———

I loved Paul still, but we had somehow lost the rhythm of our early days together. Paul, I'd come to realize, had married me with the expectation that marriage would change us. Would change me, make me less childishly shy, less unsure. He wanted me to grow up, to get a grip, somehow.

Maybe if I changed, I thought, Paul would change too, back to the man at that wedding only two years ago, the man who used to be more than willing to give me the benefit of the doubt. Trudging home in the near darkness, I resolved, for the first time in my life, to invite change, to pursue change, to court my own transformation.

You have to be very foolish or very unhappy to make such a resolution. Looking back, I can see that I was both. But sometimes it's not terribly stupid to set events in motion. Sometimes it's more terrible and more stupid to sit, paralyzed, as events slip past you. A certain kind of guardian angel must watch over fools as they rush in. I'd never rushed at anything before, but I was making a start, and I had to run full force at it or freeze altogether.

Five

The radiators were still cold. I should have phoned Donald and kicked up an unholy fuss. Instead, I decided to picnic in the bathroom.

This was my strategy for nights when Paul worked late. I would run a scalding bath in the enormous claw foot tub, then place a board (borrowed from Donald's backyard lumber stack) across the width of the tub. On it, I'd lay out my supper, a glass of wine and a long, generous, already-read book—**Marjorie Morningstar,** or **Shirley,** or one of the Taylor Caldwell sagas that I picked up in used-book stores.

Tonight, instead, I grabbed a notepad and pen. The list would be finished, if I had to stay in the tub until my skin wrinkled like a prune's.

I left "Personal Appearance" to the side for now. The only part of my body it pleases me to contemplate in the tub is my bellybutton, which is a small, elegant "inny." Delia has an "outy" like a clumsily tied knot in a child's party balloon. She has much better cleavage than I do, though.

In the great contest of life, cleavage serves you far better than bellybutton pulchritude, but my "inny" still brought me an innocent pride.

I moved on to "Community Service," not without wincing. Community service: my mother's rallying cry, writ large on her banner of virtue.

Luckily for my mother, she was free to devote most of her time to this calling, since my father had a perfectly good job. He'd worked for twenty years at the Division of Size-Limited Medical Products investigating applications for government approval of therapeutic or prosthetic gadgets, from realistic glass eyeballs to ingenious folding back braces. This weird occupation suited and sometimes amused him.

Meanwhile, Mom targeted her boundless energy at our parish, St. Catherine of Siena. She established the folk choir, and a needlepointing society who adorned the pew cushions with designs of fish and chalices. She created the St. Catherine Players, a theater troupe composed of ten thwarted actresses and two closeted gay men, which presented lively Broadway reviews every Christmas in mental wards across the city. Delia and I were recruited as extras in these performances, during which the audience had a tendency to stare fixedly away from the stage and clap in the wrong places.

"I think they liked it, don't you?" Mom would say, steering us backstage before we could be approached by patients in bathrobes who wanted to pet our hair.

Mildly traumatic, that kind of thing, but it was time to stop being haunted by my mother's example and to consider what helpful contribution I could make to society.

The problem was that I wasn't an innately helpful person. There'd been a story once on the evening news about a man who, trapped in a stalled subway car, led the rest of the shaken passengers through a smoke-filled Metro tunnel to safety. I knew instinctively that any suggestion I made in such a situation would be the wrong one, precipitating the entire party onto the third rail and a horrible death by electrocution. Clearly, whatever good works I did would have to be in a highly supervised capacity. I wrote tentatively:

Volunteer at grade school

A good mentor could change a child's life, said the commercials. But I was afraid of children, who tended to fix me with a steely gaze and ask questions I couldn't answer. I could work at an animal shelter, but I was also afraid of large dogs. It was unlikely that Portland had a shelter that specialized in Jack Russells and Pomeranians.

So much for community. There was always the time-honored Yankee tradition of study and self-improvement.

Classes

Surely the Maine College of Art had a division for adult dilettantes. And there were other subjects. Yoga, for example. I could take up yoga. Somehow, though, I didn't see myself in a leotard, smiling serenely as my joints were dislocated. I crossed out "yoga" and drank the rest of my wine.

I was beginning on a category called **Places in New England I'd Like to See While I'm Here,** when I heard Paul's footsteps creaking in the foyer.

"Cliff Walk, Newport," I scrawled hurriedly. **"Farnsworth Museum, Rockland."**

I'd flipped to a blank page before Paul appeared in the doorway, flushed and excited looking. He glanced at the remnants of my meatball sub.

"In the bathtub again?"

He was joking tonight. On some nights when he came home to find me in the bath, he assumed a worried expression that made me feel like Sylvia Plath just before she stuck her head in the oven.

"Just thinking," I said.

"Looks like Donald didn't fix the heat."

"I tried."

"I know you tried. He's a lazy, cheap jerk, that's all."

He flipped the toilet lid closed and sat down. This was a risky move, since that lazy, cheap jerk Donald had installed the hinges in a haphazard fashion, with the result that the seat slid sideways under you at the worst possible times.

"I made Ted an offer on the Explorer," Paul announced.

"Oh. How much?"

"Twelve thousand."

"And with the Volvo trade-in?"

"That **is** with the trade-in."

Twelve thousand was half Paul's savings account, though he had a separate retirement fund.

"Sophie, you can't believe the difference driving one of these things makes. The power's incredible. And say someone hits you, you're much more protected than in some little tin box. Twelve thousand isn't much to pay for that kind of safety."

The marriage manual hadn't covered what to do if your husband decided to spend half his savings on a large, polluting toy.

"Anyway," Paul said, as if reading my mind, "it'll come from my account. Your little nest egg will remain intact."

It troubled Paul that my savings were twice his. Tom's first pick had been a company about to debut a new blood pressure medication that had unexpectedly sailed through its FDA trials. We'd gotten out when the stock was at its peak. After our fifth go-round in the market, we bought treasury bonds with our profits. In bitter moments, Paul implied that there was something un-American about this.

Paul was also hurt that I wouldn't merge our money into a single account. But I recalled how my mom's friends used to gripe about having to explain every penny they spent to their husbands. I didn't want to be like Lucy in **I Love Lucy,** struggling to justify myself every time I bought a new hat.

"It's my money," said Paul. "Can't I spend it on what I want?"

"Of course you can. You like this car then?"

"It's not a car, Soph, it's an experience. It even has seat warmers."

"How hard will it be for me to learn to drive it?" I said.

"I didn't think of you as driving it too much," he said.

"I'd pitch in half," I offered.

I'd rather have purchased half a mink coat. But the thought of being stranded, in winter, without a car was too much.

Paul shook his head.

"You won't get enough use out of it to justify that, hon," he said. "I'll be taking it to work and on weekends you know I can't stand to be a passenger."

"Paul, I'm going to need a car soon. I can't walk everywhere forever."

"Why not?"

"Winter is coming," I said. "In case you hadn't noticed."

There it was again, the hostile note the manual had cautioned against. **When you initiate an adversarial communication, you are the loser.** Of course, I was feeling pretty much like the loser anyway.

"You make too big a deal about winter," Paul said. "How bad can it be?"

"Have you heard about these nor'easters?" I said. "Those are storms they get up here where it blows so hard the snow falls sideways. Donald told me about them."

"You listen to Donald too much. He gets a kick out of scaring you."

"I want to explore. To travel a little."

"On your own?"

"Yes, on my own."

"You never needed a car in D.C. You got everywhere on your bicycle."

"My bicycle won't be any good to me on snow."

"We probably won't get much. Natalie said she thinks it'll be a light winter."

"Natalie's a meteorologist now?"

"She's a Maine native."

"I know. She reminds us every ten minutes."

"Please, Sophie. Don't worry. Ted said he had to think about it. He has other interested buyers."

Ted was clearly no backwoods yokel, no matter what Paul thought. I sank back down into the water and Paul smiled at me, the faintly smug smile of a husband who thinks he's bound to get his way because he's so cute and persuasive.

"You'll love it. You can see everything from up there."

"Up in the passenger's seat, you mean?"

"You'll see. It's a great ride. Is there any ice cream left or did you eat it all?"

I stayed in the tub sulking for a long time. I heard Paul in the bedroom, clinking his ice cream spoon in his bowl and watching a news special on the upcoming presidential election. The TV was visible from the bathtub. A blond reporter in a bubble cut was interviewing a bunch of people in Ohio who still hadn't made up their minds.

"Frankly," said a man in jeans and a golf shirt, "There doesn't seem to be much difference between the two candidates, to me." A woman to his left nodded.

For six months now, both parties had been explaining in words of one syllable how the candidates were different. They'd done everything but hold up flash cards. Two weeks out from Election Day, what could possibly be perplexing these people? Had American men died in battle for two centuries so that people who never read the paper could stand in the voting booth and flip a coin?

An Amway saleswoman explained to the bubble-haired reporter that Al Gore was too smart to be president. "He knows so much he's disconnected from regular Americans like me," she said. I feared this was true.

The water grew tepid. The special finished and Paul called out in conciliating tones, "I'm getting ready for bed soon, sweetie."

Paul was going to buy an Explorer and leave me to become a human Popsicle, trapped in our apartment without transport while he and Natalie tsk-tsked over my increasing resemblance to Emily Dickinson. Some voice that wasn't my own declared inside me, "Well, the hell with that." I wrote on my list, in big angry letters that tore the paper: JOIN WALKING GROUP. I never left the house, did I? Then I added, in even bigger, angrier letters: BUY A CAR.

Six

There are no words for the difference between a cold day at 7:15 A.M. and a cold day at noon. It was Wednesday morning, two days after I'd met Stephen at JavaNet. I woke tired and chilled, with the feeling that I had cried in some dream during the night. Shuddering with fatigue, I showered and dressed myself in somewhat suitable walking clothes and tennis shoes. There was only frost on the ground. The hideous tennis shoes weren't truly necessary, but I wanted to minimize my chances of tripping on slick leaves or a gravelly trail.

Paul said, "Where in the world are you going?"

"I joined a walking group."

"You did?"

"Yes."

"That'll be good for you," Paul said, which immediately made me feel I didn't want to go.

Still, I knew I had to. Something in me can recognize a last chance when I see it.

Before I left, Paul kissed me on the cheek and said, "I'm proud of you for taking initiative this way, honey. Think of what good shape you'll get in."

I smiled back weakly and walked across the lawn with a firm, energetic tread in case he could see me from the window. A light was on in Donald's apartment. Today I would have to take him on about the heat again, a second hurdle to dread this morning.

Stephen's card had said, "Meet by west entrance of the Western Cemetery." There were two gates into the Western Cemetery: one used by dog owners whose pets were allowed to run off leash there, and another tucked into the side of a hill. This was the gate that faced west. I walked down the Promenade, my dark wool housebreaker's cap that Stephen had laughed about pulled over my ears, my stomach a little shaky.

A group of about fourteen people was standing there. Well, not standing there precisely. Three were doing aggressive stretching exercises. Another four or five were walking up and down the street, which was sheltered by a line of redbrick Edwardian mansions that broke the force of the gusts coming up over the bluff. The rest of the Happy Trailers were just standing, jumping up and down a little in the cold, drinking coffee. I could pick out the guy who'd be the lead walker from his exercise outfit, a red zip-up jacket with a white stripe down one side, complete with spandex leggings. Spandex Guy had intense faraway eyes, and the holy, abstracted look of the dedicated pursuer of physical fitness.

Everyone else was dressed in a hodgepodge of outdoor clothing: sweats, nylon pants, down parkas. The striking exception was a beautiful, hip-length chocolate leather coat on a thirtyish man with wicked brown eyes who kept complaining about the cold to his pale, quiet friend. In my boot-cut jeans and a checked knock-around jacket bought at an outlet in Leesburg, Virginia, the previous July, I didn't stand out like a sore thumb. Still, it wasn't a very friendly group.

Arriving at the meeting place, I'd smiled and said, "Is Ned here?"

"Not yet," said an overweight young woman with beautiful auburn hair and creamy skin. Her whole life, annoying people had probably told her that if she'd just lose a few pounds, she'd be a knockout. She was holding a doughnut oozing raspberry jam and floury with powdered sugar. The doughnut made my stomach curl hungrily.

Trying to be healthy, I'd eaten a nasty, vitamin-enriched peanut butter granola bar for breakfast.

I stood on the edge of the huddle, waiting for Ned to arrive. He seemed to be the guy who fired the metaphorical starting gun for these walks. It threw me that I wasn't asked to identify myself or show a registration form. Although political life looks like constant invigorating chaos in TV shows and movies, people in Washington are actually very orderly souls. They tend to look for the person in charge, to gravitate toward sign-in logs and printed schedules. I could have been a stray ax murderer joining the walking group and no one would have questioned my presence.

But maybe, I thought, the official stuff was always left to Ned. I could picture him. He'd be spare and meticulously groomed, with a precise manner and a stopwatch, I predicted. That was the sort of partner I could imagine Stephen choosing, someone who cleaned up after him and kept the books. It was a surprise to see, coming down the Western Prom at a modified trot, a rangy, bearded man somewhere between thirty and thirty-five, wearing an army jacket and work boots and pushing a baby stroller.

Surely Stephen would have mentioned if he and his partner had a baby? People with babies usually worked them into a conversation.

As the man drew up to the group he said, "Sorry, you guys. Carol and Jamie couldn't make it today, so only Matilda is joining us." Matilda, it seemed, was the baby.

She was about ten months old, a fat bundle of yellow flannel topped by a pink face and black curls. She was obviously one of those babies who come into the world with personalities that outpaced their infant abilities. My nephew was that kind of baby: voraciously curious, impatient to walk and talk. I had a weak spot for babies like this. They were so different from the sort of baby I must have been. In the few snapshots my parents took of me at that age, I appear startled and deeply apprehensive.

Matilda squirmed in her stroller and cast censorious glances at the rest of us, as if to say, "All right, I'm here, let's get this show on the road."

"Before we take off," said Ned, "you must be Sophie."

I half-raised my hand as if a teacher were calling roll, and the entire group pivoted on their heels to examine me.

"Stephen thought you might make it," Ned

said and smiled, a smile that could not be ob-
scured by his dark beard and his long, tattered
red plaid scarf. It was a wide, goofy smile, and I
found myself smiling back with a warmth that
bordered on foolishness. For the first time since
I'd come to Maine, I felt that someone was glad
to see me. Was **delighted** to see me. It was just a
trick of Ned's particular sort of smile, I thought,
but I liked it nonetheless.

Thus prompted, everyone else smiled at me
too, or at least stretched their lips—none of
them very enthusiastically. I wished I were asleep
under our flannel sheets.

"Okay," said Ned, fishing a saltine out of his
jacket pocket and handing it to Matilda, who
began to gnaw on it and shower damp crumbs
down the front of her blanket. "Today the first
half of the walk is Danforth to State Street, then
down to the corner of Commercial and India.
Then those of us who are ambitious or don't
have anything better to do can head along the
Eastern Prom trail to the East End beach."

Portland is swagged between two promonto-
ries, the Eastern Promenade overlooking the
Casco Bay, and the Western Prom, which faces
the Fore River. Between the two Proms, the hills
swoop gently down then up again, like cables

hung from a suspension bridge. The itinerary Ned outlined would be about three miles. That I could do.

As the walkers set out, with a low babble of conversation and some final rapid stretching of arms and legs, Ned and Matilda fell in beside me.

"So you're the Wal-Mart greeter," I said.

"For now. Stephen's better at it, but he has to let me be his deputy these days. I'm glad you showed up. Stephen is very keen on adding new recruits. You're new in town?"

"Very new," I said. "Since August."

"I know it's not the easiest place to come to cold," said Ned.

"Cold would be the word," I said, and he laughed.

"I won't tell you you'll get used to it, because you won't," he said. "But it gets more bearable."

"Thank you. You're the first person who hasn't told me that I'm being a baby about the cold. Besides your partner, that is."

"I think Stephen said you're from D.C.?" Ned asked.

"All my life."

"Big change," said Ned.

"Big change," I agreed. Then, fearing to

sound too negative, I added, "But it's been very interesting."

"I bet," said Ned.

"What I meant was, Maine is lovely."

He laughed and like his smile, his laugh was easygoing, casual, and kind.

"Maine **is** lovely," he said. "But you don't have to tell me you love it here. Maybe no one's let you in on this, but people from Massachusetts and people from Maine really enjoy bad-mouthing each other. Mainers say people from Massachusetts are loud, rude, bad drivers, and litterbugs. People from Massachusetts say that people from Maine are backward, unfriendly, and sleep with sheep. So if you like it here, great, but if you don't, feel free to complain, and I'll trot out all the Massachusetts stereotypes of Maine for you."

"I may take you up on that," I said. "I guess before I came here, I thought all of New England was the same region. One giant Norman Rockwell painting."

"We do that on purpose," Ned said. "To get the tourists here for summer and the leaf season."

We'd walked down the hill while we were talking, then taken a left on Danforth. Ned seemed to be humming something, so low I could barely hear it. After a minute I made it out—it was "Dream a Little Dream of Me," by the Mamas and the Papas. I looked over at him and he stopped abruptly.

"Go on," I said. "I like that song."

"It was for Matilda," he said. "Her parents said it's her favorite. They rock her to sleep with it. She was crying earlier and I tried it and she shut up."

"And it keeps us in step," I said, which was true. I'd felt off pace with him until I'd begun subconsciously moving to his humming. Ned was tall, about six feet, so it wasn't that his stride was too short for me, as some men's were. The problem was that even behind a baby stroller he loped, putting his weight on the balls of his feet for a second longer than Paul did. It took me a few minutes to catch his rhythm.

Our place was in the rear guard of the group, behind two short-haired, stocky women dressed exactly alike in jeans and knee-length parkas, and in front of the overweight girl and an elderly man who wore a hunting cap with earflaps. Back in Washington, I would have thought the earflaps very silly. Here I simply envied them.

Ned said, "Stephen said he almost knocked

you over yesterday and you were very nice about it. He sends his apologies."

It was a strangely formal phrase—"sends his apologies"—especially from someone as young and unkempt as this man. Not dirty—his hair was thick and shining with a slight wave to it, and his coat, though worn, had no marks or grime on it. His scarf was soft and clean, but threadbare. It was puzzling that Stephen let his partner wear such tatty clothes. Maybe they were a new couple and Stephen was just beginning to work on Ned's wardrobe, but for some reason I'd gotten the impression that the relationship was a longstanding one.

"Steve said you two talked for a while," Ned said.

"He's very friendly," I said.

"Yes, he'll talk to just about anyone." He paused, seeming to realize that this wasn't very flattering.

"I mean, he enjoys meeting any new people," Ned added. "That is, he enjoyed meeting you especially."

I noticed—it was a morning of new impressions, and maybe I was hyper-alert to them—that when he was embarrassed he cast his eyes down briefly, as a small boy might do, a blink so quick that if you weren't looking right at him you'd miss it. His lashes were thick and dark, and long. Marta would have killed for those eyelashes.

Block by block, the group was getting farther ahead of us. The two walkers behind us were literally at our heels.

"Am I holding you back?" I said to Ned.

"No. I can't go much faster without shaking up her stomach. Her parents said that her appetite's been a little off."

He spoke as if referring to the feeding habits of an exotic species of waterfowl.

Matilda's stomach didn't seem delicate. She'd polished off the saltine and located a chocolate-covered graham cracker in the crevices of her carriage. Chocolate was smeared over her mouth, her cheeks, and her forehead, and she was fussing loudly. What's more, she suddenly seemed to be bursting out of all her clothes. The snap that kept her hood around her chin had come unsnapped, and one of her booties was hanging from the footrest. I crouched down and set her to rights while she made buzzing noises. Ned gripped the handlebars tightly, as if he thought Matilda would zoom away under her own steam.

"I don't think it'd hurt her if we picked up the pace a tiny bit," I said to Ned. "She seems to be fidgeting around in there."

He peered under the stroller canopy.

"Oh God," he said.

"It's just graham cracker."

"It's all over her. Her parents have the flu and I'm going to bring her home a mess."

I removed the graham cracker and pulled the hem of my cotton camisole out from under my sweater to wipe Matilda's face. Then I placed in her mouth the pacifier that was hanging by a loop off the carriage rail, and curled her tiny right hand around the leg of a pink stuffed octopus that also dangled off the stroller rail. Matilda rewarded us with a contented grunt, and Ned smiled at me for the second time that day.

This time I observed that his eyes were a most unusual shade of blue-green. The color of blue eyes is often compared to the sea, but Ned's eyes were the first pair I'd ever seen that **were** actually like the sea, in the way that changing light and shadow changed their color. As we headed down State Street, the sun hit us directly, and his eyes went the blue of aquamarines. In the momentary shade made by a passing truck, they turned the mysterious green of the inside of a high-breaking wave after a storm.

It's always unnerving when you have the habit of examining faces and are suddenly surprised by something beautiful. You want to stare, but out in society it's not considered mannerly to stare. Once, in a supermarket parking lot, I'd pointed out a lovely woman to Paul and said, "What a striking face," and he'd laughed uncomfortably and said, "Are you turning lesbian on me?"

"You have kids?" Ned said. "You seem to know what you're doing."

"Just a husband," I said. "I have a nephew though."

"I haven't been around babies much," he said.

"You're doing great," I lied.

He began to answer, then grabbed my arm suddenly and pulled me out of the way of a honking pickup. I hadn't gotten used to the Maine habit of taking left turns into oncoming traffic in the first seconds after the signal changed from red to green.

"What a jerk," said Ned. "He could have killed you."

Matilda, seeing Ned's fierce expression, began to cry and hold up her arms. Ned looked at me and I looked at Ned.

✓ "They said I could just put her in the stroller and go," he said.

Matilda screamed piercingly. She had a fine pair of lungs.

"Here, now," I said to her. "What's all this fussing?"

She glared furiously at me. I unhitched her seat harness and lifted her into my arms. Immediately she ceased crying and settled herself into the curve of my hip.

"I should handle this," said Ned. "It's your first day. Stephen said to make sure you got to know people."

"You have one person to babysit. You don't have to worry about me."

"Go join the group. You should be meeting them, getting comfortable."

"I see you're under strict orders to have me socialize," I said, and I knew by his embarrassed blink that I was right. I could hear Stephen saying to Ned, "Now, she's a little shy and nervous, so get her talking. Get her mingling."

But by now the auburn-haired girl and the old gentleman were blocks ahead of us, rounding Commercial Street. Ned picked up the pacifier, the octopus, and a green enamel spoon from the sidewalk.

"Where did this spoon come from? Where is she finding all this stuff in that tiny carriage?"

He gazed after the remnants of the walking group. Spandex Guy was probably pumping his way along the Eastern Prom trail by now.

"Maybe you can even catch up with them if you really book it," he said.

I made a move to return Matilda to the stroller. She yelled with rage and clung to me. For the first time in three months, I felt capable.

"Tell you what," I said. "Let's take her to breakfast at Becky's. You know, that diner near the bridge?"

"I know it. But I can't have you giving up your free time. And it's your first day and everything."

The morning traffic whirred around us recklessly.

"You like Becky's?" I asked him.

"Who doesn't?"

"Good. Let's go before we get run over."

Matilda took eight long pulls at her bottle and dozed off. Ned and I both asked for western omelets with hash browns. Watching Ned devour his breakfast, I felt suddenly ill at ease. For his part, he seemed as casual as if he ate breakfast with me every day, but then I guessed he worked with lots of strangers on these away-from-Boston jobs.

"So you guys renovate houses?" I said to Ned. "You like that?"

He nodded with his mouth full. With his scarf off he seemed less sloppy, but still pretty rumpled, with his black hair standing up in disordered tufts all over his head.

"Is it hard work, your business?"

He nodded, and shoveled in more hash browns. The man could eat.

"Can you make a living at it?"

He waggled his hand back and forth, in the Italian gesture for "so-so," then swallowed and spoke.

"A decent living," he said. Then he grinned. "Okay, better than decent. If not, Stephen wouldn't do it. He likes money, and he wants to make a lot of it someday."

"And you two work together. That would be too much for some people."

"Well, it's not so strange where we come from. A lot of people in the Merrimack Valley have family businesses."

That was sweet, the way he referred to Stephen and himself as a family. I'd never have dreamed of describing Paul and me as a family.

"So was it hard growing up there?" I said.

"The economy's not what it was, but it wasn't that tough," said Ned, polishing off his toast and raising his coffee cup toward the waitress.

"I mean . . . was it hard being different?"

"We weren't that different."

"Really? That's great. Great. From what Stephen said . . ."

"Oh, Stephen's always beefing about Amesbury. The truth is, he'll probably retire there and make lasagna for the St. Anthony's annual benefit supper just like my aunts do, and vacation at Salisbury Beach every year. He's really just an old lady at heart."

"And you guys would feel pretty accepted living back there? It must be a more open place than Stephen implied."

"Open?"

"Or tolerant, but don't you really hate that word? It's condescending."

"I'm not quite following you," he said.

I fiddled with my fork. I could feel the mentally lacking look spreading over my face, the one that came whenever I couldn't explain myself.

"I mean," I babbled, "I thought some of these old Catholic factory towns up here, that maybe people wouldn't be as open-minded as maybe they'd be in San Francisco or New York. About lifestyles and so on."

The waitress refilled Ned's coffee cup and took his order for blueberry pie à la mode. Where did he put all this food? When she was gone, Ned said, "I think we have our wires crossed here." His brows were knotted, which gave him an air of almost comic puzzlement; he had very expressive eyebrows.

"No, no," I said. "I may seem reserved but I'm very liberal, believe me."

"Did you think I was Stephen's . . . did you think I was Stephen's boyfriend or something?"

"He told me you were, didn't he?"

"I'm not Stephen's **life** partner, I'm his partner," said Ned. "I'm Stephen's business partner. And I'm his brother."

That would have been an ideal moment for Matilda to wake up and begin to cry, the moment for any appropriate distraction. Matilda remained seraphically asleep.

"Oh Lord," I said. "I'm so sorry. Of course you're not . . . oh **Lord.**"

Ned put down his fork, which hadn't left his hand since we'd come in, and laughed. Laughed hard. I didn't think it was so funny.

"Most men don't fall down laughing when you think they're gay and dating their own brother," I said sourly. Then I said "oh Lord" again, under my breath. My mother had always hated cursing, and this had been an early substitute that I reverted to in moments of great stress.

" 'Oh Lord' would be right if I had to date Stephen," said Ned. "It's no picnic being in business with Stevie, but Scott is a saint. The whining since he broke his leg. I'm surprised Scott hasn't left him yet."

I gulped. "So Scott's the one with the salads every night?"

"Scott. Not me at any price. The doctor said if Steve didn't get his cholesterol down he'd have to go on medication. You wouldn't believe the ruckus he kicks up."

He started in calmly on his blueberry pie.

A self-confident person might have given a light laugh: Isn't that amusing! What a funny mix-up! But I found myself in these situations too often, and then it's not so funny anymore. Although Ned was taking my mix-up with good grace. Paul, about now, would have been frosting over like Queen Victoria at a burlesque revue.

Paul. I pictured myself explaining to Paul that

I hadn't even completed a single walk before being forced to quit the group, and his frustrated expression that would imply, "Can't she even do **that?**"

"Hey!" said Ned kindly. "What are you looking so tragic about?"

The waitress glanced at us and quickly away. She probably thought Ned was announcing that he was leaving me and the kid for another woman.

"I'm so sick of being an idiot."

"An idiot? I'm not insulted or anything. So what if you thought I was gay?"

"I didn't think you looked gay, you know. In any particular way."

"Well, that's good. I guess. Since I'm not."

"Of course, people have the right to be gay. I have lots of gay friends."

"Sophie, relax. It's my brother's fault. Completely. And if you act so dire, you're going to scare the baby."

"The baby scares me," I said.

Matilda let out a demented chortle and grabbed my leg. I took her on my lap and jigged her up and down. Holding her, I thought: I will never be smart enough to have my own kids. Kids needed someone who was sure of the world, someone who knew the answers, someone who didn't make embarrassing mistakes. My father, with his scientist's mind, was like that. Chatty he wasn't, but my father knew the answers to questions. If you asked him anything factual—what made grass green, or how far from the Earth was Pluto—he knew it. This had been reassuring to me as a child. I could never inspire that feeling of safety in a kid if I lived to be a hundred.

Ned sighed.

"I can't believe you're upsetting yourself like this. You should get some pie. Or at least finish your eggs."

"I'm not upset." I picked up my fork and began deliberately eating.

"It was an easy mistake," Ned said, and he smiled. Curiously, I didn't mind his smiling. There are people who, when you're feeling your stupidest, can't help showing that they agree with your own estimate of yourself. My mother-in-law was like that. Once, at her dinner table, I'd spilled some tomato bisque on a pale blue summer dress, and before she jumped up for a towel, I had seen it, that brief, superior smirk, as if I had once again confirmed some opinion she'd formed about me. Ned's smile wasn't like that.

When he smiled, his wide mouth curved sideways and his black eyebrows tilted up toward his widow's peak. It was the smile of someone who laughs at himself as much as he laughs at anyone else.

He said, "When we started in this business, Stephen was adamant that we shouldn't refer to each other as brothers because it made us look like amateurs. He's like that. Even in grade school he always had to be Mr. Cool. So we got in the habit of saying 'my partner' all the time, until it became second nature and also a joke. When he was talking with you, he used the word without thinking. It would have confused anyone."

"Not anyone," I said.

Matilda wriggled in my arms, snaffled a bit of my omelet, tasted it experimentally, and spit it out.

"Besides, my girlfriend's going to get a huge laugh out of this."

"Where is your girlfriend?"

"Back in Boston. She's getting a Masters in Educational Theory at B.U."

There was pride in his voice.

"That's a little rough. A long-distance relationship."

"Not fun, but Steve and I couldn't afford to turn down a commission like this."

"What's so special about this commission?"

"The house was built in 1919, and we're restoring it entirely, from the inside out. The owners are two Cambridge lawyers who plan to move here eventually, so they're serious about the renovations. No cutting corners, no patch jobs. We don't see clients like that every day."

"You're not kidding," I said with feeling, thinking of my own clients.

"So what do you do?"

He reached over and gave Matilda a spoonful of vanilla ice cream. I told him about my work. I didn't glamorize it. I even told him about Ann's greeting card line.

"An artist," he said.

"Greeting cards aren't art."

"She pays you, right?"

"A little."

"That counts. My girlfriend has friends who are artists. She's always after me to hawk their junk to my clients. They'd love to make money from their work."

"Is it nice stuff?"

"Not exactly. We went to an opening or whatever you call it the other week, and one guy did a painting of his mother being buried alive, and another one did a display of dismembered baby dolls in different settings—you know, scattered around a little sandbox, or floating in a bathtub. **That** was a fun evening."

"Maybe it's therapy," I said, choking back an expression of horror.

"Then they should show it in an institution, and not call it art, right? But what do I know. You probably like this edgy modern stuff. You probably get it."

"No. Which is why I'll be doing greeting cards for the rest of my life."

Ned scraped up the remains of his ice cream and sat back with an air of finality.

"Have to go," he said. "Have to get this kid back and meet this guy who's coming by to give us an estimate on laying a new hardwood floor for the porch. He speaks only Portuguese, so it should be interesting."

"It sounds like it's going to be fantastic," I said. "The house."

"It might be."

He buttoned his coat and turned to me with a serious face.

"You're not going to go home and worry about that little mix-up? And you're coming back on Friday?"

I rummaged in my purse for my half of the check.

"Come on, don't be dumb," he said. "Stephen considers you his personal recruit to physical fitness. It's me he'll blame, you know. He'll never let me hear the end of it. Have pity on a guy."

"I'll try," I said.

He was struggling with the zipper of Matilda's jacket. His hands were well shaped, with long fingers, but they were chapped and ragged-nailed. I wondered why the girlfriend didn't dress him up a little. He had such an underappreciated look about him, like Lucy in the Wordsworth poems: **"A maid whom there were few to praise, and very few to love."** In the poems, Lucy dies and only the poet cares. Ned did not seem in danger of fading away, though. Not the way he ate. It wasn't fair that he stayed so skinny.

"Come Friday. Jamie and Carol will be there to wheel Matilda so you can really walk."

"Matilda attends the group every West Prom day, huh?"

"Every day. She's a Maine baby, and they're tough."

I watched him lope off down Commercial Street. Again I noticed that odd lift to his walk, like that of someone who'd had fallen arches as a kid. As he turned up the hill by Three-Dollar Dewey's bar and grill, Matilda's stuffed octopus fell from the stroller. He stooped to pick it up and saw me watching. He held the octopus up in the air as if saluting and called back, "Friday."

"Friday," I yelled back, and he and Matilda disappeared around the corner.

Seven

It was ten A.M. when I reached home. Ann had left a message on the answering machine. Was I "up for" another three paintings?

"Chrysanthemums and MacIntosh apples," she said. "And maybe a few found objects from the sea."

I hoped that she meant seashells and driftwood rather than flat rocks or seaweed. Ann often came up with weird ideas for "organic compositions."

Fortunately, mums were in season still. I'd seen some at Shaw's, so at least I wouldn't have to dig up a stock photo. Painting from a photo is too removed for me. It always feels as if I'm trying to pass off a picture of a picture of an object.

I did the dishes, noting that the caustic solution Donald had poured down the drain a week before had had no effect. It might take time, he'd said, describing the inside of the pipes to me in revolting detail.

"Think of a clogged vein, like when someone has a heart attack," he'd said. "That's your pipes."

"Artery," I said.

"What?"

"Clogged artery."

"Yeah. Your pipes here are like a clogged artery."

"Will the patient live?" I said. Donald gave me a blank look.

It was sad how, nowadays, all my fantasies revolved around home appliances. I'd once had a few private scenarios involving pirates, et cetera, and now all my illicit dreams were of hissing, steaming radiators, and kitchen faucets gushing hot water, and showers that pounded scalding pins and needles of spray into the sore spot in my lower back.

I watered the sad row of rubber plants languishing on our kitchen windowsill, and finished designing a slide presentation on new treatments for **retinitis pigmentosa,** intended for the Washington Ophthalmologists Association's December meeting. Only after my tasks were completed did I grab Paul's coat and shuffle out to the mailbox in my moccasins. There was only a circular from a hardware store at the Mill Creek Shopping Center. **Snow shovels on sale**. If Donald's shoveling was anything like his other lawn maintenance habits, we'd need one for the back steps.

The phone rang before I had time to get depressed over my lack of correspondence. It was Delia.

"I have ten minutes," she said, "but I wanted to catch you because I found a letter for you last night, over at Mom and Dad's. It was under a stack of **Catholic Standards** on Mom's desk. She had been planning to get around to sending it to you 'sometime.'"

"A letter from whom?"

"From your old friend Rory McLaughlin."

My stomach hurt. Remembering past loves can make you ache all over, but this ache was not poetic. It was the sudden squeamishness you'd associate with a demand from the IRS or a message slip asking you to call your doctor right away about those lab results.

Delia knew better than anyone else what Rory had meant to me. She had never fallen under his spell because she was two years older than he was, and when you meet as children that slight difference sticks. But she knew his charm, the glamour that surrounded the entire McLaughlin clan when we were children.

Mrs. McLaughlin always seemed to think being a mother of seven was a party. She was the lovely mother of the neighborhood, with her long red hair and wide green eyes and that vivid mobility of expression that Rory had inherited. Rory's mother genuinely liked children, without smothering them with attention. Every kid within a mile came to play in the McLaughlins' big, grassy backyard with its decrepit swing set and falling-down playhouse. Mrs. McLaughlin sat in a canvas deck chair in the sun, and casually fed us foods my mother would never have had in the house: potato chips, Milky Ways, cheese spread, cream soda.

Rory was our leader. He showed us how to fish off the rocks at Fletcher's Boathouse, and paddle up to Great Falls in two leaky borrowed canoes. With Rory we climbed the riverfront palisades where the silver mines used to be, and rode our bikes in a long straight row all the way down to the reservoir. On the way back we'd stop at the white-clapboard Sycamore Store for candy, gobbling it down before we reached home.

We were allowed to roam, as long as we stayed in our pack. Parents didn't worry then as they do now, and my mother wasn't much of a worrier anyway. And Rory always looked out for us all. Rory. How awful it was to think of him, on another continent, married to someone who wasn't me.

"Want me to send it to you, or read it to you?" Delia said.

"Read it," I said. If she mailed it, I would only call her and read it to her anyway, and I didn't want to wait to hear what Rory had written after five years' silence.

"Fine. Let me put the phone down for a sec. It's airmail and I don't want to tear it. Here we go."

Delia read, **"'Dear Sophie, Sometimes it feels like just yesterday that I left you at that dingy apartment of yours that night in Cleveland Park.'"**

"That **was** kind of a dingy apartment," Delia said. "But how rude of him."

I didn't remember the apartment as dingy. I remembered a hot August afternoon two weeks from Rory's wedding, when we lay in bed together and the acacia leaves made watery green twilight in the room, and our bodies were dappled with shadows like the shadows in clear ocean shallows.

Delia read on: **"'I heard from my mother that you got married.'"** So, Mrs. McLaughlin thought to tell him that.

In our teen years, Mrs. McLaughlin had begun to disapprove of us. Delia developed rather startling cleavage, and I dressed strangely and sloppily in my attempts to follow the teen fashion of the time. Suddenly our friendship with the McLaughlin kids, especially the boys, was not as desirable—in their mother's eyes—as the company of the daughters of wealthy lawyers and doctors who attended the fancy Catholic "academies" rather than St. Catherine's, where Delia and I went. Delia had not forgiven Rory's mother for this shift in attitude, though she'd never admit it had hurt her.

"There's only a little more," said my sister.

"Go."

" 'This hasn't been a bad spot for a first assignment. I travel around a lot, and on better days I think we're doing some good here. Liz has learned far more Polish than I have. We're on to Moscow next. Marriage varies from day to day. She wants to talk about having a baby, and I don't. Mainly because the food here would kill any baby.' "

"Here's the closer," Delia said. **" 'Missing your beautiful eyes, Love, Rory.' "**

"Read it all again?" I said. She read it all again.

"And he's got his e-mail address at the bottom. He circled it. In red."

"Did he ask me to write to him?"

"No, he just circled it. Typical Rory," said Delia.

This wasn't fair. I'd been good. I'd made a list, I'd gone to the walking group. I'd done chores. The reward for all this industry should have been an affectionate phone call from my husband, not a letter from a man whose very handwriting, could I see it, would cause me pain.

"Are you all right?" Delia said.

"What do you think he wants?"

"What do **you** think he wants?"

"Would you write back if you were me, just to . . . just to say hello?"

"Rory's not the hello type. At some point he'll come back to the U.S. for some meeting or other and make his move. You know he will."

"So you'd say . . ."

"I'd say it's not a good idea, hon. If you want to flirt with someone harmlessly, find someone, but not Rory."

Delia clearly had no idea of just how small the pool of flirtation-eligible men in Portland was.

"He's the kind who **tries,** Sophie, not the kind who yearns and does nothing about it. Do you need the kind who tries at this particular moment?"

"No," I said. "But this is Rory."

Delia sighed.

"I'm late for a client meeting. I hate to go now because you'll brood over this and let him shake you up. All I can say is that I was there the last time Rory decided to mess up your life, and it wasn't pretty. So don't take the first sip, so to speak."

"I won't. I promise. But can you send me his e-mail address? I'll just write him a casual note to show how great my life turned out without him."

"Make him feel bad. He deserves it. And when he writes you back, don't answer."

I'd said Rory was in the past, but it was harder to put him there and keep him there than it would have been if he'd been simply a lover. Rory was more. I could not remember my childhood without remembering Rory, whom I'd adored. He had given me my first kiss. He had casually watched over me through all our teenage years, when I was an awkward late bloomer and he was the popular athlete. If I pulled all memory of him from the fabric of my recollections, that whole fabric would unravel.

We'd lost touch in our early twenties, and maybe it would have been better if it stayed that

way. I could have remembered him as you remember a childhood hero, with innocent, mellow fondness. But when I was twenty-nine, we
discovered that we were working around the corner from each other, Rory at Connecticut and L
and me at Connecticut and K, in my last summer at the PR firm. By then, of course, he was
engaged to Liz.

Rory told me of his engagement in the first
ten minutes after we ran into each other again
one May day, one lunchtime at the Front Page
on Nineteenth Street. I wasn't surprised to hear
it. Liz had been his high school sweetheart: a
sensible, kind, pink-and-white girl with big
straight teeth and pale brown hair. Captain of
the girls' field hockey team at St. Catherine's,
president of the parish teen club. Although they
had parted during college for prudent reasons,
they'd begun dating again a year earlier. People
do that fairly often: they return to some youthful romance and take it up again. Rory, Liz had
probably thought, had now sown his wild oats
and was good husband material. And Liz had always been good wife material, even in high
school. Even picky Mrs. McLaughlin liked her.

"We got engaged in April and we're getting
married in August," Rory informed me. "My

job's taking me overseas in September, so there was no point in waiting."

He gave me this news with insulting promptness. When you attracted women as Rory did, maybe it was a reflex to convey right off the bat that nothing could be expected of you. I **had** expected nothing from Rory, but my low expectations didn't protect me from falling in love that summer. He did, and so I did, with pathetic readiness.

Rory started hanging around with me after that day at the Front Page. Liz was occupied with the wedding and I was a safe old pal to pass the time with. We'd go out for a beer or a game of pool at Buffalo Bill's, watch baseball in the cool dark basement of Club Soda, drive along the river with the windows down and "New York State of Mind" unreeling into the night air. It was a small, harmless return to our childhood, when Rory was the leader and I was his sidekick. He gave no sign that he'd noticed I'd grown up.

There came a late-June night when he was dropping me off after a casual dinner at Gallagher's Pub and recalled that he needed to phone Liz for some instructions about his tuxedo. Liz went to bed early. She'd be mad if he didn't call tonight, so could he come in? He came in, I waved him to the phone, and he wrote down what she said about shawl collars versus notched collars.

Then he said goodnight to his fiancée, put down the receiver, strode over to me and said, "I can't wait one more minute to kiss you, Sophie Ann."

His athlete's timing, his Irish sense of when the hinges of fate open ever-so-briefly, told him that that second was the second when everything I felt for him, the childhood crush, the teenage longing, the bewildering attraction of these summer months, would turn at a kiss to a fierce delirium of love and desire.

His mouth was the stuff of dreams. Can I unzip your dress? he said. Could you take off that slip, Sophie darling? Can we lie down? After that he asked no more questions, and neither did I.

It was a shame that we were so good in bed together. I was so stupid that I thought that might mean he'd stay with me. One hot August afternoon two weeks from his wedding, I'd asked him, "Are things like this with Liz?"

"No," he'd said.

He lay looking at me, and his eyes were too kind.

"Then why?"

"Sex isn't everything, Sophie."

"It's not nothing, either."

"Liz has . . . particular qualities."

"What would those be?"

He sighed, and ran his fingers from the inside of my wrist up to my elbow. We had just made love, yet I felt a pang of desire. Desire, while he told me the reasons he was choosing someone else. I was far gone, I can see that now. I was crazy.

"Liz is sturdy," he said. "She's game for anything."

"Not for anything," I said. "That's obvious."

He laughed, and removed his hand. He sat up against the pillows, and held me close to him. Such tenderness. I was too young to know how tender men can be when they're already saying good-bye to you in their heads.

"Liz will be able to get by in Poland."

Rory said he'd waited a long time for this chance. Until now, his bosses at the Foundation for Overseas Democracy hadn't let him go abroad much. He'd needed seasoning, they said. Now it seemed he was seasoned enough.

Even though Poland had been free for several years now, the Poles still needed help setting up a democratic society, Rory said. His job would be, it seemed, to meet with journalists and small-town officials and help them figure out how to construct Western-style democratic institutions, such as a free local press and efficient municipal election systems. He was going to be based in a little town about a hundred miles from Warsaw. The name of the town sounded like the noises a child makes blowing into a telephone receiver, all whooshing sibilants.

He said, "They told me today that, in a few years, if I work out, maybe Zambia or Turkey."

"Zambia's the **reward**?"

He sighed, and stared out the window down into the street. An ice cream truck was passing, playing "Sidewalks of New York" in taped retro chimes. I lay there, memorizing his eyes, his hands, and felt despair at my own chicken-heartedness. I knew I wasn't going to break up the wedding by rising at the proper time to object; I couldn't even remember if Catholic nuptial masses had such a moment. I wasn't even going to phone Liz to tell her Rory and I had been together, which would have been the obvious course to someone like Marta. He'd be gone soon, while I stood by and let it happen.

There were very good reasons for Rory to

marry Liz. He'd outlined them to me when we were still merely lunchtime friends. And moreover, I was doing a sneaky, rotten, lousy thing by having an affair with someone else's fiancé. But the excellent principles I'd been raised with went to the wall under my conviction that two people could not feel this way and not act upon it. If ever a man was in love, Rory McLaughlin was in love with me. It wasn't vanity that made me believe this, nor lame hope. It was the evidence of my own eyes, which saw how his face changed when I kissed him. Of my own hands, which had felt his body tremble with fear and passion.

But to Rory, love was not a compelling enough reason to change his plans.

"If this had only happened six months ago," he said sadly.

"Guess we just missed the boat."

In my mind's eye, Rory stood at the prow of a Viking vessel, his red-golden hair gleaming, the ship cutting through the water away from me.

"I love you, Sophie Ann."

It sounded already futile, as if he were calling to me just out of earshot.

"Marrying someone else is a strange way to show it."

"Sophie, it's all set up. My mom and her mom

and all the details they've planned. The dress. The program. The cake."

Of course. True love weighed little against the cost of a hand-decorated cake, crowned with a porcelain bride and groom that had sat on top of Liz's parents' own wedding cake. I knew the details. I'd pried them out of him, wounding myself even more. Liz was going to wear ivory satin and carry pink roses. Her sister was going to play the communion interlude on her violin. There would be dinner and dancing afterward at the Chevy Chase Country Club. Then the happy couple would put the wedding presents in storage, honeymoon in Dublin, and travel straight on to Poland. It was all planned out.

"We can write each other, at least," Rory said.

" 'We' is you and Liz."

"When I'm with you, that seems impossible."

"Then be with me."

I sat alone in the kitchen, my teacup cold in front of me, looking out at the pewter sky with its patches of deep, clear blue. The German shepherds were romping in the backyard. Donald was teasing them with rawhide bones, then leaning down to nuzzle their heads and chuck them under their slavering jaws. I had changed planets since last seeing Rory, yet somehow he'd reached out and stopped me short in the middle of the day. There was only one anecdote for such foolish, paralyzing sentiment, the same anecdote as always. I picked up the phone.

"So he's resurfaced at last," Marta said. "I knew it. He tells you he loves you three steps from the altar and then disappears into the jungle."

"Poland."

"Poland, the jungle, whatever. And now he's sniffing around your ankles again."

I heard the scritch-scritch sound of Marta filing her nails. She wears five different nail polish colors in a week. She says it's her only form of creative self-expression.

"I never got what you saw in him anyway," Marta said. "The old boy-next-door thing leaves me cold."

"You never wonder about some old flame?"

"The boy who lived next door to me in Passaic loved nitroglycerine hits and wound up doing time for mail fraud."

"There's just something about someone you grew up with," I said.

She snorted.

"Oh, for God's sake, don't start reminiscing

about the old swimming hole and quoting **Our Town**. I hate that play. If Emily weren't dead at the beginning you'd want to shoot her. And don't tell me how Rory was the first man you've ever loved. No one should wind up with the first man she's ever loved. There's no basis for comparison."

Marta had considerable basis for comparison—she always had one or two besotted suitors on a string—but she was set in her ways as a spinster in a Barbara Pym novel. She could walk into her elegantly appointed living room and know if one tassel on one couch cushion was tangled. Her bathroom had a double sink, so visitors wouldn't mess up her toiletries. Her Siamese was as crotchety as she was, an unlovable beast with cold, milky-blue eyes. Men were too disturbing of this carefully maintained order if kept around on a permanent basis. Marta discussed this fact in tones of faint regret, like someone who'd love to own a golden retriever but knows her apartment is too small.

"Finish about the letter," said Marta. I reeled off Rory's words, which I could recall phrase by ambivalent phrase.

"Rory was an idiot to marry Liz," Marta said.

"Field hockey. I ask you. Why do adventurous men always pick dull wives?"

To Marta, the Liz Brodys of this world, with their unpretentious niceness, their innate knowledge of etiquette and first aid, had never been intimidating. To me, Liz had always been an unreachable golden mean of normality. Even my mother approved of her.

"Now there's a girl who's doing something with her life," Mom said to Delia and me when Liz joined the Peace Corps after college.

Liz had double majored in Spanish and environmental science, ready to enter a life of pragmatic altruism upon graduation. Delia and I were dilettantes by comparison, my mother faintly implied. So what if Delia had a degree in higher mathematics from the University of Pennsylvania. So what if my college art department chair had once written my parents a letter telling them that I had a talent that was "rare in his experience." My mother tried to be proud of us, she really did, but deep down she yearned for a daughter like Liz who'd share her drive to make the world a better place in concrete, measurable ways, and who'd stay in close touch even from Bavaria. Liz was the kind of daughter who phoned her mother six times a day just to chat. With Liz, my mother would have had not just a daughter but a friend. Delia and I were so different in temperament from my mom that she must sometimes have wondered if there had been a baby-switch at the hospital.

"Are you going to answer Rory's letter?" said Marta.

"No."

"You could, just to play with his head. But you're too nice for that."

I wasn't that nice. I'd have loved to make Rory feel he'd been a fool not to pick me. I just didn't think I could pull it off.

Marta tapped on the receiver with a newly filed nail.

"Still here, Sophie?"

"Just barely. I'm blue today, that's all. Pepper is coming for a visit."

I described recent developments on that front.

"No wonder Rory's letter shook you up, what with that she-wolf about to be inflicted on you. You should poison her turkey and giblets."

"Pepper will probably bring the turkey with her, stuffed. In a big box with Comfort Foods stamped on it in gold."

"Leave her at the outlet mall in Kittery with

that Natalie and hope neither of them ever finds her way back. And remember, Pepper can carp but a wife outranks a mother."

Marta would outrank any mother, that is.

"I don't know if I pass the wife test," I said.

"If a test is involved," said Marta, "it's not worth passing."

Eight

Maybe it was Marta, or all the coffee at breakfast. Suddenly I felt able to bear Donald in his den and demand heating of some sort.

Donald's wife Jackie answered the door. She was wearing the same clothes she'd worn on every occasion I'd ever seen her: a faded sweater and jeans. She was just about Donald's height, and just as skinny. Perhaps they were Donald's clothes. Perhaps the reason I never saw Donald in a sweater was that she took all of his.

Jackie's ash-blond hair was scraped back into a ponytail with a rubber band. I would have bet that she too had been a golden blonde in childhood. The rubber band had caught a number of split ends. I resolved to do something about my hair, and soon.

"I'm here to talk to Donald about the heat," I said, pitching my voice low and speaking slowly, as Marta had taught me when I worked at the PR firm where I was sometimes required to discuss proposed layouts for high-stakes accounts.

Jackie half-closed the door on me. In a

minute, Donald emerged, drying his hands on a grimy towel.

"The heat's not working," I said.

"It was working last night," said Donald.

"We got one blast last night and then zip. I'm getting really cold, Donald. I can't even type, it's so cold."

For the first time since we had begun our back-and-forth about the heating situation, Donald said nothing. Behind him I sensed the presence of his wife, listening. I could picture her hard face, weathered by Maine winters and decades of Camel cigarettes and a general, unvarying resentment. It suddenly occurred to me that Donald couldn't admit to me that he didn't have the money or skills to fix the heat. I'd have to find a solution that preserved his dignity—quickly, before I became a cryogenics experiment.

Donald edged out of the screen door and sat down on the railing of the steps, perching unsteadily. Any moment he'd tip over and crack his skull on the concrete "courtyard" just below, where he often barbecued in summertime. He'd fall, and Jackie would sue me.

"I could try flushing the system out again," he began.

"Look," I said. "This clearly is only a problem for me. Am I right?"

"Most people go to work in the daytime," Donald said.

"Well, you shouldn't be firing up the boiler three times a day just for me, right? Maybe we should take a new tack. What's the situation with the fuses in our apartment? Are space heaters an overload?"

Donald said warily, "Two would work. Three's a stretch."

I dreaded to think about the state of the wiring, which Donald had worked on himself. But life was full of risks, and I was more afraid of freezing than burning.

"I don't think we should have to buy the heaters," I said.

"You're the only one complaining that it's cold," said Donald, basely using my kindness against me. He examined his palms nonchalantly. At any moment he'd begin whistling under his breath, like a small town traffic cop after telling you that you could pay your speeding ticket or spend the night in jail. It was no use asking to see the judge because he was eating his Sunday dinner and couldn't be bothered until morning.

"The law says a landlord has to maintain buildings at a temperature of sixty-eight degrees during all daylight hours," I bluffed. "So I guess we have a problem."

The door moved a crack. Why did Donald's wife have to skulk that way?

"How about this," said Donald finally. "How about we split the cost?"

"We'll pay a third," I said. "That's the highest I can go."

"Fine," said Donald impassively.

"And you go out and buy them," I said.

"Fine," said Donald again, hitching his waistband up.

"It's a deal?"

"Sure, it's a deal."

"When?"

"I'll get them to you by tomorrow, how's that?"

He didn't seem angry; he seemed resigned.

"Well, thanks," I said.

In a burst of courage and independence, he added, "And I'll get you some good ones, the megavolt ones that really crank."

"That would be wonderful."

But it wasn't. This victory didn't feel good, not in front of his wife. A conciliating Donald wasn't

Donald at all. For some reason, I thought of how Paul never made eye contact with Donald, as if some important social distinction between the two men had to be reinforced: Donald, the ignorant manual worker, and Paul, a dealer in ideas.

I said, "Hey, Donald. You know a lot about cars, don't you?"

"More than most people."

"I need to buy a used car, one for me. Something small but sturdy. Do you know anyone you would trust who deals in stuff like that?"

"What's your price range?" said Donald.

"I hadn't thought about it."

"Tell you what, you come up with a figure and I'll make some phone calls. I know a few guys who'll treat you fair."

"Tell **you** what. You do that and I'll pay for the space heaters myself."

"Well, I'll go get them for you at least," said Donald. "I should have thought of this before."

In fifteen seconds, he'd forgotten that it was my idea. If the fuses blew—that was when he'd remember.

"How was your walking club?" Paul asked that night.

"I liked it. I really did."

"Are you going again?"

"Yes. Three times a week."

"Three times a week. Wow. Good for you. Show me your routes on the map. Maybe we can bike some of those trails before the snow sets in."

He was making pork chops, browning them beautifully in a frying pan. Work had gone well today—they'd had a promising phone conversation with an assistant school superintendent in the town of Bath, about an hour north, who'd agreed to see them in person in a few months. As a result, Paul was in such a good mood that he was cooking his favorite dinner: pork chops, apple fritters, and string beans in a dill cream sauce.

"That's great about Bath," I said.

"We'd be doing pretty poorly if we couldn't expand that far outside Portland."

"I'm proud of you," I said.

"Well, they'll be happy at the national office if we can pull this off."

Paul was uncomfortable with compliments. They weren't plentiful in Pepper's house. Paul had been raised to do well, and thus it was perceived as nothing remarkable when he did. No matter what his boyhood achievements—a basket at the buzzer, a near-perfect score on his college boards, being elected to student council—he was discouraged by his parents from "bragging." Often it was weeks after the fact before I learned of a favorable comment from a higher-up, or that Paul had reached some fund-raising goal he'd pursued for months. At such times it was easy to see in him the solemn, industrious little boy waiting for recognition that never came.

Tonight, with a big white apron wrapped around him and his horn-rimmed prep school glasses on, he looked about twenty-six. A rush of affection overwhelmed me. I stood behind him at the stove and put my arms around his waist.

"That smells good," I said. "When do we eat?"

"Whenever you're ready. It's almost done."

In Pepper's dining room with its faux-colonial high-backed chairs and polished-oak sideboard, food was lavishly provided: roasts and stews and clove-studded hams and corn on the cob with silver holders. But Paul was not encouraged to poke around the kitchen, which was Pepper's terrain. When Paul moved into his first bachelor apartment, he bought a set of expensive pots and pans and a starter cookbook from **Better Homes and Gardens**. Painstakingly, he learned to produce the same sort of food he'd grown up with. Then he began adding small twists. He put basil and a pinch of lemon zest in the breading for his pork chops, and he used real cheddar and Havarti in his macaroni and cheese. He discovered dill and cumin.

Pepper did not approve of this license, although Comfort Foods added similar gourmet touches to its pseudo-homey menu. Pepper worried that Paul's addition of sage to a roast capon was an indication that his sexuality might be in question.

"Who was there at this walking group?" said Paul as we sat down.

I described the group members but did not tell him about the mix-up with Ned. It was too embarrassing.

"This guy Ned runs the whole show?"

"Stephen does, actually, but Stephen broke his leg."

"Life isn't exactly thrilling for you in Portland, is it, hon. Donald is the only guy you see, and now you're in some club with men who just want to check each other out."

I smiled faintly and said, "Where do the hetero singles congregate, anyway?"

"Natalie says Brian Boru's."

Brian Boru's was the Irish bar in the Old Port. It was painted a deep, eye-catching red, and I bet it served Guinness in every variety.

"We could go there sometime," I said. "Listen to some music."

Paul thought Irish music was sentimental claptrap, but once in a while he would sit through a set with me back home at Nellie's Bar in Bethesda.

"We could," said Paul, "but Natalie says it's really smoky in there."

Paul's eyes teared up in any room in which cigarettes were present, but Natalie was still more allergic. She felt that smokers should not even be allowed to hang out in office building doorways since she had to inhale their fumes as she walked past.

"Where did Natalie meet Toby?" I thought to ask.

Toby was Natalie's fiancé. Every time she referred to him in Paul's presence, it seemed to be to complain about how Toby fell short. Toby didn't do enough work around their newly purchased clapboard near Deering Oaks. Toby wasn't putting sufficient money into his retirement plan. Toby had a silly passion for college basketball. Toby wasn't interested in joining a church, even to secure a place to hold their wedding. Every picturesque house of worship on the coast booked up two years in advance, it seemed.

"An outdoor activities club. They were assigned to the same canoe."

"That's kind of sweet. Did you tell her how we met?"

"Yeah, but she wasn't very impressed. I guess a lot of people meet at weddings."

"Well," I said, "I think it's ravishingly cute. You falling all over me like that."

He smiled at me, his old contented smile from our early married days when we thought our domesticity was such an accomplishment, when we'd sit after dinner over coffee talking about politics or naming places we'd like to travel if we ever made a lot of money.

"What's wonderful about you, Sophie, is that when you love someone, you think everything they do is unique and amazing. I passed out from a food allergy, that's all."

"Yes, but when you woke up you were very witty, if you recall."

"All I remember is you in that ridiculous dress."

I went around the table and kissed the back of his neck, my signal that I wouldn't be averse to a little after-dinner fooling around.

"Want to just leave the dishes?" he murmured in my ear. Not exactly "how do I love thee?" but good enough for me.

In a few minutes we were entwined on the sofa. Paul reached under my three sweaters and touched my breasts. His hands were cold but I didn't mind.

"Sophie," he said. "Sweetheart." He hadn't called me that in a long time.

We made love throughout the seven o'clock news. Tonight he was passionate and slow, and I was reminded of how he'd studied to please me in our first months together.

"You haven't been happy up here so far, have you?" he said, when we'd been lying for a while, half-asleep, pressed together. "You've been telling me what's been tough and I've been impatient and dismissive."

"You've had your own adjusting to do."

"But my days go faster than yours. I'm among

people. I'm sorry, Sophie. Sometimes I feel so responsible for you. Since we got married."

"That's a grim way to feel about another person," I said. "As if I were an invalid."

"Not that. But without me you'd be back in D.C., having lunch with Marta, seeing the baby, going to your painting classes at Glen Echo. You wouldn't be so lonely."

"It's one year of my life, Paul," I said. "If I'm lonely I can try harder."

"I can help you come up with ideas," he said. "We'll make a list."

I felt guilty about my own list, which I hadn't shown him, but it felt so good to have him talking as if he were on my side again. Planning strategies on my behalf.

We dozed on the couch, Paul curling his long body around me to keep away the chill that spread through the apartment as the evening blast from the radiators hiccuped away. We didn't wake up until the eleven o'clock headlines were making their staccato way across the screen. The dill sauce had to be poured down the sink, but Paul said it was a small price to pay.

That night he held me close until we both fell asleep, and when the alarm rang in the morning I hoped we had turned some sort of corner.

Surely everything would be all right. Paul kissed me three times before he left for work, and laughed at my walking shoes and socks ready by the door.

"Walking today, running tomorrow," he said. "It'll be marathons next. You'll leave me in the dust."

Nine

On Friday morning, no one in the walking group seemed to recognize me, although no one looked me over as they had the first day. I stood sipping from my portable coffee cup, borrowed from Paul, and shifted my weight casually from hip to hip as I used to at high school dances.

This time I'd deliberately arrived after 7:15, so as to miss most of the prewalk stretching period. At exactly 7:25, Ned appeared, accompanied by a man and woman. The man was pushing a baby stroller and in it was Matilda. I'd expected her to give me the distant gaze of babies you have met just once, but Matilda stuck out a fat hand and amicably smeared some zwieback crumbs on my knee.

Ned said, "Jamie and Carol, this is Sophie, who saved my neck the other day."

The woman, who was slim with a thick brown braid, said, "We can't thank you enough for helping Ned manage. We wouldn't even have thought of landing him with her, but we were sick as dogs. One of those twenty-four-hour stomach bugs."

Jamie was tall and skinny with a neat beard. His wire-rimmed spectacles and short pigtail gave him the appearance of a costumed interpreter portraying a colonial schoolmaster. He fidgeted with Matilda's hat, clearly a nervous father.

When I saw Ned next to Jamie, I realized that, though I'd remembered Ned as thin, he wasn't truly thin, not reed-thin like Jamie. Ned was lean but I could see that his shoulders were good, his wrists were strong, not snappable-looking like Jamie's, and his jeans didn't hang loose around his calves by an extra inch as Jamie's did. In fact, I saw with a clinical eye, Ned wasn't bad-looking. In my single days, this realization would have made me shy, but one nice side effect of getting married was that I'd lost some of my self-consciousness around attractive men.

Besides, Ned didn't seem to know he was good-looking, as evidenced by his fraying duffel coat, his pilly sweater, his clean but overlong hair and untidy beard. His red scarf looked as if he gave it to the dog to chew on when he got home.

Today our route was down to Park Street and over to Pleasant Street, winding up in the park at the top of Exchange Street, a patch of scruffy grass where kids skateboarded. Then, as before, those who still had fortitude or time could continue down to the trail that edged the Casco Bay at the bottom of the Eastern Promenade.

Ned seemed to have designated himself as my informal protector. Perhaps he and Stephen had concluded that I was touched in the head and needed shepherding. We were faster today, without Matilda, and stayed somewhere in the middle of the group. Ahead of us were the two men I'd noticed on Wednesday, the one with dark hair whose leather jacket I'd admired, and the other whose light locks were slicked back from his forehead with what seemed to be pomade, though no one called it that anymore.

"Ramon and Edgar," Ned said. "They run a flower shop three streets away from us on the Eastern Prom. They were two of the first people we met in Portland."

"Were you ordering flowers for your girlfriend?"

He laughed. "Fiona? She's not into that sort of thing. She's not the frilly type, she says."

"So if you weren't a customer, how did you meet them? Edgar and Ramon?"

"They came to the door to ask for our St. Cecilia statue. You know who St. Cecilia is? I didn't, but they told me."

"Patron saint of composers or music or some-thing."

"Yup. She's usually depicted with a harp, ac-cording to Ramon. The house we're doing, the former owner was a priest. A great guy, appar-ently. The whole neighborhood loved him. But our clients, the Cambridge lawyers, he's Jewish and she's a Quaker: what are they gonna do with a house full of Catholic paraphernalia? The priest's sister carted away most of it. But he had a life-size statue of St. Cecilia that stood on the porch. She refused to take that."

"Are Edgar and Ramon into Catholic kitsch?"

"No, but you see, this St. Cecilia carries a bouquet of red and white roses instead of a harp. That's why Ramon and Edgar wanted her, to fill a corner in their flower shop."

"You'll probably go to hell for letting a saint be used in a promotional capacity."

Ned grinned. "Haven't the saints always been used in a promotional capacity? Our bigger problem is still unsolved, though. It's the Virgin Mary on the roof."

"On the roof?"

A faint, cold drizzle was falling, misting on Ned's hair and beard and on my eyelashes. We were passing the Episcopal church, with its majestic spire. Next to it was the Gothic dark-red brick of the Portland Landmarks headquarters, and across the road was Mercy Hospital, smaller than Maine Medical, less hulking. In the narrow doorways of the hospital, employees in scrubs stood smoking. Natalie would not approve.

Ned said, "She hangs out over the front porch. She's fastened at the back to one of the dormer windows with chicken wire. The wire's given a few inches over the years, and now She kind of leans forward. Hovering. You have to see it to get the whole effect."

Ahead of us, Jamie and Carol were making a good pace, but Ramon and Edgar were dawdling, peering in shop windows and checking out restaurant menus.

"And would Ramon and Edgar take Her too?" I asked.

"No. They don't want to piss off the neighbors. She's practically a landmark."

At the park we assembled to determine who would peel off and who'd tackle the trail along the bay.

"Next week," said Jamie. I watched with regret as Matilda was wheeled away, trailing her belongings as she went.

"We're in," said the heavy girl with auburn

hair who'd been breathing down our necks that first day. She glanced at the elderly man in the hunting cap. He was drinking from a water fountain and waved his assent. Ramon and Edgar both nodded. The guy in spandex was almost out of sight already. The two women with the identical outfits and thermoses, with whom I was never to exchange more than hellos the entire time I attended the group, simply started off. The rest of us fell into line behind them.

The trail wasn't bad: a mile of asphalt-paved path with the water on one side and the narrow-gauge railway tracks on the other. I'd never walked here, having had a few nasty surprises around Portland already with walking trails that abruptly ended or became choked in weeds and debris.

Ramon turned around.

"Are you the artist?" he said.

His accent had a faint Castilian softness to it. Ned told me later that Ramon had been raised in Cuba, brought to Miami by wealthy relatives at age twelve, and kicked out when he was sixteen and began openly liking boys.

"Yes," said Ned. "She is."

Edgar said, "Ned tells us you paint flowers.

You want some of our slightly off stuff? It's still nice-looking, we just can't sell it."

"Like day-old baked goods," said Ned.

"We have a reputation to maintain," said Edgar, smiling. He had a crinkled, studious forehead and was obviously the introvert of the couple. He handed me a lilac parchment card that said **Floradora: A Purveyor of Fine Blooms,** with an engraving of a nosegay of roses in a Gilded Age bouquet holder.

Ned said, "Ramon also does, what d'you call that, Ramon?"

"Tooled leatherwork," said Ramon. "Ned's clients are going to buy a few lampshades and wastebaskets from me. And file holders, and hatboxes."

"Not hatboxes," said Ned firmly.

"Where did you learn to be an artist?" asked the heavy girl, who'd somehow materialized on my left.

"At school," I said. "College. Not art school."

"I do cartoons, myself. Just silly stuff," said the girl.

"Cartoons I could never do," I said. "They're a very specialized form."

She smiled at me, an exceptionally charming

smile that relieved the severity of her dark brows and the heaviness of her features.

"Alex is taking a year off between high school and college. She's going to Northeastern next fall," said Edgar.

"If I get in. And if the money comes through," said Alex.

"Maybe you can do cartooning for the school paper or something," Edgar said.

"Are you going to major in art?" I asked her.

"Accounting," said Alex. "I have to earn enough to eat, after all."

"Some artists make a living at it," Ned pointed out.

"Do you?" said Alex to me. "Make a living?"

"No," I said. "Only a very small part of one."

"Well, maybe I'll take a few drawing classes at Northeastern," said Alex. "Frankly, I don't care what I do as long as I get out of the shit state of Maine."

We ambled along in silence. To our right the bay stretched infinitely, blue water dotted with deeper blue islands. These were sometimes called the Calendar Islands, Edgar said, because there were at least 365 of them.

At the end of the trail we came to a little beach

with a boat slip and small lapping waves, where we turned around.

Alex said to me, "In winter they run a Christmas train with light sculptures all along the track."

"How pretty," I said. "I'll have to go see it."

"It's lame," she said in the indulgent, scoffing tone young adults use when they've decided you might just pass muster. This pleased me inordinately.

As we neared India Street, Ned turned to the group at large.

"Anyone for breakfast?"

"We can stop, but only for half an hour," said Edgar. "We're doing a big dinner party in Yarmouth tonight and we've hit a few snags, container wise."

"I have class," said Alex. She half-smiled a general good-bye, then seemed to think better of it and plodded off. The elderly man in the earflaps waved again and walked off in the direction of the Public Market.

"Class?" I said to Edgar.

"Bookkeeping. At the community college. Career preparation. She's very focused."

"And the elderly gentleman?"

"George. He day trades," Edgar said. "Alex made friends with him the first week she joined and they've been buddies ever since." He added, "There's nothing weird about it or anything. She's just shy, and for some reason, George can get her talking."

Ned turned to me.

"You want to eat?" he said. "You didn't try the blueberry pie the other day."

"I'm game," I said.

We four repaired to Becky's and ordered lavishly.

"I think the sea air is picking up my appetite," I said.

"Sea air?" said Ramon. "If you say so. On the Eastern Prom, when the wind blows from the west, you can smell the sewage treatment plant."

"Really?"

"It's very rare," said Edgar.

"Not rare enough," said Ramon.

Ned merely ate, though sometimes he chimed in when the conversation stuttered. He had a way, I saw, of monitoring the ebb and flow of talk, careful to see that no one was left out, or left silent too long. This type of attentiveness is so much more typical of women than men that I began to wonder how he came by it.

Yet he wasn't in the least what you'd call a "sensitive" type; he ate with a single-minded dispatch that completely hid his alertness to the conversation. It would be a mystery that lasted through my time in Portland: how Ned could seem so absorbed in his food yet never miss a trick.

For such a devoted eater he had nice table manners; he ate very efficiently and quickly, the way I ate when I was alone. The only sloppy thing about him, in fact, was his appearance. Examining him at close range, I wondered why he didn't trim his beard into a more attractive shape. He'd left off his scarf when we sat down, and it was evident that his jaw was a nice, well-cut jaw, with a good chin.

When we'd polished off our omelets, Edgar and Ramon hurried off. Ned leaned back and said, "It's good my job's so physically strenuous or I'd be one fat guy by now. I'm gonna have something else too. I'm still hungry."

"You really worry about your weight?"

"Stephen battles his all the time."

"Stephen clearly got a different genetic hand dealt to him."

"He has twenty-twenty vision," said Ned. "And of course, he's gay and I'm not, as we discussed last time."

"Please," I said. "Don't remind me."

"Are you kidding? I'll be reminding you from now until spring. You were pretty funny."

He flagged the waitress and ordered a slice of blueberry pie, just as he had last time. I asked for more coffee. When he turned around to order the pie, I saw that his hair grew in the nape of his neck in two curves, one over each side of his neck, in a modified M.

"**M** for Moore," I said. "Your hair, in the back."

"I know. I used to be teased about it in school. When I get a haircut you can really see it."

I refrained from asking when this event would next take place. I'm not one of those women who itches to make over every guy she knows, but Ned brought out the latent man-groomer in me. I yearned to drag him to the nearest barbershop.

"No pie?" said Ned. "Come on."

"I have to develop an exercise habit before I can develop a pie habit."

"You can try some of mine. Hey, I saw that Alex talked to you today. She usually hangs out only with George, so that's good. That she branched out."

"I liked her. She said she doesn't plan to come back to Portland after college?"

"No," said Ned. "Not many jobs here even if she wanted to. Not that she wants to. All Alex talks about is getting out of Maine. Meanwhile, housing prices are climbing up, up, up because all these yuppies from Massachusetts and New Hampshire are moving here to live the simple life."

"Then soon no natives will live here, just 'from-awayers'?"

"In houses that Steve and I remodel for them. We're making it easier for rich folks to buy family homes out from under people who'd stay if they could."

"You keep those beautiful old buildings from falling apart," I said. "When the economy improves someday, their kids may want to come live here again. So I'm sure you're doing nothing but good, you and Stephen."

"He never thinks about this stuff. He's like my mother. Neither of them ever appreciated towns that are left to get old. Like Lawrence. My mom grew up there. When she was a girl it was a real city. Department stores, bustle, you name it.

Then the factories closed and there was white flight. Now they say Lawrence is on the brink again, that any day the Boston commuter crowd will catch on and housing prices will jump."

"You think it'll happen?" Even my New England guidebooks, with their relentless boosterism, warned against exploring Lawrence.

"Who knows. But the day all those old Victorians on Tower Hill start getting bought up, Stevie and I will be booked solid, and Steve will be in hog heaven. He doesn't care who lives in the places we rehab. It could be yuppies or bank robbers, as long as they pay."

"And you?"

"I'll be a little sad. It won't keep me from taking the money, though. You have to make a living."

"At least your mom will have the joy of seeing her hometown revive."

"My mother died three years ago, but yeah, she would've liked that."

He dumped cream in his coffee and stirred it around and around.

"I'm sorry," I said.

"It's all right."

"And your dad?" I tried to speak gently. Those thick lashes came down over his eyes, and he began ripping sugar packets apart, the falsely idle gesture of someone playing for time to recover himself. His hands were the hands of a working-man. They had a few calluses and the skin was rough and chapped at the knuckles. But his fingers were long and sensitive.

"He's remarried, to a woman who lived down the street from us for twenty years. Her husband died of cancer a year before my mom died."

"Your mom couldn't have been very old," I said. "That's a lousy break."

"It was sudden. And yeah, knowing my mother, wherever she is she's very pissed about it."

I thought of Ann's "Sudden Death of Loved One" card and felt ashamed. Maybe there wasn't anything wrong with packaging a sentiment for someone's high school graduation, but this was different. Ann would never understand that there were emotions that shouldn't be canned. This noble misgiving wouldn't stop me from cashing her latest check, however. As Ned said, you had to make a living.

"Stephen didn't mention your mom," I said.

"Steve took it the hardest. You wouldn't know it, but he plays the piano like a genius. He was studying it, at Berkelee College of Music. In Boston."

"I've heard of it," I said. "It's famous."

"Well, the week after she died, he quit."

"Just like that?"

"Just like that."

He gulped more coffee, and I kept quiet. If I gushed sympathy, he might get embarrassed and shut right up. I had an inkling that one slight jolt would stop him.

Ned went on, "Then out of nowhere, Stevie apprenticed himself to this old Lithuanian fellow in Medford, a carpenter. The guy called himself a carpenter, that is, but he could do anything around a house. Plumbing, wiring, flooring."

If only Donald had ever come into contact with someone like that.

"He worked with the old guy for three years making nothing, learning everything the guy could teach him. Then one day Stevie calls me and says, I know you hate your job so come on, we're going into business."

"What was your job?"

"State government, in Rhode Island. Staffer to a state senator. I had no real bent for it, I just went to Providence College and stuck around afterward. But it was boring as hell. We had some savings, and Steve got us a bank loan somehow too."

"Your dad must be proud."

"He's happy as a clam. He never wanted Stephen to be a musician. No money in it, Dad thought. Or maybe he thought it would make Stephen more gay somehow."

"Is that a sore subject, with your dad?"

"It's not a subject at all. It's just sort of tacitly understood. Steve's gay, and my dad's okay with it as long as he doesn't have to think too hard about it. This is Amesbury, you know. We had a neighbor whose son was a hairdresser. The guy collected Victorian mourning jewelry and lived with his 'best friend' who was a caterer, and his mom still talks about Jimmy 'meeting the right girl' someday. That's just the way they are there. But Dad and Steve get along. They get along great. Stephen even renamed the business last year, Moore and Moore, to please him."

The pie came. There was a perfect scoop of vanilla ice cream melting on top of it, the creamy, pale yellow kind that you know without tasting it is full of fat.

Ned heaped two generous forkfuls on my plate.

"You should see your eyes," he said, grinning. "You like sweets, don't you?"

I nodded with my mouth full. The pie was

heavenly, the tart, hot berries against the cool, rich ice cream.

"You're going to love it here, then," said Ned. "New Englanders need their baked goods. Whoopie pies. Cream horns. A Dunkin' Donuts on every block. My dad eats three chocolate frosteds every morning, and his cholesterol's eighty points lower than Steve's. It drives Steve crazy."

"What does your dad do?"

"He sells insurance."

"Is he good at it?"

"Wicked good," said Ned, his accent stronger than I'd heard it before. "My dad could sell insurance to anyone."

"How do you do a job like that?" I said, liberally sugaring my coffee. "I would hate it. I hate persuading people to do anything they don't want to do."

"My dad really believes in it. He carries so much insurance himself that you'd think he expected to be assassinated any day now. When he says to a customer, "You can never be too safe," he's practicing what he preaches."

Ned's dad would like me then for I had always been too safe. It was exactly why Rory, reckless and daring, had caught at my heart. I'd wanted him, but more than that, I'd wanted to be like him.

I hadn't answered Rory's letter. Every response I came up with sounded elderly and staid.

"How old are you?" I said to Ned suddenly.

"Thirty-one."

"I'm thirty-four and I have no insurance. Do you think that's bad?"

"Does anyone count on you for a living?"

"No. My husband would be fine on his salary if a truck ran me over."

"My dad would be chomping at the bit to sell you some, but I'd say don't bother. You said you've got a nephew? Buy him a savings bond. He'll love you when he's twenty-one."

"At the least I'm going to need car insurance. Speaking of insurance."

"You don't have a car?"

"Not yet. My landlord is helping me find a used one."

"Nice landlord," said Ned.

"Not really."

He pulled off his sweater and tossed it into the empty space next to me. His sweater smelled faintly of a scent I knew but didn't immediately recognize. After a minute I placed it: wood smoke.

"You have a fireplace in this house you're fixing?" I said to him.

"Oh, the sweater. I wore it this morning to air it out. Guess that didn't work. Yeah, it has a fireplace. We were tinkering with it last night, but it'll need a sweep."

"There are sweeps still?"

"Sure," he said. "Sorry my sweater stinks."

"It's a nice smell. Very cozy and wintery. Very Currier and Ives."

"Spoken by someone who hasn't been through her first Maine winter yet."

"What do you think? You think I can do it, or will I run screaming home?"

"You'll do it," he said. "You've got what it takes."

I smiled at him. No one who knew me well thought I had what it took for any test of endurance.

Then the seat behind me creaked, and Stephen leaned over my shoulder.

He clenched my shoulder in greeting.

"Thought you'd be here, you pig," he said to Ned. "Eating fried food just to spite me."

I scooted over and he sat down next to me.

"What's this I heard?" he said. "First you join a walking group and now you're buying a car. That's what comes of making lists."

Stephen ordered coffee and ate some pie crust off Ned's plate. I saw that he was wearing a softer cast than the one he'd had when I met him. It seemed to bend more at the knee, and was less grimy.

"A car's great," said Stephen. "Some people say you're only grown-up once you've had children, but that's not true. It's after buying your first car. You eating your toast?"

I shook my head. It had suddenly hit me that when I did own a car, I would have to drive it on the freeway. On the Maine Turnpike, where people went at a terrifying speed. I'd be killed, surely, and evil Natalie would marry Paul within six months. He'd give her the antique filigree ring and bracelet that had belonged to his grandmother. They weren't very pretty, but I didn't want Natalie to have them.

"Maybe I shouldn't," I said. "Buy a car. I can't even drive properly."

"That doesn't stop anyone else up here," said Stephen.

"But I can't even merge," I said. "I can't even parallel **park.**"

"No one in New England knows how to parallel park," Stephen said.

"But the highway. I don't mind driving into easy parking spaces and hiking a mile from there, but on the highway I could actually kill someone."

I pictured a minivan full of laughing Girl Scouts, carefree and singing, unaware that one minute later I'd lose their vehicle in my blind spot and smash them all to bits.

"Tell you what. Ned here will teach you to merge," Stephen said. "He taught me."

"I got tired of being in the truck with him when he stopped dead on the entrance ramp," Ned said.

"That's a silly idea," I said. "Do you want to see your brother die young, Stephen?"

"You can't be worse than I was," Stephen said. "When I get nervous, I drop the wheel and hide my face in my hands. You don't do that, do you?"

Stephen was putting his brother in a bad spot. I could see that Stephen's personality, in a brother, could be inconvenient.

"Ned would offer more loudly himself," said Stephen, "only he's afraid his little girlfriend won't like it. She's the jealous type."

"She's not the jealous type," Ned said without inflection.

"Maybe not of specific women. Just of any part of your life not centered on her."

"Fiona would be fine with it, Steve."

"I don't need lessons," I said. "I can practice on my own."

"Naw. She's a chicken. I can see it. She needs coaching. Come on, Ned."

"Stephen," I said, "Ned could get hurt in a car with me. He could get killed."

"He'll live to be ninety," said Stephen. "He has good reflexes."

Stephen looked at Ned, and the look was as physical as a shove.

"I'll hire a driving instructor," I said. "They get paid for putting their lives on the line."

Ned smiled then, that singularly goofy smile that had put me at ease on my first day of walking group.

"I'm the best teacher you'll find up here," he said. "Not to brag but it's true."

"And what Fiona doesn't know won't hurt us," said Stephen

"I'll tell Fiona," said Ned. "Believe me, Sophie, she won't care."

I made one last attempt. I owed Ned that; he'd been kind to me.

"Ned, you have your whole life in front of you. Why take the risk?"

"A risk would be good for him," said Stephen. "He'll do it."

"Sure. Why not," said Ned. "I carry a lot of insurance."

Ten

"You're wasting your savings," said my husband. "I can drive you anywhere you want."

I was due to sign the papers on my new car the next day, and Paul was unhappy.

In the week since I'd asked for Donald's help, Donald had found me three contenders. There was a Cadillac Seville, a little too expensive for my self-imposedly meager budget. There was an affordable Toyota Tercel, but the color was off-putting, a sickly mauve.

"It's an unhealthy color," I said to Donald.

He rolled his eyes, but he didn't really care if I procrastinated. Donald would happily have trotted out cars for me to see until Christmas. As I ceased to expect the radiators (and much else around the apartment) to work, Donald grew increasingly cordial. Just two days after he'd said he would, he delivered three brand-new space heaters that were on sale at Sears. They cost me only fifty-five dollars total, and had many nifty safety features: If you tipped them over, they'd automatically turn off. If you got them near a curtain or tablecloth, they'd turn off. If you even spoke of fire in their presence, they would turn off.

Donald and I had finally settled on a Ford Escort owned by Donald's dentist's wife. She worked with her husband out of a home office, so the car had been used very little. It was the next best thing to a car a little old lady had driven only on Sundays, Donald said. It made me feel patriotic to buy American too, even if the car was used. Donald took the Escort to be checked out, over at Duval's on Cottage Road. The mechanic recommended a new muffler system. Donald talked the dentist's wife into shaving a few hundred off the price for that, and there I was, about to become a car owner for the bargain sum of two thousand two hundred dollars.

Paul had been given updates throughout this process, but he seemed to see our car shopping as an activity in itself. He hadn't expected me to actually buy one.

"You don't drive enough to justify a second car, Sophie."

"I would if I had a car available during the day," I said. "Honest."

"We'd be a two-car family," said Paul. "It's not good for the environment."

Paul's normal level of concern for the environment consisted of not littering and occasionally watching television specials about protecting the Kodiak bears in Alaska.

The marriage manual advised, **"When you must make a financial choice your partner disagrees with, include your spouse in your decision in some way. Buy him a tie that complements your new dress, or book scuba diving lessons for him if he'll accompany you to that family reunion in Florida."**

I said to Paul, "Want to come with me to sign the papers?"

"I might as well."

He asked many unnecessary questions of the dentist and his wife, and pored over the sales agreement, a simple form I'd taken from a model provided on a consumer Web site. He minutely inspected the emergency kit that the owners had thrown in with the purchase price. Two hours later we were done. Our hosts were even kind enough to keep the car in their driveway until I could go over to the DMV and get it registered.

When we got home, I told Paul he was my hero and fired up the space heater in the bathroom to make it warm for him while he brushed his teeth. Paul usually brushed his teeth for an inordinate length of time; longer still tonight, since he'd been around a dentist. Pepper had always treated her children's cavities as personal moral failings.

"It's a good little car," Paul assured me before we fell asleep.

"I should try driving next time we go out together," I said, envisioning the pleasure of not sitting, like a good poodle, gazing sedately out the window of the passenger side.

"Let's see how you do with it first."

"Ned, the guy from my walking group, offered to take me for a few test runs on the highway," I said. "What do you think?"

"Sure, sure," Paul said. "He's a nice little girlfriend for you."

I'd informed Paul Ned wasn't gay, but he couldn't seem to take it in. The night I'd shared the story about my amusing little blunder, he'd been studying some budget numbers that Natalie had prepared for a promotional video. The punch line about Ned being Stephen's brother rather than Stephen's love interest didn't seem to have sunk in.

Perhaps it was for the best. A gay friend giving me driving lessons would be, to Paul, quite cute. Conversely, a straight guy using phrases such as,

"Easy now," or "Speed her up just a little. Slowly, slowly," might, for some reason, threaten Paul's manhood.

If Paul could meet Ned, though, he might not be threatened much. To Paul, Ned's unruly hair, his varnish-stained hands, his plaster-encrusted sneakers would all disqualify him as a cause for uneasiness.

"Now you and my mother can really go places during her visit," Paul said, and fell asleep.

This dampened my enthusiasm. Pepper had hardly crossed my mind in the past week, save for a brief, pleasant phone call with Natalie about shopping plans. It was kind of Natalie to give up her Friday holiday to show Paul's mother a good time. I myself hadn't brought nearly as much hospitable energy to arranging activities for my mother-in-law. I was hoping to catch typhoid and have to be quarantined before Pepper could hop on the plane up to Manchester Airport, which she'd chosen for the cheap ticket price, not thinking that it meant a two-hour drive for Paul after a long workday.

But Pepper would be here for only a few days, and I'd have the car for good. It was mine. There was so much to see once you had a car, I thought, snuggling under our comforter. I'd skim up to

Acadia. I'd tack inland and experience the White Mountains in April. I would surely be, by then, an intrepid motorist. Maybe I'd make it as far as Vermont, even cross the Canadian border just to see if it felt different on the other side.

First, though, I'd have to learn to merge.

Marta said, "Now that you have a car, the next step's coloring your hair."

"I didn't know that one necessarily implied the other."

"Sophie, just ask yourself this. What if you were to run into an old boyfriend. Not Rory, necessarily. Any old boyfriend. Can you honestly tell me that you're one-hundred percent satisfied that how you look is how you'd want that old boyfriend to see you?"

"No one can see how I look anyway, under all these layers of clothing. And do you have to be so mean? It's fine for you. You're gorgeous."

"Oh, Sophie, I'm sorry. I was just trying some lines out on you. That was a new ad campaign one of our member companies is launching. It's supposed to be funny, with this dreary house-wife suddenly finding out her old boyfriend is in town and running out and buying this new face lotion that makes her sparkle luminously."

"You know, this is why I don't watch more female-oriented TV."

Marta didn't have to worry about meeting an old beau. She'd looked very good in college, but she looked great now. The problem was that to look as great as Marta, you had to have excellent natural material to work with and then spend a lot of time gilding the lily. For Marta it paid off. But I'd always been the type who wouldn't be **that** much more striking even if I put a lot of effort into it. I always related to women in magazine makeovers who appeared phony and wrong in the "after" shots.

I said as much to Marta.

"Don't be silly. You're just as pretty as I am."

"Please, Marta, don't let's lie to each other."

"Fine. I'm somewhat better-looking than you, but we could each have a similar visual impact if you tried. Besides, I **need** to come across more powerfully because that's my job. It's why they hired me."

"Your job is more than that."

"Let's face it, Sophie, what I do is ninety percent brazenness, and ten percent substantive knowledge. I could just as easily represent tire manufacturers."

"The office is getting you down, huh?"

"Just the usual why-do-I-do-this. What do I care if at-home chemical peels are about to get the all-clear for over-the-counter sales? Or if the new lip gloss formulas last twelve hours? Was it ever that big a deal to reapply your lipstick? Nowadays, anything you put on your face is supposed to stay there, even if a hurricane comes splat at you."

"You're cheerful today. What's up?"

"It's nothing. My stupid office Christmas party. I don't have a date."

Marta's association scheduled its yearly party, sadistically, on December 27, just when every sane person wanted to change into a sweatshirt and jeans and put her feet up.

"There are lots of guys you could invite."

"Yes, and all with expectations. I don't feel like dealing with that awkward good-night pause at the door."

"Couldn't you just go stag?"

"If I wanted to be an object of sympathy. Our meeting planning director came in my office the other day and said, 'I always feel **so** sorry for single people this time of year. It must be so stressful.' The bitch."

"Should I ask Delia if Tom has a doctor friend?"

"I'm too old for blind dates," said Marta.

"Tell you what. If it'll cheer you up I'll color my hair. I'll dye it red if you want."

"Not red. Just something with a little more oomph, something that doesn't say 'I used to be blond and now I've given up completely.' "

"I can't go into a beauty shop and ask for oomph."

"I'll give you what to ask for. Got a pencil? Write this down."

Ned asked almost as many questions about the car as Paul had. It seemed to be a male instinct.

"Snow tires?" he said.

"Almost brand-new."

"Automatic shift?"

"Yes."

"Any major repairs?"

"Muffler system. And we got a break on the price for it."

"You sound all set. When should we take her out for a spin?"

"Let's just wait until spring, Ned," I said.

He stopped in his tracks on High Street, on the sidewalk in front of the revolving door to the Eastland Hotel, causing several irate people to stumble into us. We were walking down to

Deering Oaks Park, a route Stephen had mapped out for a change of pace. Edgar, who noticed these things, said that Deering Oaks had very fine roses in June.

June, of course, was never coming. It was one of those bitterly cold mid-November mornings when it seemed that living in New England was simply a process of pretending that you didn't mind freezing your ass off since all would be perfect come summer. Roses would bloom, the water would become magically warm enough to swim in, and out you'd skip from your front door in a cambric sundress. Two months of joy was thus supposed to be worth ten months of endurance.

I'd seen my face in the mirror that morning—most mornings of walking group I avoided examining it too closely. When I got up this early my skin was the color of whey, my eyes so dull a blue they seemed almost colorless. The cold seemed to be sucking away every last bit of attractiveness I'd ever had, weighing down my feet, bleaching the pink from my lips and the remaining gold from my hair. I felt bad—sluggish, ugly, and squirmingly dissatisfied with myself.

"Spring?" Ned said. "Oh, I get it. You have cold feet, don't you?"

"I have a work assignment going."

I'd finished a research report on stock investment choices made by retirees in the Rust Belt
for a marketing firm Marta had referred. Now I
was laying out a teacher manual for the Juvenile
Blindness Center's Discover Braille Week. Unlike most of my work, the braille assignment fas-
cinated me. The center had even sent me my
own stylus and special paper to give me a feel
for the project. I'd already learned to write
my name.

"Sophie," Ned said. "What's the problem?"

"You shouldn't waste your time on this simply
because your brother put you in a bad position."

"Stephen had a good suggestion. I'm just following up."

"I don't need charity driving lessons," I said in
an enjoyable excess of self-pity.

"Is that what you think?"

"Ned, I understand why you volunteered but
it's not fair to you. Your brother is probably always conning you into being nice to strays he
picks up."

"Stephen's always pushed me into making
friends, yes. He thinks I'm too reserved. He's
right."

"Or maybe he said, 'Keep an eye on poor
Sophie or she'll never talk to anyone.' You have

enough to do as cruise director of this group without being a driving instructor on top of it."

"You've talked to **lots** of people, Sophie. You didn't need me for that. Look, here's Ramon coming back for us. Everyone probably thought we got run over."

"Do you realize that we could go out on the road and I could kill you on our first try, and then Stephen will be an only child?"

"And he'd deserve it too. I bought some low-fat cheese for him yesterday and asked him how he liked it and he said, 'It's delicious if you've never tasted actual cheese before.'"

I smiled wanly.

"You're just being nice," I said.

"Is that so suspect? I know you come from Washington but still . . ."

He put a calming hand on my shoulder. Ashamed of my whining and touchiness, I shrugged it off. Ned looked as if I'd flung boiling water at him.

"Sorry," I said, and grabbed his arm gently, a grip-and-release meant to erase the look on his face.

"I'm just crabby this morning," I mumbled. "Didn't get enough sleep."

He stooped down and peered into my averted

face, hamming it up as if he were talking to baby Matilda.

"Come on, Sophie. Smile. Smile for Ned."

"I hate people who tell me to smile."

"At least don't hold it against me that I have a bossy brother."

His face was young, entreating. I hated to think how haggard mine was. Here was a nice guy, a sweet guy, doing me a favor and here I was, snapping at him.

"Fine, I'll drive with you," I said. "I only hope it's a decision you won't live to regret."

He dropped his hand.

"We'll have fun," he said. "Before you know it, you'll be passing people in the breakdown lane, a regular Boston driver. I teach Boston style, you know."

"God help me," I said. "And you."

Ramon and Edgar had reached us.

"The natives are restless," Edgar said.

"I was just persuading Sophie to let me teach her how to drive the turnpike," Ned said. "Good idea, right?"

"Certainly," said Ramon. "If I had had Ned instead of Edgar taking his stomach pills continually, I would have passed my driving test long before I did."

"Three tries," said Edgar to me. "I **needed** antacids."

"Some of us come from other places where not every young person has a car," said Ramon. "Some of us don't learn to drive at preparatory school at Andover. Edgar should understand, not be always saying, 'The brake pedal is there for a reason,' and other sarcasms."

"I know," said Edgar. "You're horribly ill-used."

This morning Edgar was sporting a deep red cashmere scarf from which his pale face took no color. Edgar resembled my idea of an English banker, but more approachable and benign. He looked incomplete without a briefcase and umbrella.

"You'll be doing Ned a favor, Sophie," said Edgar. "He needs to get out of the house. Stephen's laying the kitchen tile himself, sitting on a dolly with his leg propped up, and he's in a mood. And Stephen's boyfriend can't get away from work much lately. It's their busy season."

Scott, Stephen's boyfriend, was a travel agent down in Portsmouth at a company that arranged themed European vacations for the affluent. "You know," Edgar had explained, "Jane Austen's Bath. Tea and the pump room and shopping for table linens. Or Dickens's London, ending up at Harrod's. Very tame and very expensive."

"Sophie," said Ramon, "agree to let Ned do this nice thing for you."

"I did agree," I said. "But after Thanksgiving."

"Why not sooner?" said Ned. "Don't be chicken."

"I'm not chicken."

He raised his eyebrows.

"Fine, I'm chicken but I can only do what I can do. My mother-in-law is coming and I won't have the strength until she's gone off again."

"Is she a good witch or a bad witch?" said Edgar over his shoulder.

"Bad," I said.

Ned murmured to me, "You didn't tell me about your mother-in-law."

"I try not to think about her."

"Sorry I pushed you on the driving."

"No, I need to be pushed. I'm a natural coward."

"I don't think you're a coward," he said, very quietly so that Edgar and Ramon wouldn't hear. "I don't think you're a coward at all."

"You don't know me," I said.

"I know you well enough," he said, and then Ramon called back to us to pick up the pace,

and Ned began joking to Ramon about his driving while Edgar filled me in on all the bad things
that were about to happen to the Dow Jones
Average.

After we'd done a brisk circuit of Deering
Oaks, I spent the rest of the walk with Alex.
She'd lost weight, even in the few weeks I'd
known her. Her features were emerging, and the
waistline of her jeans was belted where it had become too loose.

"You're looking good," I told her.

"Really? I thought I saw a difference but it's
nice to hear it from someone else. Ramon says
I'd be quite striking if I took off some pounds."

"I think you're striking now," I said. "Great
hair, great skin."

"Yeah, but I want men to think I'm striking,
no offense."

"Ramon counts over me?"

"I mean, guy-guys."

"Anyone in particular?"

"There's one in my computer science course.
And Ned's a sweetheart, of course,"

"Of course."

"But he's off-limits." Her sigh was heartfelt
and innocent. In three years she wouldn't be giv-

ing herself away like this. "Too old, and the girl-friend."

"Have you ever met her?"

This was spying, completely unworthy of me.

"Once. She was visiting and she came by for him after a walking session. She's nothing special. She had short hair, but not like Barb and Vicky. Hers was expensive."

Barb and Vicky were the group's only lesbian couple. They worked for the Parks and Recreation Department and came to Happy Trails only once a week since they had a very full, outdoorsy schedule that included mountain biking and snowboarding.

"What did you think of Fiona? Personality-wise."

"Nice but kind of earnest. She kept talking about her dissertation until I was so bored I could scream. But he was fawning all over her."

"What does George do all day?" I said to change the subject. It was vaguely distasteful to picture Ned fawning over anyone.

"Makes money, mostly. He has a younger boyfriend in Hilton Head who'll come up here when the weather gets warm."

"Do you think he's lonely in winter?"

"George? No way. He's got tons of friends and he loves the cold."

Even George could handle the cold better than I could. It was truly depressing.

That day, Edgar and Ramon decided they could stop for breakfast. George and Alex came along. It was such a large group we had to split into two booths at Becky's.

I sat back and savored the smell of bacon sizzling.

"Isn't the smell of frying food the best smell in the world?" I said to the table at large.

"Heaven," said Ramon. "You cannot cook without butter and oil."

"Well, you can," said Edgar. "But who'd want to eat it?"

Ned leaned over the back of his booth, putting an arm over the wooden divider in back of Alex to do so. I saw her face: she was in the throes of a hopeless crush. How good it was not to be nineteen. At nineteen your heart really could get broken; at thirty-four it just got bashed around sometimes.

Oh hell, who was I kidding? Rory had broken my heart when I'd attained the ripe old age of twenty-nine. You can be eighty and get your heart broken, I bet. You don't grow out of it.

Ned said, "Sophie, you have a reprieve until after Thanksgiving. But then we're hitting the road."

"Aye, aye, Cap'n," I said. He turned back to his side of the table and then he nodded almost imperceptibly, twice, as if making a note in some appointment calendar inside his head. His hair, I saw, was getting so long it was beginning to hang down his neck in loose rings of curls. The curls looked shiny and soft. I wanted to touch them, as you wish to touch a baby's hair. Then I shook myself. I was fifteen years older than Alex, and married. No schoolgirl crushes for me. Ned was only being kind.

On my solitary walk home, I thought about cars. About why I'd never bought one before.

Delia and I had had no access to a car as teenagers. My father was a nervous, infrequent driver who took the bus to work in Silver Spring. He was terribly nearsighted, with poor peripheral vision, but on long trips he always drove, he and my mother keeping up the fiction that it was the man's job. My mother gave Delia and me driving lessons in her ancient station wagon until we both got our licenses, but she wasn't keen on lending us the car, not for selfish reasons but because she needed it for her good works. Delia and I biked to school or rode the public school bus—something we did only when we absolutely had to because the public school kids made fun of our uniforms.

Before we went out, my mother would always inquire if we had rides and we always said yes. Sometimes we did, sometimes we didn't. I was a good walker, and Delia had been known to hitchhike on River Road, a truly stupid risk, though not quite as risky back then. My mother had no idea of this. We also got lifts from friends from time to time, Delia more than me. Bumming rides was no embarrassment for Delia, but I quickly realized that I'd rather walk three miles at a stretch than be beholden. Teenagers keep close track of such favors and when you can't repay them, it's remembered.

Even the McLaughlin kids, as many of them as there were, had cars, clunkers fixed up by a mechanic uncle then used by every kid in turn. In fact, it was because Rory had wheels, and Delia and I didn't, that he was the one who gave me my first kiss.

Rory spotted me as I was walking home after a high school dance at St. Catherine's. I was fourteen, and had no business trudging along Goldsboro Road at ten-thirty on a Friday night. The verge there is dark and overhung with trees, and in my jeans and black T-shirt I was nearly invisible to cars. My parents would have been appalled. But they were gone to a weekend convention for a lay group that supported the ordination of women, leaving Delia in charge, with many injunctions about the house and me.

Delia thought I had a ride home from the dance because I'd told her so. She'd have wrung my neck if she knew the places I traversed after sunset.

The dance wasn't a failure. I'd been danced with three times. This was social success to my tiny circle of friends who were all gawky and yearning like me. After the dance, cars had arrived and driven off. My friends' parents offered me rides that I refused. It was peaceful walking under the dogwood trees and acacias. I was a mile from home and unafraid.

Then a car pulled over. There was a sick moment when the headlights veered toward me and I knew a fear of dangers worse than being run over. Now Delia's story of the clown van seemed only too credible. The clown van preyed on stranded young women late at night, when there was no one to hear them scream as the clowns dragged them inside, never to be seen again.

"Sophie? Sophie Quinn?"

It was Rory, debonair in a baby blue V-necked cotton pullover and khakis.

"What are you doing here?" he said.

"I got stranded after the dance," I lied, not wanting Rory to know I did this regularly. He was just enough older than me, two years, that he might think it his duty to interfere.

"Hop in."

You couldn't hop into Rory's clunky old Dodge Dart. The passenger-side front door didn't work. You had to haul open the back door and climb over into the front seat.

I did this, ungracefully.

"Are you crazy, Sophie Ann, walking by the side of the road at this hour?"

Ann was my detested middle name, but when Rory called me "Sophie Ann," I didn't mind it.

"I'm okay," I said. "I know the way."

"Did you have a good time at the dance?"

"Yes."

"Did you dance and all?"

"With three different people."

"Three different people. Impressive."

He laughed, not unkindly. Rory had always seemed to find me very funny. I cracked him up, he said. I'd liked this fact until tonight, when it occurred to me that boys did not date girls who cracked them up.

When we pulled up to my house, Delia was sitting on the low front steps with a few of her friends. The scent of pot was faintly discernible in the warm spring air. Delia would be just mellowly stoned, enough to play her Dan Fogelberg album and eat potato chips. But next door, Rory's mother was standing on the lawn.

"Oh shit," said Rory.

Mrs. McLaughlin paced over to us, watching as I climbed out the back of the car. It was borne in upon me that my T-shirt was too tight and that my gimp bracelet, a loan from Delia, was tacky and cheap. "What is she **wearing**?" said Mrs. McLaughlin's look.

"Mary Webber has been calling for you all night," said Mrs. McLaughlin to Rory.

Mary was Rory's girlfriend at the time. This was before Liz. Mary didn't attend St. Catherine's, though her family belonged to the parish. Mary went to an expensive girls' prep school downtown, run by the Ursulines. To this school Mary wore a short, knife-pleated skirt and starched pale pink and blue blouses, with a pearl choker and various cashmere cardigans. Mary's cashmere sweaters were brought back by her mother from Scotland or Bermuda vacations. The pearls had been given to Mary by a doting father on her sixteenth birthday.

"What is Sophie doing with you?" said Rory's mother.

"Gave her a ride from the dance," said Rory.

"You said you were at Rob's."

"I **was** at Rob's. I swung by the dance to say hi to a few people on my way home, and Sophie needed a ride."

"Where are your parents?" said Rory's mother to me. "How were you going to get home?"

"She could have gone with lots of people, Ma," said Rory.

"My parents are away," I said without thinking.

"And they just left the two of you? All alone?"

"They're big girls, Ma," said Rory. "Delia's seventeen." This didn't help.

"Is that pot I smell?" said his mother.

"Incense," said Rory, trying to shepherd her back to their yard.

Mrs. McLaughlin eyed me narrowly and her expression intimated, "You are not a girl who is properly supervised. I don't want you around my son."

"I can't believe your parents left you and your sister to fend for yourselves," said Mrs. McLaughlin.

"We're fine," I said, sensing that Mrs. McLaughlin did not really care if we were fine.

I remember that moment very distinctly. It was the first time an adult had felt malice toward me and I had recognized it for what it was. Where was the exuberant woman who'd welcomed us as Rory's childhood playmates? I'd have given anything to have Mrs. McLaughlin say, "If you girls need anything while your parents are away, just run over, do you hear?"

"Ma," said Rory. "Go home. I'll be in in a minute."

Delia had risen from the porch steps and was peering toward us, trying to figure out what was going on. Stoned or not, she'd be more than a match for Mrs. McLaughlin if she joined our little group, and Rory knew it.

"Mary will be up for another hour," said his mother. "Her number is by the phone."

"I know her number," said Rory.

As she left, Mrs. McLaughlin flicked me again with that censorious gaze.

"Sorry," Rory said. "She's nuts sometimes."

"Don't mention it," I said grandly. "Thank you for not squealing on me."

He leaned over and kissed me very lightly on the lips.

"You're a good sport, Sophie Ann," he said.

He wore no cologne. Rory never used any props or mannerisms, unlike most teenage boys I knew. He didn't smoke fancy English cigarettes, he didn't drive with one hand, he didn't even drink much.

He kissed me again, more lightly still. It was the best moment of my life to date.

"I bet you were the prettiest girl at the dance," he said.

He was not to kiss me again for fifteen years.

And here I was, on this snowy November morning so long after that high school dance, still fingering over my regrets as if they were treasures. If Delia had had a car to fetch me from the dance, or my parents had given other kids enough rides that I felt free to accept one in return, Rory might never have picked me up that night. I wouldn't have had those two kisses. But the kisses were only pity kisses, after all, a trade for the damage Mrs. McLaughlin had inflicted. That was the bitter part.

The next day when I'd told Delia about this incident, she'd said, "What a bitch Rory's mom's gotten to be," and promptly forgot about it.

I wish I could be like my sister. Delia's always followed Eleanor Roosevelt's dictum that no one can make you feel inferior without your own permission. I, on the other hand, am easily made miserable by the contempt of others, so I'm still angry at past cruelties, past slights. I couldn't be trusted, if the deed were in my power, not to smear Mrs. McLaughlin with honey and tie her to a tree swarming with fire ants.

For years after that night, I cherished the fantasy that someday Rory would see me for the confident, grown-up woman I was—that we'd fall in love. He'd bring me home to his mother, who'd say, "Oh Rory, this is just the girl we'd have picked for you. We thought you'd never wake up!"

When I was twenty-nine and met up with Rory again, we began by having lunch together once a week, sitting in the park near St. Matthew's or grabbing a sandwich at some cheap spot. We were chums then, not lovers yet. But over all those chummy lunches, Rory never said anything like, "Mom says hello. She thinks it's neat you're working in PR now."

Would it really have been so difficult to own a car in the city in my twenties? I'd had enough money, and you could always find parking if you didn't mind a walk. Wasn't my real reason a less logistical one? Wasn't it my stingy determination that if I could not have what other people had, I'd have nothing? Not an attractive vision of myself, but suspiciously like the truth.

I stomped uphill, turning from Danforth to where Pine Street grows prosperous and aloof, with gardens locked behind iron fences and signs warning of home security systems. As I drew closer to our apartment, I saw my little white car parked along the street, and I was filled with a rush of the great happiness given only to grown-ups who are denied the joys of their youth at the proper time, a delight sacred to late bloomers.

I hadn't had a car all those years ago, but I had a car now. I would sail in that car. I would swoop and dip and enjoy myself in a way that a girl who had been approved of by Mrs. McLaughlin never could have done.

Ned had offered his help, and maybe it was time after all these years to stop refusing what people offered. All I needed was just a few pointers, just enough to get me started. There was nothing pathetic about that. And after I got started, there was no telling where I could go.

Eleven

New Day was a block away from the Longfellow statue, just as Stephen had said. Longfellow spent much of his childhood in Portland and had later written lines, much quoted around here, about the wharves and the crying of the seagulls. Now he had a statue too far from the docks, one that the pigeons, not the seagulls, frequented.

The shop was bigger than it looked from the street, long and narrow with soaring ceilings and brick walls. It was nice and warm, almost steamily warm.

Penny, the hairdresser, wore the same kind of clothes that I'd worn to paint when I lived in a milder climate: a V-necked black cotton sweater and drawstring black cotton pants. Her dark hair was held back from her face by a wide black-elastic headband.

She sat me down at her work station and supplied me with heavily sugared coffee.

"So we're doing cut and color today?"

"Yes."

"What do you have in mind for the cut?"

"I was just hoping to look less . . . messy."

She began fluffing my hair on both sides of my head.

"Your ends need cleaning up, that's all," she said. "What about a style?"

I had nothing to contribute on this question. It had been as much as I could do to make the appointment.

Penny brought over a heavy book with laminated cardboard covers titled, **Hair Now Expo 2000**. She flipped to a section showing sulky blondes with shoulder-length side-parted hair curved sinuously against their necks.

"You would look great in this," she said.

"Okay," I said.

"You want to think about it?"

I shook my head. It was Thursday, November 16. Pepper was coming for her Thanksgiving visit in four days, and it was now or never. Pepper was hard enough to face when I was at the top of my game. I needed a boost, badly.

Penny draped me in what seemed to be a giant garbage bag.

"Normally I'd do the cut before the color, but you seemed very, very nervous about the color on the phone, so how about we get that out of the way first?"

I nodded. If my hair emerged a trendy green, I wouldn't care much what the cut was.

Penny said, "Let's lighten up your base color three or four notches. Then add some highlights, in front especially, to draw attention to your eyes."

From the pocket of my cardigan, I took out the index card on which I'd recopied Marta's instructions and handed it to her. "My friend's advice," I said.

Penny read aloud, " 'No ash tones or ashy undertones. Warm shades only but nothing too yellow. No chunky highlights and no frosting.' "

"Your friend knows her stuff," said Penny. "Don't worry. This'll be fun. First we bleach. It'll smell a little ammonia-y."

She mixed a whitish paste in a bowl then glopped it all over my head and covered the whole thing with a plastic head scarf. The odor wasn't too bad. I only wished that the front window didn't face Congress Street directly. With my luck, Natalie would speedwalk by with Paul in tow. I'd told Paul I had a hair appointment but not what I was getting done. One discouraging word from him and I'd have canceled.

He'd been discouraging in general lately: not curt but distracted, preoccupied with work and coming out of his preoccupation only to talk endlessly about work. He was only politely interested in what he called "your doings around here."

There's definitely a loss of status when you work at home rather than in an office. The money might come out the same, but if I'd dressed in pinstripes and returned at night looking visibly exhausted, Paul would have been more impressed.

"Tell me about it," Delia said when I complained. "I'd like to see Tom try to excise a mole with Ben crawling around on the floor the whole time."

"I don't know how you do it."

"Oh, I just like bitching. Tom takes Ben a lot on weekends. I could be married to a surgeon and then Ben wouldn't even recognize Tom, he'd see so little of him."

I didn't tell my sister I was getting my hair colored. Delia had always gone for a natural look, like my mother, though Delia would hate for me to say it. Mom's hairstyle had remained the same through several presidential administrations: short and practical and chin length, with bangs. The one style neither Delia nor I had ever tried.

Half an hour passed. Penny rinsed me out. My wet hair looked lighter but not drastically lighter.

"Don't look yet," Penny said. "Now the high-lights."

She took a section of hair six or seven strands wide, slapped more of the paste on it, and wrapped it in a tinfoil sheet. She did this again and again. Around us new pots of coffee were made, the mailman came and went, and the streetlights burst on outside. It was snowing but it was a pretty, fluffy snow.

With my head covered in a hundred mini-antennae of waving foil, I sat in an armchair with three fashion magazines and read them voraciously. One featured "work clothes that really work." Maybe I was out of touch with the office world, but I couldn't imagine a job that incorporated tweed miniskirts, leather pants, and suit jackets paired with bra tops. Was this stuff now the done thing? Maybe it was lucky that I didn't need business clothes, that the only new career possibility on my horizon was a "big idea" Ann said she was playing with.

"I'm just working it out, so I'm a little shy about mentioning it to you," she'd said on the phone the other day. "It's for the card line but it's a huge jump."

"Airport gift shops?" I said.

"A whole 'nother level. I'll tell you soon."

I was curious about Ann's idea. She wasn't normally reticent about her business dreams; she'd confided that she planned to start her own home-and-style magazine someday, and perhaps run a bed and breakfast. Just hearing these plans tired me out. In fact, sometimes after talking with Ann I felt sucked dry, as if I'd been donating blood to her through the telephone wires.

Penny came back and unwrapped all the foil wads. She rubbed a bit of my hair between her fingers and held it to the light.

"Perfect," she said. "We'll cut and blow dry. Then you'll see."

While Penny was snipping, I drank a third cup of coffee and gazed anywhere but at the mirror. Two chairs down, a little girl about five years old sat perfectly still, regarding herself seriously as her bangs were evened out.

"I'm very stylish," she said with conviction.

"Yes," said the hairdresser. "You **are**. A touch of hairspray?"

Across the shop, a man in a ponytail was displaying switches of synthetic hair to a customer. The customer wanted a red that was far too bright for her sallow face.

The ponytailed man said, "It's true, reds are the word this season. But we don't want to follow the crowd entirely."

The customer settled for a dark auburn. The man made a relieved face at Penny as he passed, as if to say, "That could have been ugly," and Penny nodded emphatically. The whole time her scissors were going **snip, snip, snip,** until I wondered if I had any hair left.

"Oh, this is going to be good," she said. "Trust me."

The blow-drying took fifteen minutes.

"You have lots of hair but it's fine," Penny said. "No turning the dryer up to 'pulverize' and just aiming it. You have to set it low and move it around a lot."

Finally I faced myself in the mirror. **I** was very stylish. Penny's snipping had created a perfectly graduated cut that shimmered in two lovely wide curves around my forehead and then undulated down to my shoulders.

I could face Pepper now. I could face almost anything. "You look eight years younger," Penny said. A mere tip-hungry flatterer would have said "ten years younger," but Penny was an artist.

"With this new color, you'll want to go a little darker with your brows and lashes for emphasis," said Penny. "Go to the drugstore and get some medium-brown brow fill. Maybelline makes it. And dark-brown mascara. And Corn Silk powder in translucent."

The ponytailed man came over to assess Penny's work.

"Well done," he said to Penny. "A real change for the better."

I didn't take offense. My hair seemed gilded but softly, subtly. The blue of my eyes seemed more striking. My whole countenance seemed to have woken up.

"I like it," I said to Penny. "I like it a lot."

"Your husband will love it."

Paul did not love it. He gave me one startled look and said, "What did you do?"

"I went back to being blond," I said. "I decided it was time. What do you think?"

"I'm in shock."

"You don't like it."

"I do, I do. It's just so . . . different."

I'd bought the cosmetics Penny suggested and

put them on, along with a ruddy-brown lipstick from the dollar-sale bin. I'd thought brown tones were for brunettes, but the lipstick was more flattering than any of the wimpy sheer pinks I normally used.

"You hate it."

"No, no. It's just that I hardly recognize you."

I made dinner, feeling suddenly exhausted, as if I'd been tapping for months at a door that would never open for me. Should I mind so much if Paul couldn't praise my hair? Had I expected the honeymoon to last forever?

But I'd wanted him to pick me up and spin me around and tell me I looked beautiful. Instead, we ate our roast chicken and rice and talked about Pepper's visit.

Paul said, "Let's make a list of what we need to do to get ready."

"Get a tranquilizer prescription?"

"I mean around the place. For example, we could take down the curtains and wash them."

"That's a lot of work, Paul."

The curtains were muslin sheers that I'd bought for six dollars a panel at a white sale, just to keep Donald from knowing every detail of our lives. They did look a little grimy. Donald's work on the radiator hadn't helped.

Paul said, "My mother's going to think Portland's the Third World as it is. If the place is run-down and dingy, you know how she'll carry on."

"Fine," I said. "I'll do the curtains, but as for the place being run-down, I don't think you'll fix that unless you tear it down brick-from-brick and rebuild it before she comes."

"Funny, hon. Really funny. Now, the toilet is running for seven minutes a flush. Can you speak to Donald about it?"

"Fine."

"And the window catch in our bedroom's a little loose. Can you . . ."

"No, Paul. I am not bothering Donald about the window catch."

"He's your friend now. He'd probably jump to do it for you."

"I can jump up right now and do it myself with a Phillips screwdriver."

"**I'll** do it," said Paul, his manhood challenged.

He began to grumble.

"Strange how you have spare time to drive all over town but you don't have time to spruce the place up for my mother, who's coming all the way from Virginia."

Actually, I'd only had the courage to register

the car—a surprisingly easy process here in Maine, where DMV personnel were actually polite—and to drive it twice to the Shaw's grocery across the bridge. Meanwhile, his Explorer had arrived, massive and unwieldy. Donald had immediately complained about the room it commandeered in the garage. Riding in it, I felt cruel and unstoppable, like a German soldier after the fall of France driving a tank through the Arc de Triomphe. If it influenced me this way as a passenger, I was worried about the effect it would have on Paul's character.

"And I guess it's no use asking you to wash the sheets," Paul said mournfully.

"Paul! As if I weren't planning to wash the sheets."

"Well, you're seeming very rushed lately."

"I have three paintings to get to Ann by December 10. I have two large proofing jobs and two huge, detail-heavy layouts to get done by Christmas."

"I'll clean the bathroom then," said Paul in martyred tones.

"You hate doing the bathroom. I'll clean the bathroom. You do the kitchen. The broiler rack probably won't pass inspection the way it is now."

"My mother doesn't inspect."

"She does so. She does everything but wear white gloves to check for dust."

"Natalie said today she was looking forward to meeting my mother because my mother clearly knows a ton about running a house and she could learn a lot from her. Maybe you could try that approach. Flatter her."

"Natalie is a suck-up," I said.

"She admits that. She said it's her main fault, not being assertive and frank with people, just trying to make them feel good."

I hadn't noticed this fault in Natalie's dealings with me.

"Paul, I could learn something from your mother too, if Pepper didn't keep assuming that every stray dustball is my sole responsibility."

"It's how she worked her marriage. It was a division of labor. My father never thought less of her for that. For them it was a success."

"Pepper could move with the times a little. She praises your job and acts as if mine were a hobby. Then she picks at the housekeeping as if that's all I have to do."

"Honey, stand up to her a little. And don't say I should first because she's got me in the mother-guilt death grip. She can't use that on you."

He put his arm around me.

"It's five days and then she's gone. Okay?"

"Okay."

Lasting marriages are built on negotiating. The book I'd bought said so. Every still-married person I knew said so. Why did it seem as if I had lost yet another round to Pepper? When her visit was over, I would have the same feeling I always had after seeing her. That the scoreboard, which had been ticking overtime since we had last met, now read something like, Pepper Stoddard: one billion. Daughter-in-law: zero.

We watched a little post-election coverage until Paul said he was tired of it and went to bed. I wasn't tired of the coverage. It had been a thrill to vote in Maine, where my vote counted more than in D.C., even if Portland lacked the fevered approach to the controversy you'd see in Washington. The Gore campaign office was already closed. I'd strolled by there the day after the election and saw only a pimply advance kid toting out a last box of bumper stickers.

"That new cut is really growing on me," Paul said before he went into the bathroom to floss his teeth.

The compliment had come. Three weeks ago, I'd have kissed him for it. Only, there was a weird, deflecting impersonality in his voice, the momentary approbation of a man glancing at a car or a suit that takes his eye but which he has no intention of buying.

Paranoia. Didn't they say that was one of the dangers of a cold climate? I had seen **The Shining.** Snow could make you crazy.

Paul added, "It's just that I didn't picture you as a blond-blonde, somehow."

"Penny can take it down a shade if I want," I said.

"Why spend the money? You look fine. Really. I'm already getting used to it."

I struggled into my silk underwear and then into my favorite flannel pajamas printed all over with blue skies and fluffy clouds. I circled through the apartment, turning out lights, checking the stove twice as my nervous father had taught me. When I came back to the bedroom Paul was asleep. He's tired, I said to myself. He works hard. All marriages have their moments as Delia said. This was no more than one of those moments.

One of those moments, which I then lay awake worrying about for two hours.

The next morning, the group praised my hair. Edgar gave a mock wolf whistle. Ramon pronounced it "a flying success." Alex asked me where I'd gone and said she might splurge.

Stephen, who came by for breakfast, said, "I told you it would work." Ned looked at me for a long minute and said only, "Nice change," but his look was serious and approving.

Afterward, I sat in the kitchen with my coffee and pondered. Truly Paul was no more remote than he'd ever been. He'd always been slow to offer the spontaneous embrace, the unasked-for reassurance. I should have said, "Paul, just say you like it." Perhaps he needed a map to guide him until we were married longer. Too bad that these days, we didn't seem as interested as we'd once been in each other's guide maps.

Maybe I was the one drifting in strange waters. Lately I felt that there was no predicting what I might do next. Clearly I had embarked on something, but what?

The poet Swinburne said that spring begins "blossom by blossom." Something was beginning again in me that had been lost during that sad summer when I loved Rory and he left me. There was a change coming, a shift like the shift in a March wind, from biting cold to that spring-presaging hint of southerly breezes.

Getting dressed to go to my haircutting appointment the day before, I'd noticed that despite all those breakfasts at Becky's, my clothes were loose on me. Walking, I'd seemed to cover the length of Pine Street much faster than before, the road smoothly unreeling under my feet. It was cold enough that I had to pull my scarf over my mouth, but I did not slow my pace. I had gone from a person afraid to walk anywhere except out of absolute necessity, to a person who could walk some distance. Not a great distance, not an impressive distance, and yet—some distance.

I picked up the phone and called Paul at his office. I don't know what I wanted to ask him for: a revised estimate of my hair, a pleasant, husbandly word? I wanted to give him a chance to say the right thing, but I couldn't have said what the right thing was.

Natalie answered, as she always did. Either the office secretary never beat her to the phone, or Natalie was superalert in some psychic way to telephone calls for Paul.

I identified myself.

"How are you, Natalie?"

"I'm terrific. We're a little hectic around here at the moment but I'm terrific."

The implication being, why was I bothering them in their important work?

"And how are **you**?" she said, in a conscientious chirp.

I knew from Paul that Natalie felt personal phone calls at the office should be strictly limited to essential information, such as ringing to inform one's husband that the living-room roof had caved in or that the biopsy came back positive. Paul, who used to call me twice an afternoon from work for small chats and check-ins, now phoned me only at the end of the day to inform me of when he'd be home.

"I'm a little rushed too, actually. Can I speak to Paul?"

"He's around here somewhere," she said. "I don't know exactly where."

"Can you have someone find him, please?"

I willed myself to imitate Pepper, whose peremptory manner on the phone was legend in her family. Pepper got through to airlines, doctors, and health insurance companies on the first try. What made it work, said Paul's brother James, was Pepper's air of expecting to be helped, versus the supplicating tone the rest of us used.

"Honest, Sophie, it's just a zoo. A message might be a better idea."

She could not have been more pleasant.

"I'll hold," I said, equally pleasant.

After a two-minute pause designed to show me how I'd inconvenienced not only Natalie, but the entire hardworking staff of The Science Project, Natalie came back on.

"I'm sorry, Sophie. I just can't seem to locate him."

I'd bet that on a typical day Natalie hovered two feet from Paul with papers requiring his signature or the office lunch order waiting only for his menu choice. Now she said he couldn't be found.

Why couldn't Paul have said he'd be proud to be seen with me and my new hair? Or, "I'm so lucky that you're willing to put up with my mother at Thanksgiving, even though she does nothing but criticize you to your face."

"Shall I leave a message?" said Natalie.

"No," I said. "It can keep till he gets home."

And longer than that, I thought.

Twelve

After my talk with Natalie, and nontalk with Paul, I toiled for hours on a layout for a poster depicting major childhood health emergencies and the proper steps to take for each, from choking to hives to concussion. The poster would be a Christmas freebie from the Child Safety Division of the National Parents' Alliance: Happy Holidays, and here's a few facts about anaphylactic shock. How grim.

I'd tried to add a little visual interest by blocking off each health emergency in a different-colored square, but the project depressed me. It made me want to call Delia and warn her about every possible harm that could come to Ben. Since he'd come along I saw how vulnerable children were. You want to protect them from everything, and all you can protect them from is mostly everything, and that's not enough.

I finished my work then did what I'd wanted to do all afternoon. I opened my e-mail and reread the two short messages I'd received from Rory. **"You're a lot of trouble, Sophie Ann,"** he'd written four days earlier. **"I had to call**

your mother for your e-mail address. Drop a line if you get a chance. Old friends shouldn't lose touch."

Old friends. Hadn't that always been the problem? Rory and I were old friends who'd been lovers, and after you do that you can't get back to where you were. The connection runs deep but it's changed; like the stroke of midnight, love and sex change everything. Even Rory with his casual charm couldn't accomplish a return to our innocent days. Besides, in the letter Delia had read me, he'd said he missed my beautiful eyes. Friends didn't talk like that.

I didn't answer that first e-mail. Yesterday another one had come with a photo attached of Rory standing in front of a fairy-tale edifice with onion domes. He looked just as he always had. He was wearing a silly cap with blue and yellow stripes almost the same color as the stripes on the domes behind him. He was laughing into the camera and a lock of his hair shone bright under the cap. Liz had probably taken the picture.

This e-mail said:

"This is St. Basil's Cathedral in Moscow, in Red Square. It's even more unreal when you're standing right next to it. Your mother said you'd moved to Maine. Why? As I recall, you

used to get cold in the middle of July. Love, Rory."

It was true, I used to get cold all the time. I felt suddenly, horribly homesick, homesick for one of those hot summer days when our canoe cut through the green-brown water of the Potomac and you could smell warm earth and grass, a smell that never occurs anyplace by a cold sea.

Rory had made me homesick with a few lines on a computer, but he himself had always called D.C. a swamp and a mudhole. He'd been eager to leave. Rory was born to collect places and people, to encircle the world and let it flash by him at a heady speed.

But I was instantly longing for home. Paul and I had agreed to take our long trip south at Christmas, since Paul had only Thanksgiving Day off. Now I felt I'd give anything to sit at Delia and Tom's Thanksgiving dinner table and have my mother pass me her specialty: mashed canned yams covered with melted miniature marshmallows.

Reading Rory's letters, I wanted to be home, and twenty-nine, and seeing him, and warm. Warm all through. Every change in the weather here was just a variation in hardship: snow, sleet, ice, sunny days accompanied by ten-degree cold and gusty winds. Donald came by and added a thin line of rubber insulation to each window frame but it didn't help. And Pepper, easily chilled at the best of times—it was one of the few traits she had in common with me—Pepper would complain.

The house was ready for her arrival on Monday, down to the two pink hand towels in the bathroom (which Pepper would not know were our only hand towels) and the sparkling shelves of our refrigerator, with the egg holders and the inside of the butter compartment wiped clean. There was nothing to do but sit home and watch Rory's e-mail glow on the screen. I shut down my computer, laced up my walking shoes, and took off.

It was almost five P.M. Paul wouldn't be back until seven. I headed down Pine then down Congress to the Portland Museum of Art.

The museum was free on Friday evenings after five. But Paul, understandably, was never in a museum-going mood on Friday nights, and I had a yen to see the N. C. Wyeth exhibit for the third time. N. C., a painter and illustrator who was a master of New England light, was less bleak and more to my taste than the younger Wyeths.

The museum would chase away my blues. The flat brick façade and sterile white entrance hall were too bland, but further inside it was a peaceful place with dim, deserted upstairs galleries and a windowed stairway that looked out onto an old garden.

The Wyeth show was a little crowded, but not so crowded that you couldn't stand before a painting for a full three minutes before any other viewer edged in next to you. Unlike museum goers in Washington and New York, people in Portland didn't bump you or step between you and the painting. And the museum guards didn't look ready to slap you in handcuffs if you moved within three feet of a canvas.

Some of the Wyeth paintings on display I'd seen in books, but reproductions didn't capture the light in these paintings, the graceful accuracy of his draftsmanship, the mouth-watering perfection of his palettes. My favorite picture was one of a lobster boat in fog, a study of light on mist-shrouded ocean, hills, boat, and fisherman figure.

The lighting in the exhibit was mellow and golden, and focused fully on the paintings, leaving the viewers in shadow. I didn't see Ned and an unknown young woman coming toward me until it was too late to duck and run—as I would have if I'd been forewarned. Ned was my friend, but his companion was intimidatingly poised.

"Sophie," Ned said. "This is Fiona."

We shook hands.

"Are you up for the weekend?" I said to her.

"Only until tomorrow," she said. She had a low voice, a pleasing husky alto at odds with her serious, under-made-up face and rather intent gray-green eyes.

"Fiona has an important cocktail party at her professor's house tomorrow night," Ned explained.

"It's not a cocktail party, it's just a few people in for drinks. Cocktail party," she said, turning to me with mock disgust. "Where does he get these geezer expressions?"

Ned put his arm around her, affectionately.

"Apparently no one says 'cocktail party' anymore, Sophie."

"It's too bad, isn't it," I said. " 'Drinks' doesn't sound half as festive."

"It's more a work thing than a party thing," said Fiona.

She was about twenty-seven, I guessed. As

Alex had said, she was attractive. But her presentation seemed too severe for such a young woman: the black-framed glasses, the lack of powder on a complexion that only wanted the shine off it to be lovely, the bobbed chestnut-brown hair (it must have grown since Alex saw her), parted in the middle of a high forehead. Her look was that of a woman who operates in an environment of exalted academic types, her clothes the sartorial equivalent of a Mensa membership card.

They seemed to have checked their coats so it was easy to see that Fiona was slight and that her long black wool skirt and peasanty embroidered black cardigan were a little too big for her. Her necklace, faux-African, consisted of outsized blue and orange beads and was too heavy for her small features. The greenish eyes and white skin would have been better served by a sage-green cashmere pullover rather than the matte black of the peasant cardigan. Her cordovan-leather shoulder bag and her square-heeled lace-up shoes were deliberately dowdy, and very expensive. (Stephen, grousing about her later, said to me, "I always want to tell Fiona that everyone in the Bloomsbury group is dead, so cut the fashion-as-anti-fashion stuff.")

The shoulder bag appeared heavy. I wondered for a minute why all women under thirty these days carried bags that were so large, and what they could be carrying. Gym clothes? Some new kind of small computer? Surely Fiona wouldn't need gym clothes or a computer for one Friday night stay in Portland? Then again, maybe she would. Maybe she sweated on a treadmill at some local gym or toiled late into the night on her dissertation while Ned lay wakeful and desirous.

The image startled me; Ned in his boxers among tumbled-up sheets. I knew somehow that he'd wear boxers.

"It's warm in here," I said. "Isn't it?"

"It's never warm anywhere in this town," said Fiona. For the first time, I had an urge to defend Portland.

"Have you visited often?" I said.

"When I can't talk Ned into coming to Boston," she answered with a smile that acknowledged that she was being unfair. The smile did a lot for her, cracked the icy façade.

"What do you think of the paintings?" Ned asked me.

"Beautiful," I said.

"They're your kind of thing, aren't they?"

I saw that his beard had been closely trimmed, and his hair was brushed away from his forehead as if Fiona had combed it in the car. That was nice, someone giving a damn how Ned looked.

"You did mention the Wyeth exhibit at walking one morning," he said. "I forgot. We just came to see the museum in general."

"Is there much more than this?" said Fiona.

"A few floors above this one, according to Stephen," Ned answered.

"Let's try those," she said.

"Don't you like the show?" I asked her.

"It's a little old-fashioned for my taste."

I felt a little old-fashioned in comparison to Fiona. Her ruthlessly edited outfit seemed to rebuke my blue parka and sneakers and bulky knit scarf.

"Do you really think so?" I said. "It seems very fresh to me."

"I'm not that keen on representational stuff," said Fiona. "I like abstract pieces and work that's created on site."

Ned said, with a grin in my direction, "Yeah, like that thing you took me to at that gallery on Boylston Street, where the artist was building piles of sticks and Legos and dead leaves and soda cans, right in front of us."

"Constructions," said Fiona. "I'm not saying it was high art, I'm saying it was interesting. Unlike that Sister Wendy show that your brother watches, for example."

I liked Sister Wendy. I liked that she hadn't gotten her teeth crowned even though she was a minor television star, I liked the way she strode along with the wind whipping her habit and veil back from her skinny black legs, and I liked her fresh take on masterpieces. Her lecture on **The Arnolfini Marriage** had been a revelation to me. She'd spoken of the subtle but visible tenderness of the man in that painting toward his new wife, something I'd missed, fooled by the picture's surface formality.

"Are you going right home?" said Ned. "We could get some coffee downstairs. I don't think that there's anything upstairs that Fiona would really want to see."

"Come with us," said Fiona. If she was a serious girl, she was also rather kind. She and Ned were clearly enjoying some precious time alone, and yet she was including me in their outing.

I followed them, unable to think of a polite spur-of-the-moment refusal. This was Scrooge-like of me. But witnessing young love is no tonic when you're blue.

The museum had an informal little coffee bar in the basement, with tables wedged in among display cases of porcelain. As we three waited at the counter, Fiona said, "I just think it's so cute that Ned does this walking society. He's not much of a joiner."

"Neither am I, but it's not much of a joiners' group, that's the beauty of it," I said. "But he does a good job. He holds things together."

"I'm glad he has a hobby here, but I wish he'd hurry up on this house. He's been gone too long as it is."

"It's a living," said Ned.

"There are plenty of houses in Boston."

"More competition too," said Ned.

I wished Fiona would shut up. I didn't want Ned and Stephen to go back to Boston. Would the group even survive without Ned's reliable, calming presence, without Stephen's bossy directing in the background?

"Where's your husband tonight?" said Ned when we were sitting down. Fiona had a nasty-looking espresso, Ned had plain coffee, and I was drinking Earl Grey, which I don't like but which wouldn't give me bad breath in front of Fiona.

"Working late."

"What does he do?" said Fiona.

They were holding hands on the table, fingers intertwined. I tried to remember when Paul and I had held hands in public that way, not wanting to let go even to eat or drink, but I couldn't. Paul had never been big on public displays of affection, though in the beginning he'd grab my hand at the movies after the lights went down. Nowadays when we went to a movie, he fell into a deep absorption, touching me only to ask for the popcorn to be passed.

"He raises money for science education."

"That's good of him," Fiona said. "God knows the American public school system needs all the help it can get in the sciences."

"Fiona's getting her master's at the Boston University School of Education Policy, Planning and Administration," said Ned, as if he'd carefully memorized it. "Mostly she seems to learn about how no one can agree on why children can't read by eighth grade."

Fiona gulped at her coffee in the way of a deprived smoker. She'd brought out a cigarette when we'd sat down and put it away after a stern gesture from the cashier.

"I have to quit," she said self-consciously to me now, as she put the cigarette pack in her enormous purse.

"Habits are hard to break. I would eat sugar for every meal if my husband didn't come home for dinner," I said.

It's never nice to make a smoker feel guilty. I knew it was only luck that made me a sucrose lover instead of a Marlboro addict.

"So," I said. "You're in education. What drew you to that?"

"Ned jokes but I think education is the most important issue facing our country," she said.

"I don't joke," said Ned. "The eggheads you hang out with take the subject a little seriously, that's all."

"It is serious. American children are falling fatally behind. Think about it. **A Nation at Risk** came out in 1990, and nothing's really changed."

"It was some big fancy report," said Ned, seeing that I was puzzled. "One of those 'Why Johnny Can't Read' things."

"I don't know much about public education," I said. "I went to Catholic school. They taught us well but we had too much homework."

Fiona shook her head at such light-mindedness. "Homework is essential," she said. "Japanese children do something like eight hours of homework a day."

"Japanese children must not have much fun," said Ned.

"Or take the Scandinavian countries. We've been trailing Finland in math proficiency for twenty years."

"Finland is dark all the time. The kids there have more time for homework," said Ned. "What else are they going to do, ice skate in the dark?"

"Fine, laugh," said Fiona. "But you always bitch and moan about conservatives. You should remember that a country of illiterates is far more likely to go right-wing, and then where will you yellow-dog Democrats be?"

She said to me, "I'm Green Party myself."

"The anti-political political party," I said, and was sorry when she looked hurt. Her sincerity made her seem even younger than she was. She seemed far more trusting and hopeful, somehow, than a woman of her age would be in Washington.

"Everyone blames us for this election, for Gore not doing better," she said defensively. "But we raised some important issues."

"And made sure that the Bush administration will be the ones dealing with them, most likely," said Ned. "Much good that'll do you."

"Someone has to challenge the two-party system," said Fiona.

"Couldn't you guys have picked another time to do it?"

"What does it matter?" said Fiona. "The system's bankrupt anyway."

They were both smiling, going over their lines in a debate that had played out this way before.

"Well, with Bush in, watch out for vouchers," said Ned. "Then your public-education experts at the university will all be studying a mass exodus to Catholic schools. Who knows, maybe a few nuns would be the answer."

"Catholic schools aren't really that excellent," said Fiona. "Not when you correct for factors such as mothers' educational level and family economic status."

"At least in Catholic schools you learn English and grammar and some history," Ned protested. "You learn the old basics."

"No one teaches diagramming sentences anymore," I said sadly.

This was the kind of stupid, distracted remark I frequently made in conversation with very educated people, and a large reason why many of Marta's Capitol Hill friends assumed I was some kind of mentally challenged cousin on whom Marta took pity.

Fiona said kindly, "At least you have ideas, Sophie. Ned here couldn't care less."

"I don't have children," said Ned.

"You might someday," Fiona said. "And how about our economy? Do we want a bunch of dolts running the country when we're old?"

"There are good odds that a bunch of dolts will be running the country come January," said Ned. "Thanks to Florida and to your spoiler, Mr. Nader."

She downed the dregs of her espresso and made a face at him. Then she hunted in her wallet, which was tooled leather like her bag but clunkier, as if a child had made it at summer camp.

"One more," she said. "I'll do caffeine if I can't do nicotine."

I didn't think I could last through more handholding, or another round of political discussion in which I was forced to restrain myself out of politeness to a new acquaintance. Fiona's earnestness got on my nerves. I felt itchy and restless. My sweater was beginning to prickle on my neck, and there was a draft down here that was penetrating my socks and chilling my ankles.

"I should get back," I said, after Fiona had headed for the counter. "Paul gets home in half an hour and there's a chicken pot pie to put in the oven."

"Did she overwhelm you with her education talk?" said Ned.

"No, no," I said.

"She's wanted to meet you. I told her about you. She was curious to hear how you were surviving up here."

"A sophisticated woman like myself?" I said, gesturing at my parka.

"You always talk as if you're ashamed of yourself for getting cold," said Ned. "Why **not** wear that on a night like this?"

"Because it's hideous."

"It's practical. No one's watching."

"Then why are you all dressed up in that nice sweater?"

"A gift," he said, glancing toward Fiona.

"You look nice," I said.

"I'll be back in my real clothes on Monday."

He was wearing a thin black merino pullover, and it didn't smell like wood smoke from the chimney on the Eastern Prom house, like all his other sweaters did. This sweater and the neatly trimmed beard brought home to me that there was another Ned, a Boston Ned who wasn't just my buddy but someone who attended avant-garde art occasions with his trendy girlfriend, someone who wore paint-spattered jeans to walking group but more important clothes with his grown-up friends.

"They don't have any more espresso," said Fiona, returning. "Can you believe that?"

"Sophie's going. She has a pot pie to heat up at home," said Ned to her, a bit confusingly. She just nodded, swinging their clasped hands a little between them, smiling at him with a fond, private smile, as if I'd already gone. People in love were like that.

We parted at the entrance to the museum, after Ned and Fiona had retrieved their coats. Ned, I noticed, had on a charcoal wool overcoat much nicer than the duffel he normally wore. Fiona had a complicated violet cashmere wrap— again, too harsh a color for her delicate skin and her chestnut hair.

"I have to twine it around my body like a shroud," she joked as she put it on. No wonder she thought Portland was cold if all she wore was an outsized baby blanket.

"Well then," I said as a halfhearted leave-taking.

"I hope I see you again, Sophie," she said cordially.

"Sure," I said. "Maybe I can bring Paul sometime and we can all have dinner somewhere."

Ned was buttoning his coat and didn't seem to hear, for he didn't take me up on this suggestion.

"That would be nice," said Fiona. "His work sounds very interesting."

I was Paul's wife so I was required to find his work interesting. It depressed me that in this world there were two such different women as Natalie and Fiona who found it positively compelling. It was just more evidence that Paul could do better than me if he were single.

"So another time," I said, and walked away before I could say more. I was worried that I'd sound too eager to make a dinner date with them, too desperate for company. I didn't even want Fiona's company, not really. She didn't seem like she'd be much fun.

Yet it might be good for me to make a different sort of woman friend. I pictured Fiona and me in a lecture hall at MIT or somewhere highly pedagogical, taking in a physicists' debate on recent theories of time travel. Afterward, as we sampled a clever little red merlot in some fashionable post-grad dive, she would lean across the table and say, "I **should** confess, Sophie, that when I first met you, you seemed a bit of a lightweight, but you're so compelling on the subject of Minoan frieze iconography that I can't believe I ever thought it of you." Then we would both laugh muted, intellectual laughs and order tapas.

No, I couldn't see it.

I sneaked a quick backward glance at them. He had his arm around her, and she was laughing, brushing a lock of black hair from his forehead.

My mouth felt sour all the way home. This was what I'd turned into, a bitter, bitchy woman in a troubled marriage who resented the happiness of a pair of young lovers. If Fiona was a little intense and humorless, if it was hard to see what drew Ned to her, it wasn't my affair.

It was being a third wheel, I concluded when I got home. It would spoil any disposition. I made a pot of tea—regular tea, not perfumey Earl Grey—and watched the last half-hour of **The Lady Vanishes,** which was showing on some local syndicated channel. There is a scene in the movie where Margaret Lockwood, in terrible trouble, casts an intimate, quizzical glance at Eric Redgrave, a glance that says, "Well, we're in a mess here, but I'd rather be in a mess with

you than out drinking champagne with some-
body else."

For some reason this scene brought tears to
my eyes. It never had before, and I'd seen this
movie eight times. Winter blues, I told myself,
and dashed out to Shaw's for a really nice
Chardonnay to go with the chicken pot pie. On
impulse, I also picked up a bouquet of
discouraged-looking carnations.

Paul noticed the wine and the flowers.

"This is cheerful," he said, and gave me one of
his brief, approving hugs.

He even did the dishes. We had a calm, homey,
companionable evening, and I forgot Fiona and
her enviable self-assurance and the way she and
Ned held hands. Even Rory's e-mails kept to the
back of my mind, where they belonged. I was
done with letting Rory's memory spoil things for
me. At least, I was trying to be done with that.

Holidays

Thirteen

I sat on the toilet lid in a rest room stall at Bedrooms and More, an outlet store in Kittery. One of the many qualities that Pepper finds annoying about me is that, an hour into a shopping expedition, I'm looking for a bathroom. This doesn't happen normally, but with Pepper, it's as if my body is searching for a way to get me five minutes of solitude.

The ladies' room in Bedrooms and More had stalls with louvered doors going all the way to the ground and potpourri jars on the back of each toilet tank. Renaissance madrigals were being piped in. It was all very soothing.

Pepper's visit had not gone very well so far.

"What have you done to your hair, Sophie?" were her first words when Paul and I met her at the gate in Manchester. "Everyone I know is going blond these days, but I thought you were immune."

Pepper's own hair was a helped-along wheaten shade from a special color line provided exclusively to hairdressers of WASP matrons over fifty

in the conservative shopping enclaves of Potomac Village, Maryland.

"Let me see you," she said, holding me at
arm's length.

She was wearing a hunter-green cardigan and
a long, straight black-watch-plaid skirt with
loafers. I could see immediately that she didn't
approve of my leather-and-turquoise necklace,
slate-blue fleece pullover, and narrow black
cords.

"You're certainly going for a different look,
aren't you," she said, following up that remark
with a peculiar commentary noise she had,
rather like a distant airplane engine approaching
a landing pad: "Uhhmmmnnnng."

"I love Sophie's new hair," said Paul, taking
Pepper's monogrammed briefcase.

If Paul hadn't come through with hair compliments until now, he'd certainly done his part to
prepare the apartment for his mother's visit, not
griping even when we discovered that the rose-
colored fungus under the bathroom sink was
growing at a slow, inexorable rate, undeterred by
cleaning products. Donald came to view it, but
seemed more interested in it as a matter of sci-
entific inquiry than as a problem to be solved.

"Careful," Pepper said. "That briefcase contains every detail of every event that Comfort Foods is catering for the next week."

It had been five years, Pepper had reminded us when making her travel arrangements, since she'd left the business to struggle through a holiday without her. Pepper's second-in-command, the downtrodden and loyal Frances, was quite competent to carry on in her absence, but Pepper felt ruin loomed without her personal supervision.

On the way home, Pepper complained about the flight (turbulence), the flight crew (delayed beverage service for which the turbulence was no excuse), and the baggage porter who had checked her luggage at the curb at BWI (careless, Pepper claimed).

"I said to him, don't throw those around like that, there are gifts for my son in there, and he just ignored me."

She'd traveled with three large suitcases, none of which wheeled. On the drive home, she perched in front with Paul, cuddled in the army blanket he'd brought for her, chattering of business and family, asking Paul questions she didn't leave him time to answer. From the backseat, I could see Paul's hands clenched on the wheel.

Pepper declared that our apartment had "possibilities." She was in raptures over the linen cabinet.

"You know, Sophie, this could be a real showpiece. You could stack all your pastel sheets in one stack and tie them with a pink satin ribbon, all your white sheets with a blue ribbon, et cetera. Trim the shelf edges with eyelet and you'd have quite an appealing effect."

That was the difference between Pepper and me. She could derive pleasure from a beribboned linen cabinet that only she would regularly behold. There was a sort of nobility in this, but I wished that, just once, Pepper would show an interest in me that didn't involve burnishing my domestic skills.

Natalie had pulled up bright and early this morning for our day of post-Thanksgiving shopping at the outlets. Her Explorer was identical to the one Paul owned. Pepper commented, "It **is** a treat to sit up so high for a change, not that there's anything wrong with Sophie's little Escort."

The bathroom at Bedrooms and More was much warmer and less opulent than the rest of the store. It was a relief to be away from the displays of coordinated merchandise. These displays made it clear that the truly dedicated homemaker matched her comforter to her pillow shams to her washcloths to her bedskirt to her toothbrush holder. I had left Pepper and Natalie in a section devoted entirely to wastebaskets.

The toilet seat lid, unlike the one Donald had installed in our apartment, remained sturdily in place. Fully clothed, deliciously warm, I fished a Baby Ruth out of my purse. I'd taken to hiding candy in various locations. Paul never reproached me for my sugary diet, but I felt compelled to conceal how large a portion of my daily caloric intake consisted of chocolate. So there were Russell Stovers shoved in the top kitchen cabinets, which Paul never explored, and malted milk balls in the tea canister, since only I drank tea. And, most shaming of all, Hershey Kisses rolled up inside my socks to be gobbled eight at a time. I knew that I shouldn't use food to "medicate" my feelings, but in the face of the onslaught that was my mother-in-law's visit, it seemed preferable to Valium or gin.

I'd driven Pepper all over Portland. We'd visited the headlight, where she snapped several pictures of the famous lighthouse and immediately got back in the car, saying that the wind was far too cold to walk the cliff path. We'd wandered through the art museum, which Pepper endorsed as "having a nice little collection for an institution this size." We'd toured the Center for Maine History and the grim little Longfellow House. Pepper believed that if you were visiting a place, you bought a guidebook and ticked off the sights as you covered them. She enjoyed the period furnishings at the Tate mansion but complained because the gardens were over for the year.

"Why, at home we still have roses blooming," she informed the guide.

At night Paul cooked or took her out, while I caught up with the work I'd missed during the day. Pepper objected to this, but Paul remained firm.

"Then clearly Sophie works too **hard**," I heard her say. "Why, today we were lost on Forest Ave. and we were only two miles from this apartment! Does she get out at all?"

Over and over again, I could feel the "mentally defective" expression spread across my face, as I explained to Pepper why we did not yet possess a blender, or why I didn't know where a gourmet grocery was, or why I hadn't purchased the special brand of thermal underwear she'd recommended.

Thanksgiving was a dreary holiday. Pepper

wanted to cook a big dinner for the three of us. Paul resisted the idea of her "slaving in the kitchen" on her vacation.

"Perhaps I could just supervise Sophie while she cooks," Pepper had suggested.

"No," said Paul. "I have a surprise. I made reservations at the Wharf Street Tavern."

The Wharf Street Tavern was known for its offbeat chic and superb seafood. It had been written up in the **New York Times** and **Gourmet** magazine. Paul must have really wangled to snag reservations for an early dinner. The trouble was that fish was not Pepper's idea of Thanksgiving fare, and the only fowl offered was duck in apricot sauce.

"Do they even know it's Thanksgiving?" Pepper had complained.

She settled for broiled trout, mashed potatoes in wild mushroom gravy, and butternut squash. I'd have enjoyed my sole in sherry sauce and Paul his grilled salmon if Pepper hadn't been so patently unhappy. Again and again I saw her glance going to the garnet-and-filigree ring and bracelet I wore, a Stoddard family heirloom she'd reluctantly ceded to Paul upon our marriage. The set didn't really suit me: the silver was tarnished and gray, and garnets weren't a good stone for a blonde. They'd be better on a sparkling brunette like Natalie. But it pleased Paul to see me wear them sometimes.

"A polishing cloth will bring those right back," Pepper said accusingly.

"We should have just let her teach me to cook," I whispered that night to Paul as we lay on our borrowed air mattress.

"No way in hell was I putting you through that. Or me either. You know what a devil she is on holidays. We'd have been in that kitchen for eighteen hours."

"Maybe she missed your father," I said.

"She never seemed to notice him much this time of year. She was too busy."

Paul was suffering under Pepper's scrutiny. She had "popped by" his office and asked detailed questions about his operational plans. She'd taken him shopping one night for Italian shoes that cost him a fortune and pinched his feet because she felt his office footwear wasn't "executive enough." She had complained extensively about the neglect of James and Ellen, who traveled far too much yet did not have one night a week free for dinner so that she could get to know her grandchildren while there was still time.

"Are you sick?" Paul had asked, alarmed.

"No, but at my age you never know."

Pepper was fifty-eight, good for twenty more years. She wasn't the sort who succumbed early to cancer or heart attacks—she was the sort who caused them in those around her. The Peppers of this world would always be the last ones standing.

She hectored Paul, but me she treated with a brisk, domineering politeness that strung my nerves tighter than piano wire. If her spine had sagged once, if her energy had ever flagged, I could have dropped my pose of cheerful attentiveness, and perhaps we could have had one sincere conversation out of all the blather of that week. But it was impossible to penetrate Pepper's buzz of activity.

"I want to **do** while I'm here, not sit," she would say, when I suggested we take a break from our activities for a quiet cup of coffee.

When Paul brought out Ann's greeting cards, Pepper inspected them briefly and said, "Well. You married quite a creative woman, Paul," in tones that implied creativity was a secret vice, like tippling from the liquor cabinet. Pepper had been unimpressed by the news that Life Markings was now in every major card and gift store in the Harrisburg and Philadelphia areas. Later that evening she slopped coffee on a new card sample Ann had titled, **"A family grows in a day . . . Your adopted baby is finally arriving."**

Through it all I continued to get up in the mornings and stagger out to my Happy Trails meetings, though breakfast with the gang was out of the question. Left to herself for too long, Pepper might very well have pressured Donald into building a kitchen addition by the time I returned home. He was already avoiding her after a conversation in which she'd related a terrible mauling of a ten-year-old by German shepherds in Falls Church, Virginia, and asked him who'd trained his dogs for him.

I was crumpling my Baby Ruth wrapper into a flushable ball when the rest room door opened. Damn. I hoped whoever it was would do her business and leave fast. I'd just begun to get comfortable.

"And the thing I've tried to get through to her"—Pepper was speaking—"is that you have to be a doer. When I lost my husband, it would have been easy for me to shut myself up in my house, but I knew that would be bad, for me and for my children."

Paul had been twenty-eight when Mr. Stoddard died, James twenty-nine.

"You're very brave," said Natalie. "It can't have been easy, left alone so young."

"No, it wasn't easy," said Pepper. "But we had many good years."

Her main preoccupation at the after-funeral reception, according to Paul, had been ensuring that the caterers kept replenishing the crab dip. Of course, that was no real measure of her sorrow. Pepper would have to be dead herself not to fret about the appetizers.

"I hate to think how **Sophie** would manage if she were alone," Pepper continued. "She can be a little . . . passive."

"To give her credit, she's been taking more initiative lately," came Natalie's soprano. "That walking group is a good start. Up here, winters are so long that if you're not moving around a lot you could get very depressed. Especially in the case of someone sensitive."

"I could see that," said my mother-in-law in a prissed-up voice that indicated she was putting on lipstick. "Sophie isn't the most upbeat person at best. Now, clearly **you** take exercise seriously. You're in wonderful shape. What do you do?"

"Well, cross-country on weekends and downhill whenever Toby and I can get away. Also I run when I can, and when the weather's too bad I just get out my step box. Still, that's barely enough to get through January and February."

"Sophie needs to kick into high gear," said Pepper. "How much exercise is walking, really? Her figure may be holding up now, but once you pass forty you have to work to stay slim. Not to mention her mood, as you said."

"How **is** her mood?" said Natalie, in solicitous accents.

"Listless would be the word, I suppose. And disorganized. Her little studio is in chaos. I don't know how she gets any work done in there."

Mine was a very clean studio as studios go, with paint tubes capped and brushes washed and dried upright to save the bristles, and turpentine and varnish stored safely away from heat sources. Pepper didn't understand that watercolor palettes didn't have to be rinsed clean every night and that objects in a still life could include withered apples.

"I think Sophie is already slightly depressed,"

said Pepper. "Frankly, it's the drag on Paul I worry about. It's hard enough being the family breadwinner, without extra stress."

After a beat, she added, "And of course I'm concerned about her."

Natalie offered, in her clear, maple-syrup-on-snow voice, "Maybe she'd like to try one of our winter hiking groups. She could start with a beginners' mountain, like Bradbury."

Paul and I had walked up Bradbury one fall day. It took us forty minutes. Hardy Maine toddlers and old Yankee ladies with canes had raced ahead of us to the summit.

Pepper said, "If she'd go. One thing is sure, she'll need to be in good shape if she ever wants to keep up with children around the house."

"Are she and Paul planning that?"

"Paul would like some," said Pepper mournfully.

Paul must not have clued Pepper in that he was the one who wanted to wait until our lives were "more stable." I remained very still on the toilet seat, breathing quietly through my mouth. How grateful I was for the louvered doors, which hid my recognizable feet in their size nine black Oxfords.

"I've always felt it's better to have children on

the **young** side," said Natalie, as if I were about to qualify for AARP membership. "All the older mothers I see look so tired, which is already a problem for Sophie I hear."

"She doesn't even drive. That's going to be limiting for children."

"She has a license, Paul said?"

"But she hates it. Driving. It's almost a phobia with her. She's been very nervous every time I've been in the car with her. At least she works at home, so she won't have to deal with maternity leave. She can just take a break from her painting projects."

The water ran. I heard the familiar loud click of Pepper's patent vitamin box. She tossed back about twelve supplements a day. Now was the time, I felt, for Natalie to press home all my good points.

"I do worry about her," said Natalie. "I thought of asking the two of them to sign up for a ballroom dancing class with Toby and me. We have to learn a few dances for our wedding reception. I don't want to get up there and shuffle around like amateurs with everyone watching us."

"That's very wise. A bride wants to look her best on the dance floor."

"But I'm afraid Sophie would be too shy. And sometimes I think I lack tact around her. I make too many suggestions."

"I'm sure you have plenty of tact," Pepper said, with a note of warm approval in her voice that I had never heard. "And as fond as I am of her, truly fond, because there's not a mean bone in that girl's body, Sophie could use a little of your get-up-and-go. Do you know how long those dining-room windows would be without curtains, real curtains, if we left it to her? You'd think someone who works with color would **enjoy** picking out shades for a room, but you saw her today. No interest. Paul may find it adorable that she's the dreamy artistic type, but if I didn't push they'd never own even a decent mattress."

I'd like to push **you,** I thought. Right off the Casco Bay Bridge. For a moment I indulged in a glorious fantasy of Pepper thrashing in freezing water.

Natalie began asking Pepper's advice about some three-hundred-count Egyptian cotton sheets. Was white or cream better? Would a thin black pinstripe be too dated in a few years? Pepper's answer was lost as the rest room's door swung closed behind them.

It was hard to stand after being crouched on

the toilet lid so long. I had to rub my legs to re-store circulation. When I finally caught up with my shopping companions, Pepper was forcing a saleswoman to fetch a teetering metal ladder and explore the top shelf to see if there were actually **six** curtain panels of the gold-and-burgundy satin stripe she'd decided would be perfect for the dining room. There were only five, so Pepper had two panels special-ordered from the Boston store, to be delivered in three days.

"That way, if one gets stained, you have a re-placement handy," she said.

We bought the curtains, as well as a furry white rug Pepper thought would "reinvigorate" the bathroom, a set of blue polka dot coffee mugs, and a white pique shower curtain with shell-shaped curtain rings. At the last minute Pepper added a pair of holiday potholders embroidered with tiny white Christmas trees. Pepper's house was full of seasonal paraphernalia. I had a vision of my life passing in a yearly sequence of enam-eled Easter eggs, flag-printed napkins, and dried-gourd autumnal centerpieces.

At lunch, which we ate in a tourists' clam house along Route 1, Natalie talked pleasantly about a calligraphy workshop she was thinking of taking and a hand-knit boucle sweater she'd seen in the Old Port that would be perfect for me. If I'd mentioned that I'd heard the conversation in the ladies' room, she would have asserted that she'd defended me to my mother-in-law. She'd believe it too.

As for Pepper, she would be deeply surprised and wounded if anyone had suggested that she disliked and resented her daughter-in-law. After all, didn't she take me shopping? Didn't she worry about me? Didn't she encourage me in every possible way?

"That one's bad news, that Natalie," Marta said when I called her, late that night, after Pepper was safely asleep in the bedroom and Paul was tapping away on his computer, frenziedly trying to relax after an evening of Scrabble with his mother.

"Maybe she was just sucking up. Pepper evokes that response."

"I'm telling you, she's trouble," Marta said darkly.

Marta watched too much film noir. Her favorite movie was **Double Indemnity**. In fact, you could say that her entire love life was modeled on the great scene where Barbara Stanwyck undulates down the stairs and vamps Fred Mac-Murray until he can't think straight.

"They're both extroverts, Marta. They get frustrated with me."

"I'm an extrovert and I put up with you just fine. Just admit you can't stand her."

"All right, I can't stand her."

"Don't you feel better now?"

"Yes, actually. Hey, how are you doing with your date for the office party?"

"I'm thinking of not going."

In all her born days, Marta had never wanted to miss a party.

"To tell the truth, I'm getting tired of all this," she said. "I work like a dog. I go out at night and then I'm working too, schmoozing half the time."

"You love your job. At least, I thought so."

"Sophie, remember when we worked at the college paper? How important we thought it was? Remember how we toiled on that series on eating disorders? We were so ignorant. We thought that stupid little college newspaper actually made a difference. But I don't think I've ever enjoyed a job more than that one. Certainly not this job."

"Then why not do something else with your life?"

"After all these years making the world safe for skin-brightening foundations?"

"Come on, Marta."

"Do you know the staggering sum they put into my 401K here?"

"You've got scads of money socked away. You can afford a change."

"So what should I do? This isn't TV, where the woman lawyer gets sick of being paid tons and goes off to teach school in Detroit for peanuts and is so noble even the class drug dealer says she's his new role model."

"What **would** you like to do?"

Funny how seldom, after college has passed, you think to ask your friends that question.

"I'd like to write more, I think," said Marta. "I'd like to write for some cause or other. I used to do more writing on this job, but they promoted me. I'm a decent editor but it's not the same. Besides, cosmetics manufacturing isn't a cause."

"There are lots of writing jobs going in Washington," I said. "Lots of good causes you could work for."

"For astronomically less than I make now."

"How much do you need to make? You save and save."

"It's not that I need the money, it just makes me feel safe to make it."

"I'm thinking about school," I said suddenly. "For a real studio art degree."

It wasn't true. I'd blurted it out to keep Marta company. But I did want to get more serious with my painting.

"I'll quit my job the day you enroll in even one art class," said Marta.

"You think I'm bluffing?"

"I hope not," she said. "You've got talent, even if you can never see it. You deserve more than greeting cards and disease newsletters."

Pepper was cheerful on our way to the airport for her return flight Saturday. She had accomplished much on this visit. She'd lined the shelves of the linen closet with rose-patterned paper. She'd installed the furry rug in the bathroom. (Paul said, out of his mother's hearing, that the new rug was like stepping on a dead cat every time he got out of the shower.) She'd even had the pleasure of detecting, long-distance, a few mistakes her assistant had made on the Thanksgiving jobs.

Her last words to me were, "Let me know if the store doesn't deliver those other two panels. The salesgirl promised Monday at the latest." Her parting comment to Paul was, "I hate leaving you here but it's only temporary."

We watched with the first true thankfulness we'd felt all week as the gallant little figure disappeared down the gangway.

"You're a trooper, hon," said Paul.

As we sped up Route 101, I put my hand on Paul's knee and said, "You know what would be fun to do?"

"What?" said Paul.

"Ballroom dancing."

"You're kidding, right?"

"For weddings. It's very handy."

"You hate weddings."

"It was just an idea."

"A lousy idea," said Paul. "Not to hurt your feelings."

There. That would fix Natalie.

On Monday, Paul came home and said, "You must be psychic, Sophie. Natalie wants to do a dance class too."

"She probably saw the same advertisement I did."

"I said you'd already mentioned it and were raring to go."

My heart sank.

Paul said, "We start the third week of January. Toby's not very excited, but Natalie suggested we could all go to dinner afterward at that Vietnamese place next door that he likes. She said that if he gets something to eat at the end, he'll do anything."

The lessons were ridiculously cheap. I carried our registration forms down to the dance studio. It was my own fault for attempting an end-run. It's never smart to try to beat the competition on her turf.

Fourteen

On the Tuesday after Thanksgiving, promptly at noon, Ned came by for our freeway driving lesson. I was scatty and distracted, but Ned was determined to calm me down. Fortunately, Ned, unlike people who'd been determined to calm me down in the past, didn't go about it by lecturing me in excited tones.

"Here's the first lesson of driving, Sophie, and it's an easy one: go Zen. When you're in the car, you should forget everything else. **Become** the car, like they say about riding a horse."

Unfortunately, like a horse, the car was much bigger in actuality than it had seemed in theory. I'd learned to manage the neighborhood, and even the scary Casco Bay Bridge that led to the shopping plaza, but now I was headed to the big time: the highway with all its terrors.

"Our subject today is merging. Merging is all about what?" Ned said.

"I don't know, what?"

"Timing. Remember we talked about this?"

"It's all gone out of my head."

"No, it hasn't. You know it. Just let it come back to you."

He was carefully monotone, as if he were talking to someone on a window ledge.

"Some people just can't drive," I said.

"Some people," said Ned. "Not you."

He was back in one of his wood-smoky sweaters, and the smell soothed me. His hair was a mess today too. He was the Ned I knew again.

We were at the bottom of the Western Promenade, where it dipped down the hill into the roundabout leading up to Route 1. Ned leaned back in his seat, relaxed. During the few occasions so far on which I'd driven us, Paul had kept an arm stretched along the passenger-side window, ready to brace himself upon the inevitable impact.

"Timing," I said, as if repeating a spell.

Perspiration was breaking out along my hairline.

"Here's the sequence," said Ned easily—could nothing shake the man's composure? It was beginning to get on my nerves, his conviction that he would survive this outing.

He said, "You enter the ramp, you check traffic, you adjust your speed, you ease in."

I must have gone pretty green, because he

added, "You can do it, Sophie. You're a smart person."

"You say that now. Wait until you're in traction."

"I have no plans to be in traction. And stop holding your breath," he said. "That's one reason you're getting so anxious. You're oxygen-deprived."

I let my breath out and turned up the ramp, bumping over pothole after pothole. Winter was hard on concrete. Beneath us the Fore River was low, revealing banks that were a grim expanse of debris-strewn gray mud.

"Where are we going?" I asked.

"The Maine Mall. I have something to pick up there."

Later, I realized that he'd chosen the mall because driving to it involved only baby merges. There was one merge onto 295, then another onto the Maine Mall Road, and then the relief of the mall parking lot. I knew this because the day before, at breakfast, Ned had marked out our route in red pen on a map I'd procured at the Portland visitors' center. The map was drawn in a bright, cartoony manner, making it look like driving around the city was child's play, one of those amusement park rides where toddlers steered miniature Edsels and Model T's along a circular track.

At the entrance ramp to 295, perceiving a distant truck down the highway, I instinctively put my foot on the brake.

"No, you don't have to," Ned said. "Trust me. Just keep up your speed. You'll beat him, easily."

I kept up my speed, but while checking my rearview mirror and my driver's side blind spot, I almost let the car veer into the breakdown lane.

"Turn your wheel a little to the left," Ned said quietly. I jerked back into my lane, pressed the accelerator, and was on the highway with the truck still far behind me.

The next merge was more of a dedicated lane for the mall than an actual merge. In my elation at having completed the drive, I almost ran over a woman in the parking lot.

"That's okay," said Ned. "She'll watch where she's going next time."

I drew into a wide parking spot in a sea of empty asphalt, far from any other vehicles. Christmas shopping hadn't reached fever-pitch yet.

"You did it," he said casually, as if there had never been a question. I wiped my clammy hands on my pants, hoping Ned wouldn't see.

"I almost killed that lady."

"But you didn't."

He grabbed my hand and held it aloft in an athlete's victory signal. His hand was dry and warm, and hard with calluses. Mine, I knew, was still damp. He didn't mention it, though.

Ned's hand clasping mine felt, more than anything, trustworthy. If I were facing a jump across a deep crevasse, or being pulled up the side of a cliff, his was a hand I'd grab without a second thought.

"You can drive back," I said, taking my hand back and scrabbling for my purse.

"Are you kidding?"

"You don't have to prove your bravery, Ned."

"I'm not proving anything. I'm relaxing and being a passenger. This is way easier than what I went through with Stephen. You're good, Sophie. You just need a little confidence."

"I need more than that," I said.

"You're doing fine," he said. "More than fine. You were sweating it at that merge but you trusted me and you didn't brake and that took real guts."

His eyes were glowing. No one had approved of me in this whole-hearted fashion since I'd graduated from college and Delia and Tom had let forth their cab-summoning whistles as I crossed the stage for my diploma. I found myself basking in it, smiling like an idiot.

"I could have steered this thing with my nose and you'd have said I was an A student," I said to him.

"You bet," he said. "But as it happened, you're a natural."

"You should do this for a living."

"I might someday, when I get sick of having paint in my hair all the time and being a slob in general."

"You're not a slob. You always look very clean," I said.

"I look clean? No wonder the girls are always after me in droves."

"Aren't they?" I said. "Fiona was all over you the other night."

"You caught her in an affectionate mood," he said, but he was grinning.

As we were getting out of the car, a girl roared by us in a red pick-up truck. She couldn't have been more than fourteen. I'd been astonished on coming to Portland to see how laxly the minimum driving age was enforced. Yet these children in their pickups and vans seemed competent, savvy motorists, a match for me any day.

The heat was blasting in the mall. Families and couples strolled down the long corridors, and sun streamed in through the skylights. Ned bought a part for his sanding machine at Sears. He could probably have gotten it at any hardware store in town.

We had a late lunch at a restaurant that specialized in fried seafood in baskets. I had a basket of shrimp and Ned had a basket of fried clams, French fries, and corn swimming in butter. For someone who ate so many of the wrong foods, he was surprisingly lean. It must be the work he did.

"When you get better at this, which will be soon, you'll go farther," he said. "The day you can get past Freeport, you'll be an official pro. Do you have any questions about merging? Or any questions at all?"

Why are you here with me? I wanted to ask. But I thought I knew the reason already. Ned and I were both putting in time while we were stranded here. We were stranded with a purpose, like two passengers in the waiting room of a train station. My purpose was keeping Paul company, Ned's was making money. But I knew that the friendships of traveling companions, like shipboard romances, rarely lasted.

Only that morning Ned had said that Stephen's cast would be off in a few weeks. Then they'd speed up their work on the house and go back to Boston. I didn't like to think about that.

"So," Ned said, grabbing a few of my fries, "what did you think of Fiona?"

"She was nice," I said.

"She was worried that she talked your ear off about education policy."

"Well, grad school must be very absorbing."

"She's almost done, but she might go on for her Ph.D. It depends on some offers she might get. There are a few possibilities in Washington."

He was staring down at his food, hunting for a stray pickle slice, so it was difficult to see how the chance of Fiona's departing for the nation's capital was affecting him. I decided I couldn't stay so ridiculously anxious about what I said to him.

"Isn't it a little nervy of Fiona to kick up a fuss about your being up here for a few months when she's planning to decamp to Washington?"

"Isn't it," he said glumly. "But the opportunities in her field are fewer."

Fiona would fit in beautifully in certain academic and policy circles in Washington, where research reports were produced and meetings held and federal grant money spent with a free hand. Her shiny earnestness might actually last in such circles, where people felt they were dedicated to a higher purpose, where they brought to their work the painstaking attention to detail of medieval monks copying manuscripts. Ned wouldn't fit in as beautifully. Would she leave him high and dry?

"You didn't take to Fiona much, did you," he said next.

No one could accuse Ned of being predictable.

I said, "Driving really loosens you up, huh? We walked together for an hour this morning and you never asked me then."

"With Alex listening? And the rest of them? The way they gossip?"

"They gossip out of love," I said.

"Just answer the question."

"I'm shy around self-confident people. It's envy I'm sure."

"It's okay if you don't like her, Sophie. She knows she can be a little much. She gets carried away with her pet subjects, and it's only later that she realizes it. I didn't like Fiona when we met, actually."

"How did you meet?"

"When Steve and I were first in business together, I lived in Brookline, in an apartment building with a parking lot where you could buy a space. You know how hard it is in Boston. Well, Fiona kept parking in my spot. She hadn't bought one, she just figured there would always be extra spaces. You know, the absentminded academic. Finally I said something to her. Nothing out of line, just a 'hey, could you leave my parking space alone?' She got very offended, complained about me to the super, even wrote me this nasty dignified note I still have. Then I ran into her one day by the mailboxes and I said, 'I wasn't trying to humiliate you, you know. I just need to park.' Then she got human and baked me a tin of cookies to apologize."

"And the rest is history," I said brightly.

"That sounds so set in stone," he said. "We're in no big rush, me and Fiona."

I wondered if Fiona believed that.

On our way out the south entrance of the mall, Ned noticed that there was a game room with an air hockey machine.

I beat him three games to one. Air hockey is designed for those of us with over-reactive reflexes.

He said, "Here you look like you wouldn't hurt a fly and you're slamming away at that puck. Now you have to take me on at Skee-Ball so I can get my own back."

A small boy was playing. We waited for him to finish. The machine kept spitting out tickets and ringing when the boy scored.

"This is cool," I said after the kid walked away, his hands full of tickets as if he were holding a big bouquet. "This game."

"You've never seen a Skee-Ball machine before?" Ned asked. "Not at the beach?"

He demonstrated how to keep my wrist stiff and throw with a gentle upward motion, but Skee-Ball wasn't like air hockey. It was all about control and coordination. Ned was good at it. He routinely landed the ball in the forty-point slot. Every time he did, the sirens flashed satisfyingly and a coil of tickets was spat from a slot. I won a total of six tickets. Ned won eighty-two.

We redeemed his winnings at the counter for a hundred Tootsie Rolls, eating several on the way from the arcade to the car.

"Someday, you're going to laugh at that turnpike there," Ned said as we turned out of the parking lot.

I could see the tollbooths down the road, not far away. A sign pointed in the direction of Montreal. It astonished me: I was living in a place from which people could conceivably drive to Montreal. In Washington, Canada had seemed as far away as Europe.

On the trip back, a car tailgated us so closely that I could see the pores on the driver's nose in my rearview mirror. I changed lanes and uttered several words I'd never intended to say in front of Ned.

When we were safely back, Ned said, "You did great today, Sophie, but you can't lose it like that."

"Did you see him? He was practically in our backseat."

He gazed at me and sighed.

"I need your promise you'll keep it together better or I'm going to take your car keys," he said.

"You know I was right," I said.

"It doesn't matter. What you want to be is still **breathing**. I got Stephen this book. It's called **Drive to Survive.** It's a great book. It says that the main idea of driving is to remember that whoever makes it home alive wins."

"Shouldn't I care when people are doing asshole maneuvers, endangering us?"

"Sure you should. But concentrate on how you protect **yourself** in that situation."

"It bothers me," I said.

"No kidding."

He was laughing, his thin body bent in a little in the middle.

"Don't laugh at me," I said. "You never get mad?"

"Sure, I get mad. But I'm the teacher here, and I'm supposed to help you, not connive with you at establishing bad driving habits. For example, when I drive I like to play my Django Reinhardt tape. But you notice I didn't even turn on the radio with you, because that would be a bad habit."

"I don't know Django Reinhardt," I said. "Who is he?"

"He was the original jazz guitar master. I'll bring you a tape next time, but we won't play it in the car. That would distract you."

"What else do you listen to when you're driving?"

"Well, Django's my first choice, and Sam Cooke, and then there's an Irish favorites CD Steve gave me called **Mist Covered Mountains.** And if you ever tell anyone that last one, I'll deny it with my dying breath. Now, think about where you might like to go next. We should go places **you** like to go. It'll motivate you."

"You're off the hook, Ned. You don't have to do this again."

"Oh, this was just a trial run. Next time we'll work on lane changes. I noticed you avoid them like the plague."

"And next time maybe you'll learn something about air hockey," I said. "Take your game to a whole new level."

"Rematch," said Ned. "You can count on it."

He hopped into his beat-up Chevy Nova and waved casually at Donald, who was staring narrowly at him from the driveway. Donald was surprised into nodding back.

"Who's that?" said Donald.

"Just a friend. He was helping me with my driving."

"He needs a haircut, that guy."

"He sure does. But he's a nice guy."

"I could've helped you," said Donald.

"Maybe sometime. If you have time." I'd seen

Donald drive. Every mother of small children, every pet owner in the neighborhood knew Donald's driving.

"You're liking the new car?"

"I love it," I said. "Thanks to you."

"Hey, how's the heat in your apartment?"

"Much more comfortable. Much."

We smiled at each other. Donald and I had made an even trade, and it worked. It's rare to reach the happiness of perfect equilibrium in any relationship. Either you have things forced upon you—such as dining-room curtains from your mother-in-law, or "opportunities" for charitable giving from your mother—or you find yourself offering something that the other person has no use for, like a view of the Portland Headlight, when Pepper hadn't wanted to be in Nature.

"You have a good afternoon," said Donald as I lagged up the side stairs.

"You too."

Donald's amity would survive only until our icebox noisily expired or the water pressure in the shower disappeared completely. Still, it was nice. It was the best I'd do with Donald. He wasn't a friend, as Ned had become, but strangely enough he was someone on whom I felt I could rely—

not to fix anything, and not to confide in, yet there it was, this feeling that Donald would be there with his tool belt on if some dire, unspecified circumstance occurred. This was good, since I'd been expecting dire circumstances since I was a child of three.

Fifteen

Paul said, "I don't understand why the sudden rush to see Boston. It's been nearby for months and you haven't been down."

I didn't understand it either. But I was feeling an irresistible impulse to be in a city with bustle around me and people rushing past each other on the sidewalks. So when Stephen said that he and Ned were "making a run down" and asked if I'd like a ride, I'd said, sure, why not?

I found a little attic single in a Victorian bed-and-breakfast in Brookline, the Beltran Inn. Sixty dollars, a bargain for Boston. I planned to take myself to dinner in the North End and spend the next day at the Fogg Museum, admiring its Pre-Raphaelite collection and the lovely, excessive realism that Fiona's friends would have disapproved of strongly.

"Stephen and Ned are going. I told you. It's a free ride down and I need a treat."

"At least you're not taking the bus," he conceded.

Paul thought buses were for "lower-class," somehow shady people. He feared his delicate wife would find herself sitting next to a bookie or a pimp if she trusted a bus line.

"How are you finding time for this trip? Aren't you swamped?" said Paul.

It was November 30, and I was ahead of schedule, a holiday miracle. I proudly recounted how I'd shipped off the Braille manual, finished proofing an article on new uses for PET scans in treating head trauma patients, and gotten a note from Ann about how happy she was with my apples and mums.

I was happy with them too. Something new was happening to my painting. I was seeing more colors than I used to see, painting without as much preliminary drawing. I was painting on my own time too, not just for Ann. Every few days now, bundled to the teeth, I drove the car to the headlight or the Eastern Prom to sketch in charcoal or with my new colored pencils, bought on sale at the Art Mart downtown. On the coldest days I'd stay in the car and paint, which was cramped but not impossible. There were seven studies of the headlight and cove taped to the walls of my workroom now. I was going to give Delia and Tom the best of them for Christmas.

"You're spending a lot of time on your art stuff

these days," Paul had said the night before. He'd called from work twice that afternoon and reached the machine.

"I know. I can't seem to help myself," I'd said.

"Is there a particular reason why?" he said. "Practice for Ann? Because she doesn't pay you enough for all this extra effort."

"No, it's not for Ann. I'm just considering options."

"School? You don't need school, Sophie. Unless you want to train in something lucrative, like computer graphics.

"You know, Paul, I never pushed my painting. I never followed through."

"You mean professionally?"

"Or even to the next level of skill. There are things I can teach myself, but there are things I need teachers for.

"But where would you even go to school? Back in D.C.?"

"There are lots of places. Pratt, in Baltimore. And there are any number of working artists down there who teach too."

"Sophie, I'm not trying to discourage you. But you want to be realistic in planning your career moves, don't you?"

"Being realistic got me here, and I'm not sure I like what I do anymore."

Paul sounded alarmed.

"All I'm saying is that painting is a very competitive field. And you're not an especially competitive person. I'm not saying you don't have talent, Sophie."

"Ann thinks I have talent," I said. "You know what her big idea is? That one she kept hinting about? A book. With my pictures."

Ann had finally revealed her plan, but I'd been waiting to tell Paul about it, hoping for more particulars.

"What kind of book?" he said, skeptically.

"Well, sort of a . . . a gift book."

I swallowed, but if Ann could talk this bilge to a publishing company, I could talk it to my husband.

"She's looking for a broader purchasing base than just card buyers. So she's come up with a proposal for a contemplative journal for women, drawn from her own life. Sort of a day-to-day compendium of her thoughts and feelings."

"Yuck," said Paul.

"I know, but those reflective, gifty things are good sellers. And she'd use my paintings throughout. She has a small publishing company in Oregon very interested. Ann said they loved my stuff."

Paul's silence indicated that he was unflatteringly startled. I pressed on.

"If the book's a success, she could expand the line to paperweights, calendars, mugs, you name it."

Ann had been almost gushing on the phone. "Your iris painting was a big hit," she'd said. I hoped she'd shown them a slide, not the sympathy card version.

"She would put your paintings on coffee mugs?" Paul said.

"And she'd pay me more. **They'd** pay me. The publisher. It would be a big jump from what I make with Ann now."

"Not to be mean, honey, but minimum wage is a big jump from what you make with her now. It's a nice possibility, but don't you need something to sustain you long-term? You could work in a museum, or sell antiques. Learn that side of the business. Keep the connection to the arts but make a good solid career too."

If we had children who aspired to dance or act, would Paul steer them toward accounting or engineering instead? He was a careful person, while it was just possible that I was a person who had adopted habits of caution, but who wasn't at heart very careful at all. That might lead to some intense differences of opinion down the line.

But today I wasn't worrying about down the line. Today my overnight bag was filled with grown-up clothes: wool slacks and a navy boat-necked sweater for the museum, and for dinner tonight a rust tweed suit with a long, narrow skirt that had a dangerous back slit. I was determined to dress like a grown-up for a change.

Paul stood in the doorway, frowning. It wasn't jealousy, I knew. Just the other day he'd referred to Ned and Stephen as "your little girlfriends." He couldn't seem to take in that they were brothers, not lovers, and I'd given up trying to get the idea into his head. Not that Paul would have been jealous if he **had** known Ned was straight. He wouldn't necessarily have noticed if I were trolling the Atlantic in a fishing boat with an all-male crew of recently released penitentiary inmates. He was too preoccupied.

"You'll be late for the office," I said.

"Are you sure you know the way to your hotel once you get there?"

"I'm sure."

I'd memorized every T-stop in the guidebook. I loved Boston—I always had, ever since Delia had taken me there on the train during her first winter vacation from college. My mother thought travel should be connected with humanitarian purposes, but Delia had special-pleaded to my father, who was capable sometimes of small bursts of generosity.

In those four days we saw the snow-frosted Common, the golden gloom of the interior of the public library with its Sargent murals, the twisting streets of the North End, the slopes of Beacon Hill by lamplight. I'd visited five times since then. Boston was the city of my adulthood, the first city I'd ever explored time after time, all on my own.

"I left the hotel number on your desk," I said to Paul.

"Good, good."

He was looking at me with the same look he'd had when he first saw my new hair. As if I were a stranger he was sizing up. My camel coat and wine-colored beret seemed to mystify him, although I'd worn them often enough back in D.C. He pecked me on the cheek, a husbandly, perfunctory peck.

"Take care in Boston," he said. A melancholy expression crossed his face.

Foolishly sad too, suddenly, I put my arms around his neck and gave him a passionate kiss.

"Sophie, you're only going for a night," he said. But he kissed me back, holding me tightly before letting me go.

"I'm not used to you going off on your own that much anymore," he said. "So call me tonight. It doesn't matter if it's late."

Stephen played the oldies' station all the way down to Boston. I was glad to be distracted by music because Ned had not exaggerated: Stephen was a truly terrible driver. A soft cast had replaced his hard one, but his left leg still got mightily in the way. When a song he liked came on, he lost all concentration and gave the truck its head, as if it were a horse. During "Tupelo Honey," we almost wound up locking bumpers with a tractor-trailer labeled **Hazardous Waste**.

"For the love of God, Steve, would you pay attention to the road?" Ned said.

Stephen ignored him.

"What're you doing for dinner tonight, Sophie Quinn?" he shouted into the back seat.

"She can hear you," said Ned. "She's not deaf."

"I was going to head for the North End and eat Italian," I said.

"Care for company?" said Stephen. "I can postpone driving back until after dinner. And my little brother here loves Italian."

"Ned may have other plans," I said.

"Nope," said Ned. "No other plans."

"Fiona has a seminar," said Stephen, as if it were some sort of disease.

Stephen knew a family-style place called La Famiglia Giorgio, on Salem Street.

"We can get a few huge bowls of pasta and split them," he said.

"Sounds good to me."

"Six-thirty too early?"

"No," I said. "It's perfect."

"If we get there alive," said Ned.

My single at the Beltran Inn was an attic room with slanting walls and a window seat that looked out on pines and other turn-of-the-century Brookline homes. The walls were covered in red toile. There were braided rugs on the floor, a milk-glass lamp on the nightstand, and a tiny cream-tiled bathroom. A basket of apples was on the dresser, and crumbling vintage anthologies with gilt lettering were carelessly piled on a pie-crust table in the hall. I grabbed **An Anthology of the World's Great Poetry** for bedtime reading.

The clerk mentioned that coffee, tea, and chocolate chip cookies would be available all day in the dining room, along with magazines. I spent a luxurious hour in a tufted armchair by the hissing radiator, reading esoteric periodicals I'd never normally have bought and eating cookies with endless cups of tea. At home I'd have felt obliged to work. Here I had nothing to do but pass the time until dinner.

Even the ride on the Green Line T to the North End was a treat. I arrived early and found the restaurant with no trouble. I could see through the window that it was my kind of place, unpretentious and uncrowded.

As early as I was, Ned was there before me. His hair was slicked down, parted on the side and combed back from his face, but it was drying rapidly and the cowlick above his widow's peak was already springing up rebelliously. No barber in the world would ever tame that cowlick. He wore the same black sweater I'd seen that afternoon at the Portland Museum of Art. There was a bit of shaving cream stuck to the tip of his left ear.

"Is Stephen on his way?" I said. It felt strange

to meet Ned, just Ned, in a different city. As if we had a date or something. Of course, I'd met men friends in Washington for lunches and dinners and never given it a second thought.

Ned didn't seem to catch my sudden shyness. He was smiling, and his cheeks were a little flushed with the chill of the November evening. It was warmer than Portland, but he was wearing a lighter coat than he did there—the same coat I'd seen him in when I'd met Fiona, the charcoal gray one.

He said, "Stephen's tied up with the interior decorator at one of those to-the-trade places. Something about some sort of hand-dyed curtain fabric for the dining room that will only work if Stephen's willing to change the wallpaper he talked the owners into. It's the only room with wallpaper, and the decorator's pissed she didn't get a say in it. So they're off wrangling somewhere. He left a message and said we should go ahead and he'd be here around seven-thirty. Which means eight."

"I'm not that hungry," I said. "We could take a walk first."

"I was hoping you'd say that," said Ned. "If we wait a little, he can eat his main course while we're having dessert. Sorry about this."

"No, no," I said. "Let's stroll around. We'll pretend we're tourists."

"You're a good sport," he said.

We wandered the North End for half an hour, past dozens of holes in the wall from which delicious smells stole out into the chilly air, past cafés where the waiters stood serenely waiting for the late-dinner crowd, past benches with old people arguing pleasurably in Italian, and shop windows hung with sausages and strings of garlic.

"So, does Fiona have a lot of these seminars?" I asked as we turned onto one of those winding, deserted side streets that make the North End such an adventure. One minute you were on the tourist's strip of Hanover Street, and the next you were lost among old brick buildings with fire escapes, with the traffic noise so soft that you'd hardly guess you were in a city. I loved it all. I loved walking here with a sharp appetite on this kind of crisp but not biting November evening, all dressed up. For once I felt I belonged among the professionals hurrying home.

Ned's wits must have been wool-gathering, because he didn't answer my question about Fiona's whereabouts. He was smiling slightly and humming one of his tuneless tunes, and his loping walk had slowed to an amble.

"Did you ask me something?" he said.

"Fiona. Is she joining us or does she have to work?"

"She's stuck at that seminar. They're more like town meetings, actually. They hold them with parents in different school districts. The professor she works with sets them up and asks the people questions about how they like their kids' schools and then writes fancy reports on the session for high-paying educational foundations. Basically all Fiona does is take notes."

"Aren't there stenographers anymore?"

"There must be but the guy is too cheap to hire one, and Fiona's too anxious about her standing with him to say no. He's on her dissertation committee or whatever you call it."

"What a charmer," I said.

"Apparently academic institutions run on the hard work of people at the bottom of the ladder who are too powerless to say no."

"You don't like him much, do you. This professor."

"He works her too hard. And he's one of those bearded types."

"You have a beard, Ned."

"But I'm not a bearded **type**."

We both laughed and I said to him, "Stand still," and took out a tissue from my purse and wiped the shaving cream off his ear.

"I've been wanting to do that all night," I joked.

He said, "That's always the way with me. I think I'm all right when I leave the house, and then I find out I have on two different socks or something."

"What do you shave, anyway? The edges? Along your throat?"

"I just clean up the beard. I was starting to scare the little kids on the block. I opened the door on Halloween and one of them started crying."

"Oh, I do like Halloween," I said.

"I like it too," said Ned. "I just can't get used to being the grown-up instead of getting the loot. When Stevie and I were kids, we'd really rake it in."

"The boy at the gas station called me ma'am the other day," I said.

"That's not because you look old. He probably saw your wedding ring."

"With my gloves on?"

"You look young to me," said Ned. "I know you're thirty-four, but you always look younger than that for some reason."

I waited for a compliment on my dewy complexion, but he said, "I think it's your expression. You always look as if you haven't quite figured things out."

We had ended up in front of Mike's Pastry. There was an after-work crowd at the counter, and through the shifting masses I could see green and pink cookies shaped like leaves, and seven-layer napoleons, and in the corner, black forest and German chocolate cake under glass. At the tiny tables, tired but contented men in suits were perched on iron chairs drinking coffee. It looked very appealing.

"It's seven-fifteen," said Ned. "You want to be good, or you want to dawdle a little longer and have cannoli for an appetizer?"

"Cannoli," I said.

"I knew I liked you for a reason," he said.

We squeezed into a corner table next to the cake display, and Ned ordered two cannoli, one with chocolate chips and one without.

"My grandmother made these so they'd melt in your mouth," he said. "We used to have them for every First Communion party and every graduation."

"It must be nice to be Italian and have some sort of food tradition," I said. "When you're Irish and Welsh and Scots and English, there's not much to brag about in the realm of native cuisine."

"Haggis?" said Ned.

"Bleah."

"Steak and kidney pie? Soda bread?"

"Not to mention our way with fresh vegetables," I said.

The waitress brought our coffee and cannoli with surprising speed.

"They move a lot of people through here," said Ned. "But they don't hector you if you want to sit and linger. Now what was I saying?"

"I don't remember," I said with my mouth full. "This is **good,** Ned."

I was happy, for no real reason except that I wasn't thinking about anything in particular. I wasn't worrying about Paul, I wasn't hating Natalie, I wasn't wishing my mother-in-law would develop one of the rapidly fatal diseases I'd learned about from my clients. I was just sitting on a too-small chair at Mike's watching the people go by the window and hanging out with my friend Ned.

I reached my fork out and snagged the plump bit of filling poking out of the end of Ned's cannoli.

"Yours is pretty good," I said. "But not as good as mine."

He picked up my cannoli and took a large bite of it.

"What I meant was," he said, with his mouth full, "you don't **look** grown-up. You don't even look married."

"I try to," I said. "I wear the ring and all."

He gulped at his coffee and spoke more clearly.

"Here's what I'm getting at. Most people, they seem more fixed as they get older. They have a set of ideas they've been believing in for a while, they have some role they play. You don't seem to have a role. You seem unsure of yourself. Which is good."

"Unsure at my age is pathetic."

"Would it be so bad if you were unsure of yourself when you're ninety?" he said.

"Yes."

"No. You'd always be learning, anyway."

He brushed crumbs off his sweater and stood. "Let's go. I need my dinner. Stephen can take his chances."

At Giorgio's we got a table right away next to a large group of conventioneers who were convivial but not too loud.

"You want to get two we both like and split them, like Steve said? He can eat the rest of ours and order his own if he wants, when he gets here. If he gets here."

We decided on fettuccine Alfredo and spaghetti Bolognese with a half bottle of red wine and bruschetta to start. On second thought, Ned said, we'd make it a bottle. Neither of us was driving, as he pointed out.

"You think Fiona might meet up with us after dinner?" I asked, a little nervously, when our wine had been poured and a bread basket brought over. I'd eaten the tail ends of many breakfasts with Ned at Becky's, but dinner was different.

"No," he said. "These meetings always run late. This guy never lets her go home until she's promised him the notes typed up first thing in the morning."

"How nasty," I said, startling the waiter, who asked Ned if his wife's wine was all right, ignoring me as if I could not speak.

"She's fine," Ned said, with an evil grin in my direction.

"How's your drink, Mrs. Moore?" he said

when the waiter had left. "Is everything to your satisfaction?"

"Very much," I said, and took the heel of the bread.

"**Are** you a Mrs.?" Ned said.

"You mean, am I really married, or just faking married respectability to win your trust?"

"I mean, did you take his name?"

"I kept mine. Never thought of doing it any other way."

"How'd that go over?"

"It went over fine with Paul," I said. "Not with his mother."

"Is it any of her business?"

"You'd be amazed at the things Pepper thinks are her business."

He nodded, in the uncomprehending way of someone who's never had a mother-in-law.

"So you're Quinn. What's he?"

"Stoddard," I said.

The waiter came with the bruschetta. It was piled high with chunks of tomato and fragrant with fresh basil.

He said, "You're right, I don't see it. Sophie Stoddard. No, it sounds . . . off."

"The guy I dated before Paul, his name was McLaughlin," I said needlessly.

I was missing Rory acutely at this moment, with a piercing pain that came out of nowhere. It must have been the situation—I was with a man in a darkening restaurant, and the streets were taking on that magical golden winter night-time light outside. I still connected such moments with Rory, those moments when beauty struck me in a heap and everything seemed to pulse within the circle of one suspended minute. Would I ever stop doing that? I felt doomed and cursed.

"I don't see McLaughlin either," said Ned lightly. Then he said, "You look . . ."

"What?"

"Sad. You're not ever really the merriest girl in the world, are you? Have some more wine."

"**You** have some more."

We both had more.

He said, "Let me guess. This McLaughlin guy, he was the one that got away?"

The wine was hitting him, I could tell. It was hitting me too.

"Yes," I said. "He was the one that got away."

The waiter brought our pasta, huge steaming bowls of it. They always served you fast at family-style restaurants. For once Ned did not fall upon the food.

"Aren't you hungry?" I said.

"In a minute. Tell me about him."

"I don't think so."

"That's a little insulting," Ned said. He was frowning, the puzzled, lightning-quick frown I'd seen so rarely. "I'm your friend, aren't I?"

"It's not that. Rory—it's in the past, that's all."

"Not that much in the past," he said. Then he said "Rory" as if he'd never heard such an outlandish name before, which for a half-Irish guy who lived in Boston had to be impossible.

"We should eat," I said.

"So what was he like, this Rory, all dashing and charming and all that?"

"Well, if you must know, yes."

He piled a large mound of the fettuccine into the heavy iron spoon and plopped it on my plate, splattering a bit of cream sauce on my rust-colored suit. A guy who was a little more suave would have given me a compliment on my clothes tonight. Ned was just frowning down at the tablecloth as if I wasn't there.

I felt foolish. What was I doing, anyway, telling Ned about Rory? The only two people who knew about that were Delia and Marta.

"You know what?" he said abruptly. "If you

keep things a deep, dark secret, you never get over them."

"Thank you, Dr. Phil," I said.

In my turn I dumped a hefty serving of the spaghetti Bolognese on his plate.

"I don't want that yet," he said. "Tell me the big love story."

"Boy, are you nosy," I said. "Fine. Once, when I was only twenty-nine, which you were, what, last year?"

"I'm not that much younger than you are," he said. "Go on."

"Once I was a stupid young graphic depart-ment assistant at a PR agency, and Rory, who'd been the boy-next-door when I was growing up, worked for a glamorous international agency."

"Big deal," said Ned.

He drank more wine and I took a large bite of fettuccine. It was heavenly.

"Try this," I said.

"Just tell the story."

"Boston makes you crabby, I can see. Where was I?"

"You were twenty-nine."

"And Rory and I met up again. We fell in love. Or at least I did, and he said he did. We had an affair. He married someone else, to whom he happened to be engaged at the time he met me, which I should be ashamed of. The End."

Ned peered at me through the deepening gloom. The lighting budget at Giorgio's must have been tight.

"You mean, he just married the other girl and left you?" Ned said.

"He not only left, he went halfway across the world. That's how fascinating I am. Now could we eat?"

"What an asshole."

"You don't know him."

"I don't have to." He crammed a gigantic fork-ful of spaghetti into his mouth and began ticking off on his fingers.

"First, he . . ."

"Chew for a minute," I said.

Ned swallowed.

"First he . . . he seduces you when he's engaged to someone else."

"You make it sound like a Victorian melodrama, I **had** had sex before."

The light was dim, but he seemed to go a little redder.

"First, he does that, and then instead of letting

it be a one-night thing, a mistake he apologizes for and sets you free, which is the . . ."

"Decent, manly thing to do," I finished.

"Would you shut up, Sophie?"

I shut up and ate some of his spaghetti. I was very hungry now. My moment of misery had passed.

"He hangs around, right up to the day of the wedding, I bet, am I right?"

I nodded.

"Then goes off in a cloud of dust."

"A cloud of rice is more like it," I said.

"He probably writes you yearning letters once in a while, doesn't he?"

"None of your business, Ned. You're wasting all this food, by the way."

"I know that kind of guy," he said darkly.

"And what kind of guy would that be?"

"A real dick. A real **dick,**" he said.

"You Catholic boys start much too late," I said. "Wouldn't all of you just love to be dicks like that?"

"No," said Ned fiercely. "For your information, I get plenty of chances."

"I'm sure you do. I didn't say you didn't get chances."

"Not every guy who **could** behave that way **does** behave that way. Here, have more wine."

I drank several more sips, feeling as if I were at a wake. A wake for my lost summer with Rory. The melancholy Irish side of me comes out when I drink.

"That guy," said Ned, "is the kind of guy that regular guys hate."

"The way I hate Anna Kournikova."

"She has some sort of talent, at least."

"Yeah. Right."

"Your friend, he's just a poser."

"Hey," I said, and poured him more wine. "Why are we arguing? What do you care? It's a long time ago. In my salad days."

"You know, Sophie, it would be nice if you didn't always refer to yourself as Methuselah. In some ways you're younger than me, like I said earlier."

"Please," I said. "You're a baby. Eat your dinner."

He sat glaring at me. I glared back. There had been such scorn in Ned's voice when he spoke of Rory. Perhaps it was scorn for me too. Was Ned so sure he'd always behave nobly? I reminded myself, hazily, that Ned was just a prudish

Catholic boy from a backward mill town where the Pope's picture still hung in the parlor next to John F. Kennedy's.

"I don't think less of you, you know," he said, reading my mind. "For seeing an engaged guy. **You** weren't engaged."

"Of course you think less of me. **I** think less of me."

"I'll tell you some romantic screwup in my past life, if it makes you feel better."

"You haven't had one. Not one where you have to be ashamed of yourself."

"How do you know that?"

"I can tell. You're a veritable Boy Scout."

He frowned at me again.

"What's with that frown," I said. "You look like some Old Testament prophet."

"Okay," he said. "Maybe I've never been in exactly your situation, but I've had my feelings hurt before."

"When? In college? Did she not want to wear your fraternity pin?"

"Boy, you have a mouth on you when you want," he said. "If you knew me at all, you'd know I'd never join a fraternity."

"I'm sorry," I said. "It's just that only my sister and my best friend know about Rory."

"That's not good," he said. "Keeping his memory sacred and all that. You Catholic girls have a tendency to make shrines out of people, you know that?"

"I know," I said. "Not that it's any better to confess to you, Father Ned."

He smiled, that illuminating, sideways smile that had reassured me so much that first day at walking group.

"I don't think I'm cut out to be a priest," he said.

"Maybe not."

We were still smiling foolishly at each other when the door of the restaurant swung open, chiming a string of bells that probably hadn't been taken down since last Christmas, and in walked Stephen and Fiona.

Fiona was wearing another of her up-and-coming-young-academic outfits, a checked skirt with square pleats and a thin cream pullover with a lime silk scarf knotted around her neck. The cream would have been lovely with her hair if not for the acid lime of the scarf.

"We're too late, I see," said Stephen. "I'll have to have dessert instead. I think two portions of tiramisù would make up for dinner."

"We'll wait," said Ned. "We're only halfway

through, anyway. The portions are huge, as you can see."

"That's why they call it family style," said Stephen. "And what have you two been celebrating?"

He glanced pointedly at the empty bottle on the table.

"Just kicking back," said Ned.

"I was forcing the story of my life on him," I said.

Fiona sat very near to Ned and linked her hand through his.

"I missed you," she said to him softly. He turned and kissed her cheek. Stephen leaned over and kissed my cheek and mouthed, "I missed you," in my ear.

"Fiona had the bright idea of calling my cell to locate you, Ned," he said.

"I finished early," said Fiona. "I wish you'd get a cell phone," she added to Ned. "I don't know how you do business without one."

"Stephen has one. That's plenty. If I had one, it'd ring off the hook and I'd never get anything done," said Ned. "And you found me just the same."

"No thanks to Stephen. He pretended he didn't recognize my voice."

"I was just pulling your leg. Now we can

all have dinner after all," said Stephen. "Isn't that nice?"

"Terrific," said Ned. "If you can behave yourself."

"We're **all** terrific," said Stephen. "Fiona, tell us about your little seminar, or focus group, or whatever it was."

"As if you want to know," said Fiona, who was studying the menu. "I'm going to splurge and have the calamari."

"I hate calamari," said Stephen. "The smell makes me sick."

"You'll live," said Fiona.

It wasn't a successful evening. Stephen talked about the iniquities of interior decorators, and Fiona talked about a new report on voucher schools in Cleveland, Ohio, and Ned and I sat rather silently.

After cappuccino, Stephen said, "I'll drive you to Brookline, Sophie."

"I can take a cab," I said.

"Ned and I are going right that way. I have my car," said Fiona, who hadn't stopped touching one part of Ned or another all through dinner.

"No, Fiona, you have that tiny hatchback. I'll take her in the truck," said Stephen.

Ned gave me a rueful good-night smile.

"Forget what I said, Sophie," he said, so low that only I could hear it.

"Already forgotten, if you'll forget my big mouth," I said.

Stephen racketed through streets I had never seen before and would probably never see again. He smoked a cigar with the window open and we played his Creedence Clearwater tape.

"You can't beat CCR," he said. "So, what were you and my brother yammering about when we came upon you two?"

"Ancient history," I said.

"How ancient?"

"An old boyfriend I made the mistake of telling him about. I'd had a little wine."

"And he got to lecturing you?"

"A little. About wasting my time yearning over cads."

"Cads, cads, cads. Why are they so damned attractive?" said Stephen. "Just one more proof that there is no God."

He stubbed out his cigar and turned down the tape player.

"Ned's a strange one," Stephen said. "He has all these scruples but he does a lot of damage himself."

"What kind of damage?"

"Can't you tell? Women fall for him and he never even notices. You know the ones who fall for him the hardest? The tough cookies, like Alex in group."

"You've picked up on that, then?"

"It sticks out a mile. I had to warn him not to be too nice to her. Not that it's any problem. A crush can't hurt her for long, at that age. Alex is just an example. Ned goes along, being nice and kind because it's natural to him, and he doesn't always see that he's making, shall we say, a big impression."

Was this a warning?

Perhaps not, for Stephen went on, "All these bossy, bossy women. He needs someone softer. Someone like you. If you were available, that is. Which you're not of course, but someone who doesn't see his kindness as an irresistible invitation to boss him around. He's not that bossable, actually, but women mistake that sweet, gentle demeanor for sappiness. Some women. The current specimen, for example."

"You're hard on her, Stephen."

He swung onto Coolidge Avenue at an angle that defied gravity.

"I'm not hard on her," he said. "I'm actually

pretty nice to her face. I tell myself that it could be worse. She could be a Republican, or a lawyer."

"Is she that awful?"

"No. She probably wouldn't cheat on him, or rack up big credit card bills. She's just so damn dull. I tell a joke and it takes her a full minute to get it. I swear, you can see her processing it as if she's a robot, with this almost audible click when she gets it, and even then she doesn't laugh half the time."

"So you're screening her out for your brother because she doesn't laugh at your jokes? That's quite a standard."

"It's an excellent standard. You laugh at my jokes," said Stephen. "They're not **that** obscure."

"Well, he must see something in her."

"Sophie, Fiona has just **annexed** him. I can only hope he comes to himself before he marries her or something awful like that."

"I think you underestimate him."

"Maybe," said Stephen. "But I'm worried, I'm telling you. I don't want Fiona with those Buddy Holly glasses and that damn herbal drugstore perfume she uses staring at me across the family dinner table every holiday the rest of my life."

Fiona did smell faintly herbal. I'd noticed it at dinner. In spite of myself, I smiled.

"See?" said Stephen. "You know I'm right."

When I called home from the pay telephone in the inn, our recording answered. I left an affectionate message. Paul was most likely asleep in front of the television set. He'd been working grueling hours lately. The Project's summer teacher workshop announcement was scheduled for mid-March, and Natalie had an ambitious program of "educator outreach" planned. Natalie never called anyone a teacher—they were always "educators." Teachers preferred this moniker, she had assured Paul.

Later, after another cookie and cup of tea, I crept downstairs to try Paul again. But a group of German tourists were huddled around the phone attempting to access an information line about whale-watching expeditions that had long since closed for the season. When they could finally be heard tromping upstairs, it was after midnight, too late to call a man who rose at seven-thirty. I curled up under a goosedown quilt and read **An Anthology of the World's Great Poetry** until I fell asleep.

Sixteen

"The dogs should have one place to run free," Alex said hotly.

"It's disrespectful to the dead," said Edgar.

"They don't care," said Alex. "These historic preservationists with poles up their asses. It's not fair. The dog people are the ones who weeded, who kept the gravestones from toppling over. Before they came along it was just a hangout for . . . it was just a . . ."

She stopped, suddenly embarrassed.

"It was a cruising spot. We'd heard," said Edgar, patting her arm.

"Not that I've got anything against that," said Alex. "But now the cemetery's a real community center."

Alex had a springer spaniel she brought to the Western Cemetery most afternoons at four. It seemed like a lot of time for a young woman to be spending in a graveyard.

"The dogs make their business on the gravestones, don't they?" said Ramon.

"Not their serious business," said Alex.

It was Wednesday, the sixth of December, St.

Nicholas's Day. We were eating breakfast at Becky's. Ned was unusually silent, and without his almost imperceptible tact, the conversation had gotten slightly out of hand.

"The dog owners pick up after themselves religiously," Alex contended, "and those graves are so old. No one living remembers those people."

Breakfast came. Alex had ordered yogurt and granola and didn't snitch even a bite of Edgar's pancakes and bacon. She had visibly changed. Edgar still had the same little potbelly, and George's leathery trimness never varied, but Alex, like the baby Matilda, seemed different week by week. She'd softened her look too, no longer wearing the heavy eyeliner, her features revealing themselves as the puffiness dropped away.

"Alex," Edgar said, "someday we'll all be dead, and then someday not so long after that, no one we know will be alive to visit our graves either. Does that mean no one should care if there are canines pissing on us too?"

"You won't **mind**," said Alex, with youth's bright conviction that only other people die. "You'll be somewhere else. Waiting to reincarnate."

"I might mind," said Edgar.

"Anyway, I have a petition for you all to sign," Alex said.

All over Portland, the populace was dividing itself into pro-dog and anti-dog factions. Happy Trails was no exception. Ned, Alex, and Ramon were pro-dog. Edgar and George were anti-dog. I was undecided. If I were dead, would I want dogs running and barking and sniffing each other without heed to me below them? Or would I feel comforted to have a breath of dog life warming my sad, neglected grave?

I'd be comforted, I decided, and signed Alex's petition, although Edgar and George shook their heads at me.

"It's a matter of respect," George told Alex, who snorted.

Ned remained silent. After breakfast we lagged behind the group.

"You don't seem like yourself this morning," I said.

"Nothing important."

"Want to go somewhere this afternoon? It doesn't have to be a driving lesson."

"Maybe."

In the past week, once with Ned and several times on my own, I'd worked on my driving. I'd ventured to Yarmouth and Saco. I'd practiced lane changes in rush hour and merging onto the turnpike. I'd even tried passing, though I'd happily trundle along behind an Amish farmer's buggy from Lancaster to Philadelphia rather than do it again.

"It's fine if you're too busy to get away," I said.

I didn't want him to feel obligated to go driving with me. Since that evening in the North End, I'd been wary of claiming too much of Ned's time. Stephen's words of warning had registered, whether Stephen meant them to or not. But today Ned seemed blue, so blue that he looked a little battered, as if he'd been walking into a strong wind and it had worn him out.

"You don't have to come with me, honest," I added hastily, after thirty seconds had gone by without his replying. "You must have other things to do."

"Not really. We're waiting on the electrician, and Steve's already home watching TV, so he can look out for him. Edger loaned him the BBC's **Pride and Prejudice** on tape."

"We could go to the headlight," I said. "I can practice on Cottage Road."

"You know it by heart, Sophie."

"Anywhere, then."

He thought for a minute.

"How about Higgins Beach? Route 77's worth learning. Besides, you might want to paint at Higgins sometime. It's pretty."

"Sounds good."

"I'll swing by your place around three then."

"You're going to the beach with him?" said Marta. "In the middle of the afternoon?"

People in Washington never go to the beach, or even to the river, in the middle of the afternoon. You're no one in Washington if you don't work frantically past the dinner hour, on holidays and on your day off.

"What do you **do** with him, exactly?" said Marta. "I understand the gay brother. Every woman needs gay male friends. But what's up with Ned?"

"We hang out together," I said defensively. "We're friends."

"Hang out? What's happened to your vocabulary up there? Is there a big aging hippie population in Portland?"

"There's no other expression for it. He gives me driving lessons, we eat extra breakfast sometimes after the rest of the group has left. It's harmless."

"Let's see. He's spending his free time with

you. He's putting his hand over yours to show you the correct position on the steering wheel. He's taking you to secluded beaches. Sure. That sounds like any old platonic friendship to me."

"Marta, you have any number of straight male friends."

"Most of whom want to get in my pants. This Ned must have a gigantic crush on you."

"He's three years younger than I am," I said.

"Have you read **How Stella Got Her Groove Back**? Three years is nothing. Look at Susan Sarandon and Tim Robbins."

Every liberal woman I knew, including me, wanted the relationship that Susan Sarandon and Tim Robbins had.

"He has a girlfriend, Marta. A very nice girlfriend."

"If you really thought that, you wouldn't say 'very nice' in that prim tone."

"And finally, he's just being kind to me. He's a stranger here too."

"He's two hours from Boston, Sophie. In the time he spends with you, he could speed down there and catch some quick nookie with his girlfriend and speed right back."

"No, he couldn't because she works very hard and her schedule is very full."

"Ah **hah**!" said Marta.

"Besides," I said, embarrassed not to have mentioned it sooner, "I'm married."

"If Paul isn't respecting your marriage, there's no reason you should."

"We don't know that Paul's lack of respect has gone the whole distance yet."

"I know what it is," said Marta. "You're still pining after Rory."

"I am not."

"You are. It's like a disease with you."

"I haven't seen Rory in five years, Marta."

"But in the back of your mind, Sophie, you think he would fix everything. Isn't that true? Since that summer, some small part of you thinks that if somehow you and not Liz had married Rory, everything would have gone right."

"I thought things were going right when I married Paul. Silly me."

"Life's not a binomial equation, Soph. The choice isn't between one bad guy and another bad guy."

"I'm married. I'm supposed to be making that work out."

"All on your own?"

"For now. If it doesn't get better, I'll do something."

"By something, I hope you don't mean fleeing to Serbia with Rory to get a firsthand look at the cultural after-effects of mass genocide. Because I can guarantee you that you wouldn't like that."

Marta felt that the Balkans had been causing trouble since the Middle Ages and that there had to be a limit to how much slack the rest of the world would cut them before marching in and taking over permanently. She called herself a left-leaning independent, but her foreign policy views were more along the lines of Genghis Khan. Luckily the cosmetics industry had very little pull in world affairs.

"I told you," I lied. "I know Rory's a hopeless case."

"I think it would do you good to look at another man besides Rory or Paul. Just **look** at Ned. You don't have to do anything about it. It would be good practice."

I didn't ask her what she thought it would be practice for. It was only too obvious that Marta thought her wallflower friend would soon be back out on the market, and she was doing her best to get me in training for the big dating rat race.

Getting dressed for the beach in my warm cords and heavy sweater, I thought about what

Marta had said. It was undeniable that I felt a low buzz of attraction to Ned. Who could help it? He wasn't strictly handsome, but he had a quirky, offbeat face that I never grew tired of looking at. He was silly at the right moments, and a good listener, and unobtrusively courteous. When you told him a thing about yourself—your sister's name, your childhood career ambitions—he remembered it. Of course I felt an attraction. As Delia would say, I was married, not suddenly under chloroform. If I stayed married, such attractions might arrive in my life from time to time. They were normal; they meant nothing, I reassured myself.

It was also undeniable that I'd make a fool of myself if I ever indicated that attraction in any way. I didn't want to be yet another pathetic woman who read more into Ned's kindness than Ned intended.

And Marta, in her fiendish way, was right about Rory too. Rory, for me, was the big thing that could have gone so right and went so wrong. It was like being on **Jeopardy!** and betting too much on the final question and losing it all. It was like getting every number in the lottery right but one. It was like running for president and easily winning the popular vote only to have the Supreme Court and some bits of perforated paper come between you and the Oval Office. It hurt badly at the time, and it had never entirely stopped hurting.

My Rory fantasies conveniently ignored the fact that, as Rory's wife, I'd have a husband who wrote playful e-mails to other women. I also ignored the fact that Rory would endure any discomfort in the pursuit of the nonroutine, while I was a person who carefully put the tissue-paper shield down on public toilets and ordered the same breakfast at Becky's every time. I ignored a lot, because dreams of Rory were kinder than the present disappointment that was my marriage.

In all my old yearnings for Rory and new fears about Paul, the rest of my life **was** too prone to blur out of focus, like the view from those twenty-five-cents-a-minute binoculars up at the Portland Headlight. Ned, despite my liking for him, was a presence at my side rather than a person standing right in front of me. I couldn't really see him yet, except out of the corner of my eye.

Higgins Beach in the late afternoon light was a glory of pink and silver sand arched over by a deep blue sky barred with red-orange clouds.

"Nice, isn't it," said Ned, who'd been quiet on the way out, except for telling me where to turn off Route 77 for the beach entrance.

The turn for the beach took me by surprise. Here in Maine when they had a beach they didn't herald it with a string of strip malls. They seemed more concerned with preventing outsiders from finding it.

The signs on the shore road forbade parking between April and October.

"What do the summer crowds do?" I asked.

"Well, there aren't any. Outsiders can pay four dollars to park. There's only one lot. A good, old-fashioned monopoly."

"You've come here in summer?"

"A few times. It's better now, when it's just the strollers and surfers."

"People don't surf in these waters, do they?"

"Oh yeah, they do," said Ned. "I saw three here the other day after that big storm down in Cape Ann. They wore wetsuits, of course."

We scrambled down to the sand. Before us was nothing but sea and sky, shimmering with the aching blueness of a winter horizon before it surrenders to dusk.

"You think you could paint this?" Ned said.

"Not in a million years. But I wouldn't mind trying."

"Funny how you never see artists along this stretch of the coast. Maybe they all go farther north in the summer."

"Like geese migrating," I said. "But in reverse."

To our left, half a mile down the sand, a promontory stretched out into the ocean, its cliffs of reddish clay surmounted by inky-dark pine. To our right were haphazard piles of rock. We walked the long shining crescent of the beach, while the breakers rolled in one after another, louder and wilder than the breakers at the cove by the headlight. A coal-black retriever raced into the waves in pursuit of a stick. The owner was visible up the beach, ambling with her hands in her pockets.

"You see a dog run like this, where there's real space, and you realize that dogs are born to do just that," said Ned.

"But you didn't sign Alex's petition today."

"I signed the first copy. This is her third."

I picked up a few shells, then tossed them back again. There was no souvenir I could take from this place that would let me recall exactly this light, exactly this air, as fresh as the first morning of the world.

The only distraction was that my ears and neck were freezing. Out of a silly vanity that still hadn't given in to winter, I'd worn my beret instead of my stocking cap. Ned took off his tatty scarf and handed it to me.

"When are you going to get a decent hat, Sophie?"

"I have a decent hat."

"That black thing? That won't keep you warm. Get something fleece-lined."

"You hardly ever wear a hat."

"I grew up in New England. Put the scarf on before you turn blue, will you?"

I wrapped the scarf around my neck. It smelled like his sweaters, of wood smoke and old wool.

Ned's hair ruffled back from his face in the wind. He seemed another Ned out here, more at ease—not the sweet-natured diplomat of the walking group, not the patient teacher I knew, not the meek beau of earnest Fiona.

I wanted to take his hand suddenly, not as a romantic gesture but because we were alone at the water's edge. In that brief hour, I felt young again. I forgot Paul and my sad confusion about him, and Rory and the despairing heartache that he'd stirred up. I was only myself, breathing, seeing, walking.

Ned said, "Sorry I was quiet earlier."

"We were all talking so much, you probably couldn't have gotten a word in edgewise anyway."

"I was a little down this morning."

"Problems at the house?"

He cleared his throat, a fumbling sound not natural to him.

"My mother died three years ago today."

"Oh, Ned. That's lousy."

"It's lousier for her," he said.

"How did she die? You never told me."

His throat tightened and he looked out to sea.

"Car crash. She ran out to get something for a dinner party she was planning. Kind of senseless, huh. Dying because of a dinner party. She was off to the Market Basket to get frilled toothpicks or something, and a drunk driver plowed right into her."

I glanced sideways at him, sensing that there was more to it.

He said, "She was planning it for three weeks, this party. She'd do that, go whole hog into something and not stop. Not sleep." He paused. "She had bipolar illness."

"Manic depression?" I said, then could have kicked myself. "Sorry, Ned. I know that's the old name. Sorry."

"I'm not offended. She called it that herself, when she called it anything."

"Was it under control?"

"Not really. She'd be on medication, then she'd go off it for a while. She was heading into one of her bad spells when she got killed. I know because she was beginning to call me late at night, all excited about this or that. That was the pattern. Along with spending a lot of money, and talking too fast, and driving too fast, and everything too fast. But she was driving fine that night, the police said. There were witnesses. It wasn't her fault."

"Of course it wasn't," I said.

"She wasn't crazy, you know," he said. "Just troubled. And only sometimes."

"Was it hard for you guys, growing up with a troubled mother?" I said, then wished I'd kept my mouth shut. But he kept talking.

"Sometimes. But it wasn't all bad. When she was on an upswing she was incredibly fun. She'd drive us up to Rockport on a school day. She took us to New York once, on a whim. We stayed overnight at the Gramercy Park Hotel and ordered room service. Can you picture that? These two kids from Amesbury chowing down on filet mignon and asparagus. My mother never thought children were too young to try things. And she was gorgeous, so waiters and people like that would do anything for her."

"What did she look like?"

"She had black hair and very blue eyes, and she always wore dark red lipstick."

"She must have looked like you," I said.

"Only in coloring. Her features were more like Stephen's."

"And how about when she wasn't on an up-swing?"

"She'd get really withdrawn. Sit for hours staring at the television. Forget to pick us up at school, until my dad finally arranged for us to ride with another boy. Then she was furious. Dad just said, 'I have to watch out for them when you're in your blue moods, Stella.' That was what he called them."

"You must miss her."

"Yeah. Although it's been three years."

"Three years isn't that long."

His eyes were down, those long lashes of his a screen for his emotions. How old had he been when he learned that, I wondered. Only a child, probably, since it was done so unthinkingly. As we walked he scuffed at the sand with the toe of his workboot.

"I notice it more in daily things. Her being gone."

"Like what?"

"Like how she played cards. She got more into a card game than anyone else I ever saw. Not gambling, just how she enjoyed it."

We walked on. The breeze was very salty today, and the gulls were wheeling and squawking. Ned dodged one that was standing right in our path, obstinate and noisy.

"Gulls have terrible personalities," he said. "They're always complaining."

"Did you tell Fiona what today was? Do you talk to her about any of this?"

"A little. But she's frantically busy now, with that professor she works for."

"Well, I could see where that would outweigh something like the anniversary of your mother's death."

"You can be kind of sarcastic sometimes, can't you, Sophie?"

"In a good cause," I said.

"I don't want to bring her down," he said.

"She works so hard. Not that you don't, which is why I shouldn't be bending your ear."

"Bend away."

"Besides, last time I said something to Fiona she went and got me a stack of books on the grief process which I never read, which hurt her feelings. She means well."

"Do you and Steve talk about it?"

"No. Steve's only just now recovering. Beginning to. Scott's helped."

But you don't need any help, I thought. It's the quiet ones who suffer most.

We had paced the length of the beach now, and began again in the opposite direction. Ned's ears were growing red.

"Take your scarf back," I said.

"I'm fine."

"Your ears are the color of a boiled lobster. Take it."

He smiled and took it, the first time I'd really seen him smile all day.

"Let's sit down," he said, and we sat just above the tide line, where the sand was faintly damp but firm. Ned took a stick and made circles and squares in the sand.

"Your parents are still alive, Sophie?"

"Yes."

"Somehow I thought of you as an orphan. Did Edgar tell me that, or was that just an impression I had?"

"Well, they're around. A little preoccupied. My mother is bent on saving the world and my father barely knows there's a world out there. But they're not bad. Still, I'd have liked a charming mother, like your mother."

"Do you believe in an afterlife?" said Ned, almost offhandedly.

I thought, and the noise of the waves seemed to grow so loud there was nothing in my head but that sound, that beautiful, wild sound from before time began.

"I don't know," I finally said. "There are glimmers sometimes, but I don't know."

"Me neither," said Ned. "But you'd be surprised, when someone dies, at the number of people who think they do who want to tell you all about it."

If Ned had been one of my Washington friends, I'd have put my arm around him, attempted some mute comfort. But I hadn't known him long enough to make such a gesture natural, and I didn't want to presume. Instead, I leaned my shoulder into his, then leaned away.

His shoulder was more solid than I'd have thought, and for a fraction of a second he leaned it back into mine.

A moment later he was describing the French doors Stephen had found for the porch. We drove home in the half-light, talking about storm windows and weatherproofing for the house on the Eastern Prom. I've learned this about men: when they tell you something personal, they need time to recover themselves afterward. So I played along.

When we pulled up to my door, he said, "Thank you for suddenly needing a driving lesson this afternoon."

"I don't know what you're talking about," I said. "But if it makes any difference on this particular day, it's clear to me that you were an excellent son to your mother."

"It might make a difference," said Ned.

Again, I wanted to give some sign of condolence, but his self-contained sadness made me leery of the usual clasp on the arm or pat on the shoulder. Besides, the recently bereaved get patted, hugged, damply kissed on the cheek far too much. I knew because I'd seen my mother in action at so many funerals.

But Ned wouldn't be the one at a funeral

who'd be standing in a circle of mourners, telling tales of the dearly departed and being supplied with handkerchiefs. That was his brother, who seemed to have inherited the expressive Italian side, while Ned was a typically Irish stoic.

"You're a good listener," he said. "I guess people say that to you all the time."

"Not really." I thought of Paul, who'd loved to talk to me once about the silliest small things, and who now no longer had many stories he wanted to tell me.

"Well," said Ned, "anytime you want to babble, you know who to call."

"Hey, you listened to me the other night. In Boston."

"I was a jerk in Boston," he said. "I don't know where I got off, handing you all that guff about your friend being a player."

"Maybe he is a player," I said lightly. "It doesn't matter now."

"People have a right to their nice memories," said Ned. "Guys like that might get my goat, but that was no excuse for making you feel bad."

"You were just sticking up for me," I said. "In retrospect."

"I didn't know you then," he said, "or I'd have . . ."

"You'd have what? Kept me from making a fool of myself? That's a tall order."

He turned sideways toward me and said, "Maybe a guy friend could have clued you in about getting hurt by that type. Told you how they operate."

"At least I'm not among the walking wounded anymore. I got over it."

"I hope so," he said, doubtfully. "He's not worth it."

"No one's **worth** it," I said. "You pick someone and if you're lucky, you pick right, but if you pick wrong, it's worth the experience, isn't it?"

"I wouldn't know," he said. "I haven't ever picked really wrong, and I don't know if I've picked really right yet."

"You mean, with Fiona?"

He seemed to collect himself.

"Well, I wasn't thinking of Fiona in particular. But you liked her better this last time, didn't you?"

"I did."

I thought I'd be forgiven a little white lie in a good cause, on a day like today. It wasn't that I **dis**liked Fiona. It was just that she seemed so sure of herself. Maybe I was just jealous. With her small, absorbing role in the teeming city of a large university, Fiona had found a world in which she belonged, and would remain happily in it unless something unforeseen shook her out. I'd grown unattractively envious of such people. Fiona had something I wanted: a place and a purpose.

Ned got out of my car and into his.

"Don't stand out here and watch me off," he said. "I've noticed you do that. Do you think I'm going to have an accident on the next block?"

This wasn't so unlikely, with Donald on the loose.

"I'm an anxious type," I said.

"Get inside. You're cold already. I'm just gonna let the engine warm up and then I'll be out of here. Go on now."

I went inside and watched him through a fold of the curtain. He sat with his hands on the steering wheel, and then for a minute he tilted his head back against the headrest and closed his eyes. His face was more blank than sad, wiped expressionless by some long fatigue. Then, as if someone had called to him suddenly, he straightened up and drove off, and I paced the apartment for half an hour, wondering if I'd helped at all or just exhausted him further.

I called my mother that night. She said, "Is this about Christmas arrangements? Because your sister Delia's handling all that."

"No. I just wanted to check in. What's up?"

She complained for a little about the choir director at St. Catherine's. The choir director was my mother's sworn enemy, a man who used his classical music degree to promote his preference for organs and traditional hymns over guitars and folk music derived from Swahili chants.

"And what I say," my mother said, "is that the mass is for the people. But Mr. Donovan simply goes behind my back to Father Jim and the next thing I know we're having the Hallelujah Chorus at Midnight Mass as if Vatican II never happened."

"You do so much, Mom. I'm sure that it's appreciated."

"Father Jim did say I brought a generous, open spirit to the Christmas liturgy."

My heart went out to Father Jim.

My mother said that this year's children's pageant was going to include a reenactment of the flight into Egypt, featuring the story of King Herod and the massacre of the innocents. Mom described how she was going to convey the mood of the Egyptian desert using a length of burlap for sand and long, waving swathes of blue chiffon for a sky. She had some pretty nifty devices rigged up, and I became interested in spite of myself.

"You're a very visual person, Mom. That must be where I get it."

"It must be," said my mother, who'd never seemed to want to take credit for that quality before. "Set design is like painting, wouldn't you say?"

"A lot like it," I said. "Either way you're creating a view inside a frame, trying for a convincing illusion."

This seemed to please her. Strange, I'd never asked myself before if my mother had what she'd call "a creative side." But St. Catherine's was known for having the prettiest flowers at its May crowning, baskets and bouquets overflowing in pale blue and pink and white down the small hill on which the Virgin's statue stood. That was my mother's doing, as were the beautiful Easter banners in purple and gold satin, hung up the side aisles of the church every spring.

"At St. Pete's they've cut the pageant altogether, can you imagine that?" my mother said. "Instead the children sit around in the front pews for twenty minutes discussing their **feel-**

ings about the Christmas story. I blame the parents, really. They should insist on the old traditions."

I agreed with her. But then, St. Pete's had always had a reputation for all sorts of foolish modernisms. In the seventies they'd been one of the first parishes to initiate a Holy Thursday service in which the priests, in imitation of Christ, actually washed the feet of twelve parishioners playing the Apostles. That was taking meaningful liturgy a step too far.

Mom didn't ask about Paul, about Portland, about when I was coming home for the holidays. Well, boo-hoo. After hearing Ned's story, I wasn't inclined to feel sorry for myself. Sometimes all you want of your parents when they are faraway is to hear their voices, to know that age or distance hasn't changed them beyond your recognition. In some bedrock, unspoken way, my parents loved me. As long as they lived, I wouldn't be in want or entirely alone. That can make the difference between courage and despair, in those moments of decision that every life holds. I felt that such moments were coming for me.

Right before she rang off, my mother said, "Has there been much snow up there? I hope it's

not too big an adjustment after our easy winters."

"I'm managing pretty well," I said.

"You have a flashlight in case the power
goes off?"

"Yes," I said. "A lantern one. Heavy duty."

"Fine. Well, I'd better get back to work. I can't
be chatting all night."

You take your tidings of comfort and joy
where you can get them. In this season of goodwill, my mother wanted to know if I had a flashlight. It was not one of the questions that the
sympathetic, soft-voiced mother of my dreams
would have asked me, but for once I didn't feel
shortchanged.

"Break a leg with the pageant, Mom," I said.
"They're lucky to have you."

"I do what I can," my mother said.

Seventeen

Marta's phone message had a calm, girded-for-battle tone: "I'm calling to say that for the first time in my life I'm going to a formal event alone, and I want you, as my best friend, to be aware of this milestone."

When I called her back, the receptionist said, "Wait just one minute. I know she wants to talk to you." Gregorian chant echoed down the phone lines. It was strange that one could no longer hear Gregorian chant at St. Catherine's but could find it on the "hold" tape of the American Cosmetics Association.

Finally Marta could be heard saying offstage, "Give me ten minutes. No, I will not speak to Gail Farlow, she's had the copy for a month, she can wait for me."

Then she said, so loudly compared to the soporific drone of the chants that I jumped, "I always knew this day would come, and it has. Today's December twentieth and I don't have a date, so this is it. I'm going stag."

"What decided you?"

"I don't know. Suddenly working myself up about this party seemed silly."

"Marta, should I be worried about you?"

"No, no, I'm not depressed. It's that I don't want to pour so much of myself into minutiae anymore. Like getting my nails done."

"I can hop on a plane," I said. "We can go to a nice doctor and talk about all this."

"Honestly, I'm okay. Don't fuss. I won't get so listless that I let my roots show. Incidentally, can you talk? Is Paul coming home soon?"

"He's working late."

"Isn't this getting to be a habit with him?"

"A nasty habit."

"Speaking of nasty habits, did you ever write back to Rory?"

"No."

"You'll be hearing from him again. Ignoring him is a surefire way to have him beating down your door."

"He can't very well beat down my door when he's on another continent."

"On another continent is where a guy like that does his finest work."

"Why do you dislike him so much?"

"I dislike the type, that's all. They wreak havoc."

As if Marta hadn't wreaked her share of havoc among the Washington metropolitan area male population. She saw herself as the romantic equivalent of some scourge-inflicting Old Testament angel, sent to chasten the hearts of men.

"Why is Paul working late so often?" she said. "Does it have anything to do with that ferret Natalie?"

"Just procedural glitches, according to him. He explains but I have to confess my mind wanders off a little."

Every night Paul went over his work travails in detail, as if reliving the trauma of each just-finished day was essential to facing the next one. Textbooks and lab equipment had failed to arrive. Debates raged among the curriculum experts about the wisdom of teaching physics concepts prior to teaching those of traditional biology. The project's logo was hotly debated: a microscope was too narrow, a trailing comet too diffuse, an open book too much like the symbol of an already popular literacy program.

Paul and I had made love only three times since our night on the couch. Each time he had turned to me late at night, buried his face in my hair, and rushed through the act as if sex were merely a method of falling asleep, slightly handier than reading or TV. The previous Saturday evening, I'd tried to choreograph a slower, more intense seduction, putting both space heaters in the bedroom and changing into my one remaining item of sexy lingerie, a beige-net nightie that had seemed intriguing in the store but made me feel as if I were wearing full-body pantyhose. I'd gotten nowhere.

"I appreciate the thought, sweetie," he said, "but let's wait until I can really relax."

When this magic moment was to take place he hadn't indicated.

"How would you rate the general atmosphere around the house?" said Marta.

"Polite. He gives me these stilted little compliments, such as, 'I don't know where you got those new paper towels, but I like them a lot better than the old paper towels.'"

"And Heloise the homewrecker?"

"She couldn't be nicer. Apparently, she's thrilled that we're all going to be in dancing class together. Maybe she feels badly about dishing the dirt with Pepper."

"Or something else."

"Let's not talk about her. What are you going to wear to the party?"

I was sick of Natalie, of Paul's still-too-frequent mentions of her efficiency and initiative. Paul's boss, Dr. Kendrick, had recently enthused that hiring Natalie was the best thing the Project ever did. "She gets the whole office going," Dr. Kendrick had said. "She's a pistol." If I lived to be a hundred, no one would ever call me a pistol.

"I'll dig something up," said Marta with uncharacteristic indecision. "God knows I own enough evening clothes. Unlike you."

"I don't have an office party to go to."

"What about Paul's?"

"That's no big occasion. Four to six o'clock, right in his office."

"How chintzy," said Marta. "Don't you ever get a chance to dress up?"

I didn't care about that. When you're five feet eight and over one hundred ten pounds, you're fortunate to find something for evening in basic black that's not depressingly matronly. After years of unhappy experimentation, I'd learned to settle for simple numbers without gathers or frills—the fashion equivalent of Shaker furniture.

"Stay over with me after Christmas," Marta said. "I know you're stuck at your mother-in-law's for the holiday, but take a few extra days and hang out at my place."

Paul would protest but not seriously. In fact, he'd have been more comfortable during this busy season if I'd gone on a long cruise, leaving him to work in uninterrupted bliss. Part of me dreamed that, if I were absent for a few days, he might come to a whole new appreciation of his love for me. This sort of bathetic longing can easily crop up when your romantic imagination was formed on old episodes of **Petticoat Junction,** Georgette Heyer novels, and **Tammy** movie reruns on Sunday afternoons.

"Sure," I said to Marta. "I'll come stay. Paul will never miss me."

I didn't have to tell Marta that I was hoping just the opposite. Marta knew without having to be told.

"I get it," ran Rory's new e-mail, which I received late that night. **"You're working for the tourism department in Maine, and you think that if you give me the silent treatment long enough, I'll book a ticket to Portland and check on you in person, thereby adding a few dollars to the lousy economy."**

It was annoying how often Marta was right.

The e-mail switched abruptly to a travelog that I suspected he'd cut and pasted from his and

Liz's group Christmas e-mail. They were going to Vienna for the Christmas holidays, then taking a train to Prague for a meeting with newspaper editors from countries that were once part of the Soviet Union and were now a mess.

Vienna was beautiful, the e-mail went on, although they'd torn down too many of the buildings by their best turn-of-the-century architect, Victor Horta. I had never heard of Victor Horta. Wilkinson's art history courses had always been weak in the architecture department.

Then abruptly, the letter turned personal again:

"Maybe I shouldn't write you, Sophie Ann. You probably have some strict rule about not corresponding with old flames. You're probably saying as you read this, 'Please. I'm a happily married woman,' and those eyes of yours are going all big like when I used to dare you to do things."

He'd always been so good at that. Because of Rory I'd jumped off the Delaneys' shed roof and sprained my ankle when I was ten. Because of Rory I'd almost smoked my first and last cigarette at thirteen, with him and his now very-proper sister Caitlin, who'd looked like a red-haired Janis Joplin back then. Rory had handed the cigarette to me, lit it, then snatched it out of my hand and ground it into shreds with his foot. "I just wanted to see if you'd do it," he said. He never smoked cigarettes himself after that, either. I was too old now to be taking Rory's dares.

"I'm coming to the States in the spring. I'll be in Boston for another one of these boring meetings with the money people. They own me during the day but my nights are free. Let's have dinner and catch up. I'll tell you about my travels and fill you in on my family and you can tell me what you and Delia have been up to."

Did he really think I wanted to hear about his sisters' perfect marriages to doctors and lawyers from good Irish families, about all those McLaughlin grandchildren who'd been baptized at St. Catherine's in the last few years? Did he really expect I'd care about the gorgeous sunsets he and Liz had stood and watched, arms intertwined, on their vacations on the coast of Albania?

I felt bitter and nasty. But deep down, I was also grateful to him for this letter. Someone missed me. I wanted my sweet, calm husband back, the old Paul, but failing that, I could choose to be swept away in mindless passion. That I could have, maybe, if I waited until spring. If I answered Rory's letter in the manner in which I so easily could.

These were unhappy thoughts for a December afternoon when yet another snow was falling fast outside. To think I'd once seen snow as a treat! I forgot how beautiful Higgins Beach had been, forgot the salt air and the pink-and-silver light.

"Dear Rory," I typed. **"I miss you horribly sometimes, but that could just be the weather. You ask how I'm doing. You left. I moved on. Sometimes there seems to be such a wrongness in that. Funny how the sky doesn't fall down because we're not together. I always thought I'd die of losing you, and look at me. I can drive a car. I can walk for miles. I could even love my husband, until he began to mention another woman all the time and I began to lose faith. I miss you I miss you I miss you. Come back."**

I dragged my cursor down until the words stood out, white against the black. I touched a button and they disappeared.

"Dear Rory," I typed. **"I received your letter and e-mail. I'm fine and, as you know, in Portland, Maine, which is cold but I guess**

not as cold as wherever you'll be when this reaches you. I did get married, as you heard. My husband and I are here for a year for his job. As for your visit, it's too early for me to know my schedule for the next few months, but let me know when your plans are final. Merry Christmas and Happy New Year to you. Best, Sophie."

That one I sent. That prissy, proper note, which Rory would laugh at but understand. He'd always known what I wanted to say, even when I couldn't say it. I'd never claimed to be anything but a coward, after all. But if secret wishes counted for sins, then I had sinned—because if Rory had been there I would have fallen upon him and ravished him on Donald's cracked linoleum. I didn't care that he was a cad. I just wanted someone who felt something back at me: lust, memory, love, regret.

All through that fall and early winter in Maine, I'd been trying to coax Paul back into hailing distance, back into the orbit we'd revolved in before, the orbit of habit and affection and small acts of consideration. A smarter woman—my sister, for example—would have kicked up a dust about Paul's long hours of overtime, his inattentiveness, his lack of desire.

Anger might have reached Paul, but I was afraid to get angry, afraid he'd close a final door and lock me out for good. Instead I attempted futile, minor improvements, as if fixing Paul's favorite breakfast would change anything.

And in all those lonely hours, I never asked myself if it was really Paul I was lonely for, or if I suffered from another type of loneliness altogether. When you're struggling desperately to keep what you've lost, you don't ask yourself if you really needed it in the first place.

The night before, I'd leaned over to kiss my husband before he put the light out, and Paul had said: "Sophie, I would, I'd love to, but I'm beat."

I'd only wanted a good-night kiss.

Rory had left me, yes. That had hurt, so badly I still couldn't quite bear to remember it. But Rory had never made me feel as unattractive as my lawfully wedded husband was making me feel. Now I'd answered the signal fire Rory had lit on his distant hilltop with a faint, wavering signal of my own. I'd tapped out the repressive reply that virtue demanded, but Rory would read between the lines. He would see that a door that had been closed was now open an inch. Rory would arrive in Boston in the spring, and spring was not unimaginably far away. It was a dread, a consolation, a fact: I could, if I wanted to, see him again.

The first hurdle of the holiday season arrived: the Christmas Party at The Science Project. It was scheduled for December 22, two days before we left to go back to Washington for the holiday.

"Come anytime," Paul said. "It starts at four, but if you don't get there until five, it's no big deal. We're being very low-key."

The morning of the party, I baked a batch of candy cane cookies. These were dense butter cookies twisted to resemble candy canes, finished off with a dusting of powdered crushed candy canes. I'd learned to make them in the home of a neighbor when I was twelve. Since then they had been my one surefire contribution to holiday potluck events.

"Don't bother to cook anything," Paul had said. But I thought cookies would be a nice gesture. As I've said, I put too much stock in gestures as that grim year drew to a close.

I set aside a tin of cookies to bring by Ned and Stephen's place sometime, when I got the courage to take them up on their usual invitation to stop by. Then I thought, why not today?

This wasn't like me. I wasn't usually the kind of person who acted on impulse—but then lately I was less and less sure of the kind of person I truly was.

I brushed dabs of cookie dough out of my hair and headed for the Eastern Prom. I found the house easily, because the Virgin Mary statue was even more visible than Ned had conveyed.

"A real conversation piece," I said when he came to the door.

He said, "I'm just glad I don't drink much. Think of staggering home and seeing that looming over you."

Stephen's cast was off and I rejoiced with him. Then they showed me around the house.

"Here's where the French windows will be," said Stephen, sweeping a large hand to indicate the front wall's current tacky picture window and the expanse of bay.

"And look what we found," said Ned. "Pocket doors."

When he turned his back to demonstrate how they worked, I said, "Your hair's different, Ned."

Stephen said, "I finally talked him into a haircut."

"Fiona did, not you," said Ned. "It was a pain, anyway, all that hair."

"Looks good," I said. "I feel as if I can really see you for the first time."

"Like that's any big treat," said Ned.

He seemed younger with the haircut, and his face was lighter, more open. It startled me. I'd become too used to Ned's features hiding under that tousled mess of black hair. Suddenly I felt I was standing too close to him, and backed away a pace.

Stephen thought I was trying to get a better look at the new and improved Ned. He said, "It works, doesn't it, Sophie. Now he just has to shave that beard."

"Fiona likes the beard," said Ned.

"Fiona has no taste. The men she works with wear sweater vests," said Stephen.

They fell on my cookies and ate several with a pot of coffee. Stephen ate more cookies than Ned did, using the argument that his cast was now off.

"You shouldn't have," said Stephen with his mouth full. "We don't have anything for you. We still have to get something for our dad, even. We're getting so close on this house that it's work, work, work all the time."

Ned said, "We're not that close on it, actually, Sophie. Stephen always thinks we'll be done sooner than we've promised."

"And you always pad the schedule," said Stephen.

"It's safer," said Ned.

It was Fiona's first Christmas with Ned's family. According to Stephen, who seized the chance to complain about her when Ned was fetching cream and sugar, Fiona was already griping that she didn't have time for holiday obligations.

"Her damn thesis or dissertation or whatever it is," he said. "She talks about it nonstop."

"People are always that way when they're writing their theses," I said.

Stephen rolled his eyes at me.

"Just because it's Christmas doesn't mean you have to be insanely charitable, Sophie. You've spent time with her. You know she's a pill."

"But if she makes him happy, Stephen, who are we to fuss?"

"You said 'we.' So you must agree with me."

"I meant, who is anyone to fuss?"

"He's so keyed **up** with her. It's not like him."

Stephen's boyfriend Scott was also coming to the family dinner. He'd been too busy in Portsmouth to run up to Maine for a week now. Stephen complained at length.

"They're launching a new travel package later this year," Stephen said. "My idea. How do you like the sound of this: 'Rug Buying in Kipling's Istanbul.' "

I smiled doubtfully.

Ned said, "You're trying to remember if Kipling was ever in Istanbul, and the answer is Stephen didn't bother to find out."

"It's the **spirit** of the trip that matters, the whole Victorian adventurer mystique," said Stephen.

Ned walked me to my car.

"You seem a little tired," he said.

"Holidays," I said. "They take it out of you. I'm dreading my husband's office Christmas party tonight."

"That's all?"

"That's all."

"I can complain to you but you can't complain to me?"

"You weren't complaining that day, Ned."

"Have it your way. But you know where we are, me and Stephen."

"Have a merry Christmas, Ned."

"Merry Christmas, Sophie."

We looked at each other. It seemed that we should hug, as friends do at the holidays, but neither of us were natural huggers. I'd started to compromise by clutching his shoulder in a "hey, pal" way, when Ned surprised me by putting his arms around me tightly. He said, very low, "You **really** have a good Christmas." I smelled the scent of wood smoke that clung to his work sweaters, and turned my cheek into his shoulder for a split-second. I hadn't realized just how much I'd missed the feeling of being embraced by someone who truly meant it. Even when Paul did touch me these days, it seemed to be with stiff elbows ready to push me away if I intruded too far.

I disentangled myself from Ned's hug and pushed the hair out of my eyes.

Ned stooped and peered at me, as he had that day when we'd argued about his teaching me to drive.

"Sophie, really, is everything all right? You're too quiet today."

I opened my mouth, and God knows what unseemly confidences would have poured out.

But then Stephen waved his discarded crutch out the porch window and yelled, "God bless us, every one!"

"I'm fine," I said quickly. Ned gave me one long look.

"You know where I am," he said again.

Stephen came out of the house, and they

stood watching me down the street, their figures so different in my rearview mirror. The older brother, stout and genial. The younger brother, slighter and quieter, a most unlikely rock in times of trouble. But, it startled me a little to realize that if my power went or the dogs blocked the driveway, I would phone these two or Donald for help. Paul came in a distant third. Paul was so likely, these days, to say in pretended jest that I'd caused the fuses to blow or somehow provoked the dogs.

Well, friendship was much less complicated than marriage. You could always call a friend and say, "I need this," and there'd be no questions asked. You couldn't always tell a husband what you needed, or count on him to listen if you did.

Back at home, I packed the office party cookies inside a bright red cardboard box left over from the day of outlet shopping with Pepper and Natalie. By three-thirty, I was ready, in my blue boat-necked sweater and fawn velveteen pants. I decided to surprise Paul by being on time for once. Another nice gesture. Another bad idea.

An icy rain had fallen that morning and the roads were still a little slick. I slithered down

Pine Street and over on Congress to the Forest Avenue parking garage. This garage was my favorite because the view of the city from the open top deck was lovely, a Currier and Ives Christmas scene of spires and stars. I stood for a few moments watching the lights winking on Portland's hills, inhaling the cold air. The sullen gray sky had cleared and was deepening now to midnight blue.

Uplifted, I made my way to Paul's office in my new six-dollar boots from the Goodwill down at St. John's Plaza. I'd often been thrift shopping in Washington, but the pickings here were richer than I'd ever seen: sweaters with the tags still on and designer dresses priced for eight and ten dollars. Occasionally the Goodwill took a factory overage. Last time, I'd snagged brand-new, fake-fur-lined black leather snow boots, knee-high, the very last pair of size nines they had. Another overage had provided me with a white full-length, down-filled jacket, with a hood lined in pale apple green. It had cost seventeen dollars.

On the same trip, I'd found three lovely old bronze-gilded frames for a dollar each. I framed two seascapes for Delia and Tom, and a little watercolor of the lighthouse cove for my parents. It was simply a study in pale blue and Payne's gray of the woods and rocks meeting the ocean. They'd probably stash it away in their hall closet, there to remain until the distant day when Delia and I settled their estate.

In my six-dollar boots and seventeen-dollar coat, I slogged up Congress Street to the old converted-warehouse building where The Science Project leased a large suite with attached conference room. Music was playing through the open door, a 1960s instrumental version of "There's No Place Like Home for the Holidays." Inside, about thirty people were gently milling about. Some were gathered at a temporary bar set up on a long folding table. Some hovered around another folding table loaded down with food.

Smack in the center of the office floor stood an enormous Christmas tree. I stood before it for a few minutes, mesmerized. The towering spruce was such a contrast to the tree in our apartment. Since we were going away, we'd bought a small, chubby fir that stood in a corner of the living room, dwarfed by the high ceilings. Its decorations were twelve silver balls and a quantity of tinsel from the Dollar Store.

Even Donald's aqua-metallic artificial tree, which he'd proudly shown me while Jackie was out grocery shopping, was an improvement on our puny specimen. But the Project's Christmas tree was straight out of the **Nutcracker Suite**. There were gingerbread men and papier-mâché angels and cranberry garlands. Tiny, tasteful white lights sparkled all over the branches. At the top was a crystal star, its points outlined in more fairy lights.

The tree mercifully blocked the usual view of a wall full of charts depicting the evolutionary stages of man and undersea life on a barrier reef. All the desks had been covered with red foil wrapping paper, tied at the base with gold twine.

Sitting on one of those desks, drinking punch and singing along to "Silver Bells," were Paul and Natalie and two coworkers. She was wearing an outfit I could never have pulled off: a snug white angora sweater over a long ruby-red stretch velvet skirt with dark-green suede half-boots. A modified "sexy elf" look. Paul was in his shirtsleeves, his hair mussed. And Natalie was next to him, offering him chocolate kisses from her palm.

It was all quite friendly looking. But as I watched, Natalie dropped her head down on Paul's shoulder. If I had walked in five minutes before, I'd have missed the moment. It was like an image going by in a newscast you'd just turned on, disturbing but so briefly shown that you couldn't tell what it meant. A harmless bit of workplace flirting? Or the caress of a lover taking a small, exciting public liberty before the wife arrives?

"Sophie! You made it. I was about to call to see if you were on your way."

Natalie slipped away and Paul was taking my coat, fetching punch, leading me around to this group and that. He couldn't have seemed more natural, just a regular working stiff proud to introduce the little woman to the office gang. Natalie reappeared and took the box of cookies from under my arm.

"Look what Sophie brought," she exclaimed.

She added my puny box to a tabletop crammed with desserts. Its centerpiece was a Yule log cake surrounded by eight teensy silver-wire reindeer.

"Natalie made it," said Paul. "She was up all night."

Natalie was chattering about how someone named Rosalind had pitched in with a genuine English Christmas pudding. It looked like a sodden lump to me, but Natalie said it was authentic because Rosalind hailed from a real English town in the Cotswolds.

I glanced from Natalie to Paul. They were relaxed, convivial, chattering away.

"Did Paul tell you? Toby and I are going to
Barbados for the first week in January," Natalie
said. "I found these bargain hotel reservations on
TravelSmart."

"What's that?" I said.

"A Web site," said Paul. "Natalie saves a lot on
travel by using the internet."

"I can't wait," said Natalie. "It's the most
dreary week of the year."

"I like it," I said. "Christmas is all over with.
Time to relax."

"Sophie never makes New Year's resolutions,"
Paul said. "She hates them."

"I make a ton," said Natalie, letting forth a
trilling party laugh.

"About what?" I said dully.

"Oh, everything. Fitness. Taking cooking lessons. Toby loves Thai food and I just can't get
the hang of it."

"Why would you learn to cook Thai food
when you can go to Seng Thai and have the real
thing for seven bucks apiece?" I asked. What I
really wanted to ask was, "Are you sleeping with
my husband? Does everyone here know? How
stupid am I?"

"Oh, I like to make the effort," said Natalie. "Toby grew up with macaroni and cheese and Hamburger Helper for dinner. I like to spoil him."

Paul's face was expressionless. Either he was bored with talk of Toby, or he was hiding the pain it gave him to see his office inamorata talking about her main squeeze.

It was then that Bob came over. Bob was the office jester, the guy who made the Christmas party and the summer picnic go off with a bang. Every office I'd ever worked in had had a Bob.

He wore a Santa suit and a beard made out of yellow sticky notes, and was brandishing a sprig of artificial mistletoe. Through the corner of my eye I'd seen him making the rounds of the room, embarrassing unlikely people into embraces. Dr. Kendrick, the Project's executive director, beamed at it all. He was an elderly gentleman who'd parlayed white hair and a tall, lean physique into a reputation for wisdom and management ability. The few times I'd run into him he'd called me "Sarah."

"Paul!" Bob said. "Paul Stoddard, old pal. How's the big kahuna?"

"Fine, Bob. Just fine."

Paul grinned. He held up his glass and toasted Bob.

"I'm gonna ask you to show a little Christmas spirit. You know the drill."

Bob was waving the plastic bundle over my head.

"Kiss the wife," said Bob.

Paul swung me around, dipped me, and planted a hot, wet kiss on my lips. A few people clapped. I felt sweaty, and a little sick and dizzy.

"That's showing them," said Bob.

"I think I'll get a drink," I said. As I walked away, Bob began hacking into the Yule log with a plastic knife to Natalie's evident distress.

For an hour I drank inferior eggnog and listened to strangers lay out their Christmas plans. For another hour, after everyone else left, I helped Paul and Natalie clear up, throwing out plastic cups full of sour, cheap champagne, ripping down the wrapping paper that had covered the desks and file cabinets, watching Paul water the tree. Natalie was going to come in and water it for the four days that Paul would be home in D.C., then Paul would take over during Natalie's vacation.

"Why not just take it down?" I asked.

"It still has two good weeks left in it," said Natalie.

We heaped the trash bags near the door for the cleaning crew and locked up.

"Merry Christmas," said Natalie to Paul and me on the sidewalk. If the good wishes could have been phonetically parceled out in the frigid air above us, Paul would have received a bolded, seventy-two point "Merry Christma" and I'd have gotten just the faint tail end of a micro-scopic, six-point "s."

"Can we give you a lift?" Paul said.

"No, Toby's meeting me any minute. We're going up to Freeport. Just for silly shopping. Toby needs some waterproof hiking socks."

L. L. Bean was open even on Christmas Eve, for those disorganized souls who needed to make a last dash for a gift. Natalie probably stockpiled extra presents, wrapped in tasteful, occasion-neutral wrapping paper, for just such eventu-alities.

"Here's Toby now," she said, and skipped off toward a blue sedan with a badly dented front fender. The windshield was too shiny with re-flected neon for me to get a good look at Toby. I would have loved to see that he was dazzlingly handsome or carrying a bouquet of red roses for his sweetheart. Anything to show that Natalie had cause to prize him rather than risk her marital stakes on an office romance.

"Good party," Paul observed as we made our way to the parking lot. His Explorer was parked there too. We were a two-car couple strolling hand in hand, reviewing the details of a pleasant seasonal social event.

"Paul," I said. He was laboring up the steps of the lot, puffing a little. I was surprised to see that I wasn't. When had that happened?

"Paul. Please. Is something going on with Natalie?"

"Going on?"

He gripped the iron handrail, seemingly unbothered by the smell of urine and damp cement in the stairwell.

"When I walked in, she was being very cozy with you. She put her head on your shoulder."

"That? You were worried about **that**?"

The incredulity in his voice reassured me.

"Well, it just seemed a little odd. For the workplace."

"She'd had a few drinks."

"Is it . . . is it possible that she might have a little crush on you?" I said.

Paul was fumbling in his jacket for his monthly parking pass.

"If she did, wouldn't it be harmless?"

"Not to me."

"Oh please, Sophie. These things happen."

"They might but I don't have to like it," I said.

"I can't fire her," he said. "I'm not even her direct supervisor. Kendrick is."

"Just discourage her," I said. "Don't go complimenting her cooking all the time."

"She worked so hard on that Yule log. It took her two days. Besides, you have nothing to worry about. She's engaged. She's already booked the reception hall."

I would rather Paul had said, "You have nothing to worry about. How could I look at another woman when you're in the room?" The deposit on Natalie and Toby's wedding reception space seemed like scant security for our marriage.

He kissed me softly.

"It's Christmas. This is so nutty to argue like this when we can go home and finally relax. We'll take that train ride tomorrow if you want. That could be fun."

A week before, I'd suggested seeing the Christmas illuminations along the Narrow Gauge Railway, the ones Alex had mentioned back in October. He'd rolled his eyes. Now he was offering to go, like a parent granting a child a begged-for treat.

"I don't want to go on the train ride," I said.

"Then we'll do something else Christmas-y. I'm off for five days. Isn't that reason enough to celebrate?"

I did not feel like celebrating as I sat in my car, waiting to see Paul's headlights go on across the lot. Natalie meant business. Tonight had demonstrated that. She wanted Paul, and for more than a casual affair. Natalie wasn't a casual person. Paul could not or would not see the purpose in that piquant little face, those large, intent dark eyes.

Paul drew up, honking his horn. He rolled down his window.

"See you at home," he said. "Drive carefully. It's freezing up again."

The only signal that came in on the Escort's faulty radio was a Bowdoin College station that seemed to be staffed by potheads and insomniacs. It was playing a calypso version of "Have a Holly Jolly Christmas." Ahead of me Paul turned left onto Bramhall Street. We drove past the hospital. Its outdoor lights seemed almost festive, though they were on every single night of the year. Paul parked the Explorer in the garage. I parked on the curb twenty feet away and turned off my engine and sat still.

There was a memory I'd been chasing all the way home, a memory somehow connected to the party tonight. Now I had it. It was a memory of the first time I'd seen Rory walk down the hall of our school next to Liz Brody. I saw again his head bending down toward hers, her lessening of the distance between them until their shoulders touched. It was a statement, the public announcement of a well-regarded merger. I had seen them and been fixed to the spot with heartache, though Rory had not seen me.

Why had that hoary old fragment come to mind? Paul stood under the lamplight, waiting for me on the porch. My gloved fingers fumbled for the car door handle.

Rory and Liz walking down the hall.

Rory and Liz.

Paul and Natalie.

You shouldn't ignore the evidence. It's not wise. But what was evidence, and what was jealous fancy?

"Come **on,** Sophie hon, it's damn cold," Paul called. He whistled a little, the whistle of a man with five days of vacation in front of him and not a care in the world. The whistle faded away in white smoke around his head.

I went in and he put an arm around me.

"Thanks for coming to the party and baking those great cookies," he said.

"You're welcome."

"It's going to be a good Christmas," he said. "You'll see."

Eighteen

Pepper kicked up a fuss about the rental car.

"Where are we going to **park** that?" she said, looking out the bay window of her living room at the tiny two-door Geo, which stood alone at the end of a pristine expanse of curb. All of Pepper's neighbors had driveways. Some had two-door garages.

"Sophie could park twenty-four rental cars on this street without any problem," said Paul.

"Mr. Cantwell doesn't like cars parked on this side," said Pepper. "It gets in the way of the garbage truck."

"Is your neighbor a Montgomery County policeman?" said Paul. "Because if not, he'll have to grin and bear it."

"I could have taken Sophie anywhere she wanted to go," said Pepper, referring to me, as she often did, as if I were in the next room.

"You're worked off your feet with the Christmas rush," said Paul. "Sophie's become a wonderful driver. She'll enjoy getting herself places."

"City driving is different," said Pepper, as if

Paul and I lived in a small village in the Loire Valley.

We sat in the living room and talked about Paul's cousin Ginny, who had been married six months and pregnant for three of them.

"On the first try," Pepper said, eyeing me as if she suspected horrors yet to be revealed about my flagging fertility. I missed the days when people didn't feel free to discuss reproductive matters in public.

"Well, with those hips of hers Ginny should be a natural in labor," said Paul. "She's been porking up ever since the honeymoon."

"She's always had big bones," said Pepper, frowning.

"I don't think it's her bones that are jiggling around back there," said Paul.

"Don't talk like that," Pepper said. "Ginny is like a daughter to me. She took me with her to choose the layette. We used a lot of yellow. That way if it's a girl or a boy, she'll be set either way."

"Doesn't she know?" said Paul, squirming a little, not over the obstetrical discussion but because the couch cushions were the kind that fight back as you lean against them.

"They want it to be a surprise."

I'd met Ginny once, at a dinner party Pepper had given to celebrate—well, to announce—Paul's marriage. She was large and loud, and her hair was the same straw-blond that Pepper dyed hers. Ginny discussed her golf game for ten minutes before looking me up and down and saying, "We thought Paul would never get married." Her stare said that if this was what Paul was going to bring home, he should have waited still longer. Later, over Pepper's peach cobbler, she praised the Commonwealth of Virginia's firearms laws, which enabled regular citizens to carry handguns in their cars and jacket pockets. Someone like Ginny deserved a twenty-eight-hour labor, but she was the kind who popped the baby out in an afternoon and then didn't see what all the fuss around childbirth was about.

"She's not anxious about buying the layette so soon?" I ventured. "I know a lot of newly pregnant mothers are nervous that that's bad luck."

"That would be silly in her case," said Pepper. "She's not at the danger age for miscarriages and birth defects. It's after thirty-three or so that you have to worry. Now, are you two up for coffee? I have a delicious new raspberry-vanilla blend, or you can run up and shower first. Oh, and I have an iron, Sophie, if you want to touch up that blouse."

"Did she say that on purpose?" I said when we were safe in our room.

"Which thing do you mean? She was in top form today. I'm sorry," Paul said, taking me in his arms and kissing my forehead. I pulled away. There were moments since the Christmas party when my suspicions of him seemed like sheer hysteria, and others when they seemed the most practical certainty. Sometimes the view changed from minute to minute, that was how muddled and unsure I was.

"The thing about children," I said.

"She blurts. It has nothing to do with you."

Just before I'd tossed the marriage manual out along with the trash from my Christmas gift-wrapping, I'd happened to see the words, **"Remember that no matter how badly your mother-in-law may behave, she is the person who made your spouse the terrific person he or she is."**

This was obviously nonsense. Paul's good qualities must be inherited from his father, with no credit whatsoever due to Pepper.

"You take the first shower," said Paul, picking up one of the copies of **The National Review** on the nightstand. He began to leaf through it as if obeying a pressing need to stay informed about the latest debates on flag-burning and children of divorce. I'd have pressed my point, but we were due at Delia's in two hours.

It was thankless to be a daughter-in-law, I reflected in the shower. Pepper might gush that Ginny was like a daughter to her, but it wasn't Ginny whom Pepper would count on to take care of her in her old age. It wasn't Ginny who'd be carting her off to get her osteoporosis checked or lugging her dutifully to D.A.R. meetings. Pepper should be nicer to me, if only as a sort of an insurance policy. Men didn't take care of aged relatives. Women did. A woman with two sons had better be damn nice to her daughters-in-law.

Of course, Pepper might be counting on James's wife Ellen to fetch and carry for her when she got too old to buzz around herself. But Ellen was a dark horse. She'd been a neighborhood au pair when James met her. Having her son marry an immigrant domestic worker from Dublin had mortified Pepper, who seemed to long for the days when shops put out signs reading, "No Irish Need Apply." She'd said a few unforgivable things on the occasion of James's engagement. Surely Ellen hadn't forgotten.

Ellen had black hair, a lovely heart-shaped face, and eyes that kept their own secrets. She treated Pepper with gentle courtesy. Yet in any contest, Ellen usually got her way. She and James were living in Alexandria in a Civil War–era townhouse, instead of the 1970s faux colonial in Kensington that Pepper had picked out for them. They were raising their kids Catholic to Pepper's often-voiced horror. And they were coming from Alexandria tomorrow instead of staying at Pepper's tonight. In a standoff, my money was on Ellen every time.

This prospect, as enjoyable as it might be to watch, was not a happy one for me. In years to come, I might actually emerge as the "sympathetic" daughter-in-law, God help me. With this grim possibility looming, I should probably give some serious thought to a full-time job that involved travel. Of course, if my husband was cheating on me, I might never have to face the dreadful fate of being Pepper's comfort in her golden years.

I shampooed my hair with a little bottle of baby shampoo I'd brought with me, ignoring Pepper's almond-scented designer stuff. It was

Christmas and my heart was too filled with resentment even to use my mother-in-law's shampoo. Against my will, I had to admire Pepper's Egyptian cotton bath towels, to admire the effort that had gone into the whole guest bedroom "suite," as Pepper called it. It was like staying at a luxurious hotel. On the bathroom window ledge was a basket of individual soaps wrapped in pale gold paper. The bath mat was English sheepskin. The guest-room bed was a four-poster with feather pillows and a down comforter in robin's egg blue. If I could have forgotten that Pepper was downstairs waiting for Paul to nail the stockings to the mantelpiece and for me to give one last polish to her four silver candy dishes, I might have found our room's impersonal cushiness soothing.

The silver didn't take me long. I like small intense tasks like that.

"What else can I help with?" I asked.

Paul was gingerly tapping the stockings into place. Each was made of red velveteen with a name embroidered in white script across the cuff, except for mine, a late arrival in green sateen with "Sophie" in red braid.

"Nothing," said Pepper. "You know how I am in my kitchen."

"Any presents left to wrap?" I said. "I'm good at that, believe it or not."

"Oh, that was finished weeks ago."

"Wait till you see ours, Mom," said Paul, putting his hands on my shoulders. "Sophie's an artist with the gold ribbons and the pretty paper."

"Well, that's her calling, isn't it," Pepper said. "Artistic matters. Now give me twenty minutes before you rush off and we'll have some drinks and these herbed cheese puffs I'm testing for that party at the Deavers' tonight."

We sat on the resistant couch, Paul sprawling, me as stiff and well-behaved as a patient in a dentist's waiting room.

"That's my mother for you," he said. "I'm home for two and a half days and she's sweating over her cheese puffs instead of talking to her son who lives so far away. It makes me feel like staying in Portland for good and just having her visit us."

"For good?"

"It's only a thought. There are lots of nice places to live, a little out of town. Falmouth and Yarmouth and Cape Elizabeth. They'd probably be glad for me to put in another year, if we wanted."

He'd said, "If **we** wanted." That was encouraging.

"I like Portland proper," I said.

"Well," said Paul. "You have friends there. But you could drive in to see them. Out of town's more value for our money."

Et tu, Paul? Already thinking of the suburbs. I'd have argued but why bother? If my marriage somehow improved, there'd be plenty of time to discuss real estate. If it didn't, I'd have bigger problems.

Pepper wasn't coming with us to Christmas Eve supper at Delia's. Comfort Foods was catering six soirees that night.

It was fortunate that Pepper's traditions—presents exchanged after an elegant brunch, followed by a huge mid-afternoon dinner with thirty guests—didn't conflict with Delia's plans. Delia was cooking a Christmas Eve meal starring three different kinds of seafood to honor Tom's Italian half. Then we'd go to mass, and return to their house for hot cocoa and gifts.

Ever since Delia had married Tom six years ago, my parents had contentedly ceded to her the hosting of every holiday our family passed together. This was a relief to us all. My folks' house, with its rail-less center stairway, sliding glass patio doors, and slate-tiled living room, was no venue for celebration. At best, it might suit a Fourth of

July barbecue where the host wears an apron with a slogan on it and someone brings a sheet cake with blueberry and strawberries and Cool Whip depicting the American flag.

"If you have to go I suppose you have to go," Pepper said mournfully." 'A son is a son till he gets him a wife, but a daughter's a daughter the rest of her life.' "

"I'm still your son, Mom," Paul said wearily. "And you're working tonight. What would I do, sit here alone and contemplate my warm family feelings?"

"Of course you should go. Both of you. It's natural for Sophie's family to claim some time. Just save a little room for brunch tomorrow, if you can."

My mother hadn't altered much since I'd last seen her. She has a solid, comfortable plumpness that never varies, and her hair has been gray since I was twelve. My father was older-looking, though. His face was thinner, his hair was thinning, and there was an old-man fragility to his knees and ankles that was new.

They gave me brief hugs. My parents are not demonstrative. They came from families that believed love was expressed through what you did for a person: making breakfast, or remembering to get the storm windows installed, or giving the dog a bath.

Tom crushed my ribs with his embrace, and Delia grabbed me tight.

"Back from the wilds," Tom said to Paul, and clapped him on the shoulder.

Paul smiled weakly. He hated it when people acted as if Maine were a faraway, barbarian land.

After eyeing me solemnly for ten minutes, my nephew Ben demonstrated his walking abilities, stumbling from the coffee table into my waiting arms a dozen times. It was hard not to snatch him up and weep sentimentally all over his downy round head.

Delia had put out cheese, crackers, and red wine. Soon Paul and my father were engrossed in discussion of a unit on food preparation safety for The Science Project's sixth-grade curriculum. My mother talked to Tom about how Doctors without Borders could "certainly use" a few more dermatologists in its ranks. Tom smiled and ate cheese cubes. I picked up Ben and trailed after Delia into the kitchen.

Delia and Tom lived in Cleveland Park in a Sears Craftsman bungalow, circa 1908. It was a white elephant when they'd bought it back in

the mid-nineties, priced reasonably for that desirable neighborhood because it had been in
such bad shape. Today it was worth half a million at least. Back when I'd rented a place one
neighborhood down, Cleveland Park was a refuge
for little old ladies who needed stabilized rents
and for young singles not rich or fabulous enough
to live in Dupont Circle. Now it was a haven for
professional couples who used their deluxe baby
strollers as battering rams to push the few remaining little old ladies off the sidewalk.

"So what's up?" I said to my sister.

"Mom's driving me crazy, as always. She has
some stupid community gardening-for-charity
project up the street, on Sedgewick."

"So she's dropping by a lot?"

"Oh no. She wants **me** to put Ben in the carriage and trot up there. God forbid she ever offer
to babysit."

This wasn't the philosophical Delia who'd long
ago come to terms with my mother's faults. This
was the angry teenage Delia who felt shortchanged and wanted my mother to know it. The
holidays brought out this side of my sister.

I snuggled my nose into Ben's neck and blew
out my lips. He laughed uproariously.

"She's always going after Tom and me for contributions for St. Ann's Infant Home. Which we don't grudge, but you'd think she might stop by with a lousy teething ring for her own grandchild."

It was true that Mom was full of ideas for other people to share their wealth. Meanwhile, her wallet was as carefully sealed as an unraided Egyptian tomb.

"Remember the Christmas she gave us bike headlamps?" said Delia. "And patch kits, and whistles on cords?"

"How could I forget? The safety Christmas."

We laughed.

"At least Dad spoils him rotten," Delia said. "He can't see him enough. It makes up for the fact that Mom wouldn't be able to pick Ben out of a police lineup."

Delia lifted the lid of a frying pan and checked on the shrimp scampi.

"There's stuffed fried flounder in the oven, with steamed mussels to start," she said. "An Italian Christmas Eve dinner. Next year Tom's folks will be with us."

Tom's parents were visiting his mother's relatives in Ocean City, where many Washington-area Italians went to retire.

"And you, sweetie?" my sister said. "How are you? I like the hair."

"Thanks."

"So spill. You look great but you don't look happy."

"Problems with Paul. That girl at work I mentioned."

Delia put her slotted spoon down.

"I'll kill him," she said. "You haven't even been married two years."

"It may be my imagination, Delia. She's just very . . . cozy with him."

Delia turned back to the stove, first rubbing my head in sympathy, then rubbing Ben's round, bobbling head.

"Tom had an assistant with a big crush on him," she said. "She lay in wait for him one night at his parking garage. I just put my foot down and he got rid of her."

"It isn't that easy with Paul. Although I'm trying."

I must have sounded plaintive, because Ben began to whine in sympathy. I gave him a sugar wafer.

Delia said, "I know you're trying. Look how Rory wrote, and you didn't rush to fall at his feet."

"His feet are thousands of miles away or maybe I would."

Tom stuck his head in.

"Sophie, stop talking to Delia for a second. You talk to her nearly every day. You have to listen up, Soph. This is important. I just heard about this great new IPO. Company with a wonder drug for irritable bowel syndrome. It'll open big. Are you in?"

"What are the prospects with the FDA?"

"Almost through. Approval expected in weeks, not months."

"We've heard that before."

"I've checked around. This is solid. In the clinical trials, patients were using the word 'life-changing.' You know how common an IBS diagnosis is these days?"

"Sounds good," I said.

"How much are you in for?"

"Five thousand?"

"Done," said Tom. "Write me the check tonight and you'll be making a profit by New Year's. It's my last flutter for a while. Delia's cutting me off."

"The market's been tanking since June," said Delia.

"That's tech. Not pharmaceuticals and bio-tech," said Tom.

"Did you buy those treasury bonds, Thomas?"

"Yes, ma'am, I sure did."

"You'll thank me when the bottom falls out, you know."

"I always thank you. I thank you every day, my darling beautiful wife, my . . ."

"Okay, okay," said Delia.

Tom kissed her and took Ben from my arms.

"Let's give your aunt a break," he said, moving across the living room to Paul and my dad. Paul peered anxiously at Ben, as if Ben might spit up on him or poke his eye out.

Delia gave me a steady look.

"I know you, Sophie. You always go halfway. Whatever's wrong is Paul's fault."

"But what if it's true? What if he's cheating on me?"

"Oh honey," Delia said and put an arm around me. She didn't say anything else. When the situation looks dire, and there's no more advice to give, Delia doesn't give it. She just puts her arm around you instead.

Delia's cooking wasn't as polished as Pepper's, but it was hearty and abundant. Despite the name Comfort Foods, at Pepper's it was always hit-or-miss if the canapés would go around.

Mom attempted to say grace but Tom forestalled her, setting a time record. Soon after Tom married Delia, he'd learned to make skilled end-runs around anything my mother did or said that would get Delia fuming. This talent helped preserve the uneasy peace between my mother and her firstborn. Tonight, he'd arranged the seating so that there'd be a buffer zone around the two powers. Delia chatted about the baby with my dad. Paul and Tom talked about cars. My mother and I were left to each other.

I turned to her and said, "How'd the children's pageant go?"

"Wonderful. We had only one child sick to his stomach beforehand, the little Gabrielli boy, but he's a sensitive one. We'd made him one of King Herod's henchmen, so the play wasn't disrupted much. All he'd had to do was stand there and hold an ax."

"You'd think a child like that could get a doctor's excuse not to be in the play."

"Now, **that** wouldn't be good for him, Sophie. Children get these ideas and before you know it, they have a lifelong fear of public speaking."

Delia's eyes met mine down the table. I gave up arguing for the welfare of the Gabrielli child. His future therapy bills weren't my lookout.

"But the pageant in general?" I said. "Was it a hit?"

"A **big** hit," my mother said. "We had a full house, and the audience insisted on an encore of 'We Need a Little Christmas.'"

For reasons lost in the mists of time, the St. Catherine's pageant always ended with something secular and jazzed-up. Calls for an encore of the closing number were also traditional, probably because the audience had sat through long, uninspiring choruses of "Away in a Manger" and "Jesus Our Brother, Kind and Good" for the previous hour.

My mother was getting older, I thought as she talked on. In ten years or so, she'd be a bona fide elderly lady. Other people would be kind to her simply on the strength of that. **I** could be kind to her for that, if I chose to. My mother couldn't disappoint me anymore. She might even surprise me—although I wasn't holding my breath.

Every Christmas for all my life, my family had arrived a half-hour early for midnight mass to ensure "good seats." Tonight my mother, always chilly in church, sat huddled in her sensible gray coat, like a shivering pigeon with feathers plumped against the cold. She whispered to my father, bemoaning again that the folk choir wasn't singing tonight. My father nodded and jounced his grandson.

Paul sat on my other side, leafing through the hymnal. It was Christmas Eve so I squeezed his hand. He smiled at me, and the specter of Natalie receded for the time being.

Tom stretched his long legs under the kneeler; he'd fall asleep halfway through the sermon. Delia was discreetly peering around, trying to spot a few old stoner school friends she didn't have much time for these days but enjoyed keeping up with.

It was pleasantly sentimental to be back in my childhood church, even though St. Catherine's was ugly and unwelcoming, a steel-and-glass tent with theater-in-the-round seating and an altar made from a big slab of concrete set across two small slabs of concrete, like a miniature Stonehenge. But tonight, with candles lit, it was almost pretty.

My mother, loyal to her folk choir, made a face as the first trumpets blared out "Joy to the World," but Tom bellowed the words and my father joined in in his wavery tenor. Paul sang in his "church voice," a careful baritone.

"On this happy night," said the priest during his sermon, "let us look at our lives and celebrate the pure gifts, the gifts that have come to us, like Christ's love in this flawed world, as grace abundant. Let us bow our heads for a moment and be thankful."

Everyone bowed their heads, except Tom, who was sleeping. My mother kept glancing over at him, then glancing admonishingly at Delia, who refused to wake him up.

After Communion, my father jiggled the baby up and down while my mother prayed with a rapt, unconvincing expression that was marred by a fleeting smirk when the soprano flatted on, "O Little Town of Bethlehem."

When mass was over, people milled about the vestibule wishing each other Merry Christmas, covertly observing holiday finery. Jostled, I took refuge in an out-of-the-way recess near the baptismal font. The font was a hideous malachite basin set in black granite. It stood in a dark corner up a short flight of stairs. Here I could pass unnoticed by old classmates I wouldn't recognize and old nuns I'd been afraid of.

From behind me, an arm tugged at my coat. When I looked up, there was Rory.

He'd changed after five years but just a bit. His beautiful lion's mane was a trifle receded, and his flashing grin was subdued to a suitable church-going smile. But he was the same Rory. The same wicked blue eyes, the same square shoulders, the same sense of constant movement even when he was standing still.

"Sophie," he said. "I thought you guys might be here tonight. I saw you up front but you were looking straight ahead the whole time."

"You're supposed to be in Prague," I said stupidly.

He gestured toward the crowd below us.

"My mom had a health problem," he said. "A little scare."

I could see Mrs. McLaughlin now, though I'd somehow not spotted her before. She was leading Liz off into a gaggle of parishioners. Even from our vantage point, her pride and pleasure in her daughter-in-law were obvious.

"It turned out to be just her gall bladder," Rory said. "We'd already canceled our vacation, though. It's worth missing Prague to see your face, Sophie Ann."

Liz, I saw, was heavier than when I'd last seen her. Her face was puffy and her calves decidedly thicker. Maybe the water and food in Eastern

Europe were hard on a woman's looks. But it didn't matter how she was holding up. She was his wife.

Delia was eyeing us from the far door. Rory saw her too. He never missed anything.

"Delia's looking good," he said. "But not as good as you are."

"Thanks."

"I mean it. Where's your husband?"

I pointed to Paul, who wasn't appearing at his best. My mother was showing him a bulletin board of photos of children with severe Down's syndrome, taken at the parish Advent party. Paul's face was a little green. When he was a child, Pepper would threaten him with eternal disgrace if he ever revealed the smallest discomfort around his senile grandmother or his cousin Arnie who was retarded, as they called it then. This policy left Paul with an intense panic in the presence of the mentally challenged. A recent series of Wal-Mart commercials had ballyhooed the chain's charitable efforts in this direction, and Paul had to leave the room when they came on television.

"Looks like a nice guy," Rory said.

"He is. Very nice."

We edged farther into the baptismal nook as the crowd eddied closer.

"I'd love to see you, Sophie," he said. "Just to catch up."

"I don't have much free time this trip."

"Only for lunch. Just to hear what's happened with you in the past five years."

"Well, for one thing, I got married," I said.

"Sophie, aren't we even allowed to talk anymore? Lunch is pretty darn innocent. I have a meeting in town on the twenty-seventh, down at Seventeenth and Connecticut. Will you still be here? Could you meet me somewhere around two?"

I said, "The Mayflower does an afternoon tea, if that's possible for you."

It was a most dispassionate setting, the Mayflower tea room. I'd been there many times with Marta, who was a glutton for scones with lemon curd.

"Very ladylike, aren't you," said Rory, who could always read my mind. "You're cute. Fine then. Tea at the Mayflower, the twenty-seventh, at two-fifteen sharp."

"I'll try to make it," I said, but he'd already gone. "My son, Rory, you remember him, my son," I could hear Mrs. McLaughlin saying to her friends.

It had been years since I'd seen Rory's mother this close up. Her face was unlined still, but her cheeks had sunken in slightly, and her hair had faded from its glorious copper-penny brightness to a lackluster marmalade shade.

Liz still wore hers in a long ponytail down her back. It was too girlish a style now. But when she turned and waved at me, her wide, kind, impersonal smile was the same.

Like Rory, Delia never missed a trick.

"Careful, Sophie," she whispered as our sleepy group made its way back to separate cars. "You didn't agree to see him, did you?"

"It's tea at the Mayflower. We're not booking a room or anything."

"Didn't he work you over enough the first time?"

"You have nothing to worry about, Dee."

We had a pleasant time opening Christmas presents; I guess it was pleasant, anyway. I was still in a daze from seeing Rory.

The seascape would hang above her desk, Delia declared. "I can look at it and imagine you there."

My father said only, "You did this, Sophie?" Later, when Delia was clearing up and Tom was putting the baby to sleep, he came and perched by me on the sofa arm.

"The painting is lovely, Sophie. It must be a beautiful place."

That was all he said, but it was enough. My mother said, "Very nice little painting, hon. There are a lot of parks up there?"

"Untouched **wilderness,**" said Paul.

Untouched wilderness held no charms for my mother. There was nothing to organize there.

Back in our enormous bed at Pepper's, Paul said, "I'd say let's fool around, but there's something about being at my mother's. It's an anti-aphrodisiac."

"I understand," I said.

"When we're back at home, how about that."

After he was sleeping, I began to think again about the Christmas party. About Natalie and that comfy scene I'd interrupted when I arrived.

A woman who doubts her husband is not a woman who should be meeting a man she cannot trust. Especially when that man is, even in a brief encounter by a baptismal font, still devastatingly attractive to her.

But it was only tea, after all. How dangerous could it be?

Nineteen

"I see you've picked a real den of vice and sin for us to meet in," Rory said.

"I don't know what you're talking about," I answered.

The elderly waiter came over to describe tea varieties to us. You can debate tea at the Mayflower as you can debate a wine selection in a French restaurant: Oolong, Formosa, Jasmine, Darjeeling.

We both ordered the Ceylon blend, much to the waiter's disappointment. Such a dull choice. You could see that this waiter really cared to educate the clientele. He was a career waiter, not some punky kid who didn't know the difference between a diffuser and a slop basin. The Mayflower did not use diffusers, of course. They used small silver strainers.

That morning, I'd said good-bye to Pepper, hoping my joy wasn't too evident, and dropped the rental car and Paul at National, taking the subway back from the airport to Marta's immaculate, peaceful apartment in Woodley Park. Marta and I had spent a pleasurable two hours debating outfits for her office party that night. Marta had finally decided on a killer dress, a pale blue silk-satin number cut on the bias. She said that if she didn't have a date, she may as well make an entrance.

Paul had been understanding about my extended stay. Too understanding. "Have a good time with Marta," he'd said. "Stay longer if you're having fun."

"Stay longer." Not exactly words to keep Paul's image forcibly before me at this moment, sitting with Rory in sequestered plushness.

Our table was a corner banquette that was reflected in the gilt-framed mirrors, which also reflected the flowered carpet in moss green and pink, the rosy tablecloths, and a passing crowd of diplomats, stockbrokers, and guests returned from shopping. I loved this hotel's Gilded Age gentility, its kind staff who opened doors and answered questions whether you were minor royalty or just passing through to admire the spectacular restoration.

I'd been so sure Rory wouldn't belong there, in this hum of discreet luxury. But Rory was as natural here as he'd been at the Tastee Diner in Bethesda when he was a teenager. His loafers were polished and his socks were absolutely correct. He wore a hunter-green jacket that had always been one of my favorites, with immaculately pressed khakis, a white Oxford shirt, and (his only lapse) a regrettable tie covered in what seemed to be bright green tadpoles. Rory had always had terrible taste in ties.

Under the table he took my hand. Briefly. Rory never rushed his fences.

"You had to have missed me a little," he said softly.

"I miss all my old friends."

He threw his head back and laughed. He had the Irish trick of silent laughter, the blue eyes narrowed in appreciation of a joke.

"I'm glad," he said. "You know, I'd hardly recognize you today. You're so grown-up in those clothes. Not that I don't like how you look."

I was wearing a mulberry cashmere sweater, borrowed from Marta and just the faintest bit snug, and a close-fitting dark gray skirt. I'd also worn my camel coat and the wine-colored beret Ned had said was useless that day at Higgins Beach.

Ned seemed a million miles away in this hushed retreat for the leisured and powerful— mostly the leisured, this post-Christmas afternoon. The only other guests were a decorous bridal shower in the opposite corner, and a mother and daughter obviously just returned from shopping who kept diving among their bags to reconsider wallets and watch straps and a silver baby's rattle.

"Which tea would you like?" the waiter murmured.

Rory appeared confused, which was natural since the tea had arrived and was sitting in front of us, complete with an individual silver pot of extra-hot water for each of us. At the Mayflower, the old niceties prevailed despite the cell phones, speeding SUVs, and roller-blading messengers just outside.

"He means this," I said pointing at the right side of the menu, which gave several choices for eatables, from a modest repast of scones and jam to a four-star extravaganza that featured salmon, Champagne, and strawberries.

"Marta and I usually get the classic," I said.

"Two classics," Rory told the waiter, who nodded deferentially and padded off. Above us, the harpist started on a selection of Ye Olde English Christmas carols. Strains of "The Holly and the Ivy" floated down to us.

"How are things?" I began.

It was disconcerting how directly his eyes met

mine. An **adventurer's** eyes, said my Harlequin romance inner monologue.

"Well, we were in Warsaw all last year, and now I'm off to Moscow for a month of training and probably a stint there if the powers that be decide."

"La-di-da," I said mildly.

"It's no big deal. I'm looking forward to it because I like Moscow better than Warsaw. Warsaw, a lot of it's rebuilt since World War II, so nothing's that authentic. Moscow's much better. Of course, for authentic medieval, Krakow's the place."

"Show off," I said.

"If I can't show off to you, who can I show off to? You've been letting me show off in front of you since you were six."

He talked about his work and I watched him, enjoying the play of expression on his face, marveling at how light and easy a thing he made of recounting the passage of five years. Time couldn't matter to us, his casual, intimate voice implied. And I found it didn't. He was the old Rory, my Rory. I'd been born to listen to his stories, to hold his hand under tables in restaurants, to watch with delight as he turned even the drabbest, dullest places into scenes of adventure.

His job hadn't changed much in five years. He'd be based in one Eastern European city and travel to others, advising fledgling civic groups. Meanwhile, Liz did international relief work involving medical care for women and children, working alone from the Warsaw satellite office of some worldwide health organization.

In their time overseas, Rory and Liz had seen most of Eastern Europe, Paris, Madrid, the Greek islands. And Venice, of course. Everyone went to Venice, Rory said.

"You'd like Venice, Sophie."

"Wouldn't anyone?"

"Liz didn't. She said it smelled. The big cities don't interest her. She likes experiential travel."

I knew what that was. Backpacking up the sides of old Mayan temples. Staying with Chinese families in the Hunan province instead of buying suits in Hong Kong.

I couldn't help feeling a proprietary thrill as I saw the mother and daughter look up from their food and catch sight of Rory. He was a man who attracted female attention wherever he went, but he never cased the room, as some handsome men do, to see who was making eyes in his direction. It was one of his many endearing traits.

So many times I'd seen it, that riveted, feline

attention that Rory commanded and which he pretended never to see. Could I ever be married to this as Liz was? To these envying, hostile glances from other women?

"Do you and Liz do much experiential travel?" I said, trying to sound as if I really didn't care about the once-in-a-lifetime memories he and Liz must be racking up all over the world. After all, I was racking up once-in-a-lifetime memories in Maine too. Of sorts.

"I promised her a walking tour of Wales next year. We'll get rained on and eat some bad food and she'll feel she's really seen something."

He grinned. It was the grin of someone mocking his own failure. Rory was not giving Liz what she wanted, and he was feeling it, that rueful smile said.

"You never used to mind roughing it," I said, thinking of camping trips Rory used to take with his dad and brothers. They'd return smelly and jubilant, full of stories about bears in the night and snakes under tree trunks.

"I do enough roughing it for my job. They have a very weird idea of what decent hotels are over there."

In case we needed another reminder of the virtues of not roughing it, the food arrived. The

Mayflower teas come on tiered silver caddies, each delicious tidbit resting in a fluted gold cup set on a paper doily. Seeing Rory should have killed my appetite, in the tradition of romantic heroines, but it had been a long time since I'd had those two slices of wheat toast in Marta's kitchen. Marta wasn't much of a breakfast person, and the bread had been defrosted the night before. It had tasted of ice and cardboard.

I snagged a cream puff and scooped the cream out with my teaspoon. Not meeting his eyes, I said, "So what's your problem with Liz nowadays?"

"Was I complaining about her?"

"Well, I just got a feeling."

"I'm too happy to see you to complain about anything."

He sighed, and I had a flash of remembering how Rory used to take me in his arms after making love and sigh just like that, a sigh of complete contentment. He would lie back in my bed, hogging the pillows, his hair tousled and shining that lovely golden red against the white sheets. His face would have that angelic flush that only fair men get. I'd lean my head against his chest and kid myself that true love would overcome all.

In a moment Rory would see what I was thinking. Next thing you know we'd be asking for a room.

So I put some vinegar into my voice and said, "Talk about Liz. Tell me how things turned out. We don't have much time and I want to know."

"Why do you want to know, Sophie?"

"For my own edification, maybe."

He grinned.

"Is that the only reason?"

"You were so sure she'd make a wonderful wife. You were so sure of that, you bailed out on us."

This was putting it baldly, but when you have a half an hour of talk left after a five-year absence, you can't be coy or tactful.

"She'd make someone a wonderful wife. She's so much of a wife."

"I don't understand."

"These days Liz seems like such a . . . a State Department–style dependent. She was so intrepid once, and now she won't spend four nights in a strange city by herself."

"Maybe she's lonely."

"Plenty of Americans come through. My sister and her family came last year and we showed them around. They had a ball. I don't know why Liz is so unhappy."

He clearly hadn't paused to consider that while he was listening to the fascinating tales of Solidarnosc journalists who'd survived the Soviet dictatorship, Liz was pressing pamphlets on dental hygiene into the hands of reluctant housewives in some dingy market square. But what was I doing, feeling sorry for Liz?

"You'd have weathered it better than she has," Rory said. "You don't mind being alone. Artists even **need** solitude sometimes."

"There's a limit," I said. I told him about my autumn in Portland, not the parts about Paul but about how hard I'd found it to make friends, and how cold and broken-down our apartment was. I tried to sound wry and amused, like one of those game and plucky memoirs about an American family living in a Tuscan hilltown.

"Oh Sophie," he said. "What I let you in for when I walked out on you."

"What an ego," I said. "You act as if my life in the past four years has been nothing but an extended reaction to being left by you."

"Isn't it?"

I shook my head.

"Damn. I'd hoped. Out of sight, out of mind, I guess."

There was that smile again, that wicked, challenging smile that had led me into trouble all too often.

He dispatched six finger sandwiches—two ham and chives, three salmon and cream cheese, and one cucumber—in neat, wolfish bites.

"I kept thinking of you in Venice," he said. "I kept thinking of you in lots of places. You're sneaky, Sophie. You come off quiet but you leave a big impression."

"It must be those long hours on the road with nothing better to think about."

"No," he said. "It's not like that at all. I'll be someplace gorgeous, traveling with my lawful wedded wife, happy and contented, and suddenly I'll think of a joke I'd like to make to you, or a story I'd like to tell you, and there's Liz with her Fodor's guidebook and her bug spray, approaching everything as if it were a homework assignment."

He knocked back a seventh sandwich and took my hand again. No one saw us. The waiter had darted in once to refill the hot water, but now he stood regally at a distance, awaiting a wave of Rory's hand before approaching us again.

"Do you ever go back to that summer?" Rory said. "The summer we were together?"

"The summer of your wedding?"

"If you want to call it that. I think of it as the summer we were in love. Did you ever think we might have made a mistake by not . . . not following through?"

"We?"

"Sophie. Can you stop being mad long enough to remember you used to love me?"

"Not anytime soon," I said.

"How about by spring? I'm coming back then. Can you think about things in between now and then?"

"What things? What is there to think about?"

"I'm considering that I might have made a big mistake with Liz."

He stroked my palm with his thumb just as he used to do. He was still good at it. I felt as if my hand had committed adultery.

"Liz and I never did . . . mesh. Not like you and I did."

"You mean, in bed?" I said baldly.

He was Catholic enough still to redden.

"Among other things."

A circus monkey would have had the intelligence to know that if sex with Liz before marriage wasn't knocking his socks off, sex afterward wasn't going to break any records. But no one is stupider about sex than Catholics are. To us it's so charged with ignorance and illicit thrills that we abandon all reason and logic about the subject.

"What else then?"

"Oh, she gets clingy. Jealous."

"Jealous how?"

"I taught a course on voter outreach in Latvia a few months ago, and one of the students wrote me a letter afterward. It was an admiring letter. No big deal."

I raised my eyebrows at him.

"I swear, Sophie, I did nothing to encourage it. Liz went ballistic. Who else had I flirted with on the road, did this happen a lot, et cetera. If only she knew how homely most of these activists are, with their dirty hair and unshaved armpits. Plus, she keeps talking about wanting a baby. As if nothing counts until you start reproducing."

"What about all that adventure travel she likes? You can't do that with a baby."

"You can, she says. A lot of her friends from school have had babies abroad and they just tote them along."

Liz sure had some strong-minded, efficient friends. I felt daunted at the prospect of someday carting a baby to the grocery store, and Liz's cronies were trekking through the rain forest with infant carriers strapped to their chests.

"The worst part," said Rory, "is that everyone, including my family, thinks of her as so nice, but she can be really angry underneath."

"I wonder why," I said.

"Not just at me. General anger. She hates it when people break the rules. She never does herself so she expects everyone else to shape up and fly right."

"You know, you always did have a tendency to pick conformers, like Mary Webber. If you're conforming at a tender age, by our age you're likely to be a bit angry."

He said, "She got fat, you know. Mary Webber. She's a tank now."

"No, really?"

"Really. Didn't you see her at midnight mass? Not like you, Sophie. You don't change."

"I've changed some."

"Not in who you are. And as for looks, you're prettier than you ever were. And you were always pretty."

I cleared my throat. The atmosphere was getting thick with reminiscence.

"Tell me about Moscow. How's the food?" I said. "How are the hotels?"

"What?"

"I'm changing the subject."

He collected himself. Rory could always stop on a dime.

He said lightly, "Do you think there's only vodka and bread crusts? You do, don't you. If I know you, you think everyone in Russia still rides around in horse-drawn sleighs while the wolves howl on the steppes."

I did think that. I was a Cold War baby.

"There's even Chinese takeout," he said.

I said suddenly, "I told you not to marry her."

"How long are you going to rub it in before you forgive me?" he said very softly.

"Forever."

"You have some cream on your mouth."

He rubbed a thumb across my lower lip. Then he tilted my face up to his and kissed me, lightly, like that first kiss so long ago. My knees, my ankles, my inner elbows felt as soft as the clotted cream.

"Sophie," he said. "I've thought of you so often. I know that sounds like a line but you have to believe it."

"You're right," I said. "It does sound like a line."

"It's the truth," said Rory. "Was I ever a liar with you?"

"No," I said. "Not a liar."

He laughed.

"Worse things?"

"Just so you know, I've recovered," I said. "Completely. I only came out with you for my pride, so you could see how good I look. Eat your heart out, baby."

He laughed again, and I congratulated myself inwardly. To be soggy and reproachful with Rory would be a disaster. I had to strive for a feisty drollness, like the heroines in those old movies Marta made me watch.

The harpist began strumming her way through "Good King Wenceslas." A woman in a black-and-white checked suit hurried through my line of vision. The suit was just like a suit my mother wore to her charity banquets. I pulled away from Rory.

"I won't pressure you," he said. "But you've never said you're happy with your husband, Sophie."

"I never said I wasn't."

"You didn't have to," he said. "You came out

with me today. Think about the spring, sweetheart. I'll be back then. I'll still feel this way."

"What way would that be?"

"Still crazy about you. Getting married didn't change that. It should've but it didn't. For two cents I'd start up with you all over again. Right here, right now."

"In the tearoom?" I said.

"There are other rooms in a hotel."

"Sorry, I don't happen to have two cents on me," I said. My voice shook a little.

"Maybe you will in the spring," he said.

After he'd settled the check, he left for his four o'clock meeting. I let him pay. Rory had an expense account, and a platinum card he seemed touchingly proud of.

In the lobby, he caught me up close to him. He didn't kiss me, he simply held me tight. Right there in the lobby of the Mayflower. Rory, who used to be so circumspect.

"Don't forget me, Sophie," he murmured in my ear. Then he was gone.

Late Winter

Twenty

I got back to Portland on the afternoon of Friday, December 29. That night, as Paul ate his dinner of canned pea soup and a sandwich, I gently removed the newspaper from his hands and said, "Paul, let's talk."

"I was reading that," he said, and made to take it back. He'd been silent and preoccupied since first greeting me. It seemed that our Christmas ease with each other had been only temporary.

The kitchen was lit only by the dingy fluorescent bulb that hung over the sink—Paul hadn't bothered to turn on the other lights. The pea soup was a healthful, low-fat preparation Paul had become addicted to, without any ham or bacon in the stock to mute the green-pea odor. Paul's face was getting thin and his hair seemed dull. He did not look like a happy man.

I said, "Paul, something's wrong between us."

"Nothing is wrong, honey. I'm working myself to death, that's all. I'm worn out. I just need you to cut me some slack until I can come up for air."

"You've been saying that since August."

"We've had good times since August, Sophie."

"Not many."

"I'm sorry if I'm failing you," he said. "I'm just going through a job adjustment. It's hard."

"This is more than a job adjustment, Paul."

"You watch too many soap operas, sweetie."

"I never watch soap operas."

If I ever took to watching soap operas, I knew I'd never leave the house again.

"Sophie, this project is at a make-or-break moment. Can't you understand that?"

"I can understand that we need something, some help. Would you consider marriage counseling?"

"Marriage counseling is for people with real problems."

"We **have** a real problem," I said. "You're distant, you read the paper at dinner. You never want me anymore."

"Well," he joked, "I have ten minutes before I pass out from exhaustion but if you want them, they're yours."

"Screw you," I said, and threw the paper at him. The edge of the sports section landed in his soup. The green-spattered headline predicted a great spring season for the Portland Sea Dogs.

He stood up and put an arm around me.

"I'm sorry, Sophie."

I shrugged off his arm.

"Really, Sophie. I **am** sorry. If you could have some faith in me for a little longer, it'll all ease up. Can you have some faith in me?"

"Sure. Fine."

"Can you? Just for a little more time?"

In the dead of winter, when it begins to get dark at three-thirty and you are far from everyone who normally helps you distinguish the real from the imagined, it's seductively simple to give in and keep quiet. My common sense told me that something was going on between Paul and Natalie. A heavy flirtation, an affair, **something**. Paul would never admit this in so many words. I could either wait it out or pack my bags, but I couldn't force a confrontation with a man who refused to be confronted. So I did what a lot of women do: I kept my head in the sand. And I waited for winter to be over.

Snow came and more snow, until I forgot what grass looked like, and trees with leaves on them. Donald ran the radiators four times a day now and came by to check them, gulping down gallons of coffee and helping me finish off any sweets I was keeping around the house. There were always plenty. During this period I lived mainly on chocolate bars and doughnuts, with suppers of grilled cheese, ready-made shepherd's pie, and frozen clam strips heated on a cookie tray.

"What do you eat all day?" Paul would laugh, his head in the half-empty refrigerator. In the weeks after my return from Washington, he became less critical, but it wasn't a change for the better. He was pleasant, like a pleasant roommate, and the pleasantness struck a chill to my heart.

But I kept hoping, at some low, buzzing level that was like a motor left on in a beat-up old icebox. I hoped that Paul would return as suddenly as he'd left, that when this crazy winter was over our troubles would be over too. In the meantime, Rory wrote flirtatious, sometimes ardent e-mails, and letters on airmail sheets that had the weight of tissue paper in my hands. I wrote back once, saying that I was confused and had no plans. Yet I didn't tell him not to write. His letters reminded me that I'd once been loved, loved to distraction. I craved that proof as the days went by and my cheery, unnatural husband traveled further and further from me.

Our ballroom class with Natalie and her fiancé Toby was due to begin on the Wednesday of the third week of January. A few days before, Paul asked me if I still wanted to go.

"It's been so lousy out that I wasn't sure you were still up for it," he said diffidently.

"I'm still up for it. Sure I am."

"I just thought it would be something that would get me out of work on time once a week. Force me not to stay late."

"We'll plan on it then," I said. I did not want to disrupt even our current pained equilibrium and least of all look like wet-blanket Sophie to my husband.

The class began during a spell of weather so frigid that just stepping outside after dark was an endurance test. The cold was so much worse at night, or maybe I was just more chipper on my walking mornings.

Our Maine Dance Company instructor, Tammy, had counterfeit-golden hair in a high ponytail and wore beautiful red ankle-strap shoes.

"I don't care how uncoordinated you are, you're going to leave here knowing the box step, the swing step, and the fox trot," she said after we'd assembled, eighteen of us, in the narrow, mirrored room dedicated to beginners.

Tammy believed in jumping right in.

"Anyone can dance," she said in unnaturally bright, businesslike tones, like the nurse in our pediatrician's office when Delia and I went to get our back-to-school shots.

Tammy divided the class into two lines: the men along one wall, the women against the opposite wall, as if for a Virginia reel. Standing with her back to the men, she demonstrated how to lead in a box step. Then, standing with her back to the women, she demonstrated the female, "following" role.

"But men," she said archly, "only in dance class will women follow."

"Don't we know it," said Toby.

Toby was a "regular guy," neither handsome nor homely. An ordinary brown-haired fellow in a baseball cap. You could tell that Natalie deeply disapproved of the baseball cap.

"I got a bad haircut," Toby said to Paul and me. "I'm not taking this cap off until it grows back in."

As he spoke I saw that one of his front canines overlapped the tooth next to it. His teeth were white but not very straight, the mark of a family that hadn't had money for braces. I liked him for that. Every stuffed shirt in Washington had uniform, obediently straight teeth. D.C. was second only to L.A. as a land of people who'd had orthodontia.

Toby wasn't much taller than I was, but he was tall enough to make Natalie look wondrously small and delicate next to him. Catching a glimpse of myself in the unforgiving wall of mirrors, I wished I didn't feel so large and clumsy. When I was walking I liked my body, liked my long legs and wide shoulders and big feet that got me where I was going. Here every limb seemed outsized and puffy.

We stayed with the partner "who brung us" while we were learning the box step, during which Tammy played a tape of Olivia Newton-John singing the mournful ballad "Sam" in waltz time.

I managed the box step, but then came a maneuver in which the woman was supposed to circle the man while he stood still, holding only the tip of her fingers. Natalie performed this tricky promenade with the grace of a Dresden shepherdess, so well that Tammy pulled her out of the line to demonstrate. Meanwhile, I held Paul's hand too tightly and wound up nearly dislocating his elbow.

"Don't worry," Tammy told me in a voice audible to the entire class. "Everyone gets it eventually."

My dread in any course that involves "class participation" is that I'll be the worst in the class, a dread that dates back to gym class when the only two girls regularly picked after me were Suzanne Canova, who had a back brace, and Millie Reilly, who really belonged, we all knew, in a special education class at public school. She was just enough "on the border" that the nuns had taken pity on her family and let Millie trail through the elementary grades at St. Catherine's.

I wasn't going to be the very worst in this class, but I was going to mind being bad the most. That was because Paul wanted us to be good at this. He was the same with board games and charades: a competitor. The engaged couples weren't taking the whole stunt seriously at all. They just wanted to learn enough to get through their first dance at the wedding. You could tell that the engaged ones irked Tammy.

"Remember, you're here to have fun," she said through her teeth.

After our first dry run, Tammy had the class switch partners. The men stayed in place and the women moved down one, with the woman at the end of the line crossing back to the top to partner the first man. I wondered if orgies worked this way.

On the third switch, Paul danced with Natalie, and I saw how good he could be when he was partnered by someone graceful. By contrast, when I found myself face to face with Toby, we both instinctively stared down at his feet and counted. The brim of his baseball cap jabbed my forehead, but at least the pressure was off.

Toby's hands were sweaty but he held mine hard, as if we were holding each other up in a pitching boat. His clasp was reassuring. Here was a person who didn't want to be here almost as much as I did, but who, unlike me, could joke about it.

"All this for ten minutes at the reception," he said.

"Getting married is a lot of work, isn't it," I said.

He nodded, and continued counting.

"You could elope," I murmured.

"I could," he said. "Natalie couldn't. Neither could her mother."

When I'd moved almost all the way down the line, I found myself dancing with the oldest man in class, Graham. He looked about seventy-two, and his wife had signed them up as a retirement present, he said.

Graham came from a more courtly era. Instead of looking reproachful when I missed a beat, he forestalled my apologies with, "No, no. My fault." When I stepped on his feet he said, "A pretty girl can step on my feet anytime she wants." He said this not lecherously, but sweetly. I wished I could dance with him for every minute of every class.

"Now practice," said Tammy as we left.

"That was more fun than I thought it would be," said Paul on the sidewalk. "You're very good," he added to Natalie with a belated, "So are you, hon."

"I stank," I said, trying to sound casual about it and failing.

"Next time you'll relax more," Natalie said. I wanted to strike her.

"How about that old guy?" said Toby. Natalie gave him a "mind your manners" glance. "What's the point of learning to dance at his age?"

"He was better than I was," said Paul, fishing.

"Oh no," Natalie assured him. "You have a natural talent."

We four had dinner at the Vietnamese restaurant next door. The restaurant was uncrowded, which wasn't a surprise as an icy snow had been falling for the last two hours. Natalie had already studied the Maine Dance Company brochure describing more advanced classes. She thought salsa would be fun.

Toby finished eating before the rest of us and began asking me what I thought of their New England summers.

"I didn't get to see much of the past summer but I liked the breezes," I said. "Our summers are too hot back home."

"And the bugs you guys get down there. In the south, they put up with bugs we would never put up with here. My mom went to Charleston once and she saw a roach in a restaurant, walking right up the wall as relaxed as if he were a customer. And no one turned a hair. It's so hot and sticky down there, it's no use even trying to keep clean. They just let the flies and insects buzz around."

"It's not like that everywhere," I said, smiling. "If you're really selective."

"Toby," said Natalie.

"There were no roaches in any apartment I ever lived in," Paul said. He spoke jocularly, but there was a tiny edge to his voice.

"It's more the age of a building than anything else," I broke in. "I had an apartment once where the roaches were enormous. They'd wait in the foyer for me to come home from work, just like I owned a dog."

I turned to Paul. "Remember the first night your mother came to dinner, and one of them walked right across her shoe?"

"And how about those Madagascar ones," said Toby. "They're as big as your hand and they hiss."

"You can see them at the Insect Zoo, at the Natural History Museum," I said.

"Cool," said Toby. "I'm going there then, if we ever get to Washington. Not to the darned Smithsonian."

"The Natural History Museum is **part** of the Smithsonian," said Paul.

"At the Insect Zoo, they let you hold the roaches on your palm if you're brave enough," I said to Toby. I had been there with Delia and Tom once, and Tom had done that. "They have enormous spiders too."

"A tarantula?" said Toby, his eyes gleaming.

"**Ahem**," said Natalie. There were bright red spots high on her cheeks. What a little prisspot she was. You'd think someone that prissy wouldn't be trying to steal someone else's husband.

"This isn't a nice subject," Natalie said.

"The South is very clean," Paul said earnestly to Toby.

"Hey, I wasn't talking about Maryland," said Toby.

"Many people would define Maryland as the South," said Paul. "Our state song is is all about Confederate sympathies and the secessionist riots in Baltimore."

"Whoa," said Toby. "It sounds like you guys should change your state song."

Paul's father had been born in Philadelphia, and Pepper, though she would never admit it, had spent her girlhood in Teaneck, New Jersey. Why was Paul acting like Ashley Wilkes all of a sudden?

"But Maryland's not the **real** South, I do know that," said Toby. "My mother might have enjoyed herself in that harbor thing they have in Baltimore for the tourists. As it was, she checked out of her hotel in Charleston after one day. Last year for their vacation they were smart and just rented a place at Old Orchard Beach. I tried to

tell her. I said you have to expect the occasional
bug in those southern parts. You get swampland
and that kudzu moss and what do you expect?"

"Kudzu isn't moss, Toby," said Paul patiently.

"Anyway," I said quickly. "I can't say I ever
miss that apartment."

This remark fell on the table like a dropped
anvil.

"I hear you and your greeting card partner
might do a book," Natalie said, leaning toward
me with a warning glare at Toby.

"It's not finally settled," I said, trying to imply
by my tone that I had a contract waiting for my
signature on my desk at home.

"The book's very New Age and touchy-feely,"
said Paul. "So it should do well if it all comes off.
It's a nice break for Sophie. If it happens, that is."

I wished he'd stop with the qualifiers. But
then it occurred to me that Paul was bragging
about me and I smiled. Natalie sat up sharply, as
if pinched.

"What do you paint?" said Toby. "For this
book gal?"

"Pretty tame stuff. Flowers and fruit and
seashells. Still lifes."

"Do you ever paint birds?"

"No, that's hard. It's a rare ability. Audubon, for example, was a genius."

"Have you ever seen an osprey?" said Toby.

He finished the meal with stories of ospreys he'd sighted around Portland. They even nested in the stream near the shipping company in Falmouth where he worked as a procurement officer. I felt again that strange new fondness for Portland. In how many cities could you go to work and see ospreys nesting outside your window?

"Not everyone is dying to see your ospreys, Toby," Natalie said. She added to Paul, "Toby could sit and watch birds for hours."

"People do that, Nat," said Toby. "They even go on special trips for it."

"Oddballs do," said Natalie.

"Now practice, damn it," Toby said to me as we parted, with a creditable imitation of Tammy's upbeat, hectoring tone. "By the way, Sophie, if you really want something pretty to paint, go up to Reid State Park. You'll like it. It's just like Scotland."

Natalie interjected. "I'm sure Sophie's seen better. And you've never been to Scotland, Toby, so how would you know?"

"I just know," said Toby. "It just looks like what Scotland should look like."

Paul and I walked home, staggering into the wind. We'd thought it would be fun not to drive for a change. We'd thought wrong. The Maine Trust Bank digital readout said fifteen degrees.

"That Toby's a hoot, huh," Paul said. "All that talk about roaches."

"Roaches are like back pain. If you've had a roach experience, it creates a universal bond with everyone else who's had one."

"We couldn't have bonded about something besides how dirty the South is? Some of these guys up here think anything south of New York is straight out of **Deliverance.**"

"I thought Toby was kind of sweet."

"He's a nice fellow but he's not exactly sophisticated," Paul said dismissively, as if Toby had nothing to do with him. If it was acting, I had to admire how he did it.

I tested the waters. "He's an odd choice for Natalie."

"Is he ever," said Paul. "But sometimes these odd couples are very happy."

After that we just concentrated on walking, on making it home.

I had a dream that night. I was standing in the entrance hallway at St. Catherine's school, my old school, and in the distance, in the gymnasium, I could hear a party going on. I stood facing the enormous statue of St. Catherine, her cow-like eyes glowering down at me, and I was searching for Rory. I knew he was there. I ran by empty classrooms and then, suddenly, I was at Paul's office, in a large crowd of people none of whom I recognized. Then, in the distance by the Christmas tree, I saw Ned. He had his back to me, but I knew it was Ned because of how his hair grew on the back of his neck. I knew I had an urgent message for Ned, but I couldn't recall what it was. I began making my way through the crowd toward him. Then Rory came into view. He was talking to a lovely blonde in a pinstriped business suit and sequined high heels. She was showing him papers in a folder and smiling at him flirtatiously.

"Rory," I called to him. "I'm late but I did get here. Give me credit."

He gave no sign that he heard me.

In the dream I began to cry, and then Ned was at my side with an enormous handkerchief made of red tissue paper.

"I can't use that," I said to him. "The dye will run."

"Just keep it," Ned-in-the-dream said. I folded the tissue paper and stuffed it into a large, heavy purse I seemed to be carrying. When I looked up, Ned was gone and Paul was yelling at me from the elevator doorway.

"Hurry up," he said. "We're all going down."

Natalie was in the elevator with him, and Fiona, and Toby. I rushed toward them but the door closed in my face.

The dream woke me. It was almost dawn, and a clinical white light was filtering into the room through the flannel sheets I'd nailed over the bedroom windows to keep out the cold. I lay there, breathing hard, as if I'd been awakened by the sound of an intruder. I inched closer to Paul, just to feel his body heat. My parents used to let me come into bed with them when I was very little and had a bad dream, and I remembered how the sound of my father's snoring had soothed me.

When I woke again, Paul was just leaving for work.

"You were restless last night and I knew it wasn't a walking day, so I let you sleep," he said kindly.

"Bad dream," I said. "Sorry I disturbed you."

"Sleep in," he said. Then he pecked me on the head and left.

All week, Paul assiduously practiced the box step, with me and by himself. He even bought a tape to practice to: "Waltz Time on the Danube." He was full of the determination to excel, the same determination he brought to his job, to even the most casual game of tennis. I dreaded that I was going to pull down his performance.

"What do you care?" Ned said when I joked about my clumsiness after breakfast one day. "It's just a silly class. You won't be graded."

Everyone else had left, and we two were waiting for change. It had been a dreary day for a walk, and the group had felt it. George, who'd spent Christmas in the Southwest with his boyfriend and was tanned to tobacco color under his hunter's cap, was uncharacteristically nervous about a painting that he was having shipped from a gallery in Santa Fe. Ramon complained about Christmas with Edgar's family at their lodge near Stow.

"They're too well-behaved," he said. "What is a holiday without some drama, or at least some-

458 | Snowed In

one overeating and getting chest pains in the night?"

"How are they about you and Ramon?" Stephen asked Edgar, which was the piece of information all of us really wanted to know.

Stephen was limping gamely along with the rest of us these days, using a handsome oak walking stick that he and Ned had found in the attic at the Eastern Prom house. Ned had insisted on adding a hideous rubber plug to the ground end of the stick, for safety. Stephen plonked it down in the snowdrifts with vigor, trying to scrape off the rubber part like a dog trying to scrape off a doggie sweater.

Edgar said, "Oh, they never notice anything anyway. They think of us as just very good friends."

Alex had stayed in town to eat turkey dinner with her mother and stepfather, and to catch a movie in the evening with friends from her community college course.

"You can only hang around with your parents for so long," she said.

Now they'd all gone off to begin their busy days, and Ned and I sat among the ruins of breakfast for eight at Becky's. The toast crusts and cold egg bits were dispiriting.

Ned said, "If I'm remembering right, you're only taking this dancing class to please your husband. Which is damn good of you. There's no one in the world I'd learn ballroom dancing for. So why are you so concerned about acing it?"

His hair had been trimmed again over Christmas. The bangs were a little too short, giving him the air of a ten-year-old boy on the first day of school.

"If I said because of a much-too-pretty work pal of my husband's who's taking the class with us, would that make sense?"

He frowned, the interior-aimed frown that indicated he was figuring something out in his head. He would make a terrible diplomat or politician, I reflected. When something bothered him, he worried it like a dog with a bone and it showed in his face.

"This friend of your husband's, she's competitive, is that it?" he said.

"About everything," I said.

"Attention-grabbing?"

"She grabs attention. I don't know if it's deliberate."

"But why do you let her get to you? You must run circles around her. I don't care how well she dances the rhumba or whatever."

I got up to leave. If I stayed, I was afraid I'd express to Ned just why I was letting Natalie get to me.

"Where are you going?" he said. "Wait for your change."

"You can give it to me Friday," I said.

He pulled on my wrist, lightly, tugging me back to the table.

"Don't run," he said. "Hold on, and I'll walk up Danforth Street with you and circle back down State. I need the exercise. I ate like a pig over Christmas."

"And how did it go? Christmas?"

"Good. Pretty good. My dad liked Fiona. Fiona liked my dad. Stephen went off his diet for two days so he was happy. How was yours?"

"Not bad."

The waitress delivered our change and Ned left a large tip out of his own share, giving me back all mine.

"Ned," I said. "We always split."

"Let me be a big spender for once."

"I make decent money, you know," I couldn't resist saying.

"Did you think I thought you only made pin money with your work?"

"I didn't know what you thought," I said.

"Well, I make good money too," he said. "Hey, we actually have a waiting list these days. Stephen has three clients on hold while we finish up this place."

"So still not close to being done?"

"Not very."

I felt guilty at how pleased that answer made me. Going out and making friends was supposed to make you more willing to go out and make **more** friends, but I wanted to rest in cowardly comfort with the friends I'd made at the walking group. Even walking wasn't a given these days. So much snow had fallen since Christmas that the Happy Trails meetings had almost been canceled several times, but Ned and Stephen finally decided to let everyone who could manage it wade through the drifts. Fearless in my Goodwill boots, I turned out religiously. Jamie and Carol took turns staying home with Matilda, though. Strollers weren't made for three-foot-high snowbanks. I missed Matilda.

Ned slumped down on his side of the booth, looking lazy and contented, making no move to go. "Tell me some more about your dance class."

"It's not important."

"Yes, it is. You never complain about anyone,

so if you do she must be a real pain in the neck, this girl from work."

"Well, have you ever had someone who just gets to you? Who bothers you even though you tell yourself you don't have to allow it?"

He drummed his fingers on the table, thinking. His hands, as always, were stained with varnish and smeared here and there with streaks of dried paint.

"Fiona's professor. He's a blowhard. He had a New Year's Day reception at his house. Twenty hungover people pretending to be interested in his art collection and his bread-making machine."

"Is he gay?"

"He's single but I don't think he's gay. Being gay would be some excuse for the bread-making machine, Stephen says. Anyway, your husband's work friend sounds like a real pain in the ass."

"You could say that."

"I just wish I could tell you some quick method of neutralizing her," Ned said.

"I wish you could too. One that's not illegal."

"Yeah. She doesn't sound worth doing time for."

He was rifling through his jacket, putting away his change, which allowed me to observe him without embarrassment. I liked looking at him, even though Ned wasn't strikingly handsome. He lacked Rory's dashingness, or Paul's hail-fellow-well-met good looks, or Stephen's Medici-prince profile with its noble nose.

Ned's looks were of the quirky variety. They crept up on you, in small individualities: the way his eyes were set, rather deeply, so that their unusual color was somewhat hidden by dark lashes and the shadow of the eye socket. The angle where his jaw met his ear was a clean and interesting angle that would be a pleasure to draw. He shoved his money into his wallet carelessly, in a manner that Paul would have blanched at. Paul liked to arrange his currency in ascending order by denomination, and he always knew just how much money he had on him, while Ned frequently surprised himself by finding a stray five or ten in his pocket.

"Sophie?" Ned said. "Still in this world?"

"I was daydreaming," I said. "Fill me in some more about your break."

"It was a little tiring. I spent a lot of it making repairs at Fiona's. She lives in a rathole in Brighton that she rents for eight-hundred seventy-five a month."

"Rents are that high there?"

"Since the tech boom. You wouldn't believe it. There are people coming in from out of town who are renting places based on one photo on a Realtor's Web site. You pay fourteen hundred in Somerville for a one-bedroom. We used to call Somerville "Slummerville" when I was growing up, and now it's pricey as hell."

The waitress, thrilled with Ned's tip, came back and refilled our coffee cups.

Ned continued, "Fiona's landlord won't fix anything. So I spent the holidays unclogging the drains and installing a new kitchen faucet and spraying insulation-fill in the holes in her vents so that the smoke from the apartment next door doesn't float right through. I put in some light fixtures too."

"How long did you say you'd been dating?"

"A year. I know what you're thinking. You're thinking that we could move in together, and then she'd have a nicer place."

"It would be one solution," I said.

"She says she'll only move in with me when she has a ring. She's traditional that way."

When she had a ring? How serious were they?

"Speaking of jewelry, I have to find something for Valentine's Day," Ned said.

"You're a very good boyfriend, planning so early," I said, thinking of how casually the always-broke young men of my twenties had treated such occasions. Ned struck me as the sort of guy who'd get an engagement ring that had real meaning—a sapphire in an antique silver setting or seed pearls in old gold, not just a diamond in platinum from some jeweler at the mall. Paul and I had decided to forgo an engagement ring. I'd told him that we could spend the money on something for both of us. We'd never gotten around to that something, however.

I said, "Fiona gave you some specific hints? About what to get?"

I remembered the pair of earrings Fiona had been wearing that night in the North End, large buttons that looked as if someone had dripped layers of paint on them. Those earrings argued a woman with very particular tastes. Just any trinket wouldn't do.

"I just thought a nice bracelet or necklace," Ned said. "That's what women like on Valentine's Day, right?"

"I guess. I don't own much jewelry."

"Your husband's a cheapskate, is that it?" he said, smiling to show me he was joking.

"He'd buy it for me, but necklaces make me feel like I'm choking, and I've never liked my hands, so I don't tend to wear rings."

"What's wrong with your hands?"

He studied them with great attention. His gaze made me nervous.

I said quickly, "They're too big. And I don't do my nails, I just clip them so I won't get paint under them. And my knuckles are knobby."

He said, "I like your hands. They look . . . well-used."

"Geez. I'll put hand lotion on the shopping list."

"It's a compliment. I meant that they look as if you **do** something with them. You're a painter. What are you supposed to have, little bird hands?"

"I can come along with you to pick something pretty for Valentine's, for Fiona. If you want any advice," I said, feeling more kindly toward Fiona, who did nothing but study and produce dry academic writing no one would read while I had painter's hands.

"Stephen already offered, but she probably wouldn't like that," Ned said. "She says something I chose myself is more meaningful. You should see her doing her Christmas shopping. It takes her forever. Everything's a ritual with her."

He seemed to think this was cute.

We talked idly for a while, then he walked me nearly all the way home. We discussed the Red Sox.

"They sound like a lost cause to me," I said.

"Yes, but they're the best lost cause since the Easter Rebellion. You have to go see a game at Fenway sometime, Sophie. When they come from behind in the seventh inning after giving away six runs, and then Trot hits a double and then Nomar gets a homer and it sails over the wall, and the crowd stands up and cheers, and there's the smell of hot dogs and fried dough in the air. You have to see it."

Then he said, "But I forgot. You go back to Washington in the fall, right?"

"I may not go back," I said. "Paul likes it here. A lot."

"But you don't, I'm guessing. As something permanent."

"Not under the circumstances," I said, adding hastily, "the cold, I mean."

He gave me one of his noticing looks but didn't press me with questions. That was the difference between men friends and women friends.

Ned said only, "You should wait until spring before you decide about New England. There'll be lots of scenery for you to paint. You haven't been anywhere yet."

"There's scenery where I come from too."

"Not like this," Ned said. "Not like up here."

"You New Englanders."

"Maybe we'll take you to Plum Island some day, that's one of our Massachusetts beaches. It's only an hour away."

"Pretty?"

"More than pretty," he said. "Different from Maine but beautiful all the same. You like to swim, Sophie?"

"Ocean swimming. Not doing laps."

"Me too. I can be in the water for hours. Plum Island is nice in spring, but they get greenheads in the summer."

"What are those or do I want to know? Are they jellyfish?"

"Flies. With big green heads, which is where the name comes from. But for swimming, you try the beach at Wells. The sand goes on for miles. And the waves come in bunches, not just one or two whumping down on the shore with nothing to ride."

"I'd like that," I said.

"You would. And after you swim, you go for steamers and corn on the cob."

"Steamers are clams, right?"

"You've never had steamers? Yes, you poor ignorant girl, steamers are clams in the shell that you dip in melted butter."

"I think I'm beginning to understand the heart attack rate up here," I said.

"You wait," he said. "When you're sitting at a picnic table at one of these places in your bathing suit, and you're finishing off your fifteenth steamer, and there's a breeze from the sea. Then you'll get it."

After he'd headed off down Danforth Street I strolled home, wondering if I'd last in Maine long enough to go swimming with Ned and Stephen on the beach at Wells, where the sand went on for miles.

That afternoon Marta called. Normally Marta's voice is a cool, controlled instrument—rather like Jean Arthur's in the old Frank Capra movies. Today I could hear a hint of Passaic in her tones, and she was almost babbling, if Marta could ever babble.

"Sophie, you remember the woman I talked to at the Christmas party?"

I did. Marta had gone to her office party in her femme fatale dress and spent half the evening talking to another woman. It was rare enough to be memorable.

The woman had been in line for the bar right in front of Marta and had turned around to compliment Marta's dress. This had surprised Marta, because the stranger was quite dowdy. She wore a black, polyester-blend A-line coupled with the plainest black pumps imaginable. She also wore the kind of orange-hued hose for which Marta would have cheerfully started a charitable foundation to educate women not to buy.

This woman, Joan Caravelli, turned out to be the wife of Marta's association's convention director, and she was bored silly by shop functions. She and Marta ordered double bourbons, pulled up chairs in a corner, and talked half the night.

Joan had spent years as a doctor in rural Vermont and was head of a small, newly formed nonprofit group that aimed to improve medical care in rural areas nationwide. She'd married late and moved to D.C. to be with her husband. She was still a rookie in her new hometown, and was enthralled by Marta's tales of the inner circles of power and the follies therein. She gave Marta her card and asked Marta to keep in touch.

"And now," Marta said, "she's called me to say

that she's raised enough money to hire a communications-slash-lobbying director, and guess who she wants?"

"You," I said. "Of **course** you."

For the first time in years, Marta sounded truly thrilled about something.

"I'm interviewing with a few people this week, but Joan says it's a formality. She says that if I'm willing to take a big salary cut, they'd be delighted to have me on board."

"Oh Marta, this is great. This is just what you were looking for."

"Only I didn't go look for it, it landed at my feet."

"If you hadn't had the guts to go alone to the party, this wouldn't have happened."

We talked for a while about Marta's finances.

"I don't need the health club, and I don't need half these clothes I keep buying," Marta said. "And I've traveled everywhere, so I don't need any more fancy vacations. Anyway, Joan said I could do some field trips, see what's going on in the places this group supports. The clinics and centers."

I tried to envision Marta patting the head of some child with ringworm under a blazing Louisiana sun. Then I pictured her meeting a tall, lanky, red-haired doctor who made house calls in a beat-up pick-up truck. Someone like that could be perfect. Someone with something **to** him, not like the tailors' dummies she'd gone through in D.C.

"Keep me posted," I said before we hung up.

"Posted? I wouldn't be doing this if it weren't for you, Sophie."

Being Marta, she didn't choose that moment to remind me that it was my turn to step up and make some change in my own work. Marta could be bossy but when the chips were down, she had exquisite tact.

That afternoon and night, as I basked in the glow of the two space heaters aimed at the couch and watched **Four Weddings and a Funeral** for the tenth time, I was happy. Happy for my friend, who was beginning a new job with such hope, and happy about my own hopes for new work: Ann's book, classes, maybe even an MFA someday. Paul had called to say he'd be very late, but for once it didn't bother me. I put my feet up and enjoyed the movie, and thought not of romance but of vague and wonderful career plans. They were vague plans but while they occupied me thoughts of what my husband and Natalie might be doing did not.

Twenty-One

During this time—the first two months of the new year—there were plenty of signs and signals I couldn't help but see, since they were foisted upon me like telegrams containing bad news.

They were small things. Once when I failed to enter a check in my checkbook, Paul found me puzzling over the discrepancy.

"It's a good thing after all that we never merged our finances," he said. "Your creative accounting would have driven me crazy."

His tone was fondly exasperated, as always when he saw my checkbook. It was the tense he'd used that startled me: "that we never . . ." A few times now I'd caught him using that past tense, as if he were already looking back on us.

He was working so hard he looked almost haggard, as much as a boyish type can. The only leisure activity for which he could be diverted from the office round was our ballroom dance class. We learned the swing step and Paul played "Rockin' Robin" into the small hours, getting it right. He'd become a dancin' fool.

Tammy praised him. "See how Paul is coming along? That's the result of practice, folks."

To me she said, "Sophie, let Paul lead. You won't drop onto the floor if you relax a little."

Who could relax? Paul issued patient little reminders as we danced, but I could hear his jaw click when I missed a step. It was a relief to partner with Graham, the courtly elderly gentleman, or Toby, who praised me no matter how badly I did. Toby's hair grew in, but he continued to wear the baseball cap to class. He said it was part of his dancing routine now.

In February, against all expectations, I was good at the fox-trot. Perhaps I'd known it in a past life, or was more suited to its rolling backward gait than to the frenetic motions of swing. Whatever the reason, it came easily after Tammy's first demonstration. But Paul lectured me nervously, even when Tammy tapped him on the shoulder and said, "Paul, cut it out, okay? She's doing it perfectly."

Tammy had probably seen many marriages in trouble over the years; the professional sympathy in her eyes made me feel worse.

Yet I still wasn't one hundred percent certain that my husband was unfaithful. Not knowing for sure was starting to unravel me at the edges.

"A hit man," advised Marta. "Life insurance beats alimony any day."

"Counseling," suggested Delia again.

"A guy would be a fool to dump a woman with a stock-picking ability like yours," said my loyal brother-in-law.

Our Christmas investment had quadrupled. The first week of February, Tom sold. A week after, the stock began to drift downward a little, proving Tom right and impressing Delia and me no end.

I spent many hours that winter going over my finances. With my savings, I could afford to go to art school part-time, or take a six-month break and travel. Or join someone in Eastern Europe. I could afford—could always have afforded, financially—a divorce.

These last two thoughts I didn't often allow to rise to my conscious mind. When my spirits faltered and the weather cooperated, I drove. Me, who'd once been so afraid of driving. I drove to Portsmouth, where the narrow colonial clapboards reminded me a little of Georgetown, and to South Berwick, where the gardens of Hamilton House were blanketed in snow as white and smooth as sheets in a hope chest. I went to Higgins Beach a few times, and saw the same black

Lab running in the sunset. The owner nodded to me, in fellowship I guess, for these days few people braved the fierce winds to walk this stretch of beach. I was coming to see that winter could be beautiful up here, to love its variations in blue and ivory and pink and the simplicity of its stripped-down landscapes.

Too often, of course, the weather did not co-operate.

"And Valentine's Day?" said Delia. "What's on tap for that? As things stand."

"Maybe dinner out."

"You **deserve** a dinner out, Sophie. A nice dinner, somewhere romantic."

"So we can sit and stare at each other? Or make small talk?"

"Oh Sophie. I don't like this. It's all too quiet. Give him an ultimatum. I've said it before but now I mean it. You can't keep on like this, sweetie."

"I **can,**" I said. "But I shouldn't."

"Hey," said Delia, "Want to hear something you'll like? Something flattering?"

She spoke in her cheering-me-up voice, the voice she'd used as far back as I could remember to buck me up before the first day of school and other occasions of dread.

Delia said, "You won't believe what's happened to the painting you gave Mom and Dad for Christmas. That lovely study of the lighthouse, the Portland Headlight."

"Mom raffled it off at the church auction?"

"No."

"Gave it to a sick friend?"

"All good guesses, but no. Dad **framed** it and he hung it. In the **living** room."

The living room of my parents' house, like a parlor of old, was sacrosanct. There they kept favored wedding presents: two black vases like funeral urns, a Venetian glass ashtray, and a cherrywood kidney-shaped coffee table that had been the height of modernity in the early sixties.

Delia said, "He took down that orange abstract that that deaf guy in Mom's Bible group did and put yours up. He even showed it to his card-playing buddies."

My father had always spoken of painting as a lure that would condemn me to life in a garret while practical gals who'd learned shorthand would live on the fat of the land. Now he'd bragged about me to his friends. This information was so startling that I forgot to feel sorry for myself all afternoon.

Valentine's Day was in two weeks. I took trouble over Paul's gift but it was conscientious trouble, as if I were choosing a present for a particularly valued client. Cologne was too mundane, he had more ties than he could wear in a year, and the only book he'd shown an interest in lately was a history of the Cuban missile crisis. Finally I found a silver pen and pencil set at a stationery shop in Kennebunkport. I had it engraved, "To Paul from Sophie, with love."

Ned told me he'd gotten Fiona bookends.

"Very fancy ones, like two blocks of green glass. From that shop in the Old Port."

I knew the place. It specialized in "sculptures in crystal."

"I was scared the whole time I was there that one careless elbow, and smash, I'm ten thousand in debt. Fiona will like these, since they sort of allude to her scholarly work. And she loves that store."

"I thought you were searching for jewelry."

"I gave up on that. It was too hard. Her taste is very individual."

I said, "Are you guys doing anything? A big night out?"

"She'll be away, at a conference in New York about theories of distance learning or some such thing. We'll celebrate when she gets back. How about you two?"

Walking was tough going that day. The Portland crews did an impressive job clearing the streets, but after a while there was nowhere to put the snow but in ever-higher piles heaped on either side of the roads. Every curb was a clamber, every downhill stretch was a slide. The path along the Eastern Prom beach was still passable, however. The group was strung along it, and Ned and I were last today.

"Nothing big," I said. "I hate occasions."

"I don't like them either," said Ned. "Too much pressure to say just the right thing."

Rory had written me a long letter for the holiday, full of memories of things we'd done when we were kids together, and things we'd done during that summer we'd been in love. Rory always did say just the right thing. But Rory was continents away.

I'd hinted to Paul that I wanted chocolates, but Paul disapproved of them on principal, especially the gaudy drugstore hearts that were my secret desire. On my way home, I stopped at Paul's Grocery and bought a dozen Hershey bars. You may hope for chocolate from men, but you should always be ready and willing to provide it for yourself.

On Valentine's Day Paul arrived home by six-thirty. I had his favorite Sinatra on the stereo, and a nice little eye of round in the oven.

He hugged me with one arm then disappeared upstairs. After dinner he handed me an oblong shirt box wrapped clumsily in a paper covered in snowmen and reindeer.

"I had to use the Christmas paper," he explained. "I didn't have time to run out and buy some."

"That doesn't matter. It's cheerful, don't you think?"

My present was a gorgeous cashmere scarf, in a flattering warm rose. It was the prettiest scarf I'd ever been given, and must have been expensive.

"Oh Paul," I said. "This is perfect."

"Thought you'd like it. The lady at the store said it was right for a blonde."

Then he unwrapped the silver pen and pencil.

"These will really gussy up my desk at the office," he said, and pecked me on the cheek. "They're really, really nice, Sophie."

I leaned over and kissed him on the lips.

He said, "Hon, don't take this wrong but I'm beat tonight. Can we postpone the whole Valentine's mood until Saturday? We'll go to Starboard Sam's."

Starboard Sam's was a restaurant near Freeport that looked out over what was supposed to be a river, but was more like a bog this time of year. If you had the appetite of three men it was a good place to go, generous with rolls and salad and cuts of meat, with huge showy desserts. Some guy at the office must have recommended it. I hoped it wasn't Natalie.

"Sure," I said. "Saturday's more festive anyway."

"We'll do it up. Order drinks, appetizers, you name it. And now I'll turn in, before I start yawning in your face."

Before he went to sleep he nudged me and muttered, "Make us a reservation for Saturday, will you? We don't want to have to wait for a table."

Starboard Sam's was crowded on Saturday night with late celebrators like us. Paul was almost oddly energetic. He talked all through the potato skins about the chances of the new railroad service coming to Portland, and the possibility that Maine could one day attract large service and technology companies.

"Staying here for the long term might not be such a bad idea," he said. "Why go back to D.C. with its crazy real estate market and impossible commutes?"

Paul's commute in D.C. had been three subway stops. Twelve minutes door to door. Here it took twelve minutes just to warm up the car.

"You want to stay?" I said.

"Headquarters has been talking. They think the Project might be worth investing a few years in, to really get it off the ground."

Never in his life had Paul referred to his bosses at the national office as "headquarters." Three guesses as to where that came from.

"What would you do if we stayed?" he said.

"Keep freelancing, I guess. And get serious with some classes. Ramon told me about this little studio down by the Concord bus station, by the river. Nice, small classes, he said, and a really nice teacher."

"That's great but have you thought about a job? I've been asking around, and there are some openings out at the University of Maine. Good benefits and everything."

"You have benefits for both of us now," I said, perplexed.

"Just so you had a routine."

"Art classes would give me a routine. And I could keep freelancing that way."

"But a college job would give you a community, Sophie. You need more than your walking group."

"What are these jobs, do you know?"

"Easy stuff. Research assistantships, administrative work. You could even do research for a professor in the art history department, I bet. There's a guy at the office with a few connections at USM. I could talk to him."

"I don't think so, Paul. They couldn't possibly pay much."

"Money isn't everything," said Paul, who'd been quick to say when we moved here that I should stick with the freelancing because my rates were so high.

I had the strange feeling that Paul was offering me some sort of last chance, and I was passing it up. But I didn't want to be squirreled away in some study carrel digging up obscure references about early Edwardian dog portraitists or some such subject. I wanted even less to dress up and greet prospective students, or process financial aid forms.

"I just thought that you might enjoy an academic environment," Paul said. "Freelancing can be isolating, I know."

At every table a happy family was celebrating some milestone, or a mistily smiling silver-haired couple were holding hands, or young lovers were leaning into the candlelight the better to catch each other's smallest words. At our table Paul was giving me career advice and poking around in his salad, searching for a cucumber.

We spent the rest of the evening talking about neutral topics: the train, Paul's latest grant proposal, an operation that Paul's brother James was having to help him stop snoring. The most romantic comment Paul made all night was, "Your filet is good. Want to try the swordfish?"

At bedtime he flossed his teeth and was waiting when I emerged from the bathroom. He held out his arms.

"Happy Valentine's, hon," he said. Then he rushed through lovemaking as if someone were observing us with a stopwatch. He was asleep five minutes later. I took **Marjorie Morningstar** into the living room and read for half the night.

At the Western Cemetery where Happy Trails met, you could slip-slide from one gate to another on a glassy surface of ice. The dogs loved the makeshift rink, skittering after tennis balls and skidding after sticks.

"This is not a city. It's a day in the life of Ivan Denisovich," said Ramon one morning.

"Portland's not that much colder than Boston," said Edgar.

"Yes, Edgar, it is. In the paper every day you can compare," said Ramon.

" 'February made me shiver,' " said Stephen.

"Not just **shiver,** freeze solid," said Alex, who was too young to remember vintage Don Mc-Clean.

Alex was an inspiration to me. She hadn't let the cold become an excuse not to exercise. She'd even added an aerobics class at the Y three times a week, though she loathed it and made fun of the teacher in her color-coordinated leotards.

Failing to show up for walking, letting Alex know I was a tenderfoot and a coward—it was unthinkable. Even George turned out regularly, though we all worried he'd break a hip.

I ate boxes of Russell Stovers. I could afford to. Jealousy and walking were making me thin. In the mirror, my face seemed too pale, the blond of my hair mockingly bright against my skin. Alarmed, I indulged at the Estée Lauder counter at the Macy's in the Maine Mall. It was free gift week. Marta would've sent me a raft of samples, but asking her for freebies would have alerted her as to just how lousy I felt.

In the fourth week of February there was an ice storm the day of dance class, but Paul was adamant that he wanted to go.

"I'm not sure it's safe," I said. "It's very slick out."

"Sophie, this is the one time I look forward to all week. This is why I bought the Explorer."

We drove uneventfully to class.

"See?" said Paul. "Even in ice you don't have to worry in this vehicle."

Toby and Natalie were in the vestibule, waiting for us. Toby said he'd lost control of his car three times on the way over. It was evident that Toby enjoyed narrow escapes of this type; life was still something of a Hardy Boys adventure to him.

Natalie said nothing. As usual, she wasn't listening to Toby. She was taking off her coat, straightening her hair, adjusting her skimpy red pullover.

"How was Valentine's?" I asked Toby.

"We went to The Purple Eggplant. It was great."

The Purple Eggplant was one of the fanciest restaurants in town.

"Overrated," said Natalie. "David's, on the square, is much more eclectic."

"Natalie's like a restaurant critic," said Toby, apparently not hurt. "Even this place couldn't impress her."

"Toby forgot his tie and they had to lend him one," Natalie continued.

Forgetting a tie was one of those little faux pas that a woman found endearing in a man she was crazy about, but Natalie's grimace implied, "It's terrible to be judged by Toby's buffoonish manners. He's such a liability."

"I'm sure that happens all the time," said Paul condolingly, relieving Natalie of her coat and hanging it carefully on the vestibule rack. I hung up my own coat.

"I **reminded** him," said Natalie, and Paul nodded in empathy. This time Toby did look hurt.

It was one of those moments when I was hard-pressed to like Paul. Love still lingered but affection temporarily fled. Never before had it been so evident, Paul's assumption that people like Donald and Toby weren't quite at his social level and that their feelings by definition couldn't be injured.

I went docilely through the cha-cha and docilely to dinner at our usual Vietnamese restaurant afterward, nodding with feigned interest as Toby rattled on about a fly-fishing trip he was planning for spring.

Then Toby said to Paul, "I hear you two did okay for yourselves in that meeting at Bath on Friday afternoon."

"Fine, fine," said Paul, hurriedly.

"What did you think of the new bridge up there?"

"Very impressive."

"You know how much money that bridge cost?" Toby asked.

You had to admire the keen interest Toby took in his world. You could picture him reading the morning **Press Herald,** devouring every detail about a playground ribbon-cutting in Wiscasset or a girls' lacrosse team victory at the university in Orono.

Paul just shrugged.

Then it came to me, the strangeness of Toby's mentioning Bath.

I said, "I thought you were at the Public Market for lunch on Friday. You said you had a turkey sandwich at that counter near the Big Sky Bakery booth."

"That was Thursday," said Paul, but he shifted in his chair. Natalie took her purse and headed to the ladies' room.

"I'm sure it was Friday," I said.

"It **was** Friday," Toby said. "I was fighting with my boss about a big order, and Natalie called to say she was leaving for Bath just before all hell broke loose with him."

"They're still very keen on the Project in Bath?" I said. "Who'd you meet with?"

There was a pause.

"The superintendent of schools," said Paul. "He was very receptive."

"I'm glad," I said. "You two work so hard for these opportunities."

We ate our noodles and lemongrass beef, while Toby explained why the new coach of the New England Patriots was better in every way than the old coach. Natalie didn't meet my eyes, but then, she never met my eyes.

When the door closed on us at home, I took

off my coat and hung it up. I put some water in the teakettle and turned to Paul, who hadn't taken off his coat and was sitting thumbing through the paper, which he'd already perused once that day.

"You didn't tell me you'd gone to Bath on Friday."

"I'm sure I mentioned it. Actually, **Bath** was Thursday, now that I think of it. Toby gets confused."

He put his arms around me.

"Your dancing's really coming along," he said.

I disentangled myself from the embrace.

"Thanks," I said. "I think I'll work. I suddenly have this burst of energy. You go to bed when you get sleepy."

"Okay, hon," he said obliging—or was he relieved?

There were so many straws in the wind that I'd be a fool not to doubt him now. But maybe it wasn't . . . the whole enchilada. Maybe they'd kissed, or flirted, or "petted" as my mother put it when I was a teenager.

And maybe I was the world's biggest, most-trusting idiot.

Paul left for work the next day without waking me, before I could ask any more questions. I wouldn't have asked them anyway. Asking him questions was useless.

In March it snowed and sleeted intermittently. Paul and I spoke brightly of objective matters, like the awful weather and whose turn it was to shovel the steps. We went to our last dancing class. Tammy said that she was very proud of all of us, and then she gave a plug for Beginning Ballroom, Level 2.

"I've seen people placing in competitions who were far worse at this stage than many of you in this room," she said, by way of a parting compliment.

"Thank God that's over," Toby said when we all reached the sidewalk. We did not have dinner with Toby and Natalie. Natalie had a headache, it seemed.

Delia phoned and described a new game she and Ben played, in which Delia hid a miniature marshmallow in each lidded slot of a daily pill-taker box Tom had brought home from the office. Ben's job was to pry open the lid for each day and find the marshmallow. He could now flip the lids up to Wednesday's dose of marshmallow before losing interest. My father was speaking of early admission to Princeton.

She said that the daffodils were out and the cherry blossoms were on schedule.

"Any news from Rory?"

"He may be in Boston in April. For a brief visit. We might have dinner."

"Sophie."

"Marta says that I should get some use out of Rory. A nice recovery fling."

"And you'd listen to Marta because she's had such a stable time of it with men."

"At least she's not sitting around moping, like I am."

"You're not. You're biding your time."

"Do I have to bide it alone?"

Delia made a fed-up cluck in the back of her throat.

"Sophie, you say you can handle him. But he'll do it again."

"I'm much more hurt about Paul, so Rory can't possibly hurt me like he did. I'm inoculated."

"You can't get inoculated for Rory's type. You just have to stay away from them. You know, if you were ever single again Tom has some nice friends. Not that we should be talking about this at this point. But Rory's not the only guy out there, Sophie."

I wondered if that was what the future held for me: a nice doctor, and a home in some affordable outlying suburb, and a cousin or so for Ben, and a painting career subsidized by the nice doctor's salary but never successful enough to live on, on its own.

It sounded pretty. Pretty and impossible. If I were headed for that, wouldn't I have gotten there long ago?

Twenty-Two

On March 20, Rory wrote: **"I'm coming to Boston in the third week of April. Come to Boston for dinner, Sophie Ann. It's not Paris but we'll have a good time."**

On March 22, I sent an e-mail: **"Dear Rory, I'd be glad to see you in Boston for dinner. I'll book my own hotel and meet you at a restaurant somewhere."** I'd go back to the Beltran Inn, like a chaste wife on a shopping trip to the city.

On March 23, the heaviest snowstorm of the winter hit. It would be two straight days of snow, sleet, and hail, with heavy drifting and wild, howling winds.

That morning, four inches fell before Paul left for work.

"Couldn't you work from home today?" I asked him.

"I'll look like a wuss. People here don't stay home from work for six inches of snow. But I'll walk. No point in risking the Explorer."

By noon, the four inches were eight inches, and the schools were closing early. I called Paul, who said that visibility was still fine and what was I worried about? He'd be on foot.

Stephen phoned at two.

"Needless to say, group's canceled for tomorrow," he said. "But I thought I'd phone everyone. Besides, I'm bored."

"This is a really bad storm, huh," I said.

"Really bad. When you hear them taking it as seriously as they're taking it on the local news, you know it's a nasty one. Is your husband headed home?"

"No. He walked to work so he's staying to finish the day out."

"Tell him to get home. He's crazy if he thinks even walking will be doable soon."

"I tried already. He thinks I'm being silly."

"Well, if he winds up in a snowdrift and you need help, we're here," he said.

At three the news was reporting accidents on the turnpike and the closing of ferry service to the Casco Bay islands. "If you don't have to be out in this, remain at home," said a grim-faced meteorologist in an undertakerish black suit.

"Sophie, by 'out in this' they mean driving," said Paul.

"It's hailing. It's Wuthering Heights out there."

"You and your imagination."

At five he phoned to say that Toby was stopping by to get Natalie and give him a ride home. At six he reported in. He was "bunking down" at Toby and Natalie's until the storm let up. Toby had decided not to risk the detour to our place on Pine Street, but to shoot for his and Natalie's house in Deering Oaks, which they reached by the skin of their teeth.

"Stay where you are as long as you have to," I said.

"I was stupid not to try for home before," he said. "You have what you need there?"

"Of course."

We'd hung up before I realized that there was very little food in the house. A can of chicken noodle soup, two eggs, a box of Ritz crackers, and a bottle of spring water. I checked out the window, wondering if the Cumberland Farms was still open. The snow was coming fast now, slanting down in sheets under the streetlights. But I had my down coat with the hood and my snow boots. I could make it. Cumby's probably wouldn't close even for Noah's flood.

I was pulling my boots on when I heard honking outside. Paul was back. What a good-natured idiot Toby was to venture on the road in this!

Then into our driveway pulled not Toby's sedan but a red truck I knew. I could barely see the dim forms of Ned and Stephen as they clambered out and jogged toward me.

They'd brought groceries. Plastic tubs of frozen homemade corn chowder and fresh sourdough bread. Frozen pizza. Cornflakes. Milk and Coca-Cola and a jar of apricot preserves. Eggs, bacon, fish sticks, cheddar cheese. A coconut cake. Two bottles of cabernet and one of sherry. And, to top it off, Stephen was carrying a large copper pot.

"Beef stew," he said. "My trademark."

Ned said, "We thought you guys might need some extra food."

"Paul isn't here. He got stranded at someone's house. A co-worker's."

"To tell the truth, we thought that might be the case after you said he was being so stubborn," said Stephen. "You newcomers never read the weather right."

They dripped all over the kitchen floor. Their noses were running and their hair was in strings around their red faces, which were almost hidden by scarves and caps and hoods. They were lovely as angels.

"I hope you're hungry," said Stephen.

"I'm starved."

"Show me your stove and we'll heat this up. But first, we'll all have some wine."

I busied myself with a corkscrew and wineglasses. When I turned around, Ned had taken off his jacket and scarf. That's when I saw that he'd shaved off his beard.

"Ned? Is that you, Ned?"

"Can you believe it?" said Stephen.

"Cut it out, bro," said Ned. "You've had a day to get used to it."

I said, "What brought this on?"

"I did," said Stephen. "He was starting to look like an escaped convict."

"You don't decide when I get a shave," Ned said, mock-punching Stephen.

"More than a shave," I said. "A whole new look. Very nice."

"Stephen paid you to say that, didn't he."

"No, really. You look wonderful."

"You think so?" said Ned.

"You look so clean-cut. But not stuffy," I said.

"Next stop, wardrobe," said Stephen.

"Give it a rest, will you, Stevie," said Ned. "He's just full of himself for getting us over here."

"Was it dangerous?"

"Piece of cake," said Stephen.

I put the bread in the oven to warm, grabbed the butter dish, set the table, and thanked them again and again. When Stephen said that the stew was ready, I lit a few of the candles I'd hastily assembled when the storm first started and flipped on the album Paul had been playing the night before. It was one Tammy had suggested during our last class, Michael Feinstein's **Isn't It Romantic.**

"Feinstein," said Stephen. "What good taste you have."

"What good taste **you** have, Stephen," I said, "The stew's delicious."

"And not too unhealthy, either," he said. "I used a lot of Burgundy for flavoring and just a little oil for sautéing the meat."

We drank the first bottle of wine while Ned and Stephen told me a story about the first dog they'd ever had, a Labrador named Hoagie who'd been so much trouble he'd had to go to a farm to run and play. A real farm, not the farm that meant dog heaven, Stephen said.

"How do we know?" said Ned. "We never saw him after that."

"We did," said Stephen. "Mom and Dad took us. You don't remember?"

"I was four, Stevie."

"I remember things that happened when I was four. Don't you, Sophie?"

"I don't remember anything until I was about six. Then my first memory is of a day in school when I raised my hand to ask to go to the bathroom, and Sister Isabel yelled at me for bothering her and I cried in front of the whole class."

"What a lousy first memory," said Stephen.

Ned said his first memory was of losing a kite in a tree in the backyard and for a week watching the wind tatter it.

"Weren't you a morbid little thing," said Stephen. We drank more wine.

Stephen's earliest memory was playing on the floor of his mother's closet, pulling shoes and belts down from shelves and making a big mess.

"Mom just laughed," he said. "She thought it was funny when I was bad."

Then he fell silent. Into the silence the phone rang.

It was Paul.

"How are you holding up?" he said.

"Good. Ned and Stephen brought by some beef stew."

"Nice friends," said Paul. "They must have four-wheel drive."

"Yes. At least, I think so."

I could hear Natalie and Toby laughing in the background.

"Toby's going to teach me to chop wood," said Paul, laughing too, as if chopping wood were hilarious.

"Don't cut your foot off," I said.

Paul said, offstage, "She's worried I'll chop my foot off. She's always worrying."

"Don't worry, Sophie," Toby yelled. "I'll take good care of him."

"When do you think you might come home?" I asked Paul.

"Have you looked out the window? Luckily, they just bought an air mattress. It inflates with its own pump."

"So you're there for the night."

"It seems like the smartest idea."

"Yes, definitely. Have fun," I said, not knowing what else to say.

"I'll check in on you in a few hours," Paul said. Then I heard more laughing and Natalie's voice saying, "The lasagna's ready."

Of course Natalie had some spare lasagna lying around the freezer. Storms didn't find Natalie unprepared, relying on the kindness of strangers.

When I put down the receiver, I saw Ned and

Stephen were both regarding me with identical expressions of muted solicitude, as if I were sick with a disease that had an uncertain prognosis. For the first time I saw a true resemblance between them. Ned's eyes were blue and Stephen's hazel, but both pairs of eyes were deep-set and heavy-lidded. They both had the same widow's peak, the same wide, humorous mouth. Only Stephen's face was much rounder than Ned's, and Stephen's nose was short and broad while Ned's was a faintly aquiline type that hinted at his Italian heritage.

"That was Paul. He's still stranded at that friend's from work."

"That's great," said Stephen. "It gives us an excuse to hang around and keep you company. If you want."

I said, "I do want. Should we go into the living room? Let's break out the sherry."

We played the Michael Feinstein record twice over, because Stephen was a big fan. We drank sherry and ate coconut cake. Stephen was crooning along to "I Won't Send Roses," when he suddenly struggled up from the depths of the couch.

"Sophie, I heard you've learned to dance since I broke my leg."

"Not really dance."

"Ned said you were taking a class."

I mock-glared at Ned, who sat next to me on the floor. We were leaning our backs against the sofa where Stephen reclined.

"Stephen was impressed," said Ned. His feet were stretched out in front of him, six inches from mine. They were bigger than my feet, but not by a lot. I was so tipsy I didn't care how big my feet looked in their house moccasins.

"So show us," said Stephen.

"Now?"

"Of course now. What else are we going to do around here?"

"Scrabble?" I said, recalling the set Pepper and Paul had played with.

"Later," said Stephen. "Here are two men dying to dance with you."

"The fox-trot is all I know."

"Watch me pick it up in five minutes," said Stephen. He bounded off the couch. "Actually, I did the fox-trot for a high school play, **The Women.**"

I said, "There are no men in **The Women.** And I don't recall any dancing."

"We added in the dancing for effect, just as a

scene opener. And it wasn't a big school. I played Sylvia, in heels and a wig."

"He's kidding," said Ned. "He was the assistant director."

"But I subbed for Maureen Bouchard in rehearsal once. Although I didn't get to wear the costume. A big disappointment."

"You'd think our parents would've caught on," said Ned.

"Shut up, Neddy," said Stephen. "It's your turn next."

He pressed a button, and Michael Feinstein's gorgeous voice floated out to us singing **"I Love New York In June."**

"'I like a Gershwin tune, how about you?'" sang Stephen, tapping his foot and holding out his arms to me with a phony leer.

"You asked for it," I said. "Prepare to dance."

We shoved the dining room table and chairs aside to make room. Ned watched from the floor and poured himself more sherry.

"One, one, two-two," I counted to Stephen.

We fox-trotted across the living room and into the dining room, then back into the living room again.

"You catch on fast," I said to him.

Back and forth we went. Floating. Skimming.

"One, one, two-two," Ned counted from the floor.

"Stephen, you're a natural," I said.

"Now for Ned," said Stephen. He was getting winded but I knew he'd never admit it. So I called to Ned, "Are you game?" and he nodded. Ned was relaxed tonight, smiling, willing to be silly. I liked this version of him.

"Sit down, Stevie," he said to his brother. "We'll show you how it's done."

"Hah," said Stephen, puffing. "Great couch, Sophie."

Ned was not half as good a dancer as his brother. I couldn't seem to guess how his body would move or what he'd do next with his feet.

"You're a mile away from her," said Stephen. "Just grab him, Sophie."

I put one hand on Ned's shoulder and drew him toward me with my other hand. And for one crazy moment, I wanted to **keep** drawing him toward me. I wanted to put my head on his shoulder and my arms around his neck. I wanted to feel his neck under my palms, his beautiful neck that looked so vulnerable now that his hair was cut short.

I shook myself. All that wine.

He was looking straight down at me, into my

eyes. His were the darkest blue I'd ever seen them. Probably the twenty-watt bulbs in the living room lamps.

Stephen restarted the song. Ned stumbled.

"No, no," Stephen yelled. "You're going to mow the poor girl down."

"Could you shut up, Stevie," said Ned. His forehead was knotted in concentration and his lower lip was under his teeth.

"Tell you what, Ned," I said. "Stand on my feet."

"I'll crush them."

"These feet are a size nine. You can't crush them."

Ned gingerly put his toes on mine. Stephen started the song again.

"'...to see your name, right beside mine,'" Michael crooned. Ned's feet rested lightly on my moccasins, following my steps.

"Slide," I said, "now slide again."

"This is too fast," he said.

"Stevie," I called out, forgetting that I'd never called Stephen that. "Turn off the record. You sing for us. Sing slow."

It took twenty minutes, but Stephen sang the first verse over and over, until I could feel Ned dropping into the step, step, slide-slide of the dance.

"You did it!" I said to him, just as he'd said to me two months before when I merged onto the highway. "Now turn on the record again, Stevie."

Ned and I moved, not without clumsiness but in the recognizable steps of the fox-trot, from living room to dining room. I smiled up at him, but he didn't smile back down. His face was grave, intent.

In the dining room, away from Stephen's watchful eye, I said, "You can relax, Ned. It doesn't matter. It's just a stupid dance."

"It's not stupid," he said, and he paused in the steps for a moment, still holding me.

"What's the matter?" I said. "Are you dizzy?"

He shook his head as if to clear it.

"No. Just a little tired."

"Here, sit."

He dropped his arms but stayed close to me, almost whispering. If I had a brother with Stephen's bad hearing I'd whisper too.

"You never told me you could dance so well," he said.

"Because I can't, normally. It's the wine."

"You really can dance. Every time I think I have you pegged, you surprise me."

"What's to figure out?"

He didn't answer and we began to dance again, taking a few steps from the dining room toward Stephen in the living room. I looked up at Ned, trying to see his expression in the dark room.

"I think I'm crazy," he said. "I get the stupidest ideas in my head."

He laughed, a dry laugh I'd never heard from him before, and we fox-trotted back into the living room.

"By Jove," said Stephen from the depths of the couch. "It took a while but I think he's got it, Sophie."

"By Jove, you're an asshole, Stevie," said Ned cheerfully.

"My turn again," said Stephen.

We danced until nine o'clock, getting progressively more sober. I showed them the box step and the swing step. Stephen refused to dance to Paul's copy of "Rockin' Robin," but pounced upon the Squirrel Nut Zippers and the Ben Folds Five with joy.

When we looked outside, the snow had stopped.

"Just a lull," said Stephen, who was flipping through channels that showed a doughnut-shaped break in the storm clouds.

"I can fix up something for you guys to sleep on, or you can have our bed, if it's not too weird to sleep next to each other," I said.

"It is too weird because Stephen yells in his sleep."

"I have war dreams," said Stephen. "I've seen too many movies."

"And we can make it home," said Ned. "If you'll be okay."

"I won't finish all this food until Memorial Day. But don't go. The roads are bad."

"We're Massachusetts boys. We can drive in snow," Ned said.

I glanced at Stephen, who still seemed a bit tipsy.

"I can drive in snow, that is," said Ned. "Come on, Stevie. This is our best chance to make it. Are you sure you'll be all right here, Sophie? The storm's going to blow itself out in the next nine or ten hours, I think. But if you need us before that, we'll get here."

"I'm fine. You brought enough food for an army. Take the rest of the stew at least," I said.

"The stew is yours," Stephen said with a grand

gesture. "The stew, our hearts, you name it. At your feet."

"My size nine feet," I said.

"Your beautiful, dancing feet," said Stephen.

At the door Ned let Stephen go first and leaned back inside.

"I hate leaving you here alone," he said.

"What can happen? You guys solved the main problem. Now I have food."

"This place . . ." he said. The whole house seemed to be sighing in the wind, and I wondered if the chimneys would tumble down in the night. Wouldn't it be ironic if a chimney fell in and killed me when I'd never even gotten any use out of the fireplace?

"This house must have seen far worse storms than this," I said. "And Donald and his wife are just over in the garage if I get really stuck."

"Yeah. I can see he keeps the place up wonderfully," said Ned, who was standing on the spot in the kitchen doorway where the rubber weather stripping had curled up from the floor.

"Go, before it gets really bad again."

"The phone lines will stay up," he said. "They'd have gone down before this if they were going to go down. So call us for anything. Anything. Promise."

"I promise, Ned," I said. The wind seemed to die down. I could hear Stephen making his way to the curb, the faint chunk-chunk of his boots on the snow.

"Do you have any thumbtacks in your kitchen?"

"In my studio," I said, curiously. "They call them artists' tacks or something but they're the same."

"Get them, would you?"

I brought the box to him and he learned down and pressed a line of tacks through the edges of the rubber stripping.

"It's just a quick fix, but at least you won't pitch over down these stairs in the snow and break your neck. Tell your husband some wood glue would work on that."

He paused, seeming to consider what he knew of Paul.

"I'll bring some by myself next time we go driving," he said.

"You're good to me."

"It's easy," he said. "You don't ask for much."

"Now go. I couldn't stand it if you came to grief out here because of me."

"You won't be brave and martyrish?"

"Since when have I been brave around you?" I said.

Stephen had the truck running. I saw Ned gently shove him over and take the wheel. The brake lights flared red on the snow.

"Good-bye, Sophie darling," Stephen yelled to me. I waved my hand and hoped they could see it.

Stephen bellowed "No Other Love Have I" out the window of the truck until the wind flew up from across the Fore River bluff and his words were lost in its howling.

Paul called once more, and I assured him I was set for the night. I cleared up the dishes, drank more coffee, and watched the weather reports until Ned and Stephen phoned to say they were safely home. Then I tumbled into bed. The cold did not wake me, nor the wind's screeching outside my windows. In the morning I had no headache. All morning and afternoon it snowed, and ice spat at the windows. Then, just before dark approached, the snow petered out and a watery light spread over a scene of such immaculate whiteness that my eyes were dazzled.

I was digging out my car when Paul came back. Toby dropped him off and turned right around, waving a hand to me.

Paul gave me a kiss.

"Glad you're okay," he said. "Is there anything to eat in there?"

"Plenty," I said, and continued to dig.

"Let me get another shovel."

He slogged across the yard, the snow up to his thighs. As he walked the thin layer of ice on the snow crumpled in front of him like the melted-sugar crust on a crème brûlée.

When he returned, he said, "That was kind of your friends to bring groceries by."

"Yes," I said. "They're nice people."

"It's a nice town," said Paul. "Natalie cooked for us for two days straight."

I said nothing. Suddenly, I didn't care that Natalie could cook and I couldn't. Why had I ever cared?

"You must have been bored, though," Paul said. "Stuck inside."

"No," I said. "I practiced the fox-trot."

"By yourself?"

"I taught it to Ned and Stephen. We had fun."

"That's good," said Paul.

"Yes," I said. "It's good."

The sun on the snow was so blinding and beautiful, I couldn't help but smile.

Twenty-Three

On April 18, I left to see Rory in Boston. I'd told
Paul I was going to Boston to see an old friend
from the neighborhood who was passing
through, then sticking around to visit a few
more museums. He hadn't expressed much cu-
riosity about my plans.

I'd booked the same single at the Beltran, because having your own bed makes you less likely
to fall into someone else's. I'd had my hair cut
again and had religiously moisturized my complexion for days. I needed to feel at my best, to
guard against any hangdog gratitude over Rory's
attentions. I had been hangdog for long enough,
I'd decided. What I hadn't decided was whether
to sin or to back out. I knew I wouldn't be able
to choose until I saw Rory. There are some decisions you can't make theoretically.

You see, I was still married and I still **felt** married, though Paul wasn't currently involved in
the marriage very actively. It was like sitting
alone, up in the air, on one end of a seesaw. The
person on the other end wasn't playing the game
anymore, he was just sitting on his side—but I

was still on the seesaw. I couldn't stay there forever, though. Spring was on the way, even if it was a slow, shy spring. I had to move in some direction. I had to move.

So I was going to meet Rory in Boston.

In Maine, the wind still blew raw, but in Boston it was warmer, the weather forecasters said. I'd wear my camel-hair coat and wine-colored beret, and the thin, dark red leather gloves Delia had given me for Christmas. I also packed two pencil skirts, one dark gray, one chocolate brown, with two cashmere sweaters I'd picked up at the Goodwill on my last trip and had dry-cleaned: a close-fitting pullover in pale yellow, and a petal-pink cardigan with pearly buttons. In case Boston wasn't warmer after all, I added woolen flat-front pants in a dusty lavender tweed, which had been on sale at Marshalls.

Rory would be in the city already when I arrived. We had fixed a place to meet, another restaurant in the North End.

"So what will you do?" said Marta.

"I have no idea. Guess I'll know when I see him."

"Don't let him push you into making any commitments, or I'll hear from you next in some dump overlooking the Volga River."

"You have nothing to worry about. This is just an exploratory meeting."

"Exploring is fine," said Marta. "You explore all you want. It serves Paul right."

It might. But I didn't want to sleep with Rory while muttering imprecations at Paul through my teeth, so to speak.

We'd just have dinner and see what happened. Dinner was a step more sinful than lunch or tea, but I could always flee virtuously in a taxi back to my own hotel room.

I'd be gone Thursday and Friday, so on Wednesday morning I let Ned and Stephen know I'd be missing our next walking group.

"Boston?" said Ned. "If you could wait until Friday afternoon by any chance, I could give you a ride down. I'm going to see Fiona then."

"I can't wait until then, Ned. I'm sorry. I'm meeting an old friend who's there for a conference, and he only has tonight. I'm taking the afternoon bus."

"An important old friend, if you're going all the way to Boston," said Ned.

"Actually," I said. "The one I told you about."

Ned took my arm and let the tail end of the group go past us, except for Stephen, who was hanging back, fiddling with his three scarves and pulling his two sets of gloves up under his coat sleeves for the tenth time.

"You're seeing that guy? You're really seeing that guy?"

"For dinner," I said. "Dinner only."

Ned shook his head.

"It's none of my business," he said, "but are you sure you know what you're doing?"

"No, I'm not sure," I said. "And I'd say it's none of your business, but I already told you all about it, so feel free to chime in."

"You're setting yourself up," he said. "To get hurt again."

I stared at the ground, at our moving feet. I had walked over more of Portland with Ned than I had with Paul, I realized.

"Ned, my marriage is not exactly a huge success at the moment. I have a right to have dinner with an old . . . an old beau. It's harmless."

"It would be harmless, if it were another sort of guy," said Ned. His black brows were drawn together. He looked ridiculously young and serious.

"He's not in the States very often. He has one night."

"Well, bully for whoever it is," said Stephen,

coming up behind us. "Not in the States very often, indeed. All these world travelers are so frickin' glamorous."

Stephen was feeling low. His boyfriend Scott was off on the first of his spring trips with his sightseeing-for-the-rich agency. I asked him the theme for this time around.

"Paris in the Roaring Twenties. As if Hemingway would have put up for a minute with all these matrons from Dallas and New London with their matching luggage. They even subtitled the restaurant preview 'A Moveable Feast.' Can you believe it?"

"That was **your** idea, Steve," Ned reminded him irritably. "And Scott phones you every afternoon, so I don't know what you're beefing about."

"Easy for you to say," said Stephen. "Long distance isn't fun. Look at you. You're going all the way down to Boston to play Mr. Fix-It so Fiona won't get pouty."

"Shouldn't you be walking faster, Stevie?"

"Well, excuse me," Stephen said and stalked on, his rubber-tipped stick thudding on the now-snowless streets in protest.

Ned said, "Men like this McLaughlin guy

don't just have dinner with old girlfriends to catch up on old times."

"I know they don't," I said. "But he's about to get separated from his wife. He's not catting around. So if he holds my hand or something, it's not that sinister."

"You haven't heard that one before? The line about 'my wife and I are on the verge of separating?' Boy, are you naïve. You talk like you've seen everything and you're just as naïve as some little schoolgirl."

I ticked my arguments off on my hands.

"First of all, Ned, I'm staying in a separate hotel and meeting him in the North End for dinner. Second, of course I'm not going to agree to anything until I know his status with his wife. Third, thank you so much for assuming that I'm so unappealing that he'd only waste his time with me for some sordid one-night stand."

Ned ran a hand over his face in a scrubbing gesture, the way the baby Matilda did when she was tired.

"I didn't **say** you were unappealing, Sophie. This isn't about you, it's about the kind of person this guy is."

"You know, you can be a real prig sometimes, Ned."

"Excuse me for caring," said Ned.

"If you cared, you'd know I have every right to even the score on my husband, to be crude."

"You never told me anything about that. I had an idea but . . ."

"Well, I'm telling you now. My husband is cheating on me with his perky little friend at work, and I'm not responsible to anyone for what I do about it, understand? Not to you or to anyone. Now let's walk."

We walked three blocks in deep silence.

We had almost reached the Eastern Prom trailhead on India Street where the others were waiting when he said quietly, "I didn't know about your husband. At least, I wasn't sure. I'm just asking you to watch your back in Boston, Sophie."

"I know," I said. "But sometimes, don't you just want to be with someone who thinks you're wonderful? Even if they aren't trustworthy, even if they aren't the answer? Sometimes anything is better than the status quo."

"Not anything," said Ned.

"You have no idea how it feels," I said. "No idea."

"No, I don't. But watch it with him all the same, okay?"

"You're an awfully interfering friend," I said. "Good thing I still don't know how to manage rotaries, or I might get really mad at you."

He smiled at me but I saw him only hazily because there were tears in my eyes.

"Go on with the rest of them," I said. "I think I'll go home now."

"Sophie," he said. "Don't cry. I can't stand it."

"Go. Catch up to them. I'll see you on Monday."

"I've screwed everything up," he said.

"You haven't screwed anything up. You have every right to speak your mind."

"See you Monday," he said.

As he walked away he hunched his shoulders against the cold. The movement looked oddly forlorn.

This was silly. If Ned didn't consider it a sign of weakness to wear a warm jacket, he wouldn't be hunching. And I'd see him again in five days, see all of them. There was no reason to act as if we were saying a long good-bye.

"Where can I reach you while you're gone?" Paul had said that morning.

"Here." I had typed out my bus schedule and my hotel number, and noted in bold letters when I'd be coming home. If Paul was indeed playing around on me, I didn't want to surprise Natalie in a negligee in my own bedroom—not that Natalie owned one, I bet. She probably had the sort of cute, cap-sleeved cotton pajamas that wives used to wear on sixties' sitcoms.

Paul said, "If you get back on Friday like you're planning, we could drive down to Kennebunkport on Saturday if you like, get a little scenery."

"Sure."

I had no idea why he was planning a day trip for us. Perhaps it was in the spirit of fattening the condemned goose: give Sophie a good time while she's still around. Then a qualm assailed me—maybe Paul was having second thoughts.

"I hear the aquarium's worth looking at, if you have any spare time down there," he said.

I walked him to his car, watching as he pulled out of the garage with exquisite care. He really did prize his Explorer. It was worth, to him, what he'd paid for it.

He leaned out the window and gave me a clumsy kiss on the side of the head.

"We'll have a good time Saturday," he said, and sped off down Pine Street.

Rory had picked a very different sort of North End restaurant from the one I'd eaten in with Ned back in November. This place was one of the Hanover Street tourist-attraction eateries, with an indoor waterfall and fake Roman statues and freestanding plaster columns strewn around.

We bumped into each other, literally, in the doorway. He was dressed in a business suit and trench coat and another truly awful tie, a bilious yellow with red diagonal stripes.

"Sophie," he said, and grabbed me and spun me around. This annoyed the tiny, old lady who ran the place. She flourished menus in our direction, but Rory ignored her.

"You should have seen me dashing out of my meeting," he said. "I couldn't wait."

"Did you think I'd chicken out?"

"I didn't know. I had such a hard time getting you to meet me in D.C., I couldn't believe you'd slog all the way down here for dinner."

"I'll go far for good Italian," I said.

The proprietress surged up again. She commandeered us to the worst table in the place, in a shadowy corner next to the kitchen.

"Can we have another table?" Rory said to the woman, smiling the smile that never failed him.

She muttered no, something about a party being expected later, and we took our seats. A moment later a harried middle-aged waiter appeared with water and bread. Rory asked for a glass of the house red for each of us. There were no other customers except for a husband and wife sitting near the door, thumbing through maps and guidebooks in a weary, contented silence.

The waiter reappeared and urged us to order. From the kitchen we could see the hostess glaring at him. He was probably her son. He looked that frightened.

"I'll take the chicken parm," said Rory.

"The same," I said.

After the waiter left Rory said, "Wait a minute, I don't even like chicken parm. Oh, well. It doesn't matter."

He took my hand, right out in the open, across the tablecloth. As always, I was surprised at the extent of my sheer physical longing for him. There seemed to be nothing I could do about it. Like rheumatism or a shellfish allergy, wanting Rory McLaughlin seemed to be bred into my physiology.

He chafed my fingers in both of his.

"You're so cold," he said. "How are you surviving up there in Portland?"

"I'm surviving fine. It's not such a bad place."

He laughed.

"What a ringing endorsement."

"Honestly, I don't dislike it the way I used to."

"Grows on you, huh."

"It's beautiful there, even in the cold, and I can drive to the ocean," I said. "I've been painting again, kind of seriously."

"I can't believe you're an artist and you've never been to Italy," he said, ignoring Maine's claims to beauty. "You can't top it."

"Yes. I remember you said that when we had tea."

"I can't get the idea out of my head. Us in Venice, walking the alleys, going to look at every painting or statue you ever saw in a book, eating incredible meals."

"Holding our noses," I smiled, dismissing the image. To see Venice, and to see it with Rory; it was too tantalizing a thought.

"The smell's not that bad," he said. "People exaggerate."

"You said Liz complained about it," I said.

"She's not a painter."

"And how is Liz?"

"The same."

The waiter arrived again, bearing two platters with huge slabs of parmigiana and heaps of steaming spaghetti doused in thin tomato sauce. On the side were two salads consisting of iceberg lettuce, three radish slices, and two carrot rounds apiece.

"We'd better let this cool," said Rory dubiously.

He leaned forward. His hair gleamed in the candlelight.

"If I told you how much I care about you," he said, "you'd get a big head."

The couple at the other table had moved on to cappuccino. They were planning their next day, talking about Concord and the Old North Bridge. The wife said she'd like to see the house where Louisa May Alcott wrote **Little Women**. The proprietress evidently took to them. She was pointing to spots on their map, making recommendations.

"I've been thinking a lot in all my travels. I know now that I just didn't appreciate you," said Rory. "When we were together. I want to say this now, so you hear it. I'm so sorry I hurt you back then."

"It's all right," I said. "It really is. If we'd stayed together, who knows, I might have gotten on your nerves."

His face was flushed in the steam rising from his plate. His eyes were the same brilliant blue. He seemed young to me, younger than ever. If I stayed with him long enough, I might become young too. I might become a different kind of person.

I speared a morsel of my chicken. It was surprisingly wonderful, meltingly tender with a hint of lemon.

"God, this is great food," Rory said. "Now, why would you say that, about getting on my nerves?"

"No reason."

"Let me guess. Is that how you feel with your husband?"

"Married couples do get on each other's nerves."

"Not if you're half the couple. You're easy to be around, Sophie. You're soothing. Your husband must know that."

"It's beginning to look as if someone else is soothing him these days."

"You're kidding. He looked so square when I saw him at Christmas."

"He **is** square. Maybe he's just fallen in love. I don't know. People do fall in love."

Rory leaned forward. He held my eyes with his as if he'd hypnotize me.

"Listen to me, Sophie. Your husband is a fool. It all comes easily with you and he throws it away. Does he know how rare that is?"

"Sex, you mean," I said. "Sex was all we could be sure came easily to us, Rory. We never tried the day-to-day stuff. Anyone can be good for an hour or two in bed."

"You think sex is all I remember about you? I remember that, of course I do, but I remember the rest. I remember talking. And playing pool. And driving around—remember all those drives we took?"

"I remember our drives," I said. "Remember the night you stole the rowboat and rowed us over to Sycamore Island after dark?"

"You kept giving these little yips of alarm the whole time, and then once we were there you were the one who wanted to break into the clubhouse."

"I just wanted to look in the windows."

"Then we wound up on that tarp behind the boat shed," said Rory, with an evil grin.

"That was a nice convenient tarp."

"You should see the bed in my hotel room. The spread looks just like that fabric that tarps come in. It's huge too, from here to that window."

He gestured to indicate the size of the bed, and the waiter, thinking something was required of him, came hurrying over.

"Coffee?" he said, and eyed our still-full plates. You'd have thought that there was a line of hungry diners outsides clamoring for our table.

"Later," said Rory. The waiter left, sighing mournfully.

"Was it something I said?" Rory murmured to me. He winked, and just like that, it was us against the scowling hostess, us against the morose waiter. It was that fizzy thrill I'd always had with him, that we two were breaking the rules together.

The hostess was now seated with the other couple, treating them to a round of Sambuca.

"Is it nice?" I asked him. "Your hotel."

"It's amazing, more than nice. But the Foundation got a good rate."

He was staying in one of the big chain hotels near the business center. His room, he said, had a mini-bar and a huge television and floor-to-ceiling windows with a view of the city lights. It was full of rich businessmen and well-heeled tourists.

"It bowls me over fresh every time I come back to the States," he said. "The scale of everything over here. This hotel, it's so big, the escalators, the wall hangings, the plants. It's like that Pharoah's temple I saw at Karnak, with the gargantuan pillars. Everything the biggest possible. That's America for you."

"Supersized," I said.

"This country. No wonder everyone's obese."

Rory himself had become someone who was not **quite** American, it struck me. The veneer of foreignness wasn't glaringly obvious. It was just that the toes of his shoes weren't cut like American men's shoes. His hair was longer than he'd used to wear it in Washington, and brushed rather theatrically straight back from his forehead. He carried an odd zip-up case of yellowish leather for his business papers, and his tiepin was cheap Russian silver with an agate set in the middle. You couldn't have glanced at him and known for **sure** he was from the U.S.

"Did you see Karnak?" I asked, made uneasy by this new strangeness in him.

"Last fall. And the Valley of the Kings and Luxor. It was one of our better times together. When Liz has me to herself, she's happier."

"Who's she sharing you with the rest of the time?"

"Work," he said. "Nothing else and no one else, in case you wondered."

"I have no business wondering."

"It could be your business. But we'll leave it at that for now. About your husband. What are you going to do about that?"

"Leave, I guess. If he won't be straight with me or see a counselor."

"What a jerk," said Rory. "And don't tell me that I'm a jerk too, to be sitting here with you. That's different. I'm willing to fix my mistakes. I wouldn't leave Liz in limbo forever."

"Just for a few months while we see how we do together?"

"Everything depends on you, Sophie Ann," he said. "You know that."

My chair seat seemed very hard and uncomfortable suddenly. I leaned back, trying to seem at ease, in control, a sophisticated married woman who was propositioned all the time.

"Can we be . . . lighter for a few minutes?" I

said. "You just got here. I'm just getting my sea legs with you."

"What should we talk about then? I'll talk about anything with you."

"Your job. Your traveling. I wouldn't mind knowing more about it."

He liked being asked; he had stories for me. He spoke of people he'd met, journalists and political activists and trade union leaders and writers who'd taken big risks under the Soviet system, when risks could cost you your liberty or more.

"But it's not glamorous," he said. "A lot of the time, all I'm trying to do is funnel money really. Just keeping them going, under the guise of projects and what-not."

He'd lost a few illusions—a student in Moscow he'd been kind to had stolen the pearl earrings he'd gotten Liz for their first anniversary, and a trusted assistant had quit for a job at a rival organization. But on the whole, he was happy in his career. It showed in his face, just as a happy marriage shows.

"So the job's worked out. I'm glad, Rory. You deserve it."

"The **job**'s worked out, yes. I'm even due for a promotion sometime soon."

"A different part of Eastern Europe?"

"Or maybe Central America, or the Philippines."

"Not the Philippines. It's too dangerous."

"That's media hype, most of it. I'm not scared of where they'd send me. But I'd have more people to supervise, less direct fieldwork. I don't know how I'd like that."

"How does Liz feel?"

"She wants a baby. I'm not sure she even cares where we live. And I just don't share her urgency on that. Not now, just when things are getting interesting."

"Maybe they're not interesting for her."

"They could be. I'm pulling some strings. We're going to find her more challenging work. But the kid thing seems to be all she thinks about."

"Funny, you haven't said you don't **want** a kid. You've just said the timing's bad."

"You know it's not just timing."

The food was taken away while our forks were still in mid-air. I snatched some bread from the basket as the waiter whisked it out of my hands.

"We can have coffee at my hotel," said Rory.

"Only coffee. No pressure."

"No pressure. I just want to talk to you without the waiter coming and going."

When we left, the couple in front was still gabbing away with the signora, who ignored Rory's courteous thank you on our way out the door.

The hotel was off Copley Plaza. It was fancy in a beefy, impersonal business-traveler fashion. It could have been any upscale business hotel anywhere.

As he'd promised, Rory didn't try to persuade me into going up to his room. We had brandy— a tiny capful each in huge globe glasses—in the bar, which was filled with businessmen watching a basketball game. Not the Celtics, but another team, a team that was up and coming in the Western Conference.

"What kind of shot is that?" said one of the men, who subsided abruptly after the shot went in.

"Do you miss American sports?" I asked Rory, swirling my brandy around and feeling like an impostor in this room full of professionals and padded leather swivel chairs. I ate a Brazil nut from the bowl in front of me.

"Are you still hungry?" he said. "Because I think they have a dessert menu here."

"No," I said. It would be humiliating to down a hot fudge sundae in the midst of all these Scotch-swilling men in suits.

I peered at my brandy, making oily swirls around and around my snifter. Then I met Rory's eyes. He was watching me with such affection that I caught my breath. I'd forgotten how his eyes could turn that cloudy, tender blue.

"It's just so good to see you," he said. "Sorry. I know I've said that eighteen times. Were we talking about sports?"

"I just asked if you miss American football or baseball."

"Not much. Sometimes I get to a soccer game if we're somewhere where that's big."

I suppressed a brief flash of criticism. It was one thing to not care much who won the Super Bowl. It was another thing to think soccer was any substitute for real sports.

Suddenly he took my hand again, urgently, as if he needed to lead me from the scene of an accident.

"Sophie, what's wrong? We've written for months, but tonight I can't seem to get ahold of you. You have to tell me what you're thinking."

"I don't know what I'm thinking. I'm probably talking like an idiot."

"No, never. We have to get used to each other again, that's all."

"Also, I can't help worrying about what you expect. Tonight."

"I don't expect anything," Rory said. "Nothing you don't feel like. But can we go up to my room and just talk? This place is getting on my nerves."

Well, I knew what I was probably agreeing to but it was Rory, and the old days were coming back to me so strongly that Maine felt a little like a dream I'd had and half-forgotten. He moved to kiss me in the elevator but three businessmen got on, and he had to dart back at the last second.

"Later," I said, feeling reckless.

The room was on the thirty-third floor. It was done in sickly shades of beige but the view was stunning: the skyscrapers, the lights around the harbor, the gleam of traffic far below. For a moment, at the window, I was lost in how much I loved this city where I'd spent so little time.

"What a face you have," he said. "Look at you looking out the window. The way you enjoy things. It kills me."

The bed was as enormous as Rory had said, covered in a nylon-ish, shiny spread.

"I keep sliding off that bedspread, it's so slippery," he said. "You want a drink?"

We each had a brandy from the mini-bar, sitting in the same leather swivel chairs they'd had downstairs. These were placed at a round marble table obviously intended for in-room meetings or late nights of solitary work. It was so heavy that if you knocked into it hard and it tipped over, it would break every bone in your feet.

We stared at each other, as if wondering how to open a difficult business negotiation.

"This is awful. Let's move to the couch," he said.

We moved to the couch. He put his arm around me and I relaxed into it. He still smelled the same, moved the same, fitted my body against his body in the same old way. He breathed into my hair and I lifted my head to kiss him.

We kissed for a long time, dozens of kisses. I began to do what you do when you want more than kissing: I loosened his tie, fumbled at his shirt buttons. He slipped his hand under my sweater, up my back.

"Sophie," he said. "I miss you. I miss you all the time."

I murmured nonsense to him, half dizzy.

He went on, kissing me in between words, holding me close.

"We'll find a way to meet," he said.

I nodded, finally unbuttoned his shirt all the way, put my hand against his warm bare chest and felt the lovely muscles there and the beating of his heart against my palm.

He was going on and on, softly, deliriously, "We can even set up a system so you can call me sometimes at the office. I have to hear your voice sometimes. Then, soon, I promise soon, you can come over and we can meet in person somewhere. I take trips different places. She doesn't always come with me."

His voice was muffled in my hair. I wanted to lean back into these familiar, intoxicating kisses. I'd dreamed of him, longed for him, and yet I couldn't lean back. If only he hadn't spoken. If only, in his devastatingly charmingly conspiratorial way, he hadn't made it clear what we were planning.

I sat up.

"Rory, just say to me, are you ready to leave Liz or not?"

"Of course I'm ready. But we should see how it goes, don't you think?"

"I think we can see where it's going."

"Sophie, Liz knows our marriage is in trouble. There won't be any mess you'll get caught up in, I promise."

"Are you sure she knows it's in **this** much trouble?"

"She knows all right."

"And then what? If our affair passes muster, you'll leave Liz and then what?"

"We'll be together, that's what."

"Wherever **you** are?"

"**Wherever** I am," he said, misunderstanding me. He began to kiss me again, sitting forward, cupping my face in his hands.

"No, Rory, I mean . . . I may not want to live over there."

"It's not the moon. They have cars and houses and drinking water, you know."

He was smiling indulgently.

"I told you about my book with Ann, my painting. I told you in my e-mails."

"You can paint there, Sophie. You can mail Ann your stuff. We'll travel to the most inspiring places you could ever imagine. You can even keep freelancing, with the technology they have now."

"People in Washington won't wake up at four A.M. to call me in Zanzibar with blueline corrections."

"We'll work it out," he said, with his eternal confidence.

He'd offered me all he could, for now.

I don't know what got me to my feet and straightening my clothes. Not lack of passion and not high-mindedness. I knew his promises were sincere. The only problem was that to get from here to there with him, I'd have to slog through a lot of swamp in between. And I was tired. I'd done enough slogging; all winter I had slogged. I couldn't slog any farther.

"Rory," I said. "I'm so sorry but I can't do this."

"Can't make love with me? Because I can wait. For a little."

Then, in immediate contradiction, he began whispering to me, entreating me.

"Just tonight," he said, as he'd said five years ago. "Give us tonight."

"Tonight," I said. "But then what? Will you phone Liz before you go to sleep, while I'm lying there next to you? Will you have to leave the hotel separately from me in the morning?"

"What does it matter?" he said.

"It matters. Rory, I felt embarrassed in front of that horrible restaurant hostess."

"You're letting that old lady determine our future?"

"Not her. What she represents. Dark corners. Me and you in dark corners. Like that song from that movie **The Commitments**. You know the song: 'The Dark End of the Street.' "

He knew the whole album; he used to play it in the car. Comprehension crossed his face, then stubbornness. Rory had never met a woman he couldn't persuade. And God! He was beautiful in that moment. Beautiful not because he was the same untarnished youth I'd once loved, not because his hair was as bright and his eyes as untroubled a blue. He was beautiful because these things had worn and changed just a little; in old age, he'd be beautiful still, as a vaulted cathedral ceiling is with its gold-leaf flaking off and its painted azure sky faded soft with time. I'd never tire of looking at him. But I couldn't have him. It came over me in a great wave of grief; there was no path to him that I could travel now, not one that wouldn't leave me irreparably damaged. Maybe there never had been.

"I don't want to be without you another five years," he said.

"But Rory . . . can you see telling your mother about us? Or telling Liz?"

"I don't tell my mother anything. It's why I live across the world from her."

We laughed a little and I sensed it again, that current between us, that sense of being two people who spied on the world from our own secluded vantage point. I wanted him badly. I could see the night, how good it would be. I just couldn't see farther. I couldn't picture us doing something even as simple and public as walking down a street together. I could not picture **setting out** with Rory.

"You've always delighted me, Sophie," he said. "You're such a delight, you know that?"

"And you've always delighted me, Rory. But you're farther from breaking with Liz than you want to be, and I don't think I can be the person who helps you get farther. I'm no saint, it's just that I don't have the strength."

He drew a hand across his forehead, wearily, and I knew I was right.

"I rushed this," he said. "I'm a fool. I should have settled things and come to you afterward."

"You aren't close to settling things."

"I thought I was. I thought that we'd both know, that it'd be simple."

I sat down next to him.

I said, "Rory, it's my fault too. I'm so mad at Paul. I'm mad at him all the time now. I can't hop in bed with you and expect to feel any better."

"**I'd** sure feel better," Rory said.

"For ten minutes."

"For longer than that," he said. "Or you've forgotten a lot."

"For hours," I said. "I do remember. But then you'd feel not so good. Because the main drama is still what's happening with you and Liz, not this side plot you have going with me. Or with whoever might step in if I turn you down."

He flushed at that, and it was clear that my guess was right: there were other women waiting in the wings, ready to take up the challenge of Rory McLaughlin if I turned it down.

"You're saying that the dream of your heart is to see me patch things up with Liz? You're saying that, Sophie Ann?"

"I can't say how things will work out with you and Liz. But incidentally, Rory, if you were so set against a baby, you wouldn't be fulminating about it all the time."

"You think I'm one of those men who has to be dragged into things. Dragged into marriage and now dragged into fatherhood, and deep down I'll be relieved?"

"It's a good theory."

"You must not think much of me," said Rory.

"I think a lot of you. And I think I have to go now, before I do something stupid with you that will only throw me off."

"I'll walk you to a cab," he said.

"No. No, I don't want that. There's a stand just outside, with a bellman."

We kissed, gently and tiredly, and I put my arms around his neck, then pulled away. In a minute I'd be crying and I didn't want Rory to see me that way. I'd been crying the first time he left me.

"I'll write you," he said at the door of his room. "I'll settle things with Liz and I'll write you."

"You'll settle things," I repeated, unable to imagine it.

"Yes. Yes, I promise. One way or another. That's what you want, isn't it. It's the least I can do. But whatever happens, can we always be friends, Sophie Ann? Do you think that's possible?"

"Yes," I said. "I do."

He smiled wanly.

"You're a class act," he said. "Don't forget it."

The last I saw of him he was standing in the doorway, watching me go down the corridor. He was still standing there when the elevator came.

There were toffee chocolate brownies left out in the foyer of the Beltran Inn with a thermos of cocoa that read, "For Miss Quinn. Sweet dreams."

The bed was as soft as if it were really stuffed with feathers, like beds in the olden days. I thought of calling Paul, but there was nothing I wanted to say to him. Not, "Let's give it another chance," not, "You fool, I'm a better woman than Natalie." Maybe I wasn't a better woman than Natalie, for Paul.

When it came down to it, I just wanted to drink my cocoa and eat my brownies and heap all the blankets on top of me and get warm, warm, warm.

I slept for ten hours and when I woke, Rory's plane had already been gone for an hour and I was late. I had a bus to catch.

Twenty-Four

It began to snow as the bus crossed into New Hampshire. Portsmouth looked dingy and bleak, the river a sullen gray-green in the late-afternoon light.

At South Station, while I'd waited for the bus, a man with a steel-gray ponytail and a camouflage jacket had approached me. He sat next to me on the long wooden bench and said, "This is a hard day for me."

"Why?" I said. This was the reason I shouldn't wander around cities by myself. When a guy whose breath smells distinctly of alcohol sidles up to most people and talks about his hard day, they move to another seat.

He told me his troubles. He was entering rehab today, at a facility I'd dimly heard of, in Watertown. He was a Vietnam vet, he claimed, and I believed him. He had that look of haphazard dereliction shared by guys who were truly messed up by the war. Not the "gone" look of homeless people, but an aura of not caring on some profound level.

"My brother isn't speaking to me anymore,"

he said. "Until I'm sober. I've got a ride picking me up here in an hour to take me to this program. Where are you going?"

"Portland," I said.

"Cold up there."

"Yes."

"My brother said that if I could finish this program he'd speak to me again," said the man. "You have a cigarette?"

I bought him a pack of his brand, Lucky Strikes. He put them in his pocket and thanked me. He said he hoped he could do it this time.

"I hope so too," I said. "I know it's hard."

They announced my bus.

"Can I call you?" he said. "When I'm better. Do you have a boyfriend?"

"A husband," I said, raising my ring hand, not wanting him to think that I was lying to put him off.

"Well, you're a very pretty lady and he's a fortunate man," said the guy.

"Good luck to you," I said, but he'd already loped off. If he got sober I'd be some drifting face in his hazy recollections of those last hours on the bottle.

The ugly Boston suburbs slipped away with their unlovable strip malls and their lovable old restaurant and nightclub signs. I saw an ice cream parlor with a huge rotating cow on top of the roof, and a leaning Tower of Pizza.

I could still smell the brandy on that vet's breath. I wished I'd had the nerve to take his hand, to give him a pat on the shoulder. I wished I could have told him I'd always remember him, for having the guts to at least try.

It was still daylight when we were dumped off at the St. John's Street terminal. There were cabs but I decided to walk. I'd left a matter-of-fact message on Paul's work line that I was arriving home early. It seemed prudent.

Sunset was coming fast. I decided not to try the wooden stairway that ran up the side of the Western Prom bluff. The tramps and cruisers began to hang out there at this hour. Instead, I took the hill up Congress Street, with the back-side of the hospital on my right to assure me of lights and people in range if I should be bothered.

It was only six when I reached our apartment. It was Donald's poker night over in Gray, and the lights above the garage were off. But ours were on. I climbed the back stairs, glanced in the window.

That's when I knew that Paul hadn't gotten my message. Perhaps he'd left the office too early to get it. He hadn't left alone.

What's worse: To come home unexpectedly to find your husband in the arms of another woman, entwined on your marriage bed? Or to arrive at your kitchen doorstep, see through the window a scene of such domestic felicity that the only answer to the question "what's wrong with this picture?" is "you."

Natalie was serving pot roast and homemade rolls. The kitchen table was covered in a yellow-checked tablecloth I didn't recognize—had she possibly brought it from home, along with those yellow ceramic candlesticks and that vase of enormous daisies on the sideboard? I did recognize the big, red-and-white-striped apron that enveloped her tiny frame. It was a Christmas gift from Pepper to me. I was so close that I could hear the oven door slam shut as Natalie pulled out the baked potatoes.

Paul was sitting at the table, his legs stretched out, a portrait of ease. When she put the dish down, he pulled her into his lap, nestling his nose in the nape of her neck. They were laughing. With that lovely meal steaming in front of them and their identical expressions of delirious, domestic contentment, they could have been celebrating a first anniversary: a home-cooked dinner, with champagne in the bedroom to follow.

Oh God, they looked so right together. My husband so very happy. If a stranger had walked by at that moment and I'd pointed to that tableaux in the kitchen window and sobbed, claiming to be Paul's wife, they'd probably have hauled me off to the psych unit at Maine Medical down the block. That's how delusional I'd seem.

Fortunately, I had my car keys in my purse. I don't remember much of the drive to the Eastland Hotel. It was the only hotel I could think of in my muddled state, as it was near Paul's office. The desk clerk said that a big convention had left just that afternoon, and it would be half an hour before a room was ready. The clerk gave me a key and said he'd telephone up to the rooftop bar if I wanted to have a drink there while I waited.

I rode up many floors, and when I arrived at the top there was the bar with its glass walls, and Portland spread out below, glittering in the foggy night with a skyline as lovely as any panorama of San Francisco or New York. It seemed cruel of Portland, to hand me such a lovely view of itself just when it seemed likely I'd be leaving town soon.

I found a solitary armchair away from the few other patrons, whom it was almost too dark to see anyway, and ordered a port with lemon. My drink was only half gone when the waitress came to say my room was ready. I paid up, and cradling my wine, tripped out of the bar, pausing at the entrance to get one more look at that view.

It was that last look that allowed a dark-haired man sitting in one of the big corner sofas to look over and spot me.

It was Ned. Ned with Fiona. She was smoking, staring out the window. They seemed preoccupied—not fighting, but discussing something of sobering importance.

Damn.

I raised a hand in a casual "hello, old friend" salute, and turned to leave, but he was at my side in seconds.

"Sophie? What in the world are you doing here?"

His eyes went to my overnight bag.

"I came home early from Boston."

"You came home early?"

"It didn't pan out with my friend. I didn't feel like it."

He nodded gravely.

"Go ahead," I said. "You can say 'I told you so.' "

"What are you doing here? Why aren't you home?"

"There was an unexpected snag. At the apartment."

"Your plumbing broke or something?"

"A snag called Natalie. My husband's co-worker. I think I mentioned her before."

"I see," said Ned.

Fiona seemed profoundly engrossed in examining her fingernails.

"Join us?" said Ned unhappily.

"No, thanks. You guys are clearly in the middle of something."

"Don't stay here," he said. "It's expensive. Come home with us. We'll fix up a bed. All the mattresses and box springs came today."

Across the room Fiona had raised her head and was regarding me with a motionless recognition, her eyes fixed like the eyes of a cat on a sidewalk studying you as you walk by.

"Better not," I said to Ned.

"No, really. We were just going back anyway. We only stopped in for a drink, so Fiona could see the view."

"Thanks, Ned," I said firmly. "But I can see it's not a good idea."

"I don't think you should be alone."

"I'm a big girl. It won't kill me."

"We'll call you later," he said. "What's your room number?"

I gave it to him. It was easier than standing there arguing under Fiona's basilisk gaze. I waved a feeble hand at her. She did not wave back.

My room at the Eastland was more cheerful than Rory's hotel room had been—prettier colors, softer lighting. Other than that, I recall very little of it. I couldn't remember ever having felt such a sensation of having nowhere to go. Suspecting that Natalie and Paul might be having an affair was a very different matter than thinking of her, at this moment, sleeping (or otherwise occupying herself) in my bed, curling up with Paul on our couch. Natalie, among my things, in my place.

I could have called Delia, or Marta, but that would make it all seem too real. My friend and my sister, as different as they were in other respects, were both people who confronted bad events head-on, who made immediate plans. Plans weren't in my grasp at the moment.

If only I could stay in this nice room forever. I could picture myself living in hotel rooms the rest of my days, descending into a comfortable shabbiness, living a lush life in some small dive, like in the old song.

Songs of failure certainly seemed appropriate to the occasion. I was a failed wife, a merely adequate daughter, and a howling nonsuccess as a daughter-in-law. I couldn't even commit adultery with any efficiency. I'd gone all the way to Boston and the net effect was that a soon-to-be former alcoholic was one pack of cigarettes to the good.

When you are truly defeated, facing reality is not necessarily the best option to choose. Taking refuge, resting to fight another day—that's preferable.

Lunch at the bus station had been two doughnuts. At seven-thirty I called room service and ordered a New York strip with fries, a cup of clam chowder to start, a side salad with ranch dressing, and a half carafe of red wine. Also chocolate layer cake to finish, with a pot of coffee. "Lots of cream and sugar," I told the room service operator.

Then I watched a cable show about four bright young things gadding around New York. The theme of the show, which was clever and well-written, seemed to be that pickings were slim, and that one-night stands or vibrators were the only options for today's single woman. It got me so down that when the knock came, I nearly ran to the door.

It wasn't room service, however. It was Ned. He was carrying two bottles of wine and a corkscrew.

"I've been sent by Stephen to check on you and provide liquor," he said. "Can I come in?"

I gestured him inside. He put the wine down on the room's charming little desk and sat, without waiting to be asked, on its little overstuffed sofa.

"You remembered my room number," I said.

"You look like hell. Tell me what happened."

"Where's Fiona?"

"First tell me."

"I'm not your problem, Ned. You don't have to make mercy visits."

"Just calm down and talk," he said. "For God's sake, I've been worried all the way home and all the way back here. I thought you might be climbing into the bath tub with the hair dryer."

I laughed, a little hysterically. He was so solid on that flimsy, undersized couch. He wore a dark red flannel shirt I'd never seen before. His hair looked very black and his eyes were very blue, bluer than Rory's even.

"Well," I said. "I came home from Boston early—why aren't you there, by the way?"

"Wiring emergency at Fiona's apartment," said Ned. "She had to drive up instead. So you came home from Boston early, and then what?"

"I came home to the apartment, our apartment, and I looked in the kitchen window, and there was my husband with that friend of his from work, and they . . . they . . ."

"They weren't working?"

"No, they weren't working."

"Did you say something to them?"

"Oh no. I just got in my car and came here. Paul thinks I'm in Boston tonight."

"And why aren't you in Boston tonight?"

"It didn't go so well."

"You saw your old friend?"

"Just briefly," I said. "I lost my nerve."

"I'm glad," he said.

"Yes, because this outcome is so preferable, isn't it."

"I'm glad anyway," he said. "You can do better."

I laughed again.

"Isn't it funny how people always say that? Like they have some idea of who the perfect person for you would be. Only they've never met him. He's a figment of their imagination."

"You're upset," said Ned.

"No kidding."

There was a second knock, and this knock was my dinner.

When the waiter had left, Ned said, "At least you aren't going to stop eating and go into a decline. I was worried about that."

"I always eat when I'm down," I said defiantly. "Are you hungry?"

The steak was big, and the kitchen had piled on the fries. There were crusty rolls with butter and a salad dripping with dressing. The cake and coffee were equally lavish.

"I can't take food out of your mouth," said Ned, eyeing it all.

"As if I can eat all this. And you brought wine."

We considered spreading the food out on the little desk, but in the end we had a picnic on the bed, sitting on opposite sides and eating ravenously, as if we'd just made it back to civilization after camping in the wilderness for days. We uncorked the wine; there were plenty of extra glasses. The Eastland was a very fine hotel.

"This is good," Ned said with his mouth full.

"Did you eat dinner tonight?"

"No, Fiona and I were talking. One of those big talks."

I buttered a roll with abandon. It was no time to be counting calories.

"What did you talk about?"

"Her professor."

"Her professor?"

"The one she works with. Apparently they're attracted to each other, and she felt she should tell me about it."

"You mean she's been cheating on you?"

"Oh no. She just thought the attraction was a symptom of something wrong between us, and she wanted to tell me about it so we could fix it. She thinks it points up our issues, her attraction to her professor."

"What issues?"

"The usual. She thinks I'm not serious enough."

"About her?"

"About everything."

We were halfway through the first bottle of merlot now. It was loosening my tongue.

I said, "Boy, she's an earnest type. You're plenty serious. If anything, you need to have more fun."

I refilled his glass.

Ned drank then said, "I have plenty of fun. You don't know me when Stephen and I aren't on a job. I'm wild."

I laughed.

"You don't believe me? I'll have you know that I've been known to go to rock concerts. I've even gotten drunk at parties."

"When was the last time you got drunk at a party? In college?"

"I'm getting drunk now."

"This isn't a party."

"It's a party of two," he said.

"Tell me what else Fiona said to you."

"Well, the whole thing started because of her Valentine's present."

"That was weeks ago."

"She special-ordered mine, so we waited."

"Didn't she like the bookends?"

"Loved them. It was what **she** got **me** that was the problem. She got me a desk set, Sophie. A leather cup holder and blotter and a day planner with my initials stamped on it, and one of those big appointment books. I think it was all really expensive. So I acted, you know, pleased and all that, and I said, 'I'll use these in my home office now, and in a few years when Steve and I have a real office, they'll go with me.' She looked so disappointed. And she said did I plan to be renovating houses in ten years? She said that my business was a waste of my intellectual capacity and that Stephen was selfish to have brought me into it and derailed my career, and besides, **her** career might take her away from my 'regional' type of job and what would we do then? Then I asked her if she was ashamed of my job and she said, no, of course not, but I was underachieving my potential, or some bullshit like that. I lost my cool and said something about academics who had their heads up each other's butts all day, and she said it was clear our 'life goals were divergent.' But the gist of it was that I'm good enough to sleep with her and clean out her drains but not good enough for the long haul."

He poured more wine, and I gave him the rest of the steak.

"Hey," he said. "Don't give that to me. You're the one whose marriage took a nosedive. You have it."

"No," I said. "You weren't expecting this. I **was** expecting Paul and Natalie. Seeing them was actually a kind of relief. Now I can't pretend it's not happening. I have to do something."

"What will you do?" he said.

"Maybe travel somewhere for a few months. Or maybe I'll enter an MFA program, get a degree."

"Or you could move to Boston and just take lots of art classes," said Ned. "What do you need a degree for?"

What **did** I need it for, if it came to that? All I wanted was to study with someone who knew his or her stuff, in a welcoming atmosphere with good light and maybe a few students who weren't too much younger than I was.

"You have a point," I said.

"If you come to Boston, you'll have Stephen and me. And you won't be 'from away,' not like here. There are all sorts of transplants in Boston."

We had more wine, and Ned named semi-affordable neighborhoods: North Cambridge, Jamaica Plain, the Fens, East Arlington, Watertown.

"Rents are high and you'd have to be on a safe block, but Boston is big," Ned said. "You'll find something. We'll help you. Stephen knows everyone."

His hair was mussed and his boots were off. We finished the cake and were almost done with the second bottle of wine. I could see that Ned was getting tipsier, and I relaxed into my own pile of pillows. As I did, my hair fell forward around my face, and Ned leaned over and tucked a strand behind my ear.

"Your hair is always slipping out of place, do you know that?" he said.

"Because it's too fine," I said.

"No," he said. "It's pretty. It's beautiful. All golden."

"Thanks to Clairol," I said.

He sighed.

"The girl can never take a compliment," he said. "What were we talking about? Boston. We'll find you something. A good place in a good neighborhood."

"Enough about real estate. Did you and Fiona break up? For real?"

"She said she wanted to explore things with her professor. I said she was free to explore whatever she liked. She said she'd always sensed that I wasn't truly in love with her, or I'd be more jealous and less obtuse about myself, as she put it."

"What did that mean? Less obtuse about yourself?"

"Never mind. It's complicated. Then she got in her car and headed back. She said there was nothing more we could accomplish tonight."

"So you're through?"

"Oh yeah."

He leaned back on his side of the headboard, scooting up.

"It's no surprise, really," he said. "We weren't very well-suited. And Stephen hated her, which would've been a problem. He doesn't hate many people but once he does it's kind of hard to change his mind."

"I think Stephen is very discerning," I said. It was getting harder to enunciate properly. "Is it true?"

"Is what true?"

"What Fiona said? How much in love with her were you?"

"Women," said Ned. "They always want you to quantify your emotions."

"Well?" I said.

"She could have been right. That doesn't mean I don't feel anything."

"I didn't say you don't feel anything. You're the one who always tried to pull off that strong silent act."

"Much good that does me with you around. Now tell me about this gal your husband is carrying on with."

It was a lovely phrase, "carrying on with," so nineteen-fifties, prudish Catholic that I grinned and told him all about it, and the rest of the bottle of wine disappeared.

"And the worst part is, now I have to go home and wash all the sheets. With ammonia."

"Just buy new ones," said Ned. "You do know how to drive to the mall, thanks to me."

He paused and drummed his fingers on the bed covers.

"I'm sorry, Sophie. About what happened."

"Don't be. It was bound to, with her or someone else. I wasn't really his type."

"You're being way too brave. You should be crying or throwing something through his window."

"I'm just a little frozen at the moment."

"He's an idiot," said Ned. "You seem to be attracted to idiots. Meanwhile, nice guy like me you look at like I'm your little brother."

When he drank his eyes got bluer, I saw. They were a deep, deep blue now.

"That's ridiculous," I said. "I can see that you're attractive. Objectively speaking."

"You're very attractive too," said Ned. "Objectively speaking."

"I wasn't making a pass or anything," I said.

"I knew you weren't making a pass," said Ned. "You'd make a pass at that Rory waster, but not at me. With me, you've never even flirted."

He put out his hand and stroked my hair again. His long lashes were drooping over those deep-set eyes.

Ned said very slowly, "When you get clear of Paul, lots of men are going to go after you."

"Oh, right. The line'll be around the block."

I moved my head under his hand, and his hand dropped down to my neck, his index finger slipping down to my collarbone very, very slowly.

"You'd be surprised, Sophie."

"I've had it with men for a while," I said. "I'm going to concentrate on my career."

He pulled his hand away, and shook his head from side to side as if to clear it. Then he made to rise. He got as far as half-sitting up, propped on his elbows.

"Have to go home," he said. "I'm making a fool out of myself."

I wasn't tipsy enough to let that happen.

"You're not fit to drive," I said. "Here, you sleep on the bed and I'll sleep on the couch."

"You're too tall for the couch, Sophie."

He was talking in long syllables.

"You're not driving, Ned."

"I'll get a cab then," he said.

"It's two A.M. You'd be waiting half the night for one. We can both sleep on the bed. It's so big you won't even know I'm there."

"No pajamas. I have no pajamas."

"I do," I said, as if this was an answer.

I stumbled into the bathroom and washed my face and brushed my teeth. I had with me my flannel pajamas with the cloud print, which I took into the bathroom and changed into. When I emerged, scrubbed and wholesome and slightly less tipsy, with seven glasses of water and two aspirins in me, Ned was asleep amidst the wreck of our dinner, sprawled among the dishes and dish covers and napkins. I cleared it all onto the cart and wheeled it, squeaking, out into the hall. Ned didn't stir. He must have been pitifully exhausted. He hadn't even managed to get his jeans off.

I turned out the lights and drew the curtains. I pulled the covers up over him and crawled in on the other side.

Sometime during the night he came over to my side, and put an arm around me. Sometime even later I woke to find myself curled against him, and it would be a lie to say that I was too tipsy to move away. I lay there, feeling the warmth of him, my lips against the salty skin of his neck, thankful not to be alone, and then some. Something else that I didn't want to admit to: part of me wished he'd wake up, pull me closer, kiss me. I was one sick chicken, I told myself. Just twenty-four hours ago I'd been kissing Rory, the supposed love of my life, and now I wanted Ned. Was I that needy, that desperate for love at any price?

If Ned had woken then, who knows what might have happened? I might have made some brazen move, a move that a half-asleep red-blooded male wouldn't have been able to resist. We might have done something foolhardy that would have caused me to rush home the next morning and leave Portland altogether, in the after-blush.

But Ned kept on sleeping the sleep of the innocent, and after a while I slept too, my head on his pillow and his arm around me.

In the morning I rose before him, slipping out from under his arm. It was like a blow to the solar plexus to see how lovely Ned was when he slept. What a truism, the sappy woman turning to mush at the sight of some man asleep. If Ned woke, what would I say? He didn't wake, though. He was still sleeping the sleep of deep exhaustion.

I didn't have much appetite, but my head didn't hurt. I dressed carefully and quietly, then left him a note. It said,

> **Ned, thank you for coming to see me last night. It really helped. I didn't want to wake you so I've gone ahead and checked out. There are some things I have to do at home, as you can probably guess. Will see you at walking group Monday. Your friend, Sophie. P.S. Thank you for the wine.**

It was a mean thing to do, leaving him to wake up alone and startled, to wonder for long seconds where he was. People make fun of that moment when they're telling silly stories, but I think it's one of the saddest types of moments of adulthood, the moment that tells us we're on our own, single souls no matter who's beside us or where we've landed. And that schoolgirl-correct note with the polite, calm little postscript. It had been the best I could do, though.

For a minute I longed to crawl back into the big bed with him, to seduce him for my own comforting. Then I shook myself. I'd have to get used to ignoring these sudden, nutty impulses. I was about to be a divorcee, and I didn't want to become the unhinged, prowling kind that in my childhood had haunted the fears of my mother and her placidly married friends.

If I suddenly wanted to cry, that signified nothing.

Ned barely stirred as I picked up my bag and tiptoed to the door, and if I thought I heard my name as I closed it, it was probably just my imagination.

Twenty-Five

The apartment was quiet when I reached home, and eerily clean: bed made, dishes washed and put away, sofa blanket and cushions neatly in place. Usually when I went away, Paul left his surroundings sloppy enough to let me know he'd reverted to a son whose mother had done all the housework, or rather, supervised the maid.

The yellow candlesticks and tablecloth Natalie had brought were nowhere in sight, of course, nor was the vase with the daisies. There were two client messages, asking for minor fixes in projects just turned in. Personal dramas come and go but work lasts on and on.

Ann had left a phone message too. "Sophie," she said. "I'm almost there. I'll overnight the manuscript when it's ready, if you'll promise to be honest."

I wouldn't be. I wanted that contract more than I had a week ago. Fulsome praise was what her manuscript was going to get from me, even if I had to swallow some bile in the process. Maybe it would be good for me to be "hungry."

People up here lived closer to the bone than people in the prosperous Mid-Atlantic. Maybe that was the atmosphere Rory liked in those foreign lands where he worked: the sense that life was not a trial run, that there was no soft net to catch you if you fell.

Rory. He'd be back by now, maybe kissing his wife, having a serious talk about rejuvenating their marriage. Although if I knew Rory, such a serious talk would happen only if Liz made it happen. Still, she might sense an opening. I found that the thought didn't bother me all that much. That night in Boston seemed faraway now.

The ten o'clock sun slanted in. I could hear Donald outside calling to his dogs, and the thunk of magazines and packages being slammed down on the front hall table by our un-chipper mailman.

What to do. What to do. I could depart in a fine fit of hurt and fury, and have Paul come home tonight to an empty apartment and an accusing letter. It was Friday. He'd have the weekend to recover from the shock, if it was a shock.

But something stubborn in me didn't want to pack up my computer and art supplies and head home to Delia's or Marta's or, God forbid, my parents. If I left now, all my subsequent steps would be rushed and pressed. I couldn't see living in Portland permanently, given the chance of running into Paul and Natalie on any street corner, but I also didn't see why I should flee south at a moment's notice for their convenience.

Paul would be fine down at the Eastland or the Regency. Or there was a lovely bed and breakfast a few blocks away on Danforth Street.

On impulse, I leaned my head out the window and called to Donald.

He came ambling over, sweaterless as always in fifty-degree weather, bringing the dogs to heel with a snap of his skinny fingers.

"Wait a sec," I called, and grabbed an old cardigan. I perched on the back steps while Donald stood just below, leaning on the railing, our heads on a level.

"Donald," I said. "I think I might need your help with something."

He looked wary.

"It's not a repair," I said. "Maybe you guessed this, but my husband and I are going to be separating."

Donald said nothing. His dogs stared at me

expectantly, as if sizing me up for a prelunch snack. One of them inched forward.

"Stop," said Donald. "I gotta get them trained better. My wife says I'm too soft with them.

"I'm sorry about your husband," he added, as if Paul had died suddenly.

"Don't be. He's got someone."

"I know," said Donald. "She's been here a few times."

"You've seen her?"

"I thought about telling you, but she always had a briefcase and folders and shit with her, so I thought maybe it was work. Although I was pretty sure it wasn't."

"When was the first time it happened?"

"Sometime in the week after Thanksgiving. You need me to testify, I'm there."

"I don't think it will come to that. I just wanted to know."

So Paul and Natalie had had their first night together while I was in Boston with Ned and Stephen. All this time, Paul had been lying cheerfully to my face.

"Anyway, I'm sorry," Donald said again. "Although, to tell you the truth, I could never stand the guy, personally."

"I can't stand him much myself at the moment," I said.

"So, you need me to change the locks or something?"

"No. I need help kicking him out. He may want **me** to leave, you see."

"He can forget it," said Donald. "After what he's pulled."

"But what are my options? We're both on the lease."

"Just tell him he's out. And if he fidgets around, come get me. Landlords don't have any rights in this damn city but I can make up a few for myself if I have to."

"Oh Donald," I said. "Thank you."

"Don't mention it. You need a break on the rent, let me know."

"I won't but that's very generous of you."

"These things happen," said Donald. "My first wife left me while I was off at work. I came home, she'd taken everything. Can opener, nail clippers. You name it."

"That's lousy."

"But a month later I met Jackie, so you see?"

This did not cheer me up.

"Thanks, Donald," I said. "I owe you."

I went back inside, ready to phone Paul. Then

I stopped. There was something else I had to do first. I pulled all the sheets and pillowcases off the bed with the tips of my fingers, and grabbed the two pristinely folded towels in the bath-room. I stuffed them in a sack and headed down to the Laundromat and threw them all in a hot, hot wash.

"You've got to be kidding," said Paul.

"I need you to leave" had been my opening words.

"Sophie? I didn't even know you were back."

"I'm back. And I need you to leave."

"What's gotten into you? This is completely from left field."

"Is it? Or can you guess my reasons?"

"We haven't been doing so badly recently. Hon, you sound hysterical."

I was deadly calm. That was what alarmed him.

"Is there something you want to tell me, Paul?"

"I don't know what you're talking about."

"Yes you do, but you wanted to arrange it your own way, didn't you? You wanted Natalie to dump Toby, and then you'd go off to her house and be all set. But Natalie's holding out for **you** to give **me** the heave-ho before she tosses Toby, I'm betting."

"You went crazy in Boston, is that it?"

"I came home early. Around six last night. I came up our steps."

There was a silence.

"You must have seen us working then," he said.

"People who work together don't normally kiss. Or wear cute little aprons."

There was another silence.

"I was hoping to keep from hurting you until I had to," he said finally.

"That's real noble of you, Paul. Are you in love with her?"

"Yes. I'm sorry, Sophie. But yes."

"When did you plan to notify me of this?"

"I thought that the right time would present itself."

"Well, I'm presenting it. I'd like you to come home tonight and pack what you'll need for now and be gone by nine. I'll stay out until then."

"We should talk," said Paul.

"Eventually. Right now I want you out of here."

I was still calm, still speaking in the low firm voice I'd always tried so hard to achieve in my early days of nagging Donald about home repairs. Funny how you get what you want in life, just not the way you expected it.

"I can't rearrange my living quarters in an instant, Sophie. I have a job."

"I have a job too."

"You're more portable. If you're uncomfortable with me on the couch a few nights, you go somewhere. I'll pay for it."

"I don't think so."

"It's my apartment too," he said, as I'd known he would.

"Paul, Donald says that if I want you out, you're out. Or he'll take action."

That'd get to him. Donald could throw a punch and change a tire and make a German shepherd heel. Compared to those talents, in a situation like this, Paul's expertise at backgammon and his mastery of little-known tax deductions didn't amount to much.

"Sophie, does this have to be so acrimonious?"

"You're lucky I didn't come down to your office. Or call Toby, that poor chump."

"Fine," said Paul, "I'll get out. But using Donald is just low."

"Low?" I said softly, and replaced the receiver.

———

I spent an aimless evening in the only place where I wouldn't feel conspicuous: the Maine Mall. I ate an excellent bowl of chili at the food court, and bought new sheets at Linens-n-Things. They were pale pink, a color Paul hated. And they were cotton, not flannel. Cotton for spring. Then I dawdled over to the arcade and played Skee-Ball. I won very few tickets, and couldn't remember how to hold my wrist when throwing the ball. The only other patrons were two teenage boys who hogged the mini-basketball game.

Before I left, I picked up three magazines at the drugstore, spring fashion issues. It would be my first night alone in the apartment. I'd spent a lot of time alone there this winter, but something extra seemed called for, tonight.

When I got back, Paul had cleared out. In a mean little gesture, I'd put the Stoddard filigree ring and bracelet on the kitchen table. He hadn't taken them, and he'd left no note. I didn't mind. At least now, after months of having the rug pulled out from under me inch by inch, I knew where I stood.

Tomorrow I'd phone Delia, and Marta, and my parents. Monday I'd go to walking group, and tell Ned and Stephen that Paul was gone, which knowing Stephen meant that the rest would find out quickly.

I flipped through the magazines and drank hot cocoa. I put the new sheets on the bed. They felt cool and summery against my cheek. I was fine. I was coping wonderfully.

Then I lay down—keeled over was more like it—and cried for an hour. I cried in great big honking gulps, cried through a box of tissues and onto an old white sock Paul had left lying by the bed, an unmatched extra from the laundry. I cried until my nose hurt and my eyelids were puffed and raw and my cheekbones ached. I cried out the winter, the pain of Paul's betrayal, the ache of no longer having Rory as a light ahead, the loneliness of all these months of being a stranger in a strange land.

When it was over I tottered to the bathroom and took a hot shower. The water pressure was lousy, but I stood in the steam and let my muscles relax all down my body. At last, after the shower and a cold pill to help me breathe, I fell asleep.

And the morning after my good cry, just as other people's mothers used to say in movies and TV shows, everything looked brighter.

Ned didn't walk with me on Monday. He stayed with Jamie and Carol and Matilda, who had begun to talk in earnest. Jamie would say to Carol, "Come here," and Matilda would echo in her croaky voice, "Mere." I would miss Matilda, miss seeing how she turned out, which promised to be unusual at the least.

Ned said only, at the beginning of group, "Everything all right?" When I nodded, he moved away. Was he bashful? Repulsed by our drunken confidences? Afraid I was going to launch myself at him in a post-marital fit of loneliness?

I walked with Edgar and Ramon, and Edgar told me all about the restoration of the Portland Observatory. This was very boring, but I listened attentively because Edgar was an astronomy buff and never got to talk much about it. Ramon spoke of several upcoming wedding commissions Floradora had won. Floradora was thriving. Maybe someday in the not-too-distant future, Natalie would book them for her wedding to Paul.

At breakfast, Ned sat next to Alex and across from George at another booth. Alex laughed and flirted at Ned, who seemed oblivious as always.

In black jeans and an indigo sweater that suited her complexion, she looked pretty, and happier. She was still plump, but no one would now have called her heavy. Alex was too young for Ned, but it was quite possible that with Fiona out of the picture he might meet a nice mature twenty-four-year-old. Ned was only three years younger than I was, but he could easily wind up with someone a decade my junior. This depressed me, which was silly.

Stephen stayed with me after Edgar and Ramon left their side of the booth.

He said, "I heard about Paul. For two cents I'd deck him one, Sophie."

"For two cents I'd deck him one myself."

"What are you going to do? Ned said you might consider Boston."

"Maybe. I heard rents are high."

"But do you like Boston?"

"I like Boston a lot."

"Well, I have a friend who just joined the Foreign Service. He's going away for two years, and he owns a condo. It's a large studio on Beacon Hill, off Chestnut Street, on the top floor of a Federal-style building. He doesn't want to sell but he doesn't want the hassle of being a landlord while he's in Upper Slovenia or whereever. I told him I'd handle it for him. Collect the rent and make repairs and all that."

"That's good of you," I said.

"It is, isn't it? I'm happy with Scott and I'd never stray, but I've had a crush on this guy for years. He's very hot, in a blond, WASP-y way, and you know how it is, you'll always do a favor for an old crush. They have a power."

"I know," I said.

"So what do you think about renting the place? Very reasonably, say nine hundred, which is a steal. And it's furnished. You could bring a few pieces of your own but Jason would be thrilled not to have to haul his stuff away to storage, and he has beautiful taste."

He was handing me Boston, on a platter.

"Stephen, I'd be in the loony bin over at Maine Medical by now if you hadn't bumped into me at JavaNet, you know that?"

"Oh come on, Sophie, you'd have been fine. You're a survivor, underneath those fragile golden looks of yours. It's people like my brother I worry about."

"Your brother isn't talking to me much this morning."

"He's embarrassed. He thought he foisted himself on you the other night."

"Foisted himself? But nothing happened."

"Yes, I ferreted that out of him. But Ned's overscrupulous in such matters. And maybe he's brooding about Fiona. She's gone, you know."

"Yes, he said they broke up."

"No, I mean really gone. She felt a little blue about losing her combination boyfriend-repairman, and her mother gave her a trip to Costa Rica to cheer her up."

"But I thought she wasn't well off. What about that broken-down apartment in Brighton?"

"Did you price out her ugly clothes ever? The apartment is the kind of token show at independence that poor little rich girls make when they're young."

"I see someone has some class issues."

"You bet, sister."

"What about her thesis?" I asked.

"They're not big on deadlines in academia, you know. Anyway, let's don't waste time on **her**. Say you'll take Jason's apartment. You'll be doing us both a favor."

"You didn't already have someone in mind for

it? Your brother might have a friend he wants to give it to."

"Boy, are you dense. You think Ned wouldn't want you in Boston? He's been beefing and whining for weeks about having to leave Portland because of you."

"Me?"

"Well, he says the walking group, but who does he always walk with?"

Stephen was almost whispering, and for pure drama, because at the other booth, Alex and George were explaining a new type of treasury bond to Ned, so there was little chance of anyone overhearing us.

"Can I think about it?" I said to Stephen.

"Sure. But don't think too long. I need to let Jason know."

"I'll have an answer for you in forty-eight hours."

"Make it yes," said Stephen. "By the way, Jason has a sort of mud room that you could paint in. It's a little half balcony, but windowed in, with a cement floor, right off the main studio space. He has skis and things in there now but he'll move them."

"Stephen," I said. "You're the best."

"I am," said Stephen. "I really am."

At the door of Becky's, Ned finally spoke to me.

"I'm sorry I came barging over the other night," he said.

"Sorry, nothing. You saved my life."

"Did your husband leave already?"

"Yes, he's gone."

Ned fell silent. Always before I'd appreciated the naturalness of his manners, but now I wished he'd fill the pause with any chatter that came to his lips.

"Are you guys considering counseling, anything like that?" he said finally.

"That's a good one."

"You could try," he said.

"Are you attempting to talk me into it? Because it's no use, you know."

"Talk you into it? No. I'm just saying what you're supposed to say."

"You never have before."

"I need to grow up," he said elliptically. "I can't say anything I think all the time."

"That's what I like about you," I said.

"You might not like it, always."

I could not fathom his mood this morning. I'd tried to get us back on our casual footing and he was balking.

"Anyway, thank you for getting me through on Thursday."

"No big deal," said Ned. "You going home now?"

"Yes. I have to do some thinking. I have to decide about an apartment your brother wants to practically give me. In Boston. He's a good guy, your brother."

"He has his moments," said Ned.

He smiled at me as I walked away, but it wasn't his real smile. It was a reflex, a polite gesture.

Saturday I spent the day phoning my nearest and dearest.

My parents took the news of the separation with commendable calmness, although my mother at first protested.

"There must be priests up in Maine who could help you two with counseling."

But when I gave a brief outline of the facts, she said, "Well, at least you weren't married in the church, so you won't need an annulment."

My father, on the extension, put in, "We can clear out your room and get your old bed back in there in a day or two, if you'd like."

"Oh Dad, that's nice of you. I've got the Portland apartment for a while yet."

"Get a good lawyer," said my father. "Paul should pay since he's at fault."

My father probably thought I'd be receiving alimony.

"This'll be no-fault divorce," I said. "Uncontested. Very simple."

"No fault?" said my mother. "I would think it was clear who was at fault."

"It's just a term, Mom. Paul admits he did the cheating."

"So much for that Pepper who always thought she was so above the rest of us," said my mother. "Now this. A son who runs around."

"I don't think seeing one other woman is running around, Mom."

"Still, it's not very classy."

"Keep us posted," said my father, as we said our good-nights.

"Don't do anything rash," said my mother.

"Take care of yourselves," I said. "I love you both."

Along the line, faintly, came, "Love you," from my dad. My mother said, "Call again soon." Which, from her, was every bit as good.

Marta said nothing that was not profane for the first ten minutes.

"I always said she was trouble," she finished.

"You did."

"They deserve each other."

"They do."

"The main point is, when are you coming home?"

"I'm not sure." I told her about Stephen's offer, and about seeing Rory.

"I knew you wouldn't go through with it. Deep down, he's not really your type. He's not brave enough for you."

"He's ten times as brave as I am. Look where he works. They might even send him to a real trouble spot, you know. The Middle East, or Ireland."

"Ireland is fine these days. Ireland's laughing all the way to the bank, what with the European market. Besides, I wasn't talking about that kind of bravery. I was talking about you, how you faced things head-on."

"I faced nothing," I said. "I let this thing with Paul drag on all winter."

"You gave it a chance to play out. And remember, he kept denying everything. But are you really moving to Boston? Just when I was going to get you back? I have a new job starting. I need the moral support."

Marta's new position began on Monday. I'd never heard her so happy, so intrigued by anything, including a man. Finding the right work, for Marta, might turn out to be as romantic as any big romance she'd ever had.

"I'm sorry, Marta. If I go back now, I really will go backward."

"It's that Ned, isn't it? You've always had a little buzz of attraction for him."

"Maybe a tiny spark. It's not anything to base a new life on."

"Chemistry isn't just a trap always, you know. Sometimes it's there because you've found something good."

"Marta, if I move to Boston will you get on the train and come visit me?"

"I'll not only come visit, we'll take a trip up the coast together. There's a ferry in summer to Nova Scotia with all-night gambling, how about that one weekend?"

So we talked for a while of our projected travels when summer came, like a pair of little old ladies.

I called Stephen's cell phone, which was on the Happy Trails card he'd given me all those months ago, and said I'd take the apartment.

"I knew it," he said. "I knew you'd do it. It's a great city, Sophie. You're gonna love it. And Beacon Hill is magic. Well, you've seen it."

Stephen said he'd arrange everything.

"When would you want to move in?"

"June first?"

"It's a done deal. I'll get Jason to draw up a lease."

"Stephen, I can't thank you enough."

"Hey, just start packing. Ned and I will be finished the second week of June and we'll be right on your heels getting to town."

Delia was my last call that day because we'd talk the longest. I filled her in on my plans: Boston and a divorce.

"And are you sure about this, Sophie? I'm not defending Paul, I'm just saying, do you want to be single again? It's rough out there."

"It's been rough in here, Delia."

"But a marriage isn't something you throw out in a day."

"You're sounding like Mom."

"Take that back."

"All right. You've never sounded anything like

Mom. You were probably left by fairies on the front doorstep and are no relation to her whatsoever."

"Still, Sophie. You don't just walk out of a marriage easily, no matter what."

"We never had what you and Tom have, or anything like it."

"You guys could see someone."

I didn't tell her that my mother had suggested this too.

"A marriage counselor? To save a marriage that never jelled in the first place? He's met someone who adores him."

"Paul's under a delusion, Sophie."

"A delusion that Natalie suits him in every way better than I do?"

"This isn't about Rory, is it? Tell me it's not."

"Nope. Not now."

I gave her the story of my feeble night in Boston with Rory.

"And yet Rory's a persuasive man, and you're wounded at the moment."

"I'm not that wounded, Dee. No chance. I promise."

"And you don't want Paul back? I can't imagine ending it with Tom even if he screwed around on me."

"But that's Tom. He's rare. I don't **want** Paul now."

Delia was quiet.

"Do you have to go? Is Ben up?"

"No," she said. "No, I don't have to go, I have to apologize. It scares me. That a marriage could come apart so easily. Then I go and scare **you**."

"You didn't scare me, Delia. For once I'm not that scared."

"I'm sorry, sweetheart. I'm sorry you've gone through all this."

"I'm not," I said. "If we'd stayed in Washington, I'd have been lulled along with Paul and spent the next five years wishing that Pepper would someday like me. Now I never have to see her again. That alone is worth the whole experience. Like the old joke about the man who hits his head against the wall because it feels so good when he stops."

"You don't have to put on a brave face with me. I'm your sister."

"Oh, I'm a mess. Boston will help, though. A change of scene."

"I can come up and help you pack."

"And leave Ben with whom? It's not that big a job. As much as I appreciate the offer, a week or two of putting things in boxes would do me good."

"If you need me, I'm on a plane," said Delia.

"Wish me luck? Even if it means Boston and not D.C.?"

"Luck," said Delia. "Luck and luck and luck. You've earned it."

Spring

Twenty-Six

Spring came on shyly in Maine: wet, howling days followed by bright, blowy ones. Around the corner in a walled garden on Pine Street tulips suddenly flourished, and all along the iron fences of the Western Prom the lilacs with their velvety green leaves and the raggedy forsythia flung brilliant color through and over the black railings.

Walking got much easier, with no more ice and snow to navigate. Ned remained subdued with me, however, and often stayed at someone else's side, Edgar's or Alex's. Alex was seeing someone, the fellow student at the community college she'd told me about, but she still blushed and smiled for Ned. He didn't seem to see it.

Once I said, "Ned, have I done something to offend you?"

"Of course not. My mind's always somewhere else these days, that's all. We're just finishing up the house, and we're working too hard."

Did all men say that when they didn't want

to be straight with you? But Ned could be telling the truth. Stephen had told me that the Eastern Prom project was wrapping up amidst a storm of small finishing details: closet hooks and medicine cabinets, and panes for the small bull's eye window. Our Lady had weathered all the changes nicely, Stephen said, and the owners, anxious to fit in with their neighbors, had decided to let Her stay up for the present.

One sunny afternoon in early May, I kept an appointment with a lawyer whom I'd chosen from a telephone book—partly because I liked the restraint of her Yellow Pages ad, and partly because she was a woman.

"Do you want anything?" she said after we sat down.

"No, I had breakfast."

She smiled.

"Do you want anything from your husband, I mean?"

"Oh. No."

She had a pad out and was taking notes. It surprised me that lawyers really did use legal pads. I'd have thought it would be something more fancy, bound in leather like the office accessories Fiona had given Ned. The lawyer was in her fifties, dressed in a heather wool crêpe suit with a pale blue silk scarf. Maybe when I reached my fifties I'd have this sort of self-assured elegance too. I doubted it.

"Didn't you lose any income, following him here to Maine?"

"Not really. I freelance."

"Are you sure? Were there clients you might have lost or not had a chance to pitch to because of the move?"

"I don't pitch much. I have very regular clients. I just want the marriage to be over."

I gave her an abbreviated account.

"Sounds like a prince," she said.

"With the right woman, he might be."

"If I were her I wouldn't count on it," said the lawyer. Then she explained to me how it all worked. It was surprisingly easy, if two people agreed they were finished with each other.

Paul had phoned earlier that week, from the Sheraton near the Maine Mall. The rooms were nice but it wasn't a very convenient commute, he said with faint reproach.

"I may need to come get my spring and summer clothes."

"Come Thursday night," I said. It was the night after my appointment with the lawyer. "And leave your key when you do."

"What, may I ask, are your plans?" said Paul. "Your long-term plans?"

"I'm swamped with work right now so I'm postponing any big decisions."

This was true but I said it for my pride, so Paul wouldn't think I'd be poor without him.

"Surely you won't be staying in Portland."

"Surely that's none of your business, Paul."

"This is a small town, Sophie," he said, just like a nasty threatening character in a soap opera trying to run some young innocent out of Pine Valley or Port Charles.

"Natalie and me—Sophie, I don't want to hurt you but we're serious."

"No kidding," I said.

"Please understand, this wasn't intentional. It simply happened."

"Come off it, Paul. Affairs don't simply happen. You aren't splitting a turkey sub with someone one minute and shucking your clothes off the next."

"Be that as it may. It's now a serious relationship."

"Bully for you. Why should that influence what I do, however?"

"You could run into us, Sophie. In the street. At the mall."

"You know I'm not much of a shopper."

I could hear the intake of breath up his nose; he'd always inhaled heavily through his nostrils when he was annoyed.

"I've seen a lawyer," he said. "This could all be very easy if you cooperate."

"I'm seeing a lawyer myself. Thursday, in fact. Then I'm taking a nice long drive. So, you come at six and be out by eight and we won't even pass in the hallway."

"Sophie, could you find it in yourself to be a little nicer?"

"Not just now," I said. "By the way, I'll leave the family jewels out for you to take, in the change dish."

The change was probably worth more than the lousy Stoddard filigree bracelet and ring with those stingy dotted-Swiss-size garnets.

"I don't want the stupid jewelry," Paul said. "You keep it. It was a gift. Don't say I never gave you anything."

He laughed nervously, as he'd laughed on our

first date so long ago. We'd gone through inti-
macy and out the other side, and the far ends felt
strangely alike. It was the middle I kept forgetting. Had it ever been good?

"Speaking of which," I said. "I'm taking it that
Natalie is disease free, like the personal ads say."

"What a question."

"I do have a right to ask," I said.

"Clean as a whistle," he said with exaggerated
patience. "Just got checked, the yearly one. For
everything. Absolutely everything. She always
does, she's neurotic that way. Not that we should
be discussing this."

Finally I had discovered something I actually
liked about Natalie. I still got checked for everything, every year too. Who'd have thought that
Natalie had a bit of the hypochondriac in her? In
other circumstances, perhaps we'd have been
friends.

"And she said to tell you she's sorry it turned
out like this," he said. "You were the last person
she intended to hurt."

Then again, maybe not.

The lawyer's office was in Falmouth. I sped back
to town on Route 1, dashed into the apartment,
changed into jeans and a turtleneck, and was

back out again by three. It was the warmest day in months and the ocean was calling to me. I drove out Route 77, trying to find a place I'd seen on the map called Two Lights State Park. Alex had said it was lovely, though the lighthouses were on private grounds now.

I turned off 77 on an instinct, at a corner with a creamy pink cottage with white-trimmed windows and a screened porch. It was a real old-fashioned cottage. I wanted a house just like that, someday, by the water.

I passed yellow-green marshes on my right, and on my left a trim house next to a red barn. Over the door of the barn a sign read "Journey's End."

I unrolled the window and let in the salt air. The road narrowed, and then there was a placard that said "Two Lights State Park." There was no ranger in the admission booth. I stuffed in a few dollars anyway, and followed the road as it curved around, hemmed in by gorse bushes on either side. I hoped that some sprightly elderly driver or careless teenager wasn't coming in the other direction doing fifty.

But there was only one other car in the lot, and it belonged to some Canadians who were enjoying a picnic on the trunk and who nodded

kindly as I walked past. They must have thought
I looked mystified, because one of the men gestured.

"Up that hill and over," he said. "Then you'll
see it."

There were rock steps cut into the side of the
grassy hill face, and I climbed them to the top,
where the trees grew small and hardy in the face
of the endless wind. I went down another set of
stone steps, and before me was the ocean.

Two Lights was a massive series of rock ledges
descending to the sea, which roared over the
lower ledges and fell back again with a clatter.
The cliffs around were a dim green with new
grass, and offshore to my right I could see a few
mist-softened islands, and then blue-green to
the horizon. It was different from Higgins Beach
and Portland Headlight: far less civilized, the
slate-gray rocks terracing down to the wild sea
and then the sea stretching straight ahead, endless. It was a scene that made you understand
why men once set forth in ships to seek the other
side of the world.

Paths led down to the bigger rocks below. For
an hour I clambered and climbed. Once a wave
came crashing close and splashed my sleeve. Ned
had told me about rogue waves, and how they

could sweep unwary visitors out to sea, so I climbed a little higher, intoxicated by the air and the spray and the fun of jumping from rock to rock.

At four-thirty, a rather stern park ranger informed me that the park was closing in a half hour and she'd appreciate my leaving promptly. I felt like a kid called in to supper.

Going out, I turned right at the park entrance and stumbled across a little restaurant called the Lobster Shack. You could see the waves from there too. I ate fish and chips and drank coffee afterward. Sea air gives you an appetite.

I passed some time at the Dollar Store at Mill Creek Plaza, not buying anything, just marveling at what was for sale for a dollar. It was only seven when I crossed the Casco Bay Bridge, so I stopped in at Becky's for some coconut cream pie and more coffee. The waitresses all knew me now, and refilled my coffee without asking.

Paul was gone when I got back. His key was in the change bowl, but he hadn't taken the jewelry.

He'd left a note. It read, **"Sophie, I'm sorry. I truly am. Let me know your plans. Whatever you do is fine with me. Take care of yourself, Paul."** It was the nicest note he'd written me since our arrival in Portland.

That day at Two Lights was the day I began to recover. Not just from Paul but from everything. Two Lights had begun a cure. Like an invalid stumbling into daylight streets after months in a shadowy sickroom, I was a little dazed. But now I knew that my past hurts and illnesses weren't going to do me in. If you're the type that's going to get done in, it happens. If you're not—and sheer luck has more to do with this than anything—you come to a place where it's just irresistible to get on with things, when all you can think of is that here you are, somehow saved from the wreckage, and now what?

Two Lights was my place. I had found it. Not Ned, not Stephen, not even a sign along the way had pointed me there. If you can turn a corner on a guess and stumble upon an endless ocean, there's something to be said for keeping going, after all.

Ann called the next day.

"What did you think of the draft?"

"I thought it was extraordinary."

It **was** extraordinary, chiefly for a tone that perfectly blended hectoring, cheerleading, and quasi-Buddhist meditation. **"Take time today to plant geraniums, to bake bread, or to craft a**

bead necklace for your little girl," was one typical passage. **"Let the potting soil run through your hands. Hold a glass bead up to the light and marvel at its colors. Be in your task, and celebrate your results without judging them."**

"It has something, doesn't it?" said Ann.

"Let's just say I think there's a wide audience for a book like this."

"You're interested in doing the illustrations?"

"We'd have to talk terms but I'm interested."

"Here's what I see. The existing paintings you've done for the cards, and fifteen more due six months from now. A guy at the publishing house, in the art department, scanned one of your things and made a page mock-up I can send you."

"And what's the range you were thinking of?" I said.

She named a figure that, if Marta hadn't cautioned me to be savvy, would have made me promise to be her slave for life. It was more than I'd ever made for any one job.

"It's a place to start," I said languidly. "I'd need a percentage of royalties too."

I had no idea if this was standard, but figured it didn't hurt to try.

"Sure, sure," she said hastily. "You come up

with some numbers and I'll talk to my guy at the publishers."

"Wonderful," I said. "How's the rest of your life, Ann?"

"The rest of my life?"

"Are you seeing anyone you like? These two years we've been working together, I realized I never asked you how you're doing with anything else."

"I just bought a house," she said. "Right in town. It's already appreciating, can you believe that? People drive by and knock at the door and make me offers."

"Wow."

"And I met someone. He's an editor. For a travel magazine. He has to go away a lot but we're talking about moving in together so we can maximize our time together."

She sounded like a new bride.

"Is he nice to you?" I said.

"He's **so** nice, Sophie. I almost can't believe it."

A nice guy. This would give a whole new dimension to Ann's writing. To Ann.

Then she said, repressively, "Get me those numbers as soon as possible, okay?"

"Will do," I said. "I'm happy for you."

"We'll see," she said.

I didn't tell her about the divorce. I'd let her know my new phone and address, but no point in casting a shadow on budding romance. Ann in love. It was hard to picture and it gave me hope.

"I came to drop these off," said Stephen. He was holding a thick cream-colored paper bag, bulging with papers I couldn't see.

It was the Monday of the second week of May and it was raining, and I was packing.

"I'm not the dropping-by type, I hope you know that. I'd have called first, but you mentioned this morning that you'd be packing this afternoon, so I knew you'd be home."

I **had** mentioned it, and seen Ned's head turn momentarily in my direction, then away. I'd blown it, somehow. He wasn't my friend anymore. He didn't care if I went to Boston or Timbuktu. I'd ruined it by falling apart in front of him, by presuming too much.

"I was just starting. I'd love to be interrupted."

Stephen waded into the kitchen, which was cluttered with cardboard moving boxes from the office supply store. I'd mangled a few trying to put them together.

"You haven't moved much in your life, have you," Stephen said.

"Paul was the logistical genius. Or my friend Marta, when I was single."

"Here," Stephen said. "You make some tea and I'll finish these."

I made tea—Irish Breakfast, a new indulgence—and Stephen did some wizardry that resulted in ten boxes stacked up against the wall by the time the tea had steeped.

"You're a natural," I said.

"Yeah, if the business fails I'm gonna go to work for a moving company. In one of those elastic back braces. It could double as a girdle if I keep putting on weight. My cholesterol is way down though. Scott was over the moon. Like we'd won the lottery."

"You did. You should be proud of yourself."

He had his tea, his sugar, his non-fat cream, and a plate of ginger snaps I kept around because they never went stale.

"What's in the bag?" I said.

He spilled the contents on the kitchen table: catalogs and brochures, all describing graduate and adult courses in the studio arts. They were from all over Boston: the Cambridge Studio Workshop, the DeCordova Sculpture Park, the Arlington Center for the Arts, Summer Studies in Lexington, the Concord Painters' League.

"We collected these," said Stephen. "Ned and me. To get you started."

He opened one of the adult ed catalogs to a page marked with a paper clip.

"So You Want to Be a Real Artist" was the course title.

Stephen read aloud, "'**Want to make a real living as a studio artist, instead of just dreaming about it? We'll tell you how to find galleries to show your work, how to price and present your pieces, and where to get grants and commissions. We'll cover finding an artist's representative, and review your portfolio in a motivating and constructive manner. Making a life as an artist can be a reality, with our practical road map.'**"

The description specified that attendees should bring small works or slides.

"That seemed up your alley," said Stephen. "Were we overstepping our bounds?"

"No. Oh no. I can't believe you did this for me."

"It wasn't much work. Boston is big on self-improvement. It's a legacy from all those Transcendentalists and Bluestockings in the 1800s. Course listings all over. Libraries have whole tables of this junk."

"But you had to go find it all."

"Ned went, to be honest. It was all his idea."

I sipped my tea and got up my courage.

"Then why isn't Ned here with these? Why isn't he talking to me anymore?"

Stephen stirred his spoon around his cup.

"Can I have more cookies?"

I tipped a stack out onto a plate and handed it to him. He dunked one in and out of his tea until it crumbled into the cup in soggy driblets.

"Stephen?"

"Ned's weird. He's always been shy around women. It must be our Merrimack Valley upbringing. Flirting was not encouraged. Hell, even sex among married people was frowned on. That's why he's so backward. He has no dating skills."

"Stephen, give it to me straight."

"Sorry, no can do."

"Very funny. What's wrong with Ned? Why is he so distant?"

"He's embarrassed, like I said the other day. He thinks he made a fool of himself, during your big night together."

I opened my mouth and he waved it shut.

"Hey, I know nothing happened. He just thinks he may have hugged you in his sleep or something and that it may have traumatized you. Given your experiences earlier that night. With your husband and the slut and all."

I didn't like the word **slut** on principle, but I wasn't going to quibble in defense of Natalie when there was vital information in the offing.

"I might have curled up to him when we were sleeping. It was nothing. I thought it was nothing, anyway. For heaven's sake, Stephen, he was asleep!"

"Well, you can see how he'd be, shall we say, humiliated a little?"

"Humiliated?"

"His version is that he showed up at your room, and pushed his way into keeping you company, and made a few flirtatious comments that he now thinks were unforgivable—I couldn't get that part out of him—and then you took off in the morning because you couldn't stand the sight of him. He said you left him a very stilted, formal note."

"It was stilted because **I** was embarrassed, Stephen. Not because of anything Ned did. What has Ned ever done but be good to me?"

"That's what I said. I mean, I said you didn't mind. But now he's all shut up, and believe me, no one can close down like Ned can when he wants to. Especially when his little romantic feelings are wounded."

"What?"

"Sophie, you're either the village idiot or the most modest woman I've ever met. Ned's been hanging on your every word for months of walks now. He gave you driving lessons way past the point when you needed them. He nagged me to come over the night of the storm. 'We have to see if Sophie is okay, we have to check on Sophie.' Did you never connect the dots?"

"I thought I was a safe, married woman friend."

"You don't know much about men, do you. Ned isn't looking for someone to watch the Food Channel with, you whifflehead. He's crazy about you. More hot water, please. And a new teabag. Never mind, I'll get it."

I sat at the table at which I'd shared so many miserable breakfasts with Paul, trying to take in this information. Stephen did like to exaggerate.

Stephen found the whole milk and dumped a half cup into his tea.

"Are you surprised?" he said.

"You could say that."

"Is it a happy surprise?"

"I just separated from my husband, Stephen.

I'm not supposed to be thinking about your brother."

"Oh, come off that. If love had anything to do with timing or propriety, this wouldn't be a very interesting world."

"For you, you matchmaker."

"I've never matchmade for Ned. I did share my opinion about Fiona, tactfully . . ."

I snorted.

"I did share my opinion about Fiona with Ned, but this thing with you happened off his own bat. I didn't wake up every Monday, Wednesday, and Friday and say, 'What about falling for Sophie this morning? She's a nice girl.'"

"Are you sure you're not just imagining all this?"

"Sophie, the man went to every damn college and library and community center in Boston to get this information for you."

"He's a good friend to his friends."

"If you think this is friendship, you're loopy. He turns red when he sees you."

"That's the cold."

"It's May fourteenth, Sophie. It's not that cold anymore, although God knows it's not my idea of spring. I'll tell you, Fiona noticed it. How my brother felt about you. Right from the start, that day you ran into them at the museum."

"You're joking."

"No. I happened to overhear her asking Ned about you."

"Happened to overhear?"

"The acoustics in that old house are excellent. She was asking him all these coy questions that night. About you. What was your story, had he ever met your husband. And, of course, then she said all the rest to him when she dumped him."

"All the rest of what?"

"He didn't tell you that part?"

"No, he did not."

"She—the little weasel—blamed **him** for her crush on her professor. She said it happened because Ned was clearly 'caught up with you' and wouldn't admit it. Of course, this was after their big argument about her wanting him to quit the business. I always knew she was a snobby bitch."

So that was what Fiona had meant when she said Ned was "obtuse about himself." Ned had known exactly what that phrase signified, and hadn't told me.

"I see this rings a bell," said Stephen.

"Vaguely."

"I knew Ned wouldn't have the guts to tell you. Luckily, he has me to do it."

Stephen rose, took his cup to the sink, and said, "There's no hurry, since you're coming to Boston. Ned was very glad about that, you know."

Before he left, he said, "That strapping tape you're using is never going to hold. I'll bring some of the corded kind tomorrow."

I stood at his truck window as he revved the engine.

"This damn piece of junk," he said. "Listen to this muffler."

I leaned in and kissed his cheek.

"Bless you, Stephen."

"You won't tell Ned I spilled on him, will you?"

"I won't say a word."

"Now let me get out of here. I have a business to run. And don't tape those boxes with that crappy tape you've got, hear me? I'll bring what you need tomorrow."

"You've been doing that since I got here."

"My brother will get over his shyness, you know," Stephen said. "So stick around."

"I'm not going anywhere but Boston."

All night I thought about Ned as I made piles of books, clothes, and papers, divided into mine and Paul's (though Paul had taken most of his important papers. Even in the midst of an emotional crisis, he didn't forget his last six months of bank statements).

I thought of how comfortable I'd felt with Ned during the past few months, until his recent freeze-out. I had assigned Ned the role of Old-Reliable, but if what Stephen said was right, Ned's kindness to me wasn't a null and obligatory quality. He wasn't some version of a Canadian Mountie, riding correctly up to the rescue. He was a person who could take an interest in me and the question was, could I take an interest in him?

If Stephen was right. I had no illusions about Stephen's propensity to stretch the truth for a good cause, or what he determined was a good cause.

But no matter what Stephen thought or imagined, the question I had to put to myself was: how did I feel about Ned, once I looked at him straight-on?

I hadn't seen Ned, hadn't truly perceived him, standing there. That was because I'd never thought I'd be free of Rory. I had married Paul partly as a way of giving in to that reality, though I hadn't admitted that to myself at the time. I'd thought Paul and I had a sensible, steady adult relationship, but in truth I'd gone and chosen someone about whom I didn't feel passionately because I was convinced I could never feel as passionately about anyone as I had about Rory. For years I'd been in thrall to Rory's memory. Now that I was suddenly free, what was left of my feeling, romantic self? Like an invalid who's been confined to a couch for months on end, I was finally on my feet, but weak and tottery, unsure of my strength.

I packed until my arms were sore, leaving my studio equipment until the end. That I would stash carefully, putting turpentine and damar varnish and linseed oil all in their appointed spots in the tool kit that they'd traveled north in, sliding my watercolor sheets between layers of tissue paper in my portfolio case, stacking my canvases and wrapping them in an old sheet.

I felt ambushed by Stephen's information. He probably thought I'd run up to Ned at the next walking group and throw my arms around him, whispering, "My darling, why didn't you tell me?" That was the sort of mind Stephen had. He would like Marta. They both enjoyed the quick and easy endings of old movies where, in thirty seconds, all tension and painful confusion is ended with a kiss.

As it was, I simply strolled up to Ned at walking group the next day and gave him a big, sunny smile. I said, "Walk by me for a change," and he fell right in beside me.

When we'd gone a half mile in silence, I said, "You didn't intrude, you know. That night at the hotel."

"I'm going to kill Stephen."

"I only left that note because I was embarrassed. You had issues of your own to settle that night and I bled all over you, so to speak. And flirted with you. Lord knows what I was thinking."

"You weren't flirting. You were just trying to make me feel good after my breakup with Fiona. You probably wanted to get rid of me from the minute I showed up."

"Could you stop your fussing? Believe it or not, I was glad you showed up."

"You did treat me to a very good steak dinner," he said. "So you couldn't have been that upset with me for coming over."

"Exactly. I don't share a New York strip with just anyone."

We were covering a lot of ground. It was a beautiful May morning of the kind that tricks people into living in Portland year-round. Maybe someday it would trick me again. We strode along Danforth Street and across the Old Port, and then, after India Street, there was the Casco Bay opening out before us and the little waves breaking on the rocks with a sound I'd heard described somewhere as a chuckle, which like many such descriptions was merely accurate. Water **did** chuckle over rocks.

I would miss many things. Portland had turned out to be one of those cities that steals your heart while you're cursing it. You think you hate the place, then you wake up in the middle of the night and cry because you have to leave.

"I found a state park," I said to Ned. "It's called Two Lights."

"I've heard of it," he said. "Never been there."

"I didn't think so. Want to see how well I drive there?"

"I wouldn't mind," he said.

"The Lobster Shack down the road has the best fish and chips you've ever tasted."

"Quite the little tourist, aren't you," said Ned. Then he smiled at me, finally, his old smile, the one where his mouth curved up on one side. I hadn't realized how strung out I was until he smiled, and my very bones relaxed.

"Their soft drink refills are only a quarter," I said.

"How can I resist?"

"I'll pick you up Friday at two, how's that? I'll be done with most of my packing by then. Will the house let you go for a few hours?"

"Stephen can hold down the fort. He deserves it. I heard you took the apartment."

"How could I turn it down?"

"The best part about Boston is that it has neighborhoods that are real neighborhoods. We could go back to the North End again. It's not a bad walk from Beacon Hill. For a real walker like you."

"I'd like that," I said.

The mail was not as important to me as it had been during the dark days of winter, but I never forgot to go to the foyer and wrestle it out of its metal box. There were two letters today. One was on thin airmail paper—Rory. The other paper I also recognized. It was pale pink, and sealed with a maroon seal stamped with the initials N.P.

I opened Rory's first, happy to see his writing. I would always love him. And it was all right. My heart was no longer troubled by loving him. He was more like family now, like Delia, like Tom. He was on my side forever, even if he wasn't **at** my side.

"Dear Sophie," he wrote. **"I thought about what happened all the way back to Poland on the plane. When it hit me that you'd really left, I was pissed at you. For all of six hours. Then I realized that I had no right to be angry. I wasn't offering you much. You were right too. I didn't want to admit that I wasn't sure about my marriage. Don't get me wrong, I was sure I loved you. I just wasn't sure about leaving Liz.**

"Here's my news. Liz is pregnant. We're going to have a baby next September, how's that for a shocker? So I guess the best thing I can do is to stay with her and see how it all works out. She's so happy. She's like a different person now. So we're going to try. I'll keep you posted.

"I hope this news won't be a disappointment. Somehow, I don't think it will be. But

don't let anyone treat you badly, can you re-
member that? Not your husband, not anyone.
You're a treasure even if I can't have you, my
Sophie Ann. Stay in touch, Rory."

So. If I were bitter I'd say that Liz, who'd always played her cards well, had just laid down a
royal flush. But strangely, I wasn't bitter. Liz had
simply proven that, as much as Rory claimed
otherwise, she did understand her husband.
She'd gone ahead and made the baby happen
without asking his permission. I felt a crimp of
tenderness at the thought of Rory as a father.
He'd be a great father. Thank God I hadn't slept
with him. How cheap I'd feel now.

I opened the second letter. The wax from the
seal fell in flakes to the floor. Natalie really **was**
pretentious.

"Dear Sophie," the letter ran. **"I felt I had to
write you, although I know that Paul has told
you what regret I feel that my relationship
with Paul has caused you such pain."**

It seemed that Natalie had been reading some
book of etiquette on how the wife-to-be should
wind matters up with the almost-ex-wife.

**"Since I first laid eyes on Paul, I knew that
he and I were made for each other, as difficult
a position as that put him in. I know that,**

when some time has passed, you'll agree with me that it would have been wrong for Paul not to get what he deserved. We would all have been cheated of happiness, in the big picture."

If Paul were in front of me right now, I felt I could give him what he deserved.

"As painful as our present situation is, in the long run this change will be best for all three of us, not just for Paul and me, but for you also."

Natalie and Ann really should have met. Together they could have concocted some card for this occasion, perhaps with a title such as, "Congratulations, I've snatched your husband and it's for your own good."

"I wish you only good fortune in the future, Sophie. Please accept my apologies for any harm my actions may have caused you. Best, Natalie."

"I love it," said Delia when I read her Natalie's epistle. "The perfect non-apology apology. 'I'm sorry if you're so oversensitive that you took offense at my reasonable and wise choices.' Bleah."

"But from her point of view, the slate's been wiped clean," I said. "After a while she'll forget that Paul even had a first wife."

"Why aren't you angrier about this, Sophie? Screamingly angry."

"Oh, I'm angry. But it all depends on your viewpoint. My tale of being cheated on is Paul's tale of escape from a loveless marriage."

"Your marriage wasn't loveless. But fine if you want to let Paul go in peace. Just remember, a moment will come when you want to throw something at the wall and break it into smithereens. And when it does, make sure it's something that belongs to **him**."

"I'll save something just for that purpose."

"And one other thing. You may not have gotten it right yet, Sophie, but you're going to get it right. You're close."

"Close only counts in horseshoes and hand grenades."

"Next time around is going to be the winner for you. I promise."

Delia had been telling me things like this since we were kids. "Seventh grade wasn't your year but eighth grade will be." "Everyone gets a C-minus in freshman biology." "So you got downsized. It was a lousy job anyway. You'll find better."

"He'll be sorry," Delia said. "Natalie and Pepper will run him ragged."

"Don't you see, that's what he wants? He'll be

more secure now. He'll feel like he's on firm ground."

"**You'll** be on firm ground, with the next guy," said Delia.

I burnt Natalie's letter, holding it over the toilet bowl. It took forever to flush all the sealing wax drippings away, but when it was done I felt clean and light and finished.

Almost finished, that is. Because Delia was right about that moment of rage. You think you're not angry, and then out of nowhere comes a vicious shrew, and she's you.

What happened was this: Pepper called, the next day.

When I heard her precise, lemon-sherbet-flavored voice, I thought she was calling to be kind. I thought she'd say something like, "I can't imagine what Paul is doing. You've been a wonderful wife to him. No wonder you were too distracted to buy kitchen equipment when I was visiting at Thanksgiving. And please forget what I've said about your driving and your wardrobe. I can see now that you had more important matters on your mind."

Well, I knew she wouldn't say that, but maybe a few seemly sentiments of regret?

"Hello, Sophie. I won't keep you long. I know you have a lot to do."

"Hello, Pepper." It was weird to use her first name; I'd always avoided it.

"This must be a difficult situation for you."

"You mean, Paul's leaving me?"

"Your move, and all of that."

She spoke repressively, as if I'd tried to bring up at a dinner party the details of a brain surgery I'd watched on the medical channel.

I said, "Paul's probably told you I'm going to Boston."

"Boston is a lovely city," said Pepper. "Ballet, museums. Lovely. You'll enjoy it."

She spoke as if I were going to Boston for my own cultural enrichment. A part of me stood to one side and observed the anger roar up my spinal column, up my throat until I thought I'd shriek. Delia had warned me, but no, I had to be adult about it.

Pepper said, "Sophie, the reason I'm calling is that in a difficult situation like this, it's far too easy for items to get lost in the shuffle."

"Oh, we'll stay in touch," I said, deliberately blithe. "I'll make sure you get my new phone number. When I'm settled."

"Of course I want to keep **track** of you," said

Pepper. "You're part of the family. Just **like** part of the family still. However, the particular item I'm thinking of now is the Stoddard jewelry. The silver filigree ring and bracelet."

"Jewelry," I said, as if I couldn't quite recall it.

"You wore it at Thanksgiving," she said. "At that restaurant."

I examined my nails. They were black from all the newspaper I'd crushed in my packing. They'd be grimy for my outing with Ned tomorrow. Ned wouldn't care, though. Ned was not a stickler. In a world full of sticklers, Ned let me be a fearful driver and would-be painter who never got a manicure. He let me eat whatever I wanted for breakfast. As Pepper nattered on, Ned began to look awfully good to me.

"Valuable heirlooms can easily be misplaced," she was saying. "So if you'll just pop them in the mail, insured of course, I'd be glad to send you a check for the postage."

For a moment I was the old me, ready to rush down to UPS at Pepper's command. The new me had an evil notion.

"If only you'd thought to call sooner," I said. "I don't have the jewelry. I sold it."

"You sold it? You couldn't have sold it."

"Didn't Paul tell you? He said he'd never particularly cared for those and that I could do what I liked with them. There's the sweetest little place on Cottage Road that carries estate pieces, and so I just took them on in."

"Those were family heirlooms," she said. "You can't just throw them away."

"I got a very good price, in fact. The shop owner told me those filigree settings are very hot lately."

"I would like the number of that shop, and I would like it now, Sophie."

"You know, I can't remember it. I was a little distraught at the time."

"Sophie," she said gently. "Paul made a mistake marrying you, and he didn't choose the best possible way to fix it, but creating illwill isn't going to make you feel any better."

"They gave me cash," I said. "It felt pretty good, actually."

"Perhaps you don't realize that this is a legal matter," she said, audibly sucking in her breath. So that's where Paul had gotten that mannerism. "There are precedents."

Pepper really should have read Ann Landers more often. Ann was always sympathizing with irate former mothers-in-law whose sons gave

family engagement rings to hussies who then di-
vorced them and kept the diamond.

"Your lawyer can contact me at my new address," I said pleasantly.

"I would never have thought you could behave like this," said Pepper. "Whatever your
other faults were, you always seemed like a very
sweet person. I'm sure you'll see more clearly
down the road."

"I think I'm seeing pretty clearly," I said.

"I wasn't joking about that call to my lawyer,
Sophie. He'll be in touch with you."

"I'm rather busy at the moment," I said. "But
he's welcome to leave a message. Have a
nice day."

The phone rang for twenty minutes after that,
but I didn't pick up. And that was the last I
heard of Pepper. If I met her today, ran into her
at a department store or on a train, I'd probably
be amazed at how this small, shrill woman once
had such power over me. I'm not proud of how
I behaved in our last conversation, but you can't
be too squeamish when you're getting some of
your own back.

As for the ring and bracelet, I knew the perfect person for them.

"Here," I said to Alex that Friday at walking group, and handed her a tissue-wrapped package. "This was a gift from my about-to-be ex, and I don't want it anymore."

She opened it while we were walking. Alex was the kind of person who ripped open presents with joy and rapture. I hoped that when she came to college in Boston she wouldn't mind having lunch with me every few months or so. Maybe she'd need an auntly presence now and again.

"Sophie, I can't take this."

The bracelet was already on her wrist, the ring glowing on her pale hand. They looked perfect. I'd buffed the setting with a car chamois Paul had left behind.

"Sure you can take it. I'll throw them into the Casco Bay otherwise."

"Boy, you're pretty mad at your husband, aren't you."

"You got it. So take those. If you ever need some spending money, they'd fetch a bit at a pawn shop."

"I'd never pawn them."

"You could. I wouldn't mind."

The Stoddard ring and bracelet had found

their proper owner. It's funny how books and bracelets and husbands find their way to the right person.

At breakfast, Stephen said to me, "I saw you gave Alex a nice little present."

"A family heirloom," I said. "Only not from **my** family."

"Who needs heirlooms?" said Stephen. "If you knew your ancestors, you might not even like them. This is America, where the past doesn't matter."

Ned leaned over the back of his booth.

"Drive over at two today, Sophie," he said, almost whispering so as not to hurt Alex, who sat next to him eating dry toast and drinking orange juice. She had a boyfriend now, but crushes die hard. Alex would be fine, though. Alex had changed, slowly and arduously. You can transform yourself in a winter, I thought, looking at her.

"I'll honk the horn and you can run out," I said to Ned.

"Can I come too?" said Stephen, winking at me.

"No," said Ned. "You've made enough trouble already."

The bracken at Two Lights was greener than when I'd seen it first a week ago. The air was not balmy but it was less raw than it had been. Spring did not come in leaps and bounds here, but it was perceptible to those who had eyes to see it.

"Journey's End," said Ned, when we passed the sign.

"Hokey, huh."

"Probably some mail-order business selling Maine blueberry jam," he said.

"Or maybe just a name someone always wanted to put on their house."

There was a ranger on duty today so I paid the fee. Ned went for his wallet but I said, "This was my invitation," and he put it away.

We walked up the stone steps and reached the top of the hill. The cliffside grass was the softest of greens, the earth was dark brown, the sea a deep, sighing blue.

"So you found this," said Ned. "All by your-self."

"All by myself."

We clambered down onto the rocks. I climbed more agilely than he did, since I'd known to wear rubber-soled sneakers and he had less-flexible hiking shoes. I climbed a few rocks away from him and stood on my own rock, closer to the water. The waves were high today.

"Have you been really miserable, Sophie? About your marriage?"

"I don't look miserable, do I? Watch," I said. "Every three or four waves there's a big one, a real crashing one. It's like fireworks."

He wasn't watching the waves.

"Answer me, will you?" he said. "It's kind of important."

I met his eyes. It seemed to me that I had never looked directly at him before. It seemed Stephen had been right about how Ned felt.

"I'm not miserable," I said. "I was miserable all winter, and I don't have the heart for it anymore. And how can I be miserable here?"

"A person can be miserable anywhere."

"Or happy anywhere," I said.

"Even in Portland?"

"Or in Boston, say. With the right company."

I looked up at him. He was standing on his rock with his arms folded, staring out to sea, and his face looked as bleak as it had that day at Higgins Beach when he talked about his mother.

"Do you mean that?" he said. "What about that guy? That Rory?"

"Over him," I said. "I think you can tell I am."

"That was rough on me, you know," he said.

"I know. I missed it at the time but I do know. I'm sorry."

He came over to my rock, teetering beside me. He put his arms around me.

"Sophie," he said. "I'm the biggest chicken in the world. And the biggest fool."

"Why? Why would you be a fool?"

"Because I never let myself think about you. You always listened to me, and I had such a good time talking to you, and I never thought about it until very recently. What it meant. And then I thought about it a lot after that night at the Eastland, and I felt like a fool."

"Well, then there's two of us. I've been telling myself I like you for months now. When you were with Fiona I said, Ned is **such** a nice guy, I like him so much, why does he have to be with **her**? That's what I said to myself. That I **liked** you and so I wanted to see you happy with some lovely girl, because I just wanted the best for you. Only no lovely girl would have been quite good enough. Because I was so attached to you. As a friend, of course."

"I seem to be attached to **you**. Quite attached."

"Strongly attached?"

"Strongly. Not that I could admit it when you were still married. Still unseparated."

"That sounds like an egg," I said, and leaned against him. It was nice to lean on him with a chill wind blowing, but he wasn't just a refuge. I wanted to kiss him, but I wanted even more to hear what he would say first.

He said, "I told myself I was being kind to a stranger, that I was going along with my obnoxious, interfering brother yet again. I gave myself all kinds of stupid excuses. Then that night in the North End, when I criticized you about Rory, I went home and thought to myself, Why are you acting like this? She's married, she has the love of her life waiting in the wings. But that didn't help. When we came over during the big storm, when we were dancing together, I had an idea then of what I was getting myself into."

"What would you say we've gotten into?" I said.

"Someday soon, if things go well," he said, "I'll tell you."

The tide was coming in and I said, "We should move higher. Rogue waves."

"I taught you that," he said, and pulled me up a few feet, to a wider ledge where the spray just barely touched us. "I was always trying to look out for you. You think that would have told me something."

"It was strange," I said. "You always were, and I just thought you were being a good citizen. By the way, I wanted to kiss you that night when we were dancing."

"You never said a word."

"How could I, with your brother in the next room? Even tipsy, Stephen is very observant. Besides, I was still confused then. I wasn't finished with Rory. Or Paul."

"Are you finished with them now?"

"Very finished," I said. "More quickly and more completely than I ever thought I would be. Finished with lots of things."

"Could you start something? With me? Or am I rushing you?"

"I think we started a long time ago," I said.

The wool of his sweater scratched my face. There was no one within sight. I put my arms around his neck. When he kissed me, his lips tasted of salt. We stood on the rock together and kissed, balancing in each other's arms.

Twenty-Seven

On May 1, when I gave Donald my notice, there were still traces of snow under the trees behind Donald's garage, where the sun never reached. By May 25, when I left (giving Donald a few extra days to get the place ready for the next unwary tenant), the snow was gone. In a few months Donald's scraggly roses would be in bloom.

"You can come by anytime you're up here, you know," said Donald.

"I will," I said.

"Some bad stuff happened to you here in Portland, but don't hold that against the place," he said.

"Good things happened too," I said. "For one thing, I had a very nice landlord."

He said only, "Call me if she gives you any trouble. And change her oil every twenty-five-hundred miles. Not three thousand. Sooner. They say three thousand, but sooner really prolongs the life of the car."

Then his wife called to him through the screen door, and he slouched away.

Would I ever come back to see Donald? I might come back to Portland—especially since Ned and Stephen's success with the Eastern Prom house was already garnering more inquiries from several of their clients' friends who also aspired to Maine home ownership. But would I come back to see Donald, or would a barrier of shyness and awkwardness keep me from it? Donald was my friend, but he was the sort of friend that appears in your life as an angel might, then disappears when he's no longer needed.

The Goodwill came and carted away the furniture, and a young couple in a pickup grabbed the mattress off the sidewalk where Donald had confidently set it. "It'll be gone in an hour, you watch," he'd said. I taped my boxes with the tape Stephen had given me, and stowed my art supplies in their tool kit and tackle box.

On Friday it was my last walking group.

"I'll be right behind you. I'll be there by August," said Alex.

She was ready for school, with a suitcase full of carefully not-too-new clothes and a stack of accounting and economics books she'd already memorized.

"We come to Boston all the time," said Ramon. "For trade shows and just a change of scenery. Give Stephen your number. We'll have dinner, at a restaurant that I'll pick so you can be sure of a decent meal."

George said nothing but, "Good luck to you now," but he shook my hand in his thin dry one. Matilda was wheeled away in her baby carriage for the last time that I'd see her in it. Pretty soon she'd be walking and wouldn't need a carriage. We all changed; babies just changed faster.

I didn't stay for breakfast. I stood on the corner of High and Commercial Streets and watched them all straggling into Becky's. Stephen was ragging Ramon about something, and Ramon was laughing, and Edgar had his quiet little banker's smile, but you could tell he got the joke as much as anyone. Ned was the last one in. As the door swung shut, he turned and waved.

"See you soon," he shouted to me, and went in.

I could picture them eating breakfast, arguing and kidding around. My friends, who'd helped me make it through the winter. Godspeed, I wanted to say—but I was the one who was leaving. I said it anyway.

Ned came over for my last night in town. We had two folding chairs to sit on and could've gotten takeout, but instead we drove to the Lobster Shack and ate fish and chips overlooking the ocean. There was a fog that night, low-lying in the dips of the coastal road that led to the restaurant. It made the horizon mysterious and dim.

"I'll miss the ocean," I said to him.

"We'll come back to it."

Then we returned to my place and lay side by side on sleeping bags, talking far into the night and kissing in between, longing kisses that told me how good it would be when we made love. Somehow I couldn't bring myself to do that in this apartment that had been so unhomey, neither Paul's nor my territory, occupied instead by our joint unhappiness. Ned deserved better than to be mixed up in any way with the querulous ghost of my marriage. In Boston, we'd have our own ground to stand on, to begin on.

In the morning we gulped cereal from individual cardboard boxes, a treat my mother had never allowed Delia and me when we were growing up. I enjoyed it ridiculously.

"I could eat like this every morning," I said to Ned.

He waited for me at the door as I walked from

room to room, making sure the lights were out and the gas was off, checking everything for the last time. In a week Ned and Stephen would be done with the Eastern Prom house, and Ned would be in Boston, just a subway ride away. It was good that I'd have a week to explore the new territory on my own, to catch my breath. When he arrived, I'd be ready to see him.

The car was loaded already. Donald stood in the doorway, holding the dogs on the leash with one hand, waving to me with the other. I waved back, trying not to cry. Ned followed me to the car.

"Call me when you get there," he said. "You've got the keys to the apartment?"

"In my pocket."

"Drive safely," he said. "And don't do anything big until I get there."

You shouldn't really think about the places you're leaving as you're leaving them. Your eyes tear up and it's not safe. I concentrated on my driving, on following the directions Ned had written out so carefully. Tonight I would be sad, missing Ned, missing Portland, which I'd never thought I'd miss. Tonight I'd sleep in a bed that had been left for me by a stranger who was also going off on strange adventures in a new city, and that would be all right. I'd be a little lonely, and a little afraid, but that wouldn't kill me. I was past all that.

I flipped on the oldies station and sang along to Sam Cooke.

"Bring it on home to me," I sang. I followed the signs and merged onto the turnpike as smoothly and perfectly as if I'd done it all my life.